I0679286

BURIED SECRETS

The Buried Trilogy Book 2

VELLA DAY

Erotic Reads Publishing

VELLA DAY

Copyright © 2018

ALL RIGHTS RESERVED. No part of this book may be used or reproduced in any manner whatsoever without written permission of the author except in the case of brief questions embodied in critical articles or reviews.

This is a work of fiction. Names, characters, places, and incidents either are the product of the author's imagination or are used fictitiously, and any resemblance to actual persons living or dead, business establishments, events or locales, is entirely coincidental.

❀ Created with Vellum

CHAPTER ONE

THE SMART MOON had blanketed itself between two big, fluffy clouds, probably to keep warm. Jenna Holliday tugged close her police issue jacket wishing she could do the same. "Damn." Florida wasn't supposed to be this cold in December.

From outside the closed cemetery's gate, she peered in at the faintly lit mausoleum that housed her mom's remains. "Hey, Mom. I just finished the late shift, which was why I didn't make it in time for your birthday. I'm sorry." Jenna leaned her forehead against the wrought iron bars, gripping them tight. "I know it's late, but I wanted to talk to you. No, I *needed* to talk to you. I missed passing the exam to make detective by five freaking points. Can you believe that?" She huffed out a breath. "Dad will go ballistic when he finds out. Not that I care." She slapped her palm against the cold metal, the guilt of what she'd done so many years ago welling inside.

Let it go. You were only twelve. You had to tell Mom you saw Dad with another woman.

Keeping her gaze focused on her mother's crypt a few hundred feet up the path, she stepped back from the fence and waved goodbye. She coughed into the sleeve of her jacket as she glanced around, hoping no one caught her talking to the dead.

All clear. The lot was empty.

Just as she turned to leave, a loud crash came from the other side of the mausoleum sounding like rocks breaking. Jenna spun back to the cemetery. A flashlight traced an arc across the lawn. What the hell was going on? Whatever it was, it wasn't good.

Not thinking about her safety, she hopped onto the hood of her car and scaled the six-foot high cemetery gate, landing onto the paved walkway. *Ouch*. Her sore knee screamed.

Move. Halfway up the concrete path, more rocks exploded. Was that granite breaking? Ohmigod. They better not be touching Mom's grave—or anyone's grave for that matter. Her fingers shot to the gun on her hip.

Someone cursed. From his high-pitched voice, it sounded like a kid. She darted down the middle aisle of the mausoleum, trying to make as little sound as possible despite her breaths coming out hard and fast. She plastered her back against the far wall before making her move. The biting wind whooped and howled down the corridor.

"Let's get out of here. We already got five heads." The kid sounded scared.

"No, dumb ass. We don't get paid until we have seven."

They were stealing *skulls?* Not with her around they wouldn't. She checked around the corner. Two teens, one blond and scrawny, the other beefy and dark, hovered over a coffin that was halfway out of the bottom vault with the lid partly off. The granite faceplate lay in pieces on the ground. Dear God. Several of the coffins in the bottom row were out and exposed. The smaller kid had what looked like a king-sized pillowcase slung over his shoulder. She could take both of them if she had to.

Jenna stepped into the open, her finger on her holstered gun. "Police. Put the sack down and get on your knees—both of you. Hands behind your head." She counted the coffins. Her mother's grave was sixth from the end. Dear God. They'd broken into Mom's vault. Her stomach tumbled, but she kept her hand steady.

Before they did as she'd asked, something hard came down on the back of her head. Her knees buckled, sending her to the concrete. Her cheek planted on the ground, and a tsunami-sized ache raced down her body. When she tried to pop to her feet, her attacker delivered a sharp kick to her hip.

"Bitch." The voice was deep, ugly, mature, and quite unforgettable.

He moved back, and her police training kicked in. Jenna pushed aside the pain and scrambled to her feet. Everything hurt, but she raised her gun, nonetheless. Her damned arms wobbled. The hooded man, dressed all in black, raced away, zigzagging right, then left.

"Police. Stop." Her vision blurred long enough for him to disappear from sight. She turned around to apprehend the kids. Damn. They were gone too. *Go after the guy.*

On her second step, vomit rolled into her mouth and her legs gave way, dropping her to the ground. Crap. Police procedures raced through her mind. *Suck it up and stop him.* She stood, crouched low, and checked right, then left.

Shit. Other than the sound of the wind whipping through the trees, there were no footsteps, no voices, nothing. How had they vanished? Fuck. She'd screwed up—again.

Think. There were at least three perpetrators. Checking the surrounding area without a flashlight and being in a weakened state would be super stupid. No. She needed to call this one in, but damn, she'd have to admit she'd failed to stop the jerks.

A sharp pain stabbed the back of her head, and she touched her scalp. Gooey blood coated her hair around a wide laceration. She said a few words even her sheriff department father would have been appalled to hear.

She swiped her cell and called the precinct. "Hey, Tanner. I need backup." She gave him the rundown about the kids, the coffin, and the skulls, including the fact one of them belonged to her mother. "I would have stopped them if some dude hadn't attacked me."

"You okay?"

"Yeah, but he hit me hard in the back of the head." Bad move. She shouldn't have told him she'd been injured. Now the whole precinct would hear about her fiasco. After working hard for five years on the force to earn the men's respect, she let some creep get the drop on her and ruin everything.

"What are you doing at a cemetery, Holliday? Didn't you just get off work?" Old Tanner Trundell kept track of everyone and everything at the precinct.

No way he'd understand why she needed to visit her mom in the dead of night. "I was driving by when I saw something and stopped." That was close to the truth.

"We'll send a unit and an ambulance."

"I'm good. I don't need an ambulance." Could this get any worse?

"You're getting one anyway."

Kill me now. After she disconnected, she made her way to the end of the aisle and dropped to her knees in front of where her mom was laid to rest. A gust of cold wind crawled up her shirt, and she zippered up her jacket. Tears burned the back of her lids. The coffin sat open, the head missing. Stolen. Her throat clogged, and a metallic taste leaked into her mouth. Mom's blue Sunday dress was still neatly pressed, her leathery fingers clasped over her belly. Jenna reached out and placed a palm over where her mom's heart would be. She glanced skyward, knowing her mother's soul was with God, and that she wasn't really *missing*, but the theft dredged up the pain of mom's suicide again.

A slow boil ran from her stomach to her throat, and she pounded the walkway. "I'll get back what you stole, you bastards." She said it loud enough for them to hear, wherever they were.

She wanted to put back the carelessly tossed covers to give the dead respect, but this was a crime scene. Jenna stood and did a quick scan of the cemetery grounds. Were the boys and their leader watching her from behind some tree, and laughing about how they managed to get away? If they came back, she'd be ready.

Fists clenched, she paced in front of the coffins, trying to figure out how the man was able to sneak up on her. She should have checked the scene and taken her time instead of rushing in to save the day. She'd been stupid. Maybe she didn't deserve to be a detective.

Not true. Her father had raised her to be a cop. She knew the ins and outs better than anyone, so how had she screwed up so badly? Rotten karma, she guessed.

"Hey, Jenna?" That was fast. It was her boss, Captain Lucas.

"Over here."

Four men and two women rounded the corner. One was Lucas and the second was Larry Bernard, a veteran officer. The next two were CSU techs she didn't know personally, and the last was her father. She gritted her teeth and marched over to the captain, trying to ignore the intense pounding in her head. "Why is my father here?"

"I invited him."

"You had no right," she whispered. Everyone knew she'd joined the Tampa Police Department and not the sheriff's department to get away from the probing eyes of the man who basically had caused her mother's death.

"You were hurt," Captain Lucas said. "I thought he'd want to know. Besides, he's one of us."

Her father stood off to the side ramrod straight, not even attempting to console her. Typical. He was dressed in his sheriff department garb despite the fact it was one in the morning. He must never sleep. Other than his gray beard stubble, he looked like he'd come from work. Hell, maybe he had.

Her father nodded to her, and then stepped over to Mom's grave. He lowered his head and his shoulders drooped. Jenna never remembered seeing him anything less than the tall, straight, always-in-control dad.

She might as well get this over with and walked over to him. "Hey."

Her father faced her. The overhead light reflected off what she thought was a tear. She was about to touch his arm but then decided against it. No way would she let her heart melt toward him.

He looked up. "You okay?"

Now he asks? "Never better." *Don't show any weakness* had always been his motto.

Three camera flashes went off in succession, indicating the CSU techs were documenting the scene. The captain sidled up to her. "What happened exactly?"

What could she say? She let someone get the drop on her as two kids were stealing the skulls from the graves. Jenna explained the best she could.

"If we catch them, they'll be up for assaulting an officer too."

She didn't care. All she wanted was her mother's skull returned. "I want this case."

"No. It's too personal. Besides, Bernard here has been working another grave robbery case for the last few months."

She remembered hearing about that one. "Did the thieves only take the skulls too?" Maybe they weren't related.

Bernard stepped forward. "Actually, six coffins in four different cemeteries were dug up, but they stole the whole body."

"Any leads?" Jenna pulled her coat tighter. It was colder than a concrete slab in winter.

"We've zeroed in a particular occult store in Ybor City, called *Botanica*. Rumor has it that a high priestess is using human bones to put evil spells on people, but we don't have enough evidence to get a warrant to search the place."

She glanced one more time at her mother's grave, along with the other ransacked vaults and turned to the captain. "I want to go undercover there."

Her father drew his gaze away from Mom's coffin. "The man who hit you might work there and recognize you."

Who made him head of TPD all of a sudden? "This isn't your decision. Look, I need to do this. For Mom." *If I hadn't told her your little secret, she wouldn't have taken her life. I owe her.*

He turned away and headed to the end of the row of vaults.

Lucas nodded at her father. "I think your dad's right. You could be recognized. Besides, it's dangerous."

"I'm willing to take the risk."

Captain Lucas stared hard at her. "I will admit you'd be perfect for the undercover job. You're young, kind of hip, waiflike, and look no more than twelve."

Kind of hip? She'd been battling the you-look-no-more-than-twelve comment her whole life—all twenty-nine years of it. "I want this."

He took a big inhale and his eyes turned soft, almost as if he was regretting the words he was about to say. "I'll give you one month to bring me hard evidence. Not a day more. I'll have to reassign Phelps though."

Her partner, Greg Phelps, who she loved like a father, was due to retire in six months anyway. She had to get used to life without him soon enough. "I'll tell him if you want."

* * *

JENNA'S barely twenty-year old customer curled her lip. The girl sported a kissing snakes tattoo that peeked from under the strap of a skimpy tank top, and she had more body piercings than Swiss cheese had holes. Jenna mentally shook her head as she scanned the to-be-purchased items. Dear God, who had the money to throw away on this crap? Careful not to expose her disgust, Jenna rang up the African mask, eye of newt powder, and paper-thin snakeskin.

"That'll be fifty-seven dollars and thirty-two cents, please."

Just looking at the girl's tattoo made Jenna's fake skull on her forearm itch like hell, but she didn't dare scratch it. Too much was at stake.

The girl tossed down her VISA card. "Here you go." She turned to her girlfriend and began gossiping about the cute guys they'd met at the bar down the street. Considering the friend's purple hair and orange eyebrows, Jenna could only imagine their definition of cute.

She flashed back to last week to when her dad had come into the store to lecture her on proper police procedures when doing undercover work. First came the pursed lips, followed by the intense body scan, making it clear he didn't approve of her studded collar and pomaded hair. He acted as if she should have been wearing a plaid skirt and ponytails. In retrospect, she wished she'd dyed her blonde hair green or pink just to piss him off some more.

Jenna handed Miss Kissing Snakes a bone-shaped pen to sign her receipt and checked the clock again. Only twenty minutes until closing. Yay. On the down side, she only had a week left of her undercover job—and she still had no evidence of foul play.

Jenna leaned on her elbows. "Can I ask you guys something?"

They eyed each other. Kissing snakes nodded. "Sure."

"My boyfriend has been stalking me, and the police won't do shit." Jenna narrowed her eyes. "I really want to find someone to put an evil spell on him. Do you have any ideas who I can ask? I got money."

"Why not ask your boss? She did one for me about six months back."

Jenna's shoulders relaxed. "Really? I've been afraid to ask her. I thought she might get mad. How much did she charge?"

Kissing snakes shrugged. "She only charged me seven fifty since I'm such a good customer."

"Seven dollars and fifty cents? I can handle that." Acting dumb took work.

The girl rolled her eyes while orange eyebrows giggled. "Seven hundred and fifty *dollars*." She tugged on her eyebrow ring. "If that's too rich for your blood, I know of someone else, but he's not as reliable."

Deidra was considered reliable? Jenna widened her eyes real big. "Wow. That's way outta my league. I'll get back with you." Seven hundred and fifty dollars for some priestess to stir a pot of junk and wave a hand over it? This world was messed up.

As soon as the two girls split, the owner of the store, Deidra Willows, waddled out, her long crinkle shirt dragging on the floor. She didn't look like a high priestess to her. She was way too frumpy. A priestess should be tall, lithe, and very beautiful.

"Jenna, I need a favor." Her thick black brows creased on her too pale face.

"What's wrong? Is it the baby?" Deidra's very pregnant sister, Shelby, had another month of her term left. The sister had worked at the store the first week, but then went home to wait out her time.

"Her midwife is out of town, and Shelby's in a panic. She's gone into labor and needs me to look after the kids, and that deadbeat husband of hers won't lift a finger. Do you mind putting the money in the safe and closing the store?" Before Jenna had a chance to answer, Deidra unhooked two keys from her broom keychain. "This one's for the front door." She placed it in the palm of Jenna's hand. "And this gets you into my office. Be sure to lock the door before you go."

"Don't worry about a thing." Inwardly she celebrated.

Deidra sneezed. "Are you okay?" Jenna asked.

"Yeah, it's just a damn cold. It's a terrible time to get one, what with me having to watch the kids."

"I hope you are taking something for it," Jenna said.

"Not yet, but I will."

Jenna made a production of straightening the mess on the counter as Deidra rushed out. Jenna itched to check out the back and look around. Her boss spent hours in her one-room hideout doing who-knew-what. Twice in the last three weeks, Jenna had gone to speak with her only to find the door locked. Even Jenna's knocks had failed to rouse a response. She could only conclude Deidra was either into meditation or doing some kind of spell and didn't want to be disturbed.

Since her boss wasn't here to oversee her actions, Jenna turned off the eerie background music designed to enhance the gothic element of the place and extinguished the incense that irritated her sinuses. Not wanting anything to look out of order to an outsider, she waited until exactly ten to lock up.

"I'm going to put you back together, Mom. Don't you worry. I'll find those thieves."

With money in hand, she headed to the inner sanctum. Deidra's office sat wide open even though her boss had given her the keys. Interesting.

As she'd done for the past week, she flipped on the computer and entered the money into *QuickBooks*, happy not to have her boss breathing down her neck for a change. When she finished, she searched My Documents for something incriminating. After fifteen minutes, she shut down the machine. Cleaner than a picked bone. Damn. If her boss were into something sinister, she didn't keep a log of it here. Jenna leaned back in the chair and shoved her hands through her stiff hair. Her chances of finding her mother's skull were slipping through her fingers with each tick of the clock.

The captain made it clear Jenna needed proof someone was doing spells in this building using *human* remains before he could even ask for a warrant. She shivered just picturing her mom's head being doused with bodily fluids and other foreign substances.

"Don't dawdle," she mumbled to herself.

As she placed the money into the safe next to the closet, she got a whiff of something foul, like an animal had died. She could only hope the stench was human. But if so, how come Deidre hadn't noticed it? Oh, yeah. She had a cold.

After a quick glance over her shoulder to make sure Deidra hadn't materialized out of thin air, Jenna tugged hard on the closet handle next to the safe. It creaked open and a moldy stench blew out.

She'd expected to see a pile of stacked boxes, but instead found a dark hallway, lined with crumbing brick that led to another ancient-looking door. Determined to find out what secrets the old building held, Jenna headed down the unknown path, pushing down the knowledge she had no right to be there. The scarred, pine floorboards creaked under every step. She tugged on a ratty gray string hanging from the ceiling, and a dim bulb lit the long, narrow corridor.

This might be stupid. "Who am I? Buffy the Vampire Slayer?"

She hurried to the end of the walkway and tested the knob. Locked. Crap. The need to find out what was behind door number two overtook all rational thought. She raced back to the office and ripped open Deidra's desk drawer, regretting never having learned to pick a lock. The key to the door had to be someplace. After a two-minute search, she found a ring of keys in the fourth drawer that looked like they came straight from Home Depot. She didn't give a flip what they looked like as long as one of them let her get inside.

Rushing back down the hall, Jenna focused on the worn door. The first two keys failed to work, but the third one did the trick. She noted the time on her cell phone. She couldn't afford to waste time investigating in case Shelby's scare turned out to be a false alarm, and Deidra came back to check on her new employee. Always one to cover her bases, Jenna ran back and slipped the keys back into the fourth drawer.

Hurry. For her mom's sake, she had to push ahead. Once at the end of the hallway, it took hard pulls until the door groaned open.

"Oh. My. God." Dead fish rotting in the hot sun would smell better. She covered her nose.

Determined to find answers, she crept inside. The light switch was mounted next to the door, not that it did much good. The bulb couldn't have been more than fifteen watts. Eerie, spooky shadows danced on the wall as she stepped inside. Her stomach in knots, her eyes widened at the brownish red streaks covering a cracked wall. It could be blood. That looked like warrant material to her. She whipped out her cell phone and snapped some photos. The flash washed out the markings, but it was the best she could do under the circumstances.

One red image consisted of an arrow through a two-foot diameter circle. A second one resembled a cross that had half fallen over. Could have been an X, but the horizontal bar had fancy pointed ends. A few of the other symbols looked like some kind of Pagan secret code, but none resembled the usual pentagram used in witchcraft. Even though she'd spent much of her recent days studying different Pagan religions, she had no clue what these slash marks symbolized. If she had to guess, she'd say they were closer to the black magic cult associated with Santeria rather than the more benign Wicca.

A whisper sounded behind the side wall, and she stilled. If she believed in ghosts, she would have sworn her mother was trying to tell her something. The reasonable side concluded the noise probably came from a bunch of kids outside. She half jogged over to the far side of the room where the stench grew stronger and images of dead bodies came to mind.

A loud bang behind her made her jump. She whipped around and slammed a hand to her chest. A wooden altar lay on the ground. Her swingy skirt must have knocked it over. "Stupid thing."

Get out of here. Now.

"One more minute." Please God, let me find something to help my mom.

Against the opposite wall sat another altar covered in dark stains. More blood, she bet. Her pulse raced. She'd find these thieving kids and take back what belonged to the families if it was the last thing she did. While she didn't have a CSU kit to test for blood, she could scrape the wall with her fingernails and hope the small flakes would be enough for the test. She stepped closer and reached out a hand.

"What are you doing here?" said a voice behind her. The blood drained to her belly. That voice. Low, dark, evil—and totally unforgettable.

She whipped around and froze.

CHAPTER TWO

OH SHIT. Think fast.

"What am *I* doing here? I work at the store." He sounded just like the guy who'd attacked her at the cemetery, but she couldn't be positive. And the gun aimed right at her chest wasn't helping one bit. Jenna could only hope the spikes in her hair made her look different from when she was at her mom's grave. She stepped forward. Aggression always served her well in the past. "What are *you* doing here?"

"None of your goddamn business."

Okay.

The funky chime from over the front door sounded. Yes! It had to be Deidra since Jenna had locked the door. If not, she was in big trouble. "That's the store owner." *So go.*

His eyes widened, then his gaze darted to the right.

"Jenna?" Deidra called.

For once, she was happy the old witch had returned. A flick of what might be concern, or possibly fear, flashed across his face, but in this dim light, it was hard to tell. She judged the distance to the door and prayed she could reach it before he decided to shoot her. Her 22mm was strapped to her ankle, but if she used it, her job here would be finished—or her life if he shot first.

Taking advantage of his apparent indecision, she dashed to the door and wrenched it closed behind her. No shots. Thank God. Or maybe she should thank the goddesses. Why she thought a flimsy, unlocked door would stop the guy from coming after her, she didn't know. *Go.*

Her feet pounded on the hard wood floor as she ran toward the office. No footsteps sounded behind her. Something wasn't right, but she had no time to figure it out. She slid to a stop inside the door next to the safe just as Deidra appeared.

"Jenna! Everything okay? You look out of breath."

What gave it away? The deep gulping breaths or the red face? "I'm good. I thought I heard something behind the door. I went down the hallway, but the second door was locked. It must be my imagination running wild." She ran a hand over her forehead. "So how's Shelby? Did she have her baby yet?" In less than thirty minutes? Something, or someone had brought Deidra back.

Where the hell was the guy? He must be waiting until they locked up, though she had no idea how he'd been able to enter the room in the first place. Some kind of secret panel must exist, or she would have heard him break into Deidra's office.

A tick tugged at Deidra's cheek. "No. False alarm. Go figure. You sure you're okay?"

If she admitted to her boss she'd seen a man, she might as well confess to everything, and that wasn't going to happen. The other possibility was that Deidra had hired the guy to check up on Jenna, but there was no way he could have notified the boss so quickly about her trespassing.

Decision made. Keep her mouth shut. "Yup."

"Everything go okay after I left?"

Did she suspect something? "Fine. No other customers showed up." That wasn't a lie.

Deidra pulled out a tissue and blew her nose before moving back toward the safe. Jenna scurried out the door. She didn't take a breath until she was in her car with the doors locked.

* * *

FOUR OFFICERS FLANKED Captain Lucas at the large wooden conference table when Jenna stepped into the room. She'd just come from speaking with Greg, catching her partner up on the intruder incident and then listening to his valued opinion. Now she had to face the fact she'd failed to bring back evidence when it was right in front of her. Damn. Many more slip ups like this and she might end up directing traffic instead of investigating.

On the far end of the table sat Larry Bernard who was working his own coffin case. Next to him was Sheldon Meyers, Larry's rookie partner. Marlon Giombetti was on the Captain's left. Poor guy. He screwed up more than any cop she'd known. He might be great looking, but he had the personality of a stick. She'd learned that fact from an up close and personal experience. Live and learn. To his left was Andrea Maken, his unfortunate partner.

"Now that Jenna's here, we can begin." Lucas flipped through a manila folder.

It's not like she was late or anything. She sat in the remaining empty chair, directly across from the captain. Larry passed down a steaming cup of coffee to her. Bless him. Her unsteady hand tilted the cup and coffee overflowed onto her fingers, scalding her. "Damn." Every rustling paper and mumble ceased. All eyes darted to her. Super. "I'm fine. Thanks for asking."

Her face hotter than the burning drink, she plastered on a smile only a cheerleader could muster. She wouldn't let any of the guys see her flinch.

The captain cleared his throat and turned to Detective Giombetti. "What about the Creighton Jackson case? Did he show up at his home yet?"

Giombetti looked startled he'd have to go first. "No. Andrea and I spoke to the man who owns the yacht next to his. He's sticking to his story. He claimed a real bad odor was coming from the boat. When he went to investigate, he found nothing, so he called us."

"That's when you found the corpse?"

"Yes, sir." Marlon shoved a photo toward the captain.

Even with the picture upside down, the image was ghastly. Jenna schooled her features, pushing aside the image of her mother's body without her head. The corpse didn't have his either. Then again he didn't have any hands or feet for that matter. For a brief moment she wondered if some high priestess had ended up with the missing body parts.

The captain slid the picture back to Marlon. "You need to find the yacht owner to help identify the body."

Marlon scribbled his pen on the yellow legal pad. The ink seemed to have run out. That was why she only used mechanical pencils. They were more reliable.

"According to his neighbors, he's out of town," Marlon said. "They all claim he takes the month of December off to ski in Telluride, Colorado." Andrea handed him a pencil, and Marlon tossed her a feeble smile.

"Anyone have a Colorado address or cell phone number for the guy?" Captain Lucas asked.

Marlon waved a hand. "Yes. I phoned him, but he hasn't returned my call."

Lucas's gaze shot down to the photo. "Let's pray HOPEFAL can pull a name out of the hat for us."

She hadn't been to the Henry O. Pomerantz Center for Excellence Forensic Analysis Lab (HOPEFAL) yet, but she'd heard they could process a body nearly as fast as any TV show claimed they could.

None of the other officers said anything for a moment, obviously trying to digest the horror.

Jenna leaned forward. "How do we know the headless man isn't the boat owner?"

"We don't." The captain shot a look at Giombetti, probably wondering why he hadn't asked that question. Score one for her.

"Larry, what progress have you made in the grave robbery case?" Lucas asked.

"Other than some very upset families, we have squat. No viable prints on the mausoleum, or footprints nearby. I have no leads until this guy strikes again. Jenna's really the one working the case."

The captain turned to her. "Want to fill us in on your findings?"

All eyes peered at her. She passed around her cell phone to show them the wall drawings. "I didn't get a chance to download the photo yet." Lame. "I was about to obtain a sample of the dried blood when some guy appeared out of nowhere with a gun and asked why I was there." His brows rose, though she didn't know why. "I put everything in the report." All except the fact she had no legal right to be in the backroom.

"Did you ask him his name?" her boss asked.

"Nope. His gun had one though. Smith and Wesson." She could have sworn Lucas rolled his eyes. "As soon as the front door to the shop chimed and Deidra, that's the owner, called out my name, he backed off."

"It says here, you returned to your boss' office. Deidra came in, but that the guy just disappeared."

"That's right. Though I swear there was only one door, and he didn't go through it. He was like some ghost."

"Could he be the same guy who attacked you in the cemetery?"

"Good possibility. He had the same raspy voice."

"You didn't list any description in your report."

"It was real dark in there. I can say he was Caucasian, about five ten, beefy, and no more than twenty-five."

Lucas made a note. "What did this Deidra say about the guy?"

Groan. "I didn't tell her. I wasn't sure if she was in cahoots with him. Besides, I didn't want to let her know I was snooping." She waited for his lecture on evidence collection but none came.

Lucas tapped his pencil on his pad. "While you were *snooping*, did you see anything that resembled human remains?"

"Not specifically. A putrid smell was coming from the back of the room, but this guy appeared just as I was about to investigate. I'm hoping to have another chance sometime this week."

That would mean she'd have to sneak back in. If she were caught though, anything collected would be inadmissible in court if Deidra complained. That would suck.

"Good. Do that."

* * *

No head. No hands. Legs cut off below the knees.

Forensic anthropologist, Dr. Sam Bonita, hoped like hell the dismemberment was post mortem and not the cause of death. What was left of the yacht man was covered in a gray, waxy material, which confirmed the body had been in the boat's cold, damp hull for days, if not weeks.

It was no wonder the Tampa PD had sent the body over to HOPE-FAL. The forensics facility, like the staff, was high tech and state-of-the-art. It still amazed him he'd landed a part-time job here. Too bad Sharon never lived long enough to see this place. His wife would have been so proud.

As he decided on his plan of attack for identifying the body, he turned off the piped in jazz music floating above the whir of the enormously powerful exhaust system. He was a classics kind of guy more than a jazz aficionado. Grabbing his digital Canon 5D Mark III from beneath the counter, he photographed the corpse from the neck down. Eric Markowitz, one of HOPEFAL's forensic pathologists, had told Sam he'd removed the organs and run several tox screens, the results of which would be ready soon. All Sam had to do was inform the police who'd been murdered—a job that wouldn't be easy since there were no prints and no chance of obtaining dental records. He cursed the bastard who nabbed the head for a souvenir and then cut off the hands and feet.

Even though his expertise was in studying the bones and not on the soft tissue, his room had all the luxuries of a pathology lab. In cases such as this one, he would need to use its super powerful disposal to get rid of unusable parts of the putrefied body once he was finished deboning the victim.

As he took the last shot, a knock sounded on his key-coded door. Sam put down his camera and note pad and stripped off his latex gloves. Before he could answer, the heavy door swung open.

His thirty-year old boss, Phil Tedesco, wheeled in with wet hair and nylon athletic gear. Freshly showered from his morning of physical therapy, Phil sat up straight in his wheelchair, looking more upbeat than he had in weeks. "I have a visitor for you, Doc."

"You said the lab didn't do tours." Rules were rules. At least that's what the Navy Seals had drilled into him.

"I invited him."

Worked for him. A tall, athletic man, around his own age, stepped into the lab and smiled. "Remember me?" The jovial guy swung out his arms in a big embrace.

"Chance Taveres?" He was a blast from the past. Freshly cut blond hair and well groomed in expensive clothes had never been his friend's style, but the new look fit him. "You son of a bitch. How the hell are you?"

"Good. Real good." His friend stepped forward and encased Sam in a bear hug.

Not used to demonstrative overtures, Sam moved away after a second. "It's been what?" He did the quick math. "Fourteen years? What have you been up to?"

Phil propelled his wheelchair forward. "I just hired him to join our forensic pathology team."

Sam's eyes widened. "No shit. You're a doctor? I'll be damned." Sam couldn't decipher the look that crossed Chance's face.

"Watch it. I know I was Mr. Party when we hung together, but those days are in the past." He turned to Phil. "If it's okay with you guys, I'd like to watch the master at work." He nodded toward Sam. "Perhaps my old buddy can finish showing me around when he has a minute."

Sam nodded. "I have no problem with that as long as you're willing to suit up and help me with my new project."

Chance glanced over at the corpse. "I'd love to."

Phil shook his head. "Knock yourself out." He spun around, his wheelchair tires squeaking on the tiled floor.

Sam pulled out a fresh pair of plastic scrubs, along with booties to cover Chance's polished loafers. "Here."

Shit. Chance knew everything about Sam's background, both the good and the bad. Sam didn't need his major fuck up to be exposed. "Did you tell Phil how we met?"

Chance clasped a hand on his shoulder. "You would have been proud, my man. I told him the truth. Explained how we rowed on the same team together in Ohio. And to answer your unasked question, I didn't mention your family—or your wife. I'll keep that info to myself."

"Thanks." Sam's wife had died because he'd been too damn self-absorbed drinking with his buddies to help her. "Do you ever see Carl Rodriguez?" Only three of the four-man crew team were still alive. Bill Butler had died in a car wreck two years after he'd graduated.

"Carl and I keep in touch every once in a while. He's a firefighter in Chicago now and has a wife and three kids."

"Wow. That's great. And you. Ever marry?"

"Tried it. Failed. I'm here to move on."

"I hear ya."

His friend ran a gloved finger over the dead man's chest. "So what do you know about this guy?"

Glad to be back on solid ground, Sam straightened. "Police found the body about fifteen miles south of here on Davis Island. The vic was crammed into a storage compartment in the hull of a forty-foot sailboat."

"Did the police talk to the owner?"

"They couldn't find the guy. A neighbor said he was in Colorado skiing."

"That'll be a shock when he comes home. His boat will never smell the same again."

Sam chuckled. "Amen."

"What's your next move?" Chance asked.

"I want to X-ray this guy." Sam pulled the portable X-ray over to the body.

Chance whistled. "You have two machines?"

The larger X-ray sat in the corner. "We have everything here. The portal X-ray comes in handy, especially when I can't get the body to the big machine."

"Impressive." Chance smiled. "Now I know I made the right move to come here."

Together they lined up the contraption over the body. Before they could examine the results, Eric Markowitz came in waving a brown evidence bag, which he placed on the counter. "Dr. Tavares, Sam. I thought you might like to see what was in the victim's pocket when I prepared him for autopsy."

Apparently, the two had met. He wouldn't be surprised if Eric would be Chance's mentor. Eric opened the bag with gloved hands and pulled out the contents. "The vic was wearing a University of Florida ring. I didn't find a wallet or any other kind of identification, unfortunately, but I sent his clothes over to the Trace lab. His shirt, and what was left of his pants, were well-made, but other than the victim's blood, I don't think the lab will find anything useful to point us to his killer."

Eric set the large, gold ring with the gleaming blue stone, displaying the initials, UF on the counter, the graduation date clearly visible.

"That puts our victim at about fifty-five." Sam cleared his throat. The dry room air made him perpetually thirsty. "Did the autopsy reveal cause of death?" Eric had performed miracles before.

"If the victim's cause of death was a direct result of a series of blows or a gunshot wound to the head, it would be difficult to determine on the headless corpse."

Smart ass. "But you figured it out, anyway, right?"

Eric shook his head. "The body was too putrefied to get a good read on him. I did find an enlarged heart, which was probably due to hypertension, but the rest of the organs were too far gone to draw any conclusions. I was hoping for something simple, like a bullet hole through his heart or a stab wound, but no such luck. The tox screen might show if the man was poisoned, but I wouldn't hold your breath. I had to extract the fluid from unconventional spots on his body since the head was missing."

Sam firmed his lips. "That's good to know."

Eric blinked a few times. "I can see you two are busy." He turned to Chance. "When you're done, come to autopsy room number four. I'll show you my world."

"Sure thing."

Once Eric closed the door, the room returned to tomblike silence. Sam turned to his friend. "I'd like your opinion on the X-rays."

He waited as Chance studied the images, curious to see if he'd notice the peculiar oddity.

Chance ran a finger along the screen. "The cuts around the severed limbs are particularly clean. It doesn't look as though any of the bones were damaged."

"That's the problem. I was hoping the instrument used would have left a mark on the bones themselves. That would make it easier to figure out the murder weapon."

His face transformed from one of question to realization. "Only a very sharp instrument could deliver that level of precision. Maybe it came from a hunter's knife."

"Or a scalpel," Sam said.

"Now that's a scary thought."

CHAPTER THREE

BALANCING THE UNGRADED SCANTRON SHEETS, test booklets, and the skull the kids had dubbed, Waldo, against his left side, Sam unlocked his university office door. He set Waldo on the clutter free desk, careful not to bump into either George or Georgiana, his two hanging skeletons that resided against the right hand wall. Tired from an afternoon of watching his students take their forensic anthropology final, he dropped down onto the worn, high backed chair, ready to begin grading.

The sterile office was devoid of photos or any personal effects for a good reason. He didn't need a reminder of his wife's death or how he'd fucked up his life. His dad's suicide still pissed him off, and while he loved his mom, she was often too drunk to remember his name. All the more reason for no pictures. Chance's arrival had brought back more than college memories, and not many of them were good.

Just forget.

The longer he procrastinated grading, the shorter his winter break would be and the more time he'd be wasting when he could be investigating the identity of the yacht man.

As he sorted the essays from the multiple-choice section his phone rang. Sam glanced at the screen and groaned. It was his mom. She probably wanted more money to feed her habit, money he didn't have, especially after buying the much-in-need-of-repair duplex. "Hello, Mom." He kept his tone upbeat.

"Sammy, you haven't called me in a while." Same refrain, same whine. At least she sounded sober.

He'd called last week to tell her he'd mailed her a check to help her through December. Too bad she'd been drunk and obviously forgot the conversation. "Sorry, how are you?"

Guilt ripped through him. He wanted to find some real help for her, but a rehab center was out of his budget, and she wouldn't qualify for Medicaid for four more years. Though in all honesty, what she needed was for his father to resurrect from the dead.

"Okay, I guess, but I miss hearing your voice." His mom coughed, a dry cigarette laden hack. "I wanted to see how my favorite son was doing."

He knew she wasn't referring to the criminal son who was locked away for armed robbery. "Great. I'm in the process of grading the semester exams as we speak." He didn't want to spend an hour on the phone, but if their conversation made her feel better, he'd stay on as long as she needed. His mom seemed to receive a lot of comfort from their weekly chats.

"That's wonderful."

Not really. A knock sounded on his door and his department chair poked in his head. "Hey, Mom, can I call you back? My boss needs to talk to me."

"Sure, Sammy."

"Talk soon."

He disconnected and pushed away the grief that grabbed him every time he spoke with her.

"Can I have a word with you, Dr. Bonita?" Rolf Hoffman tugged on his bowtie before smoothing the five gray hairs on his head.

Rolf never called him Dr. Bonita unless the conversation was serious. Sam didn't need this. "Sure, Rolf, come in." Sam refused to address him as Dr. Hoffman. He knew what his egotistical boss wanted.

Sam motioned to the one chair in the closet-sized office before straightening the stack of tests on his desk. He dropped his hands on his lap to give Rolf his undivided attention. "What's up?"

Rolf sat straight-backed in the chair. "You know the tenure committee will be meeting in March."

"Of course." Not a day had passed that he hadn't been aware of the impending deadline.

"I understand Tammy and you had a study going, but since I never saw the report before she left, you'll have to come up with something soon or there's no way the committee can grant you tenure."

Sam flinched at the pointed comment. The thought of opening up Tammy's betrayal would be like rolling in a swarming anthill. She'd published the work as her own like the good little backstabber she was. "I'll have something to you soon." Or so he hoped.

Rolf's eye's widened. "You're working on a paper?"

The man didn't have to sound so surprised. "No, I'm developing a handheld device that will enable scientists to scan a person's remains and tell the age of the skeleton."

"That's excellent, but I understand the last two patents you received took you years." Rolf's brows pinched.

"True."

"You haven't been doing any other research? I thought you were consulting on a project for York University in England."

"I was invited to work on the forty-four bodies they'd unearthed, but I had to cancel my trip. I had a family emergency." Mom had fallen after being drunk. Her broken hip required him to fly up to Ohio to see to her care.

He guessed it didn't matter that he'd already published ten articles before he came to work here, won numerous awards for his contributions to forensic anthropology, or had been given a commendation from Stanford for his work in the field.

Rolf stood, looking uncomfortable. "Well, good luck on your new invention." He swiped a hand across his jacketed arms as if he'd gotten dirty while in Sam's office. "I know how much the students like you as a professor. We'd hate to lose you. Give me a draft of your findings as soon as you can. And Merry Christmas."

Sam swallowed. "You too."

As if Rolf could walk through walls, the man disappeared down the empty corridor, his steps making no noise. Sam leaned back in his chair and refused to let the claw of despair get to him. He would get tenure. He had to if he planned to pay back his loans in the next century. HOPEFAL paid well for the time he was able to work there, but it wasn't enough.

Sam patted Waldo on the head, took a deep breath, and began the tedious chore of seeing how much his students didn't know about the human body. He was on his first essay when his cell rang again.

Christ. Sam dropped his pen. It clanked on the wooden desk and rolled to the floor. He'd never get these papers graded if the interruptions didn't stop. He grabbed his cell without looking at the display. "Yeah?"

"Hey, Doc, it's Phil."

Sam's muscles relaxed. "What's up?"

"Do you have a moment to stop by the lab?"

"Sure." He checked the small alarm clock on his desk. The time had sped by. "I have to run over to my duplex first. I'm renting the other half to an elderly lady, and she's wheelchair bound and is all alone. I shop for her once a week."

"Good for you. I'll be here for a few more hours. Stop by anytime."

Sam packed his papers and straightened his desk before locking his door. At the store, he purchased the few items Mrs. Delansky had requested. Since she basically asked for the same items every week, her list was easy to remember. He tried to add some variety to her diet by sneaking in some fresh vegetables or an extra helping of fruit with every purchase. Nutrition was so important at her age.

In less than thirty minutes, he arrived at her side of the duplex. He knocked, even though she always left the door unlocked at one p.m. every Thursday. He went in. "Hey, Mrs. Delansky."

She wheeled over to him. "Hi, Sam. Just leave everything on the table. I'll put it away. I know you're busy."

She had a hard time moving around the kitchen so Sam stashed the frozen food, milk, and eggs in her pint-sized refrigerator. "How are you feeling today?" She'd been suffering from gout and a bad cold for the last week.

"I still have a little cough, but otherwise I'm doing fine." She moved over to her desk. "Here's the rent check. It's still two hundred, right?"

He didn't know why she asked since he never changed the price. "Sure is." He could have charged some college student five hundred, but she reminded him of his grandmother, and Mrs. Delansky's only source of income came from social security. "Listen, I hate to drop these off and run, but my boss at the lab wants to talk to me about something."

"Go. Go. I appreciate all you do for me."

He gave her hug and hurried off. He was at the lab in less than an hour after Phil's call. With a quick greeting to the guard on duty, Sam took the elevator to Phil's office on the third floor. When he knocked and entered, Gina, his assistant, was hovered over his boss like a mother hen. She looked up and smiled. "Hey, Sam." She tapped Phil on the shoulder. "I'll get that report you want." In a flash, she was gone.

Phil leaned back in his chair. "I'll get right to the point. I'd like you to consider working here full time."

Stunned, Sam let the success wash over him. "I thought you said you didn't have enough work for me to be full-time. You admitted that bones weren't discovered on a regular basis."

"Times are a changing."

He couldn't believe his good luck. "Where do I sign?"

Phil held up a hand. "Take you time to think about the offer first. I know you like to teach, so I thought maybe we can set you up as a mentor to one of our new recruits."

"Sounds great. I'll let you know for sure tomorrow." Though he didn't need any time to decide.

"Then get going. And find who that yacht man is."

Sam nearly skipped down the hallway and slipped to his lab. The gurney with the headless man had been resting over the lip of the sink to allow any remaining fluids to fully drain from his body. He ignored the rancid smell and gowned up. After he dragged the sink's sprayer over the corpse, he turned the temperature to hot in order to melt the waxy covering off the body. While the remaining soft tissue had turned dark from putrification, what looked like a once colorful tattoo on the man's hip materialized.

Taking a hint from his predecessor and fellow Braham University professor, Kerry Markum, he dabbed a mixture of bleach and water on the skin's surface to bring out the tattoo. After he rubbed the skin in a series of slow circles, an anchor appeared, and his pulse quickened. This tattoo might provide a means to identification.

He grabbed his digital camera and snapped a picture. Needing a hard copy for identification purposes and for the police report, he plugged the camera into the computer. A minute later, he had what he hoped would be his corroborative proof of the man's identification.

Once he finished washing the body, he began the tedious chore of scrapping the skin off the yacht man's bones, careful not to leave any damaging marks. Two hours later, he carried the pile of bones over to the maceration station and placed them in the simmering water. He added a little Adolph's Meat Tenderizer and bit of Biz Laundry detergent to quicken the cleaning process, and immediately shut the clear hood to prevent the stench from knocking him out.

His sense of smell had deteriorated over the years, but simmering human meat still eroded his nasal passages and set off the gag reflex. Unless this man was one tough cookie, the cleaning process would take about two days on low. In the mean time, he wanted to collect some information from Creighton Jackson, the owner of the yacht.

Sam stuffed his outer coveralls, gloves and footies in the biohazard trash and washed his hands. Praying he didn't smell too bad from the dead man's vapors, he headed to Davis Island in the midst of rush hour traffic. Phil informed him that a Detective Giombetti was in charge of the murder investigation, but sometimes a non-uniformed officer was able to extract more information from a civilian than a cop.

The bumper-to-bumper traffic gave him time to think through Phil's offer. Sam's mother had wrapped her pride in the idea that the *good* son was a professor. Why she didn't think researcher held the same esteem, he didn't know.

Forty minutes after he left, Sam pulled up to Creighton Jackson's townhouse, the back of which faced Sedan Channel. It had an impressive view and was way out-of-his-league expensive. The report said Jackson was on vacation during December, but perhaps news of the murder had reached him, and he'd flown home early.

If the dead man in his lab was the owner, the neighbors might be able to describe Creighton, or better yet, provide him with a photo. Not that he had a face to match it to, but the man's coloring and size would help establish if the body might belong to him.

It took him three tries to find a neighbor at home. The woman who answered his knock was slightly out of breath. She was in her late twenties and wore Spandex mid-calf pants and a low-cut top. Her not so neat blonde ponytail together with the slight sweat on her forehead implied he'd interrupted her workout. He flashed his HOPEFAL badge, hoping the woman wouldn't scrutinize his ID too carefully. To most, a badge meant authority.

She dabbed a fluffy white towel down her chest, her long red nails extended, acting as if she didn't want to mess them up. "The police have already been here." His ploy seemed to have worked, or she didn't care who he was.

"I know, ma'am, but I wanted to see if you could give me a description of Creighton Jackson."

She looked at him for a moment before motioning him inside. Her immaculate, upscale house looked professionally decorated, almost as perfectly put together as she was.

"Can I offer you something to drink?" Her smile was suggestive, as if the wedding ring on her hand didn't matter much.

"No, thanks. This isn't a social call."

"Oh, too bad. I didn't catch your name."

"Dr. Sam Bonita."

"A doctor? Ooooh." She closed the gap between them and held out her hand. "I'm Sheila Gradkowski."

Leaving entered his mind, but he needed the information. "Mrs. Gradkowski. Creighton Jackson. What did he look like?"

"Creighton?" She sucked in a big breath and clasped a hand over her mouth. "I heard they found a dead guy on his boat. It wasn't Creighton was it?"

"I'm not sure, ma'am. That's why I'm here."

"Dear God." She glanced up to the left, and then back at Sam. "Let me see. He was nice looking, but he could stand to lose a little weight around the middle." She pointed a finger at his midsection. "He wasn't fit like you."

Sam held his frustration in check. "What else?"

"Well, he had sandy blond hair, fair skin, and lots of freckles." She waved a hand. "I kept warning him about being in the sun without sunscreen, but did he listen? No." A slow smile materialized on her face as she studied Sam from head to toe like a snake to its prey.

"How old would you say he was?" he asked.

"Old. Mid fifties. I only know because he was counting the days until Social Security, not that he needed the money. The guy was loaded, but there was something about free money that appealed to him."

"Do you know if he went to University of Florida?"

"Oh, my yes. He was a mega Gator fan. He and my husband both graduated from there, though Creighton graduated eons before Jeff." Her face looked horrified, as if Sam would think she'd married someone other than a young, handsome stud.

"Can you tell me how tall he was?"

She tapped her pink manicured finger on her bottom lip. "Maybe two or three inches shorter than you."

Estimating the man's height from the length of his torso put Sam's guess at five eleven. His gut churned. Creighton Jackson would never return his call. "Did he have any distinguishing marks on his body?" He wanted to see if she knew about the tattoo on the victim's hip before showing her the photo.

Her cheeriness disappeared. "How would I know? I never slept with him if that's what you're implying. That would be Deidra Willow's job."

"Where can I find this Deidra?" He hoped this new woman would be a safe topic.

Sheila calmed down somewhat. "She runs *Botanica* in Ybor. It's on 22nd Avenue."

He entered the information in his cell phone. "One last question. Did Creighton have any relatives in town?"

A loud engine rumbled up her driveway. Sheila raced to the front window, peered out and let out a gasp. "Crapola. It's my husband. You have to get out of here." She acted as if her husband would beat her if he found another man in the house.

"No problem."

Sam was halfway to the front door when she yanked on his arm. "No. Go out the back, so he doesn't see you."

From the look of panic on her face, he didn't have time to ask why. Since Sam had parked a few doors down, the husband wouldn't guess anyone was inside his house. He saw no reason to upset that apple cart. He'd grown up in a home of domestic turmoil and didn't need to cause Sheila any more grief, so he slipped out the back, happy to inhale the fresh salt air and be on his way.

Next stop, Ybor City, to visit the strange sounding store—and hopefully to locate Deidra Willows. The trip there took no more than fifteen minutes. At six thirty, few people walked the streets. From what he'd heard, the bar scene didn't heat up until nine or so. The couple of times he'd ventured here for dinner, the mostly Cuban cuisine had been great, but the rowdy crowd had been too noisy for his tastes.

Dusk had settled over the tops of the buildings, casting a shimmering gold layer over the hundred-year old brick buildings. Christmas lights were strung across the street from ornate lamp to ornate lamp, giving the neighborhood a festive look.

Sam turned onto 22nd Avenue and spotted *Botanica* two blocks from the main drag. There were plenty of metered parking places in front of the store. Raised a Catholic, he'd never had a reason to visit an occult store before.

Determined to find out if Creighton was the man in his lab, he stepped through the entrance and almost laughed when a weird, ghoulish sounding bell announced his arrival. A combination of mustiness, incense, and something he couldn't put his finger on permeated the air. Given how the place was crammed full of merchandise and small knickknacks, he figured the dust quotient would break the air quality meter.

Two teenager girls were browsing the back of the store and a forty-something year old woman was leafing through a book. A pretty pixie, keeping sentinel over the cash register, looked bored. She glanced up, and it was as if she'd shot out a tractor beam right at his chest, ready to reel him in.

CHAPTER FOUR

SAM CHECKED out the girl at the counter even though he had no plans to take her up on her open invitation. The studded collar and tattoo on her arm was not his style, but she deserved to express herself however she chose.

His mission was to speak with Deidra Willows, not get a date. Given Creighton Jackson was in his fifties, Sam figured the cashier most likely wasn't Jackson's lover, nor did she look old enough to own the store. He stepped toward the counter to ask for the owner and realized the girl appeared closer to thirty than twenty, which put her a few years younger than him. It didn't matter. He'd had enough of women on the prowl for one day.

"Hi. I'm looking for Deidra Willows."

She leaned over the counter giving him quite a view. "Are you sure I can't help you?"

He chuckled. "Positive."

She straightened and popped the gum in her mouth. "Deidra's in the back. I'll get her."

Interesting place. While he waited for the owner, he slid over to a table that drew his attention. Several jars were jammed to the brim with bones, and he fingered through them. They weren't human, but he wasn't sure which breed of dog they belonged to. Most were bleached white, meaning the owner had more than likely purchased the bones over the Internet.

"You need to speak with me?"

Sam turned to find a rather homely woman, forty-five to fifty, smooth brow line, wide set eyes and equally wide mouth. Her jaw was a little small for her face, but that didn't take away from the woman's presence.

He held out his hand. "I'm Dr. Sam Bonita with the Henry Pomerantz Center for Forensic Science." He shortened the name. The real title was a mouthful.

"Yes?" She didn't even blink, as if she knew of the place.

"Could we speak somewhere in private?"

"What's this about?" The woman didn't seem to care if the clerk or customers overheard what he had to say.

"I'm here about Creighton Jackson."

Her body stiffened, but her face didn't twitch a muscle. "What about Creighton?"

The use of the first name meant she knew him rather well. The two teenager girls giggled and sidled up to the checkout counter. The clerk chatted with them, but he blocked out the conversation, needing to word his statement correctly. "One of his neighbors said you and he knew each other... rather well. I was hoping you'd have a photo of him."

No concern crossed her face. "Not at the store, but at home, I might. Why would you want a picture of Creighton?"

She didn't seem to connect the dots between the forensic science lab and death, nor did she seem aware of the body found on his boat despite the news stations blasting the story ever few hours. "Did you know if he had a tattoo on his hip?"

She frowned. His change in topic seemed to distract her for a moment. "Yes. He had one on his hip in the shape of an anchor. Why?"

Damn. Though the body in the lab was in all probability Creighton Jackson, he wasn't happy about it. He wished he could leave the tell-the-girlfriend to the police, but once she thought about the conversa-

tion and realized Creighton was dead, she'd be devastated and would
need some answers.

"I'm sorry to have to tell you, but the police found a man in the
bottom of Creighton's boat who had an anchor tattoo on his hip."

She said nothing for a moment, her eyes searching the air. "Are you
telling me Creighton's dead?" Her voice came out raw.

"We believe so. Once I find a relative and obtain a DNA sample, I
can make a positive identification." No need to mention the man's
head was missing, making a photo ID near impossible.

She shook her head several times as if she wished hard enough,
what he'd told her would turn out to be false. "I can't believe it. Are
you sure? Creighton goes to Colorado this time of year. You must be
mistaken."

Surely, she couldn't believe that two people had anchor tattoos on
their hips, both of whom were friends. "Apparently, he never made it
there. Did you receive a call from him after he arrived in Colorado?"

"No. I haven't spoken to him in a while. We weren't seeing each
other anymore." Maybe that explained why her breakdown wasn't as
emotional as he'd anticipated. When Sam had found his wife bludgeoned to death, he'd sobbed for days.

She leaned back, almost as if she was about to fall. Sam reached out
his hand to steady her, but she caught herself on the table. "If you'll
excuse me." Without asking any more questions, she spun around and
disappeared down a dark hallway. He bet she'd be calling the police as
soon as the news registered. For now, he'd wait, ready for her questions
to surface. Shock had a way of short-circuiting reason.

He moved away from the table with the bones toward the front
door in order to notify Phil in private. He kept his voice as low as
possible.

"Are you sure it's Creighton Jackson?" Phil's comment came out
crisp and tight.

The last of the current customers whooshed by him, and he waited
until the door closed. "Strong chance it is. Maybe that cop, Giombetti,
can get something of Jackson's to test the DNA."

"I can give him a call."

"Thanks."

Sam stuffed his cell in his top pocket and pretended to study the other artifacts on the table. The cashier rushed over to him. "Did I hear you right? Did you say a friend of Deidra's is dead?" Her brow creased and her mouth pinched.

"It's possible."

She stepped back and raised a brow. "Are you a cop or something?"

"I work at a forensic lab."

"Oh." Her nose notched up. "How did he die?" A question Deidra should have asked.

"I'm not sure. Even if I knew, I'm afraid I couldn't tell you. It's confidential."

She blew another bubble. "I get it." He could almost see the wheels in her mind spin.

"Have you ever met Mr. Jackson?"

"Me? No, but I only started working here three weeks ago."

"So you probably have no idea if Mr. Jackson had any relatives in town." A long shot, but worth a try.

"Nope. Would you like me to ask my boss?"

"That would be helpful. Thanks."

"Don't go anywhere. I'll be right back." Her smile was as pretty as a spic and span room.

Hips swaying, she glided toward the office and disappeared around the corner. While he waited, he checked out the scent section in the store, though he wasn't sure why he found the strange fragrances so appealing. Maybe it was because he'd spent the last few years surrounded by the stench of decomposing bodies.

"Dallas Brockton. He's Creighton's son."

Sam whipped around at the sound of the cashier's voice. Gone was the cute, flirty girl. Instead, she appeared more focused and direct.

Because they had different last names, he might be a stepson.

She handed him a slip of paper. "That's what Deidra said. Here's his number." She stood so close she had to crane her neck to look up at him. "I'm Jenna Richman by the way."

He waited another second to see where her little game was headed, but when she kept silent, he dipped his head and lowered his voice. "Thanks again for you help."

She ran a hand over her spiked hair. "You from around here?"

He recognized the pickup line, but decided he'd play along for the fun of it. God knows he could use the levity. "I live north of here."

She caught her bottom lip with her teeth in a provocative way that almost made him question whether he should take her up on her offer. He shouldn't—couldn't. He had a job to do. Besides, it would certainly look bad if he failed to provide Phil with an answer on Sam's first big case.

"So what do you do at this lab? Dissect bodies or something?" Her tone implied she wanted to dissect him.

"I'm a forensic anthropologist." He hoped she wouldn't make any suggestive bone(r) jokes like so many of his female students used to.

"For real?"

An unexpected laugh escaped. "For real." He hadn't anticipated finding anything about her attractive, yet she intrigued him.

Jenna's light brown eyes morphed into the color of deep, rich coffee. She stepped back and let out a breath then edged over to a large storage bin that resided near the front of the store. After removing the cover, she pulled out a femur. "Is this human?"

Sam lifted the bone from her grasp and inspected it, acting as much like a professor as he could. "Yes. It's a human thigh."

She leaned in and sniffed the bone. "It doesn't smell. Do you think it's real?"

The only detectable aroma he noticed was her fruity perfume—a mixture of lemons and peaches. His wife always wore strong scents, and he was surprised he liked the lighter aroma. *Answer her question.* He juggled the bone to determine its weight, and then studied the epiphysis, which was at the end of the bone. "I'm afraid not. It's a very good replication though. This is definitely plastic."

"Oh."

Two customers, a woman and who he guessed was her daughter, wandered in. He cleared his throat. "I better let you get back to work."

She glanced over at them. "They can wait."

The woman eyed them with a scowl, and he raised his brows at Jenna. "Don't lose your job on my account."

As if he'd told her the place was on fire, her eyes widened and her body stiffened. She spun around and raced up to them. That wasn't the reaction he'd expected, but then, he didn't understand much of what women did.

It was time to get back to work anyway. Since Deidra didn't seem to be in need of answers, and Jenna was involved in conversation with her new customers, he left. Instead of heading back to the lab though, he sat in his car and dialed the number Jenna had handed him. He would have gone to Creighton's son's place and spoken to him in person, but he didn't have an address. He disconnected after two rings. How insensitive could he get? What if the body wasn't Creighton Jackson's? Sam needed a positive ID before giving the son such horrible news over the phone. He speed dialed Carla Pendowski—the technological wonder woman of HOPEFAL. While those computer geeks on TV seemed to be able to break into any and every computer across the county, Carla wasn't far behind.

"What's up, Doc," she answered.

"Funny." He liked Carla, even though she too wasn't his type. She wore her grandmother's vintage dresses, had an IQ at least twice his own, and loved hard rock music. A relationship like that would never work—not to mention she celebrated her twenty-third birthday only two months ago. A thirteen-year age difference was too much for him to grasp. "I have a job for you."

"My fingers are at your disposal."

The image of Jenna's fingers being at his disposal quickly came to mind, but he pushed aside the erotic thought. His first order of business was to make a positive ID on the body in the lab, not wonder what would have happened if he'd asked for Jenna's number.

"Doc, you there?"

Christ. His mind hadn't wondered like that in forever. "Yeah. I need to see if you can find an address for a Dallas Brockton, son of Creighton Jackson." He gave her the man's cell phone number.

He could hear the keys typing. "Got it. What are you going to give me for the address?" Carla loved playing games.

"How about a Starbuck's Mocha Latte?"

"Done." She gave him the information. He rarely remembered to buy her the drink, but she didn't seem to care. It was the challenge that mattered to her.

* * *

JENNA CLOSED the book she'd been reading for the past half hour and rubbed her temples. The incense seemed particularly intense tonight, or maybe the impending migraine came because once Sam Bonita left, no one of any interest had stopped in. Thursday nights at the shop were the worst. At least the tourists on Friday and Saturday made her job more interesting.

Stop daydreaming. Time was ticking. She was desperate to get into the back room for a sample of the blood, but Deidra remained glued in her office. If Jenna didn't come up with some evidence real soon, she'd be back on the street doing parking meter duty. As she sorted the cash register money, her mind zoomed in on the good doctor. He was smart, had a job that paid above minimum wage, and did she mention, hot? There was no question the man worked out. A runner perhaps, but he also must lift weights. He ranked a twelve on a scale of one to ten in the looks department. She especially liked his sandy blond hair and how the bangs fell over his forehead. His eyes were a rich, chocolate, and those lips—wow. Were they kissable or what?

The bell above the entrance rang cutting short her daydream. Her breath hitched at the thought Sam might have returned. She cut a glance to the door. Oh, no. Charlotte Evert, her BFF since third grade walked in. If she blew Jenna's cover, their friendship would die a painful death. "What are you doing here?" Jenna whispered.

"Chill." Charlotte looked around and squealed. "Wow. This place is cool. You learn any spells yet?"

"No." At least her friend wasn't in one of her lawyer suits. Her jeans and tight tank top might fool Deidra if she ever came out of her bat cave.

"I'm worried about you. We haven't gone out in weeks."

"That's because I'm working a case. I told you that."

"Yeah, so you said." Charlotte leaned on the counter. "So what's new? I miss our gossip time."

No one else was in the store, thank God. If she didn't give Charlotte some tidbit, she'd hang around and cause trouble. "Okay. Here's the scoop. This really hot guy came into the store a few hours ago needing to speak with my boss. Get this. He works at a forensic lab, and he's a freaking doctor. Can you believe that?"

"Shut up." Her eyes had that dangerous look in them. "You dragged him behind one of the tall bookcases and did him, I hope."

"Char, you know that deep inside I'm not like that."

Her friend rolled her eyes. "Fine. Don't tell me all the details. You asked him out at least. Right?"

Why had she ever confided in Charlotte in the first place? The whole gang would hear every word of what she said within the hour. "No. I lost my courage, but I did learn where he works, and that's good enough."

"He knows you like him though, right?"

"He'd be blind not to."

"You know what happened the last time you led someone on."

"I didn't lead Sam on, I only flirted with him a little." She scrunched up her nose. "Besides, he didn't act really interested." At least not yet.

"Then he's not alive. What's he like?"

Jenna stacked the postcards next to the computer. "The usual combination of Hugh Jackman and Brad Pitt."

"Oh that."

"Doesn't matter. He left without asking for my number."

Charlotte fingered the plastic skull heads in front of her. "I'm putting my money on you. I say you have him in bed by the first of the month."

That would give her fifteen days, which was completely doable. "You know I can't resist a challenge. And if I do? What then?"

Her friend's eyes sparkled. "The first pitcher of Margaritas is on me."

The headache that had been brewing vanished. "You're on."

Char checked her watch. "I have to go. Billy's down the street buying cigars, and I told him I'd only be a minute. We'll touch base this weekend, okay?"

"Promise."

Charlotte blew air kisses before scooting out the door. Jenna chuckled. Char and she were night and day in so many ways, but she never had a better friend.

It was time to get to work—on Sam, that is. Jenna jiggled the computer mouse that sat next to the cash drawer and clicked on the Internet. Customers often wanted to do research on some item from the store, so Deidra had provided wireless access. Go boss. Jenna typed in "forensic lab, Tampa, Florida." Up popped HOPEFAL, a recently constructed lab that sat on the University of Braham's campus. What do you know? Her alma mater. Sweet. Perhaps a visit to her former haunt was in order. Within minutes she found all the information she needed to put her plan into action.

"Jenna?"

She looked up. Deidra's eyes were rimmed red. "Are you okay?" When Jenna had gone in to ask for Creighton's son's number, Deidra had appeared fine. But that was a few hours ago.

Her boss waved a hand. "Just being sentimental. Creighton and I broke up months ago, but I'm having a hard time understanding why someone would want to murder him."

Stoic Deidra looked genuinely upset, an emotion Jenna never thought she'd see from her. Without thinking, Jenna shot into cop mode. "Did he have any enemies?" Sam never mentioned anything about murder, nor did he say anything about the decapitation.

She shook her head. "No. He was such a generous man."

"What did that forensic man say when he came in? Did he tell you *how* Creighton died?" Maybe Dr. Bonita was more forthcoming with Deidra.

"He didn't seem to know much."

Apparently, Sam didn't share with anyone. Interesting. "Maybe you could call Creighton's son. I bet that forensic dude will tell him every-thing—being next of kin and all."

"That's a good idea." A faint smile lifted her lips. "I'd love to be able to help the police find the killer, but...." Her eyes glazed over and she clutched her purse to her chest. "I think we should close early. I need to go home and rest." She sniffled again.

"I'll be happy to close at ten." Which would give her complete access to the back room.

Deidra shook her head. "No. No. I'll close now and worry about reconciling the money tomorrow."

So much for gathering evidence. "Whatever you say."

Jenna's Google search had already uncovered that Sam's Forensic Anthropology class already had their final exam, but his other class didn't end until two—tomorrow. And she didn't have to come into work until six. Now that was what she'd call perfect timing.

CHAPTER FIVE

BACKED BY A DEEP BLUE SKY, the sun beamed high in the sky over Braham University. Jenna parked across from the library, slipped out of her car, and inhaled the crisp air, happy to be outside for a change. She strode toward the Sociology building where she would hopefully find Sam—in room 153. Wasn't the Internet an amazing tool?

As she shot past his room, she glanced inside to make sure her information was correct. Bingo. There he was in all his splendor. Pumped, she turned around and walked by a second time, stopping at the windowed door to admire his tight butt and muscled shoulders. Fortunately, his back was to her as he bent over to help a student. As though he could sense her presence, Sam stood, and turned toward the door. With cat like reflexes, Jenna ducked out of sight. Getting caught now would blow everything.

Heart racing, she sped down the hall and out the front door in case he came out of the room to investigate. No way could she come up with a plausible explanation for stalking him. The adrenaline had blocked her ability to come up with a lie at a moment's notice.

Once in the clear, she tried to control her breathing. When was the last time she'd taken the effort to pursue a guy like that? A long ass time, that's for sure. Men always hit on her, not the other way around.

Too bad none of the ones who'd asked her out had jetted her libido into overdrive like Dr. Sam Bonita did. Generally, those who hit on her had been cops—understandable since that was who she worked with. She'd accepted a date from someone in her office—once. Okay maybe twice, or possibly three times, but never for more than a couple of dates. Giombetti had been the exception. They'd hooked up for close to a month. Talk about a mistake. Thank God he bought her story about why she didn't want to go out with him anymore. No way could she tell him he sucked in bed. The guy was too aggressive, even by her standards, not to mention his unwillingness to do his half of sixty-nine.

She glanced toward the exit door trying to decide if Dr. Bonita would hide in his office to grade papers or leave the building where she would conveniently bump into him. Even though the December air had a chill to it, she opted not to wear her heavy jacket because it made her look dumpy. Jenna had vainly worn a thin, tight sweater instead, which in retrospect was rather dumb.

Resigned to wait until he showed, she moseyed over to a cozy bench in the direct sunlight and pulled out a paperback on Wiccan religion she'd stuffed in her backpack. After finding her spot in the book, she read about the circle of protection. A half hour later, she looked up, wondering if she'd become so absorbed in the material that she'd missed him exiting the building. Other than a few cars driving by, no pedestrians were ambling about. Exams were finishing up, so it was no wonder the campus was basically empty.

Jenna checked the time on her cell again. Was she being stupid chasing this guy? Could be, but he might prove useful if she ever did locate what she thought were human remains.

After another half chapter, she closed the book. Forget it. No man was worth waiting this long. Especially in the cold.

She stood and was slipping on her backpack when something big slammed into her. Coils of injustice shot through her. She spun around. Holy shit. "It's you. The guy from the backroom at *Botanica*. What are you doing here?" He had no gun this time, thank God.

He had on a black leather jacket over a white T-shirt, dirt crusted boots, and blue jeans with holes in them. "I'd like to ask you the same thing."

Her scalp hadn't completely healed from the blow she'd received in the cemetery. If she knew for certain this was the same man, she'd cuff him and drag his ass down to the station. Pronto. "How did you get into *Botanica's* backroom anyway? I didn't see any door."

"For me to know."

Asshole. The back of her thighs touched the bench. Crap. Her damned weapon was snuggled deep in her pack. Even without his weapon aimed at her chest, he was big, strong, and mean looking.

Before she made a decision what to do, the man grabbed her arms and dragged her toward him, her face inches from his chest. "Just stay out of there if you know what's good for you."

"Jenna?" The call came from the walkway, some twenty-feet away. Sam! Footsteps pounded the pavement.

She struggled, and the guy released her. She cut a hard glare at the ghost man. "How did you find me?" She asked before Sam could reach her.

"Easy." He shoved her backwards. "Be careful if you know what's good for you." He then took off.

Jenna debated what to do. Yes, she wanted more information from him, but Sam had arrived. Well, it was too late now. The jerk had already jumped in a white pickup truck and peeled out of the lot.

Sam took hold of her upper arms. Gently. "Jenna? Did he hurt you?"

"No. He might have if you hadn't saved me." She wanted to give him a sexy look, but none of the muscles on her face seemed to work.

His gaze glanced downward for a moment. "Do you know him?"

She turned her attention back to Sam. "Kind of. I caught the dude in the backroom of the store. He was up to no good." She wouldn't mention the gun. Sam would be the kind to insist she report the incident to the cops. Wouldn't that suck? "He scared the crap out of me. That's all." f

"Let's get you out of here then."

Exactly her plan. "I could use a cup of coffee." She held out hands and planned to shake them, but real tremors raced up her fingers. Christ.

"Me too." They headed to the Jefferson Center that not only

housed the bookstore, but a mini food court. "Why are you on campus? Do you go to school here?"

"I do. I wanted to see if my professor had graded my exam. Some clerk told me my teacher wouldn't be back in her office for another few minutes so I was waiting outside, enjoying the day." Jenna waved her book to give credence to her lie." She hoped he didn't ask her any specific questions on religion or he'd seen through her charade.

She waited for him to ask the name of her professor, but he didn't. Good. One less lie to tell.

His cell rang. "Bonita." The conversation was brief. He faced her. "I'm sorry. I have go. My boss over at HOPEFAL just called and said something new was being delivered I have to handle." A combination of excitement and remorse skated across his face.

Just the in she was looking for. "I've always wanted to see that facility. I've heard about all the high tech stuff you guys have over there. I was even thinking of changing my major to criminology so I could work in a place like that." She delivered her little speech with just the right sprinkling of awe and youthful ideal.

His eyes widened. "You'll probably need to have a biology background if you really want a job there."

He acted as if there was no way she could handle the tough subject. If only he knew. "Oh. I took two bio classes, but they definitely weren't my favs." Yes, they were. She excelled in anything that had to do with science. Statistics was her downfall.

He hesitated for a moment. "I'm sorry, but we don't do tours."

"I don't want a *tour*." She hooked her arm around his bicep. "I just want a quick peek at the place."

He untangled their arms. "I'm sorry, Jenna."

She stood there while he walked away, not even glancing back at her over his shoulder. Fine. Not one to take no for an answer, she followed him. He seemed oblivious to the tail. Good. As he walked up the steps to the lab's front door, she ran up behind him. "Boo."

He spun around. "Jenna. What are you doing here?"

She tried to look contrite. "How much can it hurt to look? It's not like I'd wander off on my own." Before he answered, she slipped by him, pulled open the door to the lobby and dashed inside. He jetted in behind her.

"You shouldn't be here."

"Afternoon, Dr. Bonita." The grizzled guard sent them an engaging smile.

"Harold."

He lowered his voice. "Jenna, you really don't want to see what I do for a living. It smells. Really bad."

"I'm fine. I think my nasal passages died years ago."

The older gentleman struggled with the bow on a large package. Sam pointed a finger at her. "Wait here." He strode over to the guard station. "What do you got there?"

The guard glanced down to his package, and then back again and smiled. "A present for my wife, Dr. Bonita."

"Oh yeah? Is it her birthday?"

"Anniversary. Our thirtieth. She' coming home from the hospital tomorrow. She had breast cancer surgery."

"I'm sorry to hear that."

Harold nodded.

The bow on the package remained untied. "Do you need a finger?"

"I'd appreciate it."

What a nice guy. Few of the officers at the station ever stopped to converse with Tanner to see how he was holding up. Hell. She'd bet her badge no one knew the names of the janitors who kept the department clean either. Fools. Not only were workers a wealth of information, they were people too—people with families and hopes and dreams.

The old guy set his package off to the side, crooked a finger at her and held a pen over the logbook. "You'll have to sign in, Miss, and I'll need some I.D."

Sam let out a huff. "Jenna's not really with me."

He was so not going to get rid of her. Without thought to the consequences, she leaned up and kissed his cheek. "Oh, sweetheart, stop kidding." His heavy cheek stubble came as a surprise given his fair hair.

Sam let out a big breath and leaned over. "Fine, but only for ten minutes. Nothing more."

"Okay." She squeezed his arm.

Uh, oh. She had to show ID. Her license had her real name on it, not the name she'd told Sam. Maybe she could say Richman was her maiden name if her asked. Clever, if she did say so herself.

Fortunately, she was able to keep her back between the sign-in log and Sam's probing eyes. Before the guard said anything, she hurried to Sam's side. "Show me this wonderful place."

He cocked a brow. "Don't even think about sneaking away."

"I'll stick so close, you'll be calling me Ms. Adhesive." She turned her head and winked at the guard who was beaming.

Too bad someone else stepped into the elevator just as the doors were about to close or she might have stolen a real kiss. Darn.

He unwound her arm from around his and stepped away. "I have no idea what my surprise package is going to be. It could be quite shocking."

"You mean your surprise might be a dead body?" She swallowed a laugh at the concerned look on his face.

Even before she joined the force, her father made her go to the morgue with him when he had to identify a body. He called it decompression. Fortunately, he never insisted she go with him when he needed to watch an autopsy. That privilege came later.

"I'm afraid so."

Would she see Creighton Jackson by any chance? Perhaps she would learn some inside information on the man. That would make Captain Lucas take notice. And make Marlon Giombetti, the lead on the case, happy. Given how much his life had sucked, Marlon could use a break. He'd broken down once and said after his mom divorced, life had gone downhill fast.

Once off the elevator, Sam used his badge to open the doublewide, heavy-duty doors in the middle of the foyer.

"Why all the security?"

"We do a lot of testing and research here. Some of the work is for the police and sheriff's department, and some is for private citizens. It wouldn't do to have the lab results stolen, and more than just me would be devastated if my bones disappeared."

"I see your point."

After a series of turns down well-lit, concrete block corridors, Sam pressed several buttons to enter a room. The fresh cool air was spoiled by the unpleasant odor of formaldehyde and rotting bodies, partially masked by room aerosol.

She listened a moment to the soft jazz. "Kenny G? I like it." That wasn't a come on. She seriously enjoyed the music.

"I'm more into the classics myself."

Ah, one more difference between them.

She'd been to the city of Tampa's crime lab, but it didn't compare to HOPEFAL. Every counter gleamed, and the room was bigger than the house she'd grown up in. "Nice digs."

He chuckled, and she liked the sound of it. "I think I could put twenty of my college offices in here. I really don't need all this space, but I won't complain." He stepped over to a hooded region, looked inside, and flipped off a switch. "I won't open this because the fumes will make you gag. But there lies your boss' ex-beau."

She sucked in a breath. "You cooked him?" She peered through the glass at the large bubbling vat. Though she prided herself in her strong stomach, this grossed her out. Big time.

Sam looked a little sheepish. "Had to. I needed to see the bones, and the soft tissue prevented me from doing a thorough examination."

Her admiration for him grew. "I guess someone has to do it." She leaned forward and smiled. "Where's this surprise you're expecting?"

As if her wish were her command, the door swung open. A tall black woman rolled in a good-looking guy in a wheel chair. On his lap sat something wrapped in pink shrink wrap, only the plastic hadn't been shrunk. It was a cauldron, just like the ones the Santerians used to do spells. It was the type of cauldron she'd been looking for. With bones and sticks sticking out and everything.

How the hell had HOPEFAL gotten a hold of this? And from where? Her fists clenched. This gave her one more reason to stick like glue to Sam Bonita.

"Merry Christmas," the man said. He then noticed her. "Who's she?"

Sam's body tensed. Uh, oh. Jenna stepped between them. "I kind of forced my way in. I'll go. I don't want to get Sam in trouble."

The man waited a beat. "If you'll excuse us then?"

She needed to ask Sam out. More so now than before, but the window of opportunity was closing fast.

"I'll walk you out," Sam said. Thank God for chivalry, or maybe because the doors were controlled by a fob.

"Thanks." She rubbed her palms down her side. Why was she so nervous about asking a guy out? She'd done it tons of times but standing next to Sam Bonita made her feel like she was fourteen again. Perhaps it was because the stakes were so high, or because all the men she'd ever slept with had a bicep measurement bigger than their IQ. Sam was different. He was smart, but not arrogant—a rare combination.

Sam remained silent as he swiped his fob through several doors. Once they were in the foyer, the tour ended. "Be careful now." His attitude came off cool but not angry. "And watch out for men trying to knock you down." A long beat later, he smiled.

Relieved, she leaned closer, acutely aware the guard could hear every word. "If you're free this weekend, do you want to catch a movie or something?"

To his credit, he took a good five seconds before he answered. "Sorry." He nodded behind him. "Work calls. There's no telling how long I'll be with the witch's brew in there. Once I start, I lose all track of time." He studied her for a moment longer. "If you give me your number, I'll call you once I come up from the deep."

A lie if she ever heard it, but it was better than nothing. Jenna pulled a scrap of paper from her backpack and scribbled her number on it. "Here ya go. Don't be a stranger!" She tried to act cool, but from the way he avoided eye contact, her attempt to flirt fell flat. Sam Bonita was a straight arrow—a really cute straight arrow.

He stuffed the paper in his pocket, and then headed back down the hall. She knew he'd never look at the paper again, and the rejection hurt.

CHAPTER SIX

JENNA SLAPPED a hand on Larry Bernard's desk. "Why didn't you tell me?"

He looked up, his mouth slightly open, acting as if he had no idea what she was talking about. "Oh, you mean about the cauldron?"

"Yes, the freaking cauldron—the one with the bones inside. Bones that could belong to my mother."

He had the courtesy to look sheepish. "Pull up a seat. I'm sure the captain would have told you if he knew you were here."

"Ever hear of a phone or a text?" She nearly toppled the chair as she dragged it from a vacant desk. "Spill."

"Late last night, a call came in about someone spotting a person putting a witch's cauldron in a storage unit."

"Where?"

"At a facility on Dale Mabry Highway. Unit owner's name is Christine Reynolds." He held up a hand. "We contacted her, and she had a solid alibi for the time of the sighting. She said she's the only one to have a key and keeps nothing in the unit but furniture and boxes of paper. Christine has no idea who had the key or why someone would put a caldron in her unit. I checked it out this morning, and what she said was true. We're looking into the storage facilities' workers now to see what they know."

"Who called it in?"

"I have no idea. The call came from a pre-paid cell phone."

Untraceable. "Damn."

"The cauldron is over at HOPEFAL now. They'll find out if the bones are human." A sad smile filled his face. "Don't worry. We'll get your mom's ... your mom back."

Once her anger at Larry diffused, she thanked him for letting her know. "Keep me in the loop, okay?"

He pointed the tip of his pen at her. "Promise."

The door to the captain's office was closed, but the light was on inside. Voices sounded, meaning he wasn't alone.

Jenna leaned against the wall next to Lucas' door waiting for his meeting to end. A smile crept onto her face. They'd found actual evidence. The cauldron might lead to finding the bastards who were stealing bodies.

The captain's door opened five minutes later and Richard Melmont, the head of Internal Affairs, strode out. Bummer. That would put Lucas in a not so good mood. She'd been about to step away, when her boss called to her. "Jenna?" He checked his watch. "I thought you'd be on your way to work."

He kept track of when she worked? Scary. "The store's just a ten minute drive. Can I talk to you for a sec?"

"Sure." He stepped back into his office. "Did you learn something last night?"

"Not yet."

"We need to tie *Botanica* to the thefts."

"I know." She took a slow breath, not able to contain her news. "I saw the cauldron at HOPEFAL."

A spark of interest appeared in his eyes. "How did you manage that? The place is locked up tighter than Fort Knox."

He must not understand the power of female persuasion. "The forensic anthropologist working the case came into my store. We talked. He gave me a tour." Kind of.

He sat in his chair, pulled a file closer, and opened it. The photo of the cauldron was on top. "What was a scientist doing at a store full of superstitious crap?"

She repeated how Sam had found out Creighton Jackson's identity by his tattoo and had come to the store to speak with her boss. "Deidra used to date Creighton."

"Interesting. You tell him you're a cop?"

"Not yet." She'd figure out later how to explain to Sam all the lies about school and lies about her job.

"We don't need an undercover person at the lab. They aren't hiding anything from us."

"I know." Now came for the hard part. "I stopped by to see if I could partner with Larry on this case. I think if the two of us work together, we'll get results faster."

"He has got a partner. Sheldon Meyers. You know that." He leaned back and wrapped his hands behind his head. "What I need is for you to do your job."

"I realize that, but—"

"Jenna." She knew that tone.

"Fine."

When her boss opened the folder on his desk and studied it, it was her clue to leave. Once out of his office, she looked inside her backpack to make sure she had the tube to test for blood. Though how she would work the cash register and find her way to the back for a sample while Deidra sat in her office was anyone's guess. But Jenna Holliday, super sleuth, was no quitter. She'd figure out something.

The ten-minute drive to *Botanica* turned into twenty. Either a hockey game or a concert must be drawing the people to the Channelside district, the area sandwiched between downtown Tampa and Ybor City. She had to park two blocks from the store and race to arrive there in time. As she rounded the corner, a large, casually dressed black man excited the front door and scurried into a beat-to-shit white car. Odd. The store wasn't supposed to open for another fifteen minutes.

Deidra stood at the door smiling. Now that was a rare sight. Deidra and smile didn't go together very often. The woman was as stoic as a

Puritan. Except she had broken down a little when Sam told her of Jackson's death.

Jenna's boss glanced up and spotted her. Instead of waiting for her to reach the front door, Deidra flipped the CLOSED sign to OPEN and disappeared inside. Jenna brushed off the slight and took note of the customer motoring down the street. She squinted to identify the Florida license plate number, but he took a right so fast, she was only able to catch the first three digits: XMA something. Between the make and model of the truck, however, she should be able to identify the man.

Slightly out of breath from the sprint, Jenna rushed inside. "You had an early customer?" That would be another first.

Deidra halted. The once radiant smile evaporated. "He's an old friend."

Couldn't be that old. The guy was a good ten years younger than Deidra. "Okay."

"Excuse me." Deidra waddled back to her office, leaving Jenna to open the store.

Whatever. Jenna slipped to her usual place behind the counter and opened the cash drawer. Empty. Thanks Deidra. Now she'd have to disturb her for the cash, something Jenna didn't relish.

She tiptoed down the hall to Deidra's office not wanting to be accused of being Big Foot. The door was slightly ajar. Deidra withdrew a wad of cash from her pocket and locked it in the safe. Whoa. Where had the much cash come from? If the man had purchased something from the store, the money would be in the drawer until closing time.

Her recent customer/old friend didn't appear to be flush with dough, if his crummy car was an indication. Oh, shit. She bet the dude paid Deidra seven fifty to do a spell. Not that Jenna had proof, but the conclusion was logical.

Regardless, she needed cash for the till. After thirty seconds, she knocked.

"Come in."

Jenna received a frown for the second time today. "Cash?" She held up the drawer.

"Sorry. I forgot." Deidra opened the safe but used her body to block the view.

Jenna glanced over at the door leading to the mysterious back room. It looked like it was ajar. Deidra might have conducted some kind of business back there, and then forgot to close it. Good for Jenna, bad for *Botanica*.

"Here ya go." Deidra handed her the cash, and Jenna went back into the store. A guy dressed in tattered jeans and a big beer belly fingered the merchandise on one of the tables.

"Can I help you?" she asked.

He puffed out his chest. "Deidra hired me to work here."

No way. Had Deidra fired her but had forgotten to tell her? Or was he here to spy? On Jenna.

* * *

"So, tell me about your cute new girlfriend." Phil had wheeled into Sam's lab so silently, he hadn't heard him—or else he'd been too wrapped up in analyzing the bones to notice. Surely, his mind hadn't been on perky Jenna. She was wrong for him, or so he tried to convince himself. She was too bold, too curious, and definitely too sexy. He was used to woman who wanted him to make the first move, though he had to admit, her assertiveness was refreshing. Just not right now.

His face warmed. "I hardly know her." The fact Sam didn't have to ask which cute girl made him sound guilty.

"Where did you meet?"

Sam told Phil about how he'd found the identity of Creighton Jackson. "The owner of *Botanica* identified the tattoo as his."

"So Jenna's a cashier over at *Botanica*, and she goes to school here part time."

"Yup. Given we need to find out the cauldron and its contents, I'm thinking she might be a source of information about the occult."

"Good thinking." His boss scooted his chair up to the gurney. "Tell me what you've found so far."

Thank God Phil seemed willing to drop the personal digging. "I had Kirkpatrick fingerprint the cauldron and the bones before I sorted the pieces. I'm not expecting any prints on the bones themselves, but we might find something on the cauldron. If we do, Nathan will put the prints through AFIS." [Anja: **AFIS** stands for Automated Finger-print Identification Systems

"Don't hold your breath."

"We could get lucky."

Phil grumbled something as he craned his neck to look at the find on the gurney. Sam pressed a lever to lower the table to make it easier for Phil to view.

"Thanks. I see one skull and a skullcap. I take it we're talking human here."

"Definitely. There may be more than two people, but I won't know until I compare the bones with the skulls."

"Do you know how long ago these two died?"

"I was working my magic when you can in."

Phil smiled. "How can you tell which bones belong to which body?"

Sam drew an imaginary line across the gurney. "These seven bones are from the same body. Note the color. They're different from this stack."

Phil waved a finger as if he suddenly recalled something. "Two sets of bones would be different colors if they were in the ground for different lengths of time."

"Or if the bodies were embalmed. The amount of formaldehyde would affect color. Bodies that are dressed in different material affect the bone color too."

Phil shifted in his seat. "Can you tell if these bones originated from bodies that were snatched from coffins or could the bodies have been dumped and left in the open?"

"I haven't gotten that far yet. It'll take me days to figure out if we have a killer or a grave robber on our hands."

"Sounds good." Phil wrinkled his nose as he looked into the caul-dron. "Is that dried fruit?"

"Banana, best as I can tell. I did a little Internet search and found some groups combine the elements when they do spells."

"Like wind, earth and fire kind of spells?"

"Something like that." He'd ask Jenna. She probably knew.

Phil shook his head. "Still don't get the fruit." He pointed to the cup of red liquid and sniffed. "Is it blood?"

"Yes. The bones were found floating in the stuff. I'm not sure if it's animal or human. I sent a sample to Trace. "

Phil sat back in his chair. "You aren't much help today."

Sam couldn't tell if Phil was serious or just yanking his chain. Then his boss smiled and Sam relaxed.

"I'm trying."

"Well, you keep at it, Doc. Let me know what you find. Maybe you can write a paper on how Salem witchcraft came to Tampa."

"I just might do that."

Having missed lunch, his stomach grumbled, and he let his mind turn to food—a much safer topic than the mysterious Jenna Richman. She intrigued him, but call him old fashioned, he didn't feel comfortable with a woman asking him out. His father had drilled into him all the roles men should play and being subservient wasn't one of them. His mom had been such a doormat it might have provided him with a distorted view of the man-woman relationship though. What he did believe in was safety, and Jenna was a high-voltage live wire, the opposite of safe.

Then why couldn't he keep his mind off her?

* * *

SAM HAD SPENT the weekend grading his final exam papers and sending in grades. He'd called Dr. Hoffman and announced he was leaving the University to work in the lab. To Sam's surprise, he actually seemed upset. Here he thought his boss was chomping at the bit to let him go.

His lab door swung open. Gina Andries, Phil's assistant, waltzed in carrying some X-rays. She handed him the folder. "Officer Larry Bernard is working a case involving the theft of bodies at Peaceful Sanctuary. Franklin Manchester's body was stolen from there three months ago and TPD still has no leads. As you can imagine, his son and daughter-in-law are quite upset. We're hoping his skull might be one of those in your kettle."

"I'll take a look."

He expected Miss Efficiency to leave, but instead she leaned against the counter and crossed her arms. "It's possible some of your bones came from the recent theft at Fairlawn cemetery. The cops are working on getting medical records of the six stolen skulls now. I'll drop them off when I get them."

"Great."

Gina's mouth looked more drawn than usual, but this case was getting to everyone. She tossed him a weak smile and left. No wonder Phil had hired him full-time. These thefts could keep him busy for quite a while.

For the first time in days, Sam pushed the image of Jenna aside and focused on the first piece of good news. He'd already loaded the photos of the skull and skullcap into the computer. He now scanned the X-rays Gina delivered into Photoshop and dragged the first one on top of the image of the skull. He had to nudge the X-ray until the maxillary teeth lined up. At first glance, the two images appeared to be a match, but when he zoomed in on the teeth, they were slightly misaligned. The nasal width and maxillary prognathism weren't quite right either. Damn. Maybe this did come from the recent theft.

A small knock sounded on his door. Gina must have forgotten something. He waited for the musical sound of the keypad, but a second knock erupted, harder this time. He walked over and opened the door. "What are you doing here?"

CHAPTER SEVEN

JENNA WAS the last person Sam expected to show up at the lab, especially after Phil had basically booted her out. He had no idea how she'd made it past security, unless Phil had left her name with the guard. It was one more thing to investigate.

"I hope you don't mind me stopping by," she said, half out of breath. "When I called the Center to speak with you, they patched me through to your boss." As she breezed by him, her floral scent tightened his groin. "He said I was welcome to stop by anytime."

The matchmaker would hear about this. Only Chance knew about what happened with Sam's wife and why he didn't want or need another relationship.

Jenna leaned over the pile of bones on the gurney, her hands clasped behind her back. He didn't have time to socialize, and he certainly didn't have time to think about her or her scent. "I hope you don't mind if I work while you look around. I have a lot to do." He thought that came off well—welcoming, but not inviting. A non-scientist would become bored in less than five minutes. She'd be saying goodbye in no time.

Jenna frowned and nervously ran her finger through her hair. Damn. He hadn't meant to hurt her feelings, but he wasn't convinced he'd proven himself to Phil yet, and time was of the essence. Alienating her wasn't his goal either. Jenna might be able to help with what went on in *Botanica's* back room.

"No problem." She strutted over to the computers. "What's this?"

The superimposed X-ray over one of the skulls gleamed a bright blue. "I was trying to match some dental X-rays to the skull in the cauldron."

"Cauldron?"

"The pink shrink wrapped item you saw the other day when you were here."

"Oh." She bent over the computer screen. "Those two look like they match."

Apparently the fact the cauldron contained a skull didn't seem odd. He supposed it made sense since she worked in the business. He walked over to where she stood. "I thought so at first too." He tapped the screen. "See how the teeth don't line up precisely."

"Yes."

"Means those two are the wrong people."

When she continued to study what was on the screen, he moved back to the gurney and slid his magnifying glass over the cranium.

"Now, what are you looking for?" He almost jumped. He hadn't noticed she'd stepped close. Too close in fact.

"I'm trying to identify the victim's age."

She eased back to give him room. "How can you tell that from just a skull?"

He debated suggesting he explain at a later date, but since she seemed so interested, he didn't want to extinguish her enthusiasm. The teacher in him had kicked in. "See these cracks in the skull?" She nodded. "The smoother they are, the older the person. This one is no teenager."

Jenna leaned back as if someone had pushed her. "Male or female?"

"I can't tell yet." The color in her face had gone from slightly pink to death white. "Are you okay?"

She looked up and he could have sworn her eyes were watering. "Sure. Why wouldn't I be?"

"Do you want to sit?" He nodded to the stool.

Her smile faltered. "No, I'm good." She pointed to another skull-cap. "And this one?"

She might sound fine, but her clenched fists told him otherwise. "This person was late twenties to early thirties."

Jenna's brows pinched together as if she were trying to do a complex mathematical formula in her head. "I can't imagine the connection between those two. How did they end up in the same melting pot, so to speak?"

He had to hand it to her. She was clever. "I have no idea, nor is it my job to figure that out. I'm just here to find the identity of the people."

"Any evidence of trauma?"

Her question surprised him. Even taking into account all the CSI shows, Jenna's deathly serious tone set off an internal alarm.

"On the older one, yes."

Sam's stomach let out a loud grumble. Jenna grabbed his arm and tugged, as if the previous conversation had never existed. "I'm famished too. What do you say we get something to eat?"

"You go ahead. I've got work to do."

She leaned closer and poked his arm. Her large, brown eyes searched his face. She was such a tiny thing, and her clean scent raced to his groin. Stupid body.

"You are human. Right? You have to eat sometime."

Before he answered, a series of beeps, indicating someone was entering his lab, interrupted them.

Jenna's eyes widened and her mouth half opened. "Oh, I'm sorry. I guess I should go and let you do your thing."

Carla Pendowski, the computer guru never made a lab visit—at least not to his lab, but he was glad she'd chosen that moment to enter. The tech glanced over at Jenna. "Hi, I'm Carla."

"Jenna Richman."

Carla turned toward Sam, winked, and held out an envelope. "I have a letter addressed to you. It looked important so I brought it right over."

He looked at Jenna. "Give me a sec, and I'll walk you out." Though if she got in through the security doors without his help, she probably could get out. He took the #10 envelope with his name typed in large bold letters, set it down, and pulled off his gloves. There was no return address or stamp. "Who's it from?"

"What do I look like? A snoop? I didn't open it." She shot Jenna a conspiratorial smirk. He figured woman did that kind of thing. What did he know?

He ripped open the short end and emptied the contents on the counter. A tri-fold letter fell out. When he reached out to pick it up, Jenna stopped him.

"Maybe you should use gloves."

Who was this woman? "Why? Do you think the envelope is tainted with anthrax or something?" He chuckled, but she didn't return the smile.

"Well, it's been done before." If only she knew how much he respected her insight, she wouldn't have acted insulted.

Carla planted a hand on her hip, her brows raised. "Ever hear of fingerprints?"

Sam shook his head and smiled. "You women. Why must you think in such sinister terms?" Both of the women's eyes widened. He must have overreacted. Being near Jenna made him lose his tight reign on logic.

"You don't know where the envelope has been," Carla chimed in.

"Fine, but how do you know it's not from a female admirer?"

Carla chuckled. "I haven't seen you glance at a female since you've worked here. Until now, I hear."

God. He didn't need Jenna thinking she was the exception to the rule. "You girls win." Sam pulled on a clean pair of latex gloves and picked up the letter. He read the short message, not quite under-standing why anyone would have sent it to him—or what it meant.

As Jenna peeked over his arm. "Who's it from?" she asked in a sultry whisper.

"I have no idea."

"Read it out loud."

He cleared his throat. "Beware the bones you seek to identify. I will curse you if you disturb their souls." He tossed the letter on the table. "That's dumb."

Silence passed between Carla and Jenna until a small sound eked out of Carla's mouth.

"What's wrong?" he asked.

Her eyes glistened. "It's a curse. You should put the bones back into the cauldron and tell Phil you refuse to work on the case."

He couldn't help but laugh. "You believe in that black magic stuff? This is a joke. I wouldn't be surprised if Phil sent this because I have the cauldron."

"I don't think so." Carla wrapped her arms around her waist, and her large, gaudy ring caught in the mesh of her shawl. She tried to pull it out, but that seemed to make things worse.

Jenna shot over to Carla. "Stand still. I'll help."

As Jenna freed her, a tear dripped down Carla's cheek.

"Carla, did something happen to make you fear spells?" he asked. There was more to the story than some witch's spell.

She spun around and punched the door open button. "I can't talk about it." She ran down the hall.

Had Jenna not been with him, he would have followed her. Perhaps Gina could offer some insights on Carla's odd behavior. The women in the lab seemed to stick together.

When Sam turned back to Jenna, he caught her reading the note he'd left on the counter. Fortunately, she had the sense not to touch the paper with her bare hands. She too was acting as if this threat was for real.

She glanced up. "Could you make a copy of this? I have a friend who might be able to help with the meaning?"

"Not a problem, but I don't believe I'm in harm's way."

"Think about it. You receive a cauldron full of bones. How many people were even aware you're working on this case?"

"Besides you?"

She opened her mouth, and then shut it. "Yes, besides me."

"The Tampa Police Department. They recovered the cauldron. And Phil, my boss, who assigned me to the case, along with his assistant, Gina."

"How about the owner of the cauldron? Where did the police find these bones?"

"In a storage shed on Dale Mabry, why?"

"Do you know for sure the owner didn't see the police take possession of the cauldron? Or follow the cops to this facility?"

He liked her sharp mind. Sam didn't think like a criminal, but Jenna apparently did.

She ran her fingers through her hair. From the softening of her face, the silky texture gave her pleasure. His mind jumped to doing the same thing until she dropped her hands.

"It's worth looking into, but how did they know I was the one with the cauldron. I'm not the only forensic anthropologist at HOPEFAL."

Jenna's right shoulder jutted forward. "Do you know if the police checked the logs for who entered the storage area last?"

"How should I know? I just analyze bones. I'm not a detective, nor do I interface with the cops. That's Phil's job."

She rolled her eyes. "You can lower your shields, Scottie."

Okay, so she nailed him. It just wasn't a topic he wanted to discuss. Bottom line, the cops had failed his wife, and he didn't trust them.

She snapped her fingers. "Could someone here at the lab have leaked the information?"

He stared at her wide-eyed, innocent face. To his knowledge, no outsider other than Jenna had been in his lab. Could she be the leak? "I wouldn't know." But he sure as hell would find out.

CHAPTER EIGHT

"You tossed her out?" Phil set his Coke can on the desk and frowned.

"Damn right I did." Sam tucked his thumbs in the pockets of his lab coat as he paced Phil's office. "You tell me how someone other than the police and you knew I had the cauldron. Jenna was the only one in and out of the lab who wasn't an employee. She had to have mentioned it. Remember she works at an occult store. Perhaps she recognized the cauldron and is here to find out what we know."

Phil appeared to ponder his comment. "A student could have seen the cops drag in a pink shrink wrapped pot."

"Even if someone had noticed the cauldron being delivered, a casual passerby wouldn't put a curse on me, and a casual passerby wouldn't know I'd be the one assigned to check out the cauldron." Sam couldn't stop pacing.

"Do you have any proof of Jenna's involvement?"

Before Sam could come up with a good response, Gina breezed in. "Dinner."

Phil's face brightened. "Thanks." He took the plate of meats and fruits and placed it on his lap. The tempting aroma reminded Sam he hadn't eaten since breakfast.

Gina stood behind Phil. The two looked like a solid team, but they couldn't have been more different. Phil had on his pale blue buttoned down shirt with the HOPEFAL logo and beige slacks that blended in with pasty white skin. Gina wore skin-tight black pants and a low cut red top that contrasted well with her ebony skin.

Sam still hadn't figured out their relationship. He'd heard Gina's dad had been Phil's captain when he worked at the sheriff's department, and Gina had confided in Sam that she'd been a history teacher before deciding she wanted to be a cop. After Phil was shot apprehending a killer, she gave up her aspirations to go into law enforcement and agreed to help Phil run this lab.

Phil looked up at Gina and smiled, and a small surge of envy surfaced at their tight relationship. He thought he and Tammy had been tight too, until she turned on him with no apparent remorse. He'd been used, plain and simple.

"I hear you have a new girlfriend," Gina said.

Not again. "Hardly a girlfriend, or even a friend. I think she's a plant, though I don't know her agenda."

Her brows creased. "What happened?" Gina stepped from behind Phil and perched a hip on the edge of Phil's desk, showing off a long, lean leg.

"Ask Phil, who hopefully will find out what he can about this chick. She's dangerous."

Sam knew his response was rude, but he wasn't very rational when it came to women.

* * *

CARLA LEANED over the bathroom sink and wiped her mouth with a rough paper towel. She'd vomited every day for the last week and knew why after last night's test. She grabbed her stomach. The bastard who'd raped had gotten her pregnant. While having a child was a dream come true, she didn't want to have a baby under these circumstances. She was single, only twenty-three, and had dreamed of falling in love with Mr. Right.

Her parents had drilled into her that Catholics didn't get abortions.

To make matters worse, her attacker had been black. That alone would kill her folks when or if they ever found out. Her older sister went missing six months ago, and Carla doubted they could handle any more grief.

She'd have to keep her problem from them until after the baby was born, and then give the child up for adoption. She sniffled and swiped a tissue across her nose. Enough. *Suck it up, Carla.* What's past is past.

She peered into the mirror to see if any telltale sign of her vomit episode showed. Other than her red eyes, she appeared normal—well as normal as she could be. Once she redid her ponytail, she headed out of the bathroom.

As she turned right to head back to her office, she bumped into a wall of a man. He grabbed her upper arms, probably to steady her, but the restriction caused a need-to-flee so strong her heart nearly jumped out of her chest. She pushed away from her attacker and nearly tumbled on her butt. Somehow, the man managed to catch her before she hit the floor.

"Excuse me," the mystery man said in an unexpectedly soothing voice. His tone didn't sound anything like the man who'd attacked her, nor was he an African American, but that didn't matter. Her distrust of men had hit a high a few months ago.

He searched her face. "Are you okay?"

Carla took a deep breath. "I think so." Stupid. All men weren't bad, just the one who'd violated her.

"You look pale," he said. "I'll walk you back to your office."

Carla couldn't remember the last time anyone had bothered to help her. Most people called her four eyes, geeky, or gawky. She couldn't help it if she was good at math and computer science.

"Sure. Okay." She didn't need help finding her way down the hall, but she'd been stupid to turn down his offer. He was a hunk with a capital H. "My office is the last one on the right."

He walked close beside her, acting as though she might stumble at any moment. They stopped at the office entrance, and she turned to face him. It was almost like a date. "Thank you."

"You're welcome." Her door nameplate was glued next to the door. "Carla Pendowski."

"That's me." She smiled and waited for him to say something inappropriate about her nationality since she'd spent her childhood being the butt of Polish jokes.

Instead, he smiled back. "Chance Tavares. Nice to meet you."

"Chance. What a wonderful name." Maybe she'd get lucky. Ha. Ha. Not going to happen.

For a moment, he almost looked uncomfortable. They shook hands, hands that were warm with slightly callused palms and strong fingers. He was definitely all male.

Before Carla could come up with something pithy to say, the tall stud placed a hand on the small of her back, and she nearly swooned from the intimate contact. It must be the dehydration or the ranging hormones that were affecting her equilibrium.

He led her over to her desk and pulled out her chair. "Can I get you anything?"

"No, I'm fine." While she wanted to say something smart sounding, her mind came up blanker than a zero megabit file. "So what brings you here to the lab?" *Oh, that was exciting.*

"I just started working here with Dr. Eric Markowitz."

"You're working for Eric, huh. I'm sorry."

He laughed, and then pulled up a chair. "Why do you say that?" He winked. "Give me some dirt."

Her heart beat faster. Why was he bothering with her? He was so cute. "He's a stickler about everything."

"Cool. He'll help make me be a better pathologist."

What a great attitude. Carla wanted to tell him he had the most beautiful dark brown eyes, but she wasn't good talking to drop dead gorgeous men—especially ones with fit bodies. She wished her body didn't have all those bumps and lumps, but that's what she deserved from sitting at a computer all day.

Feet pounded outside her office and Sam rushed in. Chance jumped up. "What's wrong, Sam?"

"Carla, who gave you the letter?"

"I told you I saw it on the front desk. Harold was somewhere else, so I picked it up. Why?" Surely he wasn't freaked out over the note now.

"I went out to the parking lot to retrieve something from my car, and I found my car windshield broken."

She gasped. "It's the curse."

*　*　*

CARLA AND CHANCE rushed after Sam as he sped outside. Both acted as though he might punch out someone—and he'd been tempted. Actually, he'd been more tempted to yell at Harold for leaving his station.

Two cops were stationed next to his car, filling out paperwork. Fixing the windshield would put a strain on his already tight budget, and he needed his car in case Mrs. Delansky had a doctor's appointment or required her prescription to be refilled.

"You have any idea who would do this?" one of the officers asked. "An aggravated student perhaps?"

Sam ran through the list of names in his class. "No." He was damned if he was going to mention the cursed note. After the cops copied down his insurance information, they told him they'd follow up.

"That's all?" Sam wanted the perpetrator caught—now.

"Sir, we'll let you know when we find out something. The rock on the seat looks like it came from that flowerbed over there. We won't be able to get prints off a surface that rough."

Same lame excuse they gave him when his wife called to complain about someone trying to break into their house.

Carla touched his shoulder. "Come on. There's nothing more you can do out here. The vandal isn't going to walk up and admit he did this." She looked around the campus, acting as if the window smasher was hiding in the bushes. Her eyes watered and she swallowed hard.

"You nervous about something?" Sam asked. He shouldn't have freaked over a broken window. Sheesh Carla seemed to be the one chasing a bigger demon.

"Heck yes, I'm nervous." She turned to Chance. "I want to go back inside. Curses are bad things." She whispered the last sentence.

For a scientist, she believed in this New Age stuff a little too much.

To make matters worse, Chance seemed to side with Carla. He and his friend needed to have a talk.

The moment his two cohorts disappeared, Jenna stepped out from behind the bushes, as if she'd been lying in wait. "Hey."

"Jenna, what are you doing here?"

Her bottom chin wobbled a little. "I go to school here, remember?"

She wasn't studying botany. "Someone broke my car windshield. You know anything about that?" He hated himself for his cruel tone, but she always seemed to be in the wrong place at the wrong time.

Her brow furrowed. "No. Why would I?"

"You've been here a while, right?"

A genuine look of surprise crossed her face. "Not really."

Jenna was involved somehow; he could sense it. "Didn't you tell me you used to play softball in high school?" When he'd walked her out of the lab, the topic of her high school athletic career had popped up.

"Yeah, so?"

"Someone just threw an ace shot through my window with a big fat rock."

Her mouth dropped opened. "And you think I would do that to you? You're shittin' me, right?" He winced at her foul language.

"I'm deadly serious."

"What's my motivation?" She held out very clean hands. His pulse lowered, but she could have used some wipes to clean off the dirt.

"How the hell should I know?" She planted her hands on her hips, and then lowered her arms just as suddenly. "Look, I'm sorry someone harmed your property. I have a cousin who does real good car window repair work. Would you like me to call him?"

"No." He did, but he didn't want to be indebted to her.

"Did you call the sheriff's department at least?"

"The campus police are taking care of it."

"What are you going to do?"

"Do? Wait for the cops to find out who did this." If history meant anything, he'd be waiting a long time.

Jenna smiled. "Have you eaten?"

Sam couldn't believe her moxie. He was about to say no, when his traitorous stomach growled. Again.

She tugged his arm. "Come on. My treat."

The word treat enticed him, but he wanted to investigate Jenna more thoroughly before he gave into her sexy ways. "Another time." He pulled out of her grasp.

She cast her gaze downward. "Look, we got off on the wrong foot. I need to talk to you about something."

"I'm not interested in what you have to say." With that he strode toward HOPEFAL's entrance and disappeared inside.

"You'll be sorry," she called after him as the door clicked close.

Sam's back stiffened. He wanted to believe she was the innocent woman she portrayed, but his sixth sense told him she was up to something. Instead of heading to his office, he went to speak with Carla. When he reached her office, Chance wasn't around. Good. Her pale skin didn't look healthy. "You okay?"

"Oh, hi, Sam. Sure thing."

Liar, but he wasn't in the mood to discuss her issues today. He had his hands full with Jenna. He pulled up a chair. "Do me a favor?"

"You know I will."

He needed to buy her something special to thank her for helping him so often. "I want all the information you can dig up on Deidra Willows, the store in Ybor called *Botanica*, as well as Jenna Richman."

Her fingers stopped typing and she looked up at him. "Jenna? You want me to spy on your girlfriend?"

"She's not my girlfriend."

Carla winked. "Oh. Okay. But it's going to cost you."

CHAPTER NINE

CARLA BLEW into Sam's lab the next afternoon. "Deidra Willows isn't the sole owner of *Botanica*. She's a co-owner with two others." She pulled up a chair from the computer station and sat down. There were bags under her eyes, and her cheeks seemed to sag more than usual.

"Who else is?"

"Her sister, Shelby Vivaldi, along with, get this, Creighton Jackson."

"I'll be damned." Sam hadn't expected that name to surface, though if the two dated, it made sense. "Did you tell Phil?"

"I thought I'd let you handle it."

Sam paced in front of the empty gurney. "I wonder if his death could have been a result of a lover's quarrel or a business dispute."

Carla rubbed her hands together. "Sounds like soap opera material to me."

"Do you know the percent of the store each person owned?"

"Fifty, twenty-five, twenty-five. With Creighton being the largest owner."

"Who stood to inherit his portion? His son maybe? Or the two sisters?" Carla was thorough to a tee.

She shrugged and stood. "Gotta get back to you."

"Sure." That was the first time since he'd been here the super tech didn't have a ready answer.

Carla turned her back as though she didn't want Sam to see the defeat on her face and disappeared out the door. Something was wrong. Carla would have dug and dug until she knew which movie Deidra and Creighton had last seen, how much their electric bill was last month, and who they had a crush on in high school. Must be a woman thing—something he was never good at figuring out.

Shit. He'd forgotten to ask her about Jenna. He stripped off his gloves and opened the door, hoping to catch her before she reached the elevator to her office. Instead, he ran smack into Nathan Kilpatrick who wore a frown on his face.

"Nathan." The short, squat man with the frizzy red hair and thick black glasses handed him a folder. Without as much as a hello, he stepped on by. Okay. "Something wrong?"

"I have the results of the fingerprints on the cauldron. Almost died getting here though. That idiot janitor forgot to put out a wet floor sign up and I slipped." He brushed his rear end to emphasis his anger.

"You okay?" He seemed to be asking that question a lot lately.

"Nothing broken."

Good. "What did you find?"

"You aren't going to believe this. The only prints on the cauldron belonged to Creighton Jackson. He's your dead guy, right?"

"I'm afraid so." Now that put an interesting twist in his black pot of goodies.

* * *

CAPTAIN LUCAS WALKED by Jenna's desk. Without changing speed or glancing at her, he said, "Three more days."

Wonderful, but he didn't have to remind her. She understood full well the need to find warrant material. The backroom held the key, which meant what she needed was a distraction for Deidra while Jenna found what she needed.

Sam.

Or not.

Her faux boyfriend seemed to be convinced she was evil incarnate —as in throwing rocks at his car and writing stupid curses. As if. She needed to change his mind somehow. Ignoring the ringing phone on the empty desk next to hers, she discarded one plan after another. Then it hit her.

Without further thought to her newfound scheme, she slipped out of the station and headed to Braham University. It was close to noon, and she had no idea if Sam ate lunch inside, or if he ate lunch at all, but she was determined to find a way to talk to him.

The HOPEFAL guard posed no problem, as her name happened to be on some special list. She signed in and he buzzed her into the inner sanctum. Though she had no proof, she suspected Captain Lucas had called Phil to tell him why Jenna was wandering about.

Fortunately, she remembered the way to Sam's lab through the maze of corridors. However, she had to wait about fifteen minutes before someone exited the hallway door to Sam's lab, because the hall required a fob for entrance. The last time Phil had let her in.

Once inside, she hurried to Sam's door and rapped hard. Thirty seconds later, the door swung open. He must have been expecting someone else, because his face turned hard the moment he laid eyes on her.

Man, did she have her work cut out for her.

"May I come in?" she asked with an extra dose of sweetness.

"How did you get in?"

"Hi, to you too."

He turned around and headed toward the gurney in the middle of the room. She followed. Talk about a foul mood. Not that she really blamed him, especially if he believed she was responsible for the recent troubles. There was no way to convince him she wasn't without breaking cover.

She rubbed her arms to increase the circulation. "Don't you want it a little warmer in here? It has to be hard to work under these conditions." She couldn't think of anything witty or flighty to say.

"Dead bodies need the cooler temperatures." His tone sounded colder than the room.

"Or they'll what? Turn to bone? Turn to stone?" He swiveled

around and glowered. Whatever. He wasn't making this easy. Okay, maybe it was time to cut the snark. "I stopped by to see if you'd learned who'd tossed that rock through the windshield." Another lie, but so what?

"No."

"Any more curses arrive?" She needed a break here.

"No." Sam rearranged some of the bones on the gurney.

Jenna moved in close. "I was talking to my boss's sister this morning, and she told me something you might find interesting." Actually, Jenna had called Shelby to see how the pregnancy was going and they got to chatting.

Sam continued to mess with the fragments. "Yeah, what was that?"

"That Deidra is into performing rituals with bones." Okay, so that wasn't exactly the truth, but it could be true. Jenna didn't think Deidra had it in her to kill someone though.

His hands stilled. "Do you know this for sure?" Finally, she got his attention.

She turned his shoulders toward her and ran her hands down his chest. "And if I do?" God help her for stretching the truth.

"Then maybe we should talk to your boss." His eyes sparked with interest.

"I kind of doubt she'd admit she's the owner of that pretty black pot of yours if that's what you're thinking." Jenna stared at his lab coat, wondering what his skin tasted like hidden underneath.

"You're probably right." When he stepped back from her, Jenna worked to ignore the small rejection.

"You know, one time I snuck into her backroom and found a sacrificial altar."

"Really?" The man might actually be thawing toward her.

"Guess what else I found?" She tilted up her chin.

"What?"

"Blood."

"Blood?" Sam placed his hands around her hips, and her heart zipped into over drive. "What kind of blood?"

"What kind? Oh, I don't know, but I bet you could find out."

Jenna leaned into him and raised her lips, hoping he'd take the bait.

She wasn't so dumb to think he didn't have his own agenda regarding her.

"Can you get a sample for me?" he asked.

She'd given her plan more thought on the way over. "Sure, but you'll need to come with me."

His interest deflated like a popped balloon. "Jenna, I need to work. Unless it involves solving this case, I can't afford to take the time. You can't do it yourself? You work there."

She wasn't going to let his attitude ruin her day. Time for part two of the plan. "No." She refused to explain why. "Come on." She tugged on his arm.

"You want to go to the store now?"

The stubborn man was infuriating. "No. I have a surprise for you."

"Jenna, I can't."

"Yes, you can. Surprises imply spontaneity. Let it go. For once."

The tension in his body seemed to release, as if she'd broken through a barrier of resistance. A small smile lifted his lips. "Okay. You win, but this better be good."

Joy sliced through her. "I promise."

Jenna didn't know why it was so important to prove herself to him, but it was. She led him to the parking lot, but she had no intention of telling him her surprise would take all day.

"Where are we going?"

"To see dead bodies."

* * *

JENNA FINALLY PULLED into the drive of his duplex and cut the engine. Sam had offered to chauffeur them the last hour, but she'd refused. Driving through the on-and-off rains in the dark took concentration and Jenna's eyelids had started to droop. He should have insisted he take over.

He unclipped his seat belt and faced her. "You are one unique woman, Jenna Richman. I've never had a date take me to a body farm before."

"I guess it's not exactly the romantic first date many would dream of, huh. I know I loved seeing the bugs feast on the bodies. Dr. Ranfield really takes pride in documenting the effect of the environment on corpses."

"That was my favorite part too." She was sweet to pick a place he'd appreciate.

She climbed out of the car, and he stepped around to her side. She'd expect a kiss, but neither of them was fit for anything intimate. They both smelled. Bad. Stomping around dead bodies had its drawbacks.

Jenna clasped his arm, and a breeze blew between them lessening the odor. "Did you really think I'd puke my brains out when I saw the rotting corpses?" She turned her face upward.

"At first, yes, but you're a lot tougher than I'd given you credit for." She'd changed his mind about a lot of things. "You said you'd tell me how you knew the manager." She'd mentioned she'd been to the farm before, and that's how she'd been given permission to land a tour. He wondered if she took all her dates there? Or just him?

"The owner's an old friend of my dad's. We used to go there when I was young."

His stomach clenched. "Kids shouldn't be exposed to the horrors of death." Didn't matter Jenna didn't seem any worse off for it.

"Dad wanted me to get used to the *realities* of life." She crooked her fingers around the word.

"I don't agree with his tactics. If I ever have kids, I'll protect them for as long as I can." He waved a hand. "On a different note, may I say your choice of restaurants was fantastic." Even if they ate the meal in the car. Not that they had a choice. They would have driven off the patronage. She'd picked a quaint Mexican cafe whose food was superb and cheap. He placed his hands on her hips. "I had a great time, Jenna." No lie.

"Me too." Her smile her face lit up.

How could he have thought she'd throw a stone at his car window or send that stupid curse? Jenna was a warm-hearted woman who happened to turn his best laid plans awry.

"You want to come in for a drink or something?" God, he sounded like a teenager, but he hadn't perfected the art of picking up women, especially after dating Tammy for three years.

"You bet." She dragged him to his front door, and he let a laugh escape. The sparkle in her eyes told him Jenna had one thing on her mind—sex. While she might not like it, Sam wouldn't take advantage of her on a first date. Keeping his distance though would take every ounce of strength he possessed.

He unlocked the front door and Jenna shot through the foyer, and then stopped. "Wow. It's so neat. And nice."

Neat? Hardly. The newspaper lay open in the dining room table and his breakfast dishes were still in the sink—not to mention, he needed to wallboard the kitchen, patch two holes in the dining room, and paint the living room. The duplex's best attribute was the new laminate flooring the previous owners had installed.

"Thanks." Sam flicked on one of the living room lamps. "You want some wine?"

She looked up at him and tilted her head. "Maybe later." Her fingers began working their magic on his shirt buttons.

He grabbed her hands. "What are you doing?"

"Doing?" She laughed, the sound reverberating in his head.

"Well, I know what you're doing, but now's not a real good time. For starters, I stink."

"I don't smell anything." On tiptoes, Jenna threaded her hands under his opened shirt and around to his back. God, he'd forgotten what a warm touch could do to him. Her fingers on his bare skin set him on fire. Then she kissed him. Hard. Then soft. Then hard and soft again. Her assertiveness combined with tenderness turned him on like no one had ever been able to do. His willpower was crumbling one cell at a time.

She parted her lips in an open invitation. He accepted, darting his tongue in and out. She tasted like hot sauce and spice. Jenna was sweetness and innocence all rolled into the cutest package. He kept kissing her, praying he could stop at the right moment. When she came up for air, her eyes glassed over then blew a strand of hair from her eyes, but the pesky strand returned to its position.

"Let me help you with that." He was able to do what he'd been wanting since the moment he saw her—touch her hair. It was silky soft, yet had hard ends, but not as hard as him.

Jenna kissed him again, full on the mouth, and then leaned back. "Thanks."

Sam sucked in a lungful of air. "Now it's my turn to say, wow."

Grabbing his hands, she backpedaled until her knees hit the sofa edge, and they tumbled onto the large cushions. Sam landed on top of her but made sure to catch himself before he squashed her. If she didn't find his smell offensive, he'd go with it. Jenna's breath came out ragged as she fumbled with the zipper on her jeans.

"Let me help you with that," he offered. Only his fingers didn't move, because reason intruded. Jenna deserved more respect.

She blinked and shook her head. "I can't wait." Sam held himself above her as she wiggled under him. Jenna ripped off her jeans in ten seconds flat. She held them out with one hand while she pulled a condom from the side pocket with the other.

"You came prepared?" He didn't know what to think. No woman had ever brought a condom to bed, but her act ratcheted up his anticipation. Hormones blocked his resolve to keep them apart.

"Damn straight I did. I didn't need you using that as an excuse."

Jenna dropped her pants on the floor, whipped her t-shirt over her head and flung it toward the coffee table. She missed. He wanted to pick up her clothes, but he couldn't take his attention off her bra. Plain white. No lace. No frill. He expected her to wear something red hot or lacy and black. And most definitely whimsical and impractical—like Jenna. But he liked her pure, simple choice.

She sat up and unhooked the back. The bra went flying behind her, landing on the lampshade. He was tempted to retrieve it, but her perky breasts drew his attention.

He touched her pointed nub with his finger. "Nice."

That was an understatement, but his mouth was too dry for a long conversation. Amazing, perfect mounds came closer to the truth.

"Now it's your turn to get naked." She lowered her chin and looked up through her lashes.

"You won't get an argument from me." Why did he say that? It was like some devil had put a spell on him. War raged inside. The good soldier told him to stop. The erect one forced him to proceed. Sam jumped up from the sofa and held out his hands to help her up, and her smile disappeared. She must not have understood. "Let's take this to the bedroom."

"Bedroom? That's so conventional." She raised her arms and wiggled her fingers, luring him to get back to the sofa.

Sam jumped out of his pants and shirt, and then pulled off his boxers. Jenna whistled and he tried not to smile. He picked up his jeans from the floor to fold them, when her hand shot out and grabbed him.

"What are you doing? I can't wait."

"Give me sec."

She jutted out her breasts and chin. "Are you kidding me? You've got a raging hard-on and a naked woman ready to do the nasty with you, and you have to fold your clothes?"

"Chill. Putting things away makes cleaning up later much easier."

She sighed, and then rolled her eyes. "Well, as long as you're into being the neat freak, we might as well take a shower. I don't want you getting halfway there and have you decide I smell too bad."

Her slightly nasty tone hurt, but she'd read him dead on. "Bathroom's down the hall, first door on the right."

"You're joining me? Right?"

He nodded. "I'll be in there in a minute."

She scrunched up her face. "After you fold your clothes I suppose?"

"You got it."

"Whatever."

Buck naked, she wiggled her way out of the living room. Only when he heard the water run, did he breath a sigh of relief. Jenna was right. Something was wrong with him. He should have taken everything she offered, but something stopped him. Fear, maybe, of being too close again and then ruining it.

Perhaps he should forget everything and hop in the shower with her, but who knows what kind of ideas she'd come up with. He imagined them writhing on the shower floor with Jenna on top. Or perhaps he'd press her against the wall, hot water streaming over them, and drive his cock into her. His dick twitched. No, he didn't think he was ready for the wild side—yet.

Ten minutes later she came out of the bathroom with a towel wrapped around her body, hair all wet and pretty. His erection sprung to life again.

"Next," she announced.

At least she didn't criticize him for not joining her. In fact, she didn't appear phased by his nonappearance. The shower stall was only four feet by three feet, which would have made a dual shower a tight fit—a very tight fit.

Sam hurried his washing so Jenna wouldn't have to wait too long. The logical half expected her to leave when he came out of the shower, but the emotional side prayed she'd stay. Once finished, he threw on clean clothes and rushed out to the living room. He smiled. There she was, sitting pretty on the sofa, munching on a piece of left over chocolate cake he'd brought home from Gina's birthday party two days ago. A glass of wine sat on the coffee table without a coaster and next to her was her crumpled t-shirt and bra she'd picked up. One point for Jenna.

CHAPTER TEN

WAIT A MINUTE. Sam was dressed? In jeans and a buttoned-down shirt? Did he really think putting on more clothes would keep her out of his bed? No way. Once Jenna had seen those ripped abs, she was hooked—on him. She wouldn't be surprised to learn he had a calendar that listed which exercises to do and at what time of day in order to keep him in such good shape.

Looks weren't the only thing that attracted her to him. He'd treated the guard with kindness and had talked with her like she was a person and not some stupid little girl. His straight-arrow attitude made her want to throw something at him at times, but his strong beliefs appealed to her.

"You didn't leave," he said, with a hint of surprise.

"Were you hoping I would?" If he thought that, he didn't know her very well. Then again, how could he know her well? She was pretending to be someone she wasn't.

He had the decency to look a little embarrassed. "No, not at all. It's just that—"

Jenna held up both hands. "You don't need to explain. You're not used to women who are so forward, am I right? I get that all the time." Not true, but she understood him, maybe better than he did.

"It's not that." Sam slipped down next to her on the sofa. Heat radiated off him from his shower, and he smelled like fabric softener.

Jenna curled her feet under her butt and faced him. The towel slipped a little lower on her breasts, but she didn't adjust the material. She saw no use hiding what he'd already seen. "I give, tell me why you thought I'd leave."

His jaw clenched for a moment, and then he seemed to relax. "Well. You're...so uninhibited, and I'm... not. You're also not...intense like I am."

Ohmigod. She was both uptight and intense, sides she'd kept hidden. "I guess you don't know me very well." Now there was an understatement of the year.

"It's not you. I saw your eyes when I neatened up. You're into spontaneity. I work so much, I wouldn't appeal to you."

She nearly choked. "Do I act like you don't appeal to me? I'm not asking for a wedding ring, you know. Ever hear of friends with benefits?" The lie churned inside her. She wanted commitment, a family, and someone to love her, but she'd never say those words out loud. To anyone. Disappointment would only follow.

He opened his mouth, and then smiled. "You win." Sam stood, slipped his hands under her legs and carried her to his bedroom. Despite the traditional location, she'd go with the flow. *E-ticket ride, here we come.*

The overhead light blazed bright. The bed was made, and no clothes were on the floor. The dresser was neat and the desk immaculate. Go Sam. In those respects, he was very unlike her.

Sam carefully placed her on the comforter as if she were some delicate flower. He stepped back and began to unbutton his shirt.

Jenna made a T with her hands. "Time out."

His brows furrowed. "What?"

"Okay. It seems to me like you have no clue what to do with me. Don't you know it's my job to undress you?"

"Is that so?" He cocked a brow. "It just so happens, I do have a clue. A very big clue." He peeled off his shirt and hung it up in the closet. His broad shoulders and muscular body made her pant. Sam was a feast for sore eyes.

"I'm dying here. Let the clothes go for once, okay? All your stall tactics make me feel like you don't want to make love to me."

Sam stared at her as though she were some alien. "That's not true. Look at this." He pointed to his erect cock.

"I can see that, but..." She waved a hand. "Never mind! Come here."

Sam shrugged, and then turned off the lights.

"No." Aargh. "Keep the lights on. I like to look at you." At this rate, they'd never get to bed.

Sam obeyed. He stepped out of his jeans but left on his boxers. She wasn't worried. They'd be easy enough to remove.

He pulled back the comforter on his side and slipped in. "Slide under the covers with me."

Finally.

* * *

SAM SCOOTED to the opposite side of the bed and watched as Jenna eased in next to him. God only knows how much he wanted her, but she deserved to have more than a one-night stand, which this was stacking up to be.

She snuggled next to him, grabbed his erection, and nuzzled his neck. He sucked in a breath and stilled her hand. "Jenna, I don't think this is a good idea." The shower had given him time to think through the possible repercussions of their act.

"Oh...my...God. Are you a virgin or something?" Or something? What would that be? He could tell her tone was pure bravado. He'd hurt her feelings—bad. Damn it.

He wanted to right his wrong. "No. I'm widowed as matter of fact. For the record, I do want to sleep with you but making love should be special between two people, not some one time occurrence."

She shook her head as if to say he was too full of shit. "This doesn't have to be a one-time thing. I'm willing to have a repeat performance, you know." She ran her palm down his chest and he held in a groan.

He'd seen too many men hurt his mom after his father died. He wouldn't do that to Jenna. "Come here."

He gathered her in his arms and held her tight. Her soft skin molded against his body and her hair smelled like lemons. She was so sweet and so special. Jenna deserved to be cherished, just not by him— a workaholic.

She rocked out of his arms. "I think I should be going."

The alarm clock on the side table glowed bright. "It's late. Stay the night. I don't want you driving home in the dark."

She pressed her lips together. "I'm a big girl, and remember I just drove two hours in the dark."

Sam shoved backwards to rest his back against the headboard and gathered her to his chest before she had a chance to escape. "Please stay. I think it would be nice to have you sleep next to me."

When she looked up at him, he could read the debate in her eyes. "Really?" A small smile caught her lips.

"Really." He slipped out of bed to flick off the light knowing he wouldn't sleep tonight with Jenna snuggled up against him, but he figured the sacrifice would be worthwhile when he woke up to her all warm and cuddled against him in the morning.

He must have dozed off, for when he opened his eyes, his arm had fallen asleep. Jenna was lying on top of him, one leg slung over his body. Hormones kicked into high gear once he realized he was naked with a beautiful woman on top of him. How had she taken off his briefs without him knowing?

He tried to slip his arm out from under her when a flash of light outside his bedroom window caught his attention. He blinked, straining to figure out what would have created the odd vision.

Then he smelled it.

Smoke.

Shit. Something was on fire.

He shook her and jumped out of bed. "Jenna. Wake up."

"Hmm."

He flicked on the overhead light, but she remained cocooned in the blankets, looking snug. "Jenna. Fire!" he shouted.

She rolled over and opened an eye. "Why are you up?"

"The house is on fire. We have to get out of here." Sam wasn't sure the extent of the crises, but he wanted to check it out clothed. He rushed into the closet and tossed out a white, buttoned down shirt to Jenna. "Put this on."

The horror must have sunk in, for she sat up and looked outside. "Sam!"

In a flash, she flew out of the bed and pulled on her jeans and his shirt. Sam tossed on pants and a pullover, and then shoved his feet into topsiders.

The moment Jenna was decent and had put on her sneakers, ties still undone, he grabbed her hand. "We need to go out the front."

The heat blasted them the moment they exited the hallway and stepped into the living room. Sam checked each window. Flames licked every pane.

"Fuck." It was worse than he'd imagined. He spun Jenna toward him. "Call 9-1-1 and I'll find something wet to cover us." Without protection, they were dead.

Jenna sprinted to the sofa where she'd placed her purse on the floor. Relieved she'd followed his instruction without arguing, he ran to the hall closet and grabbed two beach towels. Every second he spent preparing, the harder it would be to get out of the burning house, but if he didn't, they'd never fight their way out.

"Sam, hurry!"

He ran the shower over the towels for no more than ten seconds, and then raced out to the living room. He surveyed his options. The bedroom window was out of the question. The fire raged outside.

Jenna tugged his arm. "Out back," she yelled. He tossed her the wet towel, and she held it over her head as she went toward the sliding glass door.

"Wait. This looks pretty bad. Let me check the front first." Sounds similar to gunfire punctuated the night. He sprinted to the front door and ripped it open, the handle already hot to the touch. Thick smoke and flames jumped out at him. He slammed the door, and his heart nearly exploded. Heat seared his lungs, and Sam coughed. His lungs burned and his field of vision dimmed. "Go out the back," he yelled.

Halfway past the living room sofa, a wall of glass exploded from the heat. Shit, Jenna was near the sliding glass door.

"Jenna?" The smoke grew so thick he couldn't see her or anything.

He could only hope she'd made it outside already. Blood pounded in his ears, as spikes of fear nearly paralyzed him. "Jenna. Where are you?"

No response.

With the wet towel over his head, he rose to his hands and knees for more air, but it didn't help. His lungs screamed in protest from the lack of oxygen. He crawled around the sofa to where Jenna might be. He couldn't breathe, forcing his heart to race. Sam failed to clear his chest. His brain fogged.

Where was she?

Two feet in front of the door, he found her on the ground bleeding. "Jenna?" Heat burned his skin. If he didn't get them out of the house now, they'd both die. He shook her. "Can you hear me?"

Sam wrapped her up in the beach towel and stood on wobbly legs. Blood dripped down his elbows and hands from the exploding glass. The fire had burned through the front door and was licking its way toward them. His only hope was to go through the broken sliding door, through the wall of flames.

He held Jenna tightly against his chest, took a breath, and plowed through the fire, forcing his feet to move. His breath nearly gone, his muscles contracted from the heat. Then. Air.

He broke through the flames with his precious bundle clasped against his heaving body. Cleansing tears leaked out of his eyes. He blinked, but all he saw was black smoke in front of them. Intermittent flames snaked through the mist. He dodged to the right, praying he wouldn't run into the patio furniture and drop her.

Mentally picturing what was in his back yard, he angled to the left to avoid the hedge. Heat scorched his back, and his lungs demanded more air. In the distance sirens blared. He held Jenna tighter. He couldn't lose her. "Hang on, Jenna."

Sam tripped over something protruding from the ground. It was the sprinkler system. Damn. He stumbled forward, trying to regain his balance but then slammed into his back fence. Trapped. He had to get out of the yard. Where was the damned gate?

The stench of burnt flesh made him gag. Was it his flesh—or Jenna's?

She wriggled in his arms. Thank God Jenna was alive. "Hold on. Help's on the way."

He moved along the fence, looking for the opening, but he didn't dare put her down. From the blood on the towel, he knew he had to hurry if he wanted to save her.

There. The gate. Rolling Jenna closer to him, Sam reached out from underneath her and touched the latch to lift it. The hot metal pierced his skin causing him to drop the lever. "Damn."

Using the edge of Jenna's towel, he covered his hand and tried again to escape from the fenced in yard. The gate swung open a moment later, and he sprinted with Jenna as far as his legs would take him, gulping in large mouthfuls of semi-clean air.

Once out of immediate danger, he dropped to his knees and placed Jenna on the ground. The raging fire crackled and popped close behind him. His ragged breath scared him. The streetlights from the road behind his house illuminated her face. Small cuts littered her cheeks and neck. Poor Jenna.

"Sir?"

Sam looked up. A paramedic, med kit in hand, stood over him. "You have to take care of her," Sam pleaded.

"Yes, sir. Is there anyone else in the house?"

Oh, God. "Mrs. Delansky, a paraplegic, lives on the other side." He couldn't tell if the fire had spread to her half yet. "She never leaves the house." Panic tore at him.

A paramedic took Jenna's vitals. Seeing she was in good hands, Sam headed toward the other side to help save his friend.

Someone grabbed his arm. "We'll take care of your neighbor."

Two more paramedics appeared at his side. One took hold of his shoulder, but he shook him off. "I have to help her."

"We're already in." The words sunk in. He was too late. Again. "Come with us, please."

"What about Jenna?" He couldn't fail her too.

"She's being taken care of."

Jenna probably didn't need him hovering. As the medics escorted him toward the awaiting ambulance, he looked at his burning house. He'd lost everything. His heart broke, and then anger bubbled up inside. Someone had tried to kill him, and he sure as hell was going to find out who was responsible. And if anything happened to Mrs. Delansky or Jenna, he'd turn the world upside down to make him pay.

CHAPTER ELEVEN

THE DOCTORS MADE Sam spend the night in the hospital for observation, because they suspected he might have lung damage since he'd inhaled so much of the cloying smoke. This morning, the tests showed no immediate issues. How he'd escaped the silent killer, he didn't know, but he was thankful. The hospital released him, but he was advised to return in a few days for a follow-up visit.

He sustained two small burns on the back of his calves and a few minor cuts on his elbows and hands, which involved cleaning and suturing, but in the big scheme of things, he'd been damned lucky to get out relatively unscathed.

Jenna was a different story. Unfortunately, no one would tell him anything about her condition, other than she was being watched closely. The bad news was that Mrs. Delansky didn't exist in their system. Either she was dead or her daughter had driven down from Jacksonville to visit before the fire started. He'd never forgive himself if she died.

Sam had searched the phone book for Mr. Richman's number so he could inform Jenna's father what had happened, but he found a whole column of Richmans. He'd borrowed another visitor's cell phone and called four names before she needed her phone back. If *Botanica* hadn't been closed, he would have contacted them to see if they had an emergency number for her.

Out of options, there was nothing more he could do than wait until the hospital allowed him see her. Sam flipped through some home magazine in the waiting area but failed to notice any of the pictures, and he sure as hell wasn't in the mood to read any of the articles. Hell, he couldn't concentrate. Worry had stopped the blood from flowing to his brain.

With no cash, he couldn't even buy a stupid snack from the machine. He dropped his head into his hands and wracked his brain trying to figure out who'd wanted to harm him. No doubt arson was involved. Houses didn't spontaneously go up in flames without an accelerant.

He could almost hear Carla's ranting about how the curse must have caused the fire, and that he needed to halt the investigation if he wanted to stay live. As a man of science, he didn't believe in magic or voodoo nonsense, but someone was determined to stop him from investigating the contents of the cauldron. Only who? Deidra Willows? She wasn't his first choice. Jenna's boss acted too uptight to be a killer, but crazies didn't always follow a specific pattern of behavior.

Sam checked the wall clock for the tenth time. He refused to leave the hospital until he'd at least had a glimpse of Jenna. He didn't want to believe that his investigation might have caused harm to an innocent woman. It was his duty to make sure she was okay. Besides, he liked her. A lot.

"Sir?"

"Yes?"

"You can see Ms. Richman now. She's in room 307."

Thank God. They must have moved her out of ICU. When he stepped off the elevator, full-blown antiseptic blasted him. He neared Jenna's room, and the hum of television sets from the other rooms saddened him. There were so many ill people. Most of them were alone.

He tapped Jenna's door, and when he stepped in, his heart wrenched. One tube stuck out of her right arm that ran to a bag containing a clear liquid that hung on a stand, and another went to a collection pack on the side of her bed. A positive was that she wasn't intubated. His anxiety lessened at bit.

Jenna's cheek, chin and throat were covered in gauze and her hair was matted in blood. Damn it. He should have been the one in the bed, not Jenna. If only he'd let her leave last night when she'd wanted, she wouldn't be here now, suffering.

He stepped close to the bed. "Jenna?"

She opened her eyes and half smiled, her upper lip trembling from the effort. "Hey. You're okay."

"Yeah. You?" Dumb question, but his heart had collided with his speech center. He pulled up a chair and eased into it, careful not to knock the back of his legs as he sat.

"Good. Kind of." She reached out her hand, and he wrapped his fingers around her palm. Damn gauze bandages prevented the skin-to-skin contact he wanted. "I want to thank you for saving my life." Her tongue peeked out to wet her lips, and his mind raced to a forbidden place.

"I'm no hero." He'd been one once and had been shot for the effort. "I was saving both of our asses when I raced out of the house." Sam nodded to her face. "Does it hurt bad?"

"Not so much. They gave me something for the pain."

Her speech didn't possess its usual crispness, and she seemed to be having a hard time keeping her lids open.

Footsteps pounded down the hall and an older man barreled into her room. "Jenna." He looked at Sam and stopped. With care, Sam returned Jenna's hand to her side.

"Hi." Her throat sounded raw, but her eyes sparkled.

"My God. When we heard what happened, I raced right over. Lucas said he'd stop by later."

Was this her father? And who the hell was Lucas? "Sam, this is Larry Bernard. He's a friend of the family."

Something passed between them that Sam couldn't decipher.

Sam stood to give the visitor the seat. "How did you hear about the fire?"

Larry smiled. "I got people."

Sam was unsure if he should leave, but she seemed comfortable with this Larry guy. "Jenna, call me later at the lab, okay? My cell burned up in the fire." She nodded.

He wondered if Jenna's car had even survived the blaze. In his haste to get the hell out of the burning house, he hadn't even thought to grab his wallet. His pants were stained red at the knees, and his shirt was streaked with blood. Man, he was a mess.

A nurse pushing a man in a wheelchair slipped by him, and an old woman moaned in the room near the nurses' station. Sam halted.

Chance. He could stay with his friend until he found a place. Too bad he didn't remember Chance's number. No cash meant he couldn't even hail a cab even if he knew his friend's location. His only choice was to call his boss. That number he knew by heart.

The nurses' station was kind enough to let him use their phone. Phil answered right away. His boss kept his phone attached to his wheelchair and rose early to work out. Once Sam explained his situation, Phil said he'd send Gina over with a clean set of clothes and a small advance. He had to hand it to Phil. The guy cared about his employees.

Sam waited outside the hospital entrance for Gina to arrive. The cool air felt good on his burns but did nothing to calm the ache in his gut. Poor Jenna. She didn't deserve this.

In less than half an hour, his savior strutted toward him with a small suitcase. "Well, you look like shit," Gina said with slight laugh.

"Thanks. It's a new style I've adopted." He held up his bloodied shirtsleeve. "Jenna says I'm too uptight and need to dress down."

"She's got that right." Gina plopped the suitcase by Sam's side and planted herself on the steps next to him. "So what are you going to do now?"

He shrugged. "I'm not sure. I have insurance on my duplex, but it could take months before I'm reimbursed."

"That's tough. By the way, Phil did a little digging. He just called me on my cell. I'm afraid your neighbor didn't make it."

His gut nearly exploded as anger roiled inside him at the unfairness of it all. "Goddammit. She was like a grandmother to me. Mrs. Delansky was the sweetest woman on earth."

Gina squeezed his hand. "I'm sorry for your loss. The arson investigator is a personal friend of Phil's. He'll make sure they catch the guy."

"We hope. Will someone notify her daughter, or should I?"

"I'll ask Phil and let you know."

A strong breeze whipped through the palm trees and the sound of an approaching ambulance broke his melancholy. "Damn it. I want to find the identification of the people in my cauldron so bad I can taste it. I believe the bones hold the key to the arson and to my windshield smashing."

"I hope you're right." Gina stood. "You need a ride somewhere?"

Racing footsteps sounded behind him. "Mr. Bonita?"

"Yes?"

"I'm glad I caught you. I'm Jenna's friend, Charlotte Evert. She just called me and told me what happened. I'm so sorry about your house."

He was surprised she identified him, though his bloody clothes probably gave him away. "Thanks."

"The floor nurse told me Jenna would probably be released later today once the doctor sees her, but that she needs supervision. I'd take her, but I have got two little ones at home, along with three dogs. I have a spare key to Jenna's place. She wanted you to have it since you don't have a place to stay."

Jenna's generosity took him aback. "I couldn't."

"You have to. Someone needs to take care of her while she heals. She's too stubborn to do what the doctors tell her."

He hadn't been thinking. Jenna needed help. "Sure."

She smoothed her hands down her jeans. "I didn't see her heap in front of her house when I drove by. Was it at your house?"

"Yes, but I have no idea if it survived the fire."

"I'll ask a couple of my friends to check and drop it off at her house if it's drivable." She pulled out her Blackberry and took down his address. "Just take good care of her." Her cell buzzed. "I gotta go." She handed him the key and written directions to Jenna's place. And then she was gone.

Gina picked up the suitcase. "Come on. I'll drive you to your new abode."

* * *

SAM KEPT TELLING himself he owed Jenna for possibly scarring her for life but cleaning toilets was about as far as he'd go for any woman. To call her place a pigsty was an understatement. And the kitchen? Yikes. Dishes sat in the sink, but at least the counters were clean, and he hadn't found any roaches. His hours of waiting had been spent scrubbing and vacuuming. His back ached and his cuts started to bleed again from the hard work, but he hated disorder too much to sit around and do nothing.

Sam found her refrigerator basically bare, which implied she ate out a lot. Didn't she know how much money she could save by cooking herself? If he'd had a car, he would have taken a trip to the store and stocked up on some staples—like eggs, milk, and bread. All he'd been able to scrounge was enough supplies for tuna noodle casserole using powdered milk no less.

Around two, two well-built guys returned Jenna's soot-covered car, and a shot of jealousy stabbed him until he recalled these were Charlotte's two friends.

"How did you get the key?" Had they come from the hospital?

The beefier of the two curled his lip. "Jenna always keeps a spare in a magnetic box on her back bumper."

"Oh." Anyone could steal her car. He'd have to talk with her about safety, though the chance of some thug stealing a heap covered in girly stickers was slim. "Thanks for delivering it." A thorough wash would return her car to looking like new.

They handed him the key and took off in the shorter man's truck.

Once back inside, he checked the answering machine. No call from the hospital yet. Had the doctors discovered an infection? The lack of a call didn't bode well for her. Sam decided he'd first clean the second bedroom, which he speculated was an office/spare bedroom since it came with a pullout sofa, and then wash the car. After that he'd take a trip to the market for some much needed food.

He placed Phil's donation of two pair of pants, two shirts, and new underwear in a file cabinet drawer in the extra bedroom since the closet was too crammed with stuff to fit even one more hanger. Phil hadn't been able to replace Sam's bloody, fire damaged shoes, but beggars couldn't be choosy.

By the time he'd sanitized the spare bedroom room and their shared bathroom, he took a shower to remove the smell of smoke from his skin. He'd finished toweling off when Jenna called. Thank God she sounded alert.

"I'll be right there."

Damn. He hadn't washed her car, though in all likelihood, she wouldn't notice. She'd have more important issues on her mind.

Checking Jenna out took about an hour. The red tape frustrated not only him but Jenna as well. She paced the entire time the nurse asked her questions. Jenna promised to return the next day and deliver her insurance card that she kept in her desk at home. Sam handed her a jacket he'd found in her closet. "You don't want to get chilled."

"Thanks. Right now, all I care about is a shower, and then going over to your place to see if maybe the person who set the fire left a clue."

She had to be kidding. "My boss is in contact with the arson investigator. He'll find out who did this. Let the cops handle this."

"I am a..." Her face turned a pretty shade of pink—at least the part exposed to the air.

"You're a what?"

"Um. I'm...I'm anything but happy. I'm not going to wait around while the stupid cops put us last on their list of people to help."

He had to smile at her poor view of our men in blue. Finally they had something in common. If the cops hadn't blown off his wife's 9-1-1 call, she might still be alive. "I'm sure Phil will give them a nudge."

Her grumpy mood stemmed no doubt from her pain and probably from a lack of sleep. The hospital had cleaned her cuts, but her hair contained soot and blood. Her stomach sent out a loud grumble. He bet she hadn't eaten since last night, something he'd rectify soon.

When they approached her car, she shrieked with glee. "Nellie survived!"

Nellie? She named her car? "It needs a good washing."

"She always needs a wash. I was worried the fire might have done her in."

Maybe he should thank the rock thrower for doing him a favor. His vehicle had stayed in cozy comfort in the repair shop this past week and not in his garage—make that his burned down garage—while the shop replaced the windshield.

The five miles to Jenna's place seemed to take forever since she remained quiet the whole time. Sam surmised she was trying to keep it together until she got home.

"Do you need for me to pick up a prescription?"

She shook her head. "The hospital gave me something."

He didn't dare suggest she might need more in the days to come. When and if she wanted a refill, he'd get it for her. When he pulled into her drive, Jenna refused any help getting out. Stubborn woman. She did allow him to open the front door, however.

"Wow. You cleaned! The place has never looked better. Thank you."

Her smile made him forget the toilets and the tossed clothes. "If you're okay by yourself, I'd like to go to the lab and work on the cauldron people. Whoever placed them in the pot might have started the fire." He opened the refrigerator and pointed to the individually covered glass containers. "I made a casserole for you."

Her eyes sparkled. "You did? That's so sweet." Jenna came over to him, lifted up on her tiptoes and kissed him on the cheek. "That's the nicest thing anyone has done for me. Can you wait while I shower? I want to go to the lab with you."

Heat raced up his face at her sincerity. "You, young lady, need to rest."

"Come on. It was my life that was threatened too, you know. How can you be so sure you were the target? My car was sitting outside your house. The flower stickers on the bumper make it kind of stand out, don't you think?"

"Yes, but—"

"No, yes buts. I could be in danger if I stay all by my lonesome." She slid next to him and placed her hands on his chest. She smelled of smoke and antiseptic, but he didn't mind. In fact, his heart jumped a few beats.

What could a store clerk have done to cause someone to come after her? "Did you put a curse on someone and they want revenge?"

She rolled her eyes. "No. I don't do that kind of thing." She dragged a finger from his chest to his waist and glanced up at him with her pretty brown eyes. "I'm scared. I need you to protect me."

He didn't buy her innocent act one bit, but if she had been the target, and they came after her again, he couldn't live with himself. "Fine. But all you'll be doing is sitting and watching."

"Okay." She flashed him her pearly whites. "I'll be out in a flash."

Worry was replaced with joy. She was so easy to please.

As she rushed down the hallway, his stupid body reacted. He was half tempted to sneak into the quart-sized bathroom and watch her shower, only he wouldn't. That would create expectations on her part —expectations he didn't need.

* * *

JENNA WRAPPED her arms around herself wishing she'd remembered Sam's workplace was so freaking cold. "How can you stand working in this meat locker hour after hour?"

"You get used to it. Tomorrow, bring a sweater."

Jenna hopped up on the black counter, hoping there wasn't any left-over blood or anything under her. Knowing Sam, he disinfected the place hourly. While she wanted to get close to him for many reasons, she wasn't sure suffering in the cold was a good enough reason to stay here. Unfortunately, she couldn't think of an excuse to leave. It wasn't as if she could announce that she needed to stop by the precinct to see where they were with the fire investigation. Nor did she need to be reminded the doctor made her promise to stay away from work and stress for two weeks. Like that was going to happen. "I'm famished."

"There's some snack food in the break room. It has donuts or other bad stuff."

Not the response she wanted. "Come with me. I can't go into the room and steal a donut. Only three people out of a gazillion here even know me."

He raised a brow. "Give me a sec to wash up."

"You know you've been looking at those dumb bones for hours. Have you learned anything?"

Sam motioned her over to the gurney. "I'll show you."

Even though she slid off the counter as gently as she could, her body complained nonetheless. "Ow."

Sam raced to her side. "Are you okay?"

"Yes, I'm fine." Her father had taught her not to show pain, because it gave the enemy an advantage. "So show me."

She waved off a helping hand. If he touched her, she might have to seduce him right here in the lab, pain or no pain.

Jenna moved to the middle of the expansive room. Man, the smoke inhalation had done a number on her ability to breath. The doctor claimed it would take time—the one thing she didn't have. She needed to find out who'd set the fire, and whether or not she'd been the target. She also needed to discover if the attack was related to the stolen bodies.

Sam tapped the edge of the gurney as he kept a careful watch over her. "You wanted to know what I've learned." Jenna nodded. "I only have a bone here, a bone there, but since most of the bones I do have come from this victim, I can tell you the woman's right leg was about three-fourths of an inch shorter than the other. This would indicate she walked with a limp."

"Unless she wore a lift in her shoe."

"True, but it gives us a good place to start for identification purposes."

"Do the police have a list of missing persons you could compare to the bones?"

"Sort of. I don't know if you've read it in the papers, but there's been a rash of grave robberies. We're thinking maybe these belong to one of them. We're getting the X-rays from as many as we can."

"Cool." She rubbed her stomach. "I don't think donuts are going to cut it. Do you think we could get some real food?"

Sam gave her a tired smile. "Sure." The tick around his eye told her he was as exhausted as she was.

Beeps rang out from the door. A moment later, the tech girl she'd met earlier, and some other man, strode in. Worry lined their faces.

"Carla and Chance. To what to I owe the honor?" Sam said. It was obvious from the way he puffed out his chest that he didn't want them to know the extent of his injuries. He nodded to her. "You remember Carla. And this is a college buddy of mine who is our new pathologist, Chance Taveres."

They shook hands. The good-looking pathologist placed a hand on Sam's shoulder and gave him the once over. "My God, man, why didn't you tell us about the fire? You should have called me."

"I had your number programmed into my cell, but I lost it in the fire." Sam went into how he'd come to be at Jenna's house.

Carla slid next to her. "I can't imagine being trapped in a burning building. That's my worse nightmare."

"Mine too. To be honest, I wasn't aware of much after the living room glass blew out. When I woke up, I was in the hospital. Sam saved me." She smiled, and then swallowed the pain in her cheeks from the effort.

Carla planted her hands on her hips as she faced Sam. "It's the curse."

Sam rolled his eyes. "This has nothing to do with a curse. A curse didn't set the fire."

"Maybe not, but the curse was a warning you didn't heed. You should have told Phil you couldn't work on these bones. I bet he would have found someone else."

"And admit defeat? No way. I'm not going to let some cauldron wielding weirdo scare me."

"You don't look so good. You should take time off and rest." Then Carla swung a finger at Jenna. "And you too." Back at Sam. "My computer and I are going to do everything in our power to find the jerk who did this."

"Thank you," Sam said. They exchanged a look of friendship, and Jenna relaxed. She didn't need any competition.

"Phil said he has something for us and will be right down," Chance said.

A few minutes later, the boss swung into the room with Gina right behind him. "We have some news about Franklin Manchester."

Jenna stiffened. His family had been the first ones to contact the department about the cemetery robbery.

"Good news, I hope," Sam said.

"Laxman did the DNA comparison and your young male is indeed Mr. Manchester."

She experienced a short burst of relief. Maybe now his family could have closure.

Sam's shoulders relaxed. "That's great. One down, one to go." He leaned back against the counter. "Do the police have any news on the arsonist?"

Jenna held her breath.

"No, but we did find footprints outside the garage," Phil said. "They'll want to take your prints to rule them out. We also found an empty gas can tossed next to where your garage used to be."

"Can's not mine."

"We figured." Phil shook his head. "Some people are too stupid to live. Whoever did this probably wasn't a seasoned arsonist, which will help the cops catch him."

"My boss, Deidra Willows, has big feet. I wouldn't be surprised if she was the culprit."

"Sorry, Jen," Phil said. "We checked her out too. She was at the hospital with her sister at the time of the fire."

"Shelby had her baby?" Her energy spiked.

"I didn't ask."

"Is Deidra Willows was a person of interest?" She knew she was, but asking too many insightful questions would send up a red flag.

Phil tossed her a strange look. Oh shit. She shouldn't have used the phrase, *person of interest*.

"Yes. Ever since we connected her to Creighton Jackson, we've kept an eye on her."

"Have you made any progress on the identity of Jackson's killer?" Sam said.

"Not yet." Phil nodded to the table. "Any luck on the other cauldron victim?"

"Just that one leg was three-fourths of an inch shorter than the other, and that the victim was around thirty."

Carla stepped over to the gurney and looked ready to pass out. "How did this person die?"

"Blunt force trauma to the head. If you look at the radial nature of the cracks, you can see the damage was pretty severe."

Carla's face paled. "Can you tell what the killer hit her with?"

Jenna studied Carla. The woman's respiration rate jumped to at least twenty-four breaths a minute, way too high for someone her age.

"I never said the vic was female."

She looked up, her mouth half open. "I just thought—."

"Well you're right. Part of her pelvis was in the cauldron, which helped me identify the sex. As for the wound, I haven't matched any particular weapon, but it was a rather large one."

Carla grabbed the edge of the counter as if she needed support. "I need to go."

Chance wrapped an arm around her shoulder. "You okay?"

"Not really." She turned and left with Chance right behind.

A flash of concern crossed Gina's face. "Hope Carla's going to be okay."

Sam nodded. "She's been acting strange lately."

"I've noticed it too. I'll speak with her." Gina placed a stack of photos on the counter. "Here's what we have in regards to the Missing Persons who fit your initial biological profile. Happy hunting." She turned to Jenna. "Is there anything we can do to help you two?"

How thoughtful of her. "No, thanks." She held up a hand. "On second thought, could you order us some pizza?" No way would Sam leave now and get food.

Sam lips scrunched up and his brows pinched together. Phil and Gina laughed. "My pleasure."

Guess he didn't do junk food. His loss.

Sam handed her the package. "Would you mind looking through those to see which women were reported missing in the last year?"

"Sure. I'll do anything I can to help bring this guy to justice. I'm even betting the same person who stole the bones is the same person who torched your house."

"I wouldn't be surprised."

Jenna moved back over to the computer area and cleared a space. She separated the photos according to date. She was less than half way done when Carla came back into the lab and handed Sam a picture.

"It's Daphne. The damaged skull belongs to my sister." She gazed long-ingly at the woman's remains on the table.

He studied the photo. "The nun? The one who disappeared six months..." Realization shimmied across his face.

"Yes. That one."

"And you think—"

"Yes. She was driving down from Ohio to visit, but never made it here. She fits your description to a T."

CHAPTER TWELVE

Carla raced back to her office, bile rising in her throat, with Chance right behind her once more. She spun around. "Why are you here?" That was rude, but her mind wasn't thinking straight.

"Did you think I'd leave after you announced you believed your sister was dead?"

Yes. "I don't know." What was it in for him?

He helped her sit. "How can you be sure the remains belong to your sister?"

Carla sniffled. Overwhelmed with the reality, she began to sob. Her heart knew Daphne was gone. "How many people have one leg shorter than the other and are the right height and age as my sister? Besides, she disappeared a little over six months ago. Everything fits."

"I'm sorry. You said she was driving down to visit you. Did the police ever find her car?"

"No. That's what gave my parents hope. I knew Daphne wanted out of the convent. She was confused and thought I could help her figure out her life." She swallowed and grabbed a tissue. "But she never arrived. At first I thought she'd changed her mind and returned home."

Chance knelt down in front of her. "Could she have moved to another state and not told anyone?"

"No. Not Daphne. It's bad enough to find out your beloved sister is really... dead, but to have someone steal her bones is horrifying." Carla wiped the tears from her cheeks. "She gave her life to God. That shouldn't happen to her. *He* shouldn't have let anyone do that to her."

Chance rubbed her arm and, for a moment, her mind moved away from the tragedy.

"Are you going to tell your parents what you suspect?"

She shook her head. "I can't. Not yet. I'll have to receive definitive proof it's her before I expose them to the grief."

"They can compare your DNA to those in the bones."

"I know." Carla broke down again. Stupid hormones. "This is going to kill my parents."

Chance closed the blinds covering her office window before pulling up a chair. He took her hands in his. "Carla, isn't knowing the truth better than living in limbo?"

Could the man read her mind or what? "For me, yes. For my parents? I'm not sure. They still live with hope in their hearts. I'm not sure I want to take that away from them." Carla searched Chance's face.

Sympathy poured from his eyes. "Eventually, they'll have to be told."

"I know, but not now."

"Are you going to keep the fact you're pregnant from them too?"

She jerked up. "Pregnant?"

"I haven't known you long, but the flushed face, the rushing to the bathroom, all tell me you might be." He pointed to a stain on her blouse. Vomit.

She squeezed his hand tight. "Please don't tell anyone."

"You don't sound happy about it."

He didn't promise. "It's not under the best of circumstances."

"I'm guessing there's no reliable father around."

"No." She inhaled, needing to get it out in the open. "I was raped."

"Oh, Carla. I'm so sorry. Did you report it?"

All she could do was shake her head. Her throat had closed up.

Carla was tired of being alone. If only Daphne had been here, she'd know what to do. "I couldn't. My parents would have found out. They were still upset over Daphne being missing. Learning about the rape and my pregnancy would have sent them over the edge."

"Honesty is the best policy. They'll find out about the baby at some point regardless of how hard you try to keep it a secret. These things have a way of coming out. Perhaps not right away, but in two, three years from now. They'll be hurt you didn't think enough of them to ask for their guidance."

Carla had never met a man with such compassion. She'd opened up to Chance about her attack, and amazingly, he seemed to understand what she'd been through.

"I hadn't thought of it that way." She rubbed her stomach. The baby wasn't in a good mood. "Once I figure out who did this to me, I'll talk with them."

"Go to the police now." He trailed his fingers along her shoulder. "Did you get a good look at him?"

"Yes. I see him in my dreams every night."

"They'll fade." She didn't deserve such kindness—especially from someone so good-looking and smart. She was a geek. And fat. Not someone he'd find attractive. Chance slapped his thighs. "I need to get some work done, and you need to tell the police."

"I will." Someday. She wanted to ask him to stay but then thought better of it. "Thanks for listening."

"Anytime, princess." Chance winked and slipped out.

Princess? She knew he didn't mean anything by the endearment, but the way he said it made her feel special. Why couldn't she have met him two years ago when she was slim and whole?

Enough. She had a stack of informational requests from the department to handle. Carla turned back to her monitor and noticed the file she'd labeled in pink—Jenna Richman's file. She'd uncovered the information Sam had requested but couldn't muster the courage to tell him his new female friend was really Jenna Holliday, an undercover cop.

To double-check the accuracy of her report, Carla had called the precinct and pretended to be someone else. They'd confirmed Jenna's status. Damn. She guessed she could tell Sam about Jenna's mom's death too but shouldn't Jenna be the one to tell him about her other life?

Crap. Sometimes this job sucked.

The only good news was that Sam hadn't hooked up with someone who might have had it in for him. Jenna was as upstanding as they came.

* * *

JENNA HAD PLACED the last of the photos in the pile labeled *two years or more* when her phone rang. Sam glanced over at her, and she mouthed, "A friend." This was awkward. "Hello?"

It was Captain Lucas. Damn. "Jenna, we received another headless body. I need you to meet me at Ballast Point Pier—and bring Sam."

"I'm afraid that won't work for me."

There was a long pause on the line. "I take it he still doesn't know you're working on the graveyard case."

"Among other things."

Sam was, in theory, searching through the database in the computer next to her. He'd told her he wanted to see if he could match the skull to one of the photos, and she could tell by the angle of his head he was listening to her conversation.

"He's within hearing distance then."

"Yes."

"Can you get away? I need you to photograph the scene. My two best CSU photography techs are out on another case."

"The doctor said I need to take it easy for the next few weeks."

"Shit. I forgot."

"If you need me, I'll come."

"I do. Thanks," Lucas said.

"Sure." The captain disconnected. "What are your symptoms?" She waited a beat. "I can pick up your medicine no problem. I'll come over now." She punched the off button. Now for the best acting job in the world.

"What's wrong?" Sam asked.

Jenna stored her phone and stood. "My aunt is having some heart problems. I need to pick up her medication, and then stay with her for a while. Do you think you can catch a ride back to my place?"

Sam studied her for a moment. "Yeah. Hope everything works out."

"Thanks."

God. Jenna hated lying to him, but now wasn't the time to tell him she was a cop. Not that it should make a difference, but men as straight as Sam would never forgive her. The lie would sever their tenuous bond, and that would be terrible on many levels.

She met the captain forty minutes later at Ballast Point with her camera in hand. Police cars rimmed the park. Giombetti and Maken were there too. Blue skies and a pleasant breeze would have made for a pretty day. The spoilers were the lack of children around the swings, and the hoard of fishermen across the street, smoking up a storm, complaining the police were preventing them from catching fish off the pier. It was a shame, but the cops had a job to do.

One man whistled as she ducked under the tape. Please. With her face bandaged, she hardly looked the picture of health or sex appeal.

She spotted her boss and made her way to him. "Hey."

"You sure you're up for this?"

"No, but I was going stir crazy doing nothing. What have we got?" She glanced at the body covered in chunks of cement with one exposed hand, heaped next to the mangrove bushes.

"The white power on his fingers is lime. Someone was in a hurry. He forgot to hide all of the victim. After you take the pictures, we can uncover the guy. Troy has already videoed the scene."

Jenna squatted next to the body and snapped away from the head to his feet. Seaweed, fish, and algae dampened the smell of the decomposition. It took her all of five minutes to complete the job. "I'm finished photographing the rocks." And the exposed hand.

Bill Trundell and Johanna Ross, two CSU techs, carefully removed the rock-like cement around the body, storing the pieces in a clean dumpster-sized container. She wondered why one of them couldn't have taken the photos. She'd seen their work. It was good. Maybe her boss wanted to make up for not telling about finding the cauldron right away. He was considerate like that.

Once the techs lifted the last of the rocks, Jenna recoiled at the site. The headless man had no legs. A Creighton Jackson clone. Almost. "Christ."

John Ahern, the Medical Examiner walked up to her and the captain. "The lime did a real number on the body, didn't it?"

Lucas nodded. "Ate away most of the flesh."

Jenna swallowed and sucked up her revulsion.

Lucas nodded to the M.E. "Will you be able to tell time of death with all the lime?"

"Not accurately. Besides the lime, there's the salt air and wet soil." John Ahern lifted the torso and checked the victim's back. "From the lack of pooling blood, the guy wasn't killed here. If the killer hadn't taken the head and legs, we might have a more accurate time frame."

"Take your best guess."

Dr. Ahern circled the body. "Two, three days?"

"Thanks."

What's wrong with people? She stood next to her boss. "Are you going to send the victim to HOPEFAL for identification?"

"No need. We found an insurance card in his pocket but no wallet. Good thing the killer was sloppy or we never would have learned who he was. Guy's name was Rodrico Evans." The body was too thick to be the man from *Botanica's* backroom. Too bad. He was still lurking. She wouldn't be surprised if the lurker had set the fire.

"Never heard of him. Let's hope the ID isn't a fake."

* * *

SAM STOOD at the stove and watched Jenna pull up the drive. He'd been worried sick she'd exhaust herself waiting hand and foot on her aunt. He wished her aunt had found someone else to care for her. She should have known better than to put undo strain on Jenna—unless, the aunt hadn't been told about the fire, which, knowing Jenna, was probably the case. Next time, he'd ask for a number where he could reach her—or come with her.

The porch light cast a shadow over Jenna's face. Fatigue and what appeared to be anger flooded her face. She winced when she stood up straight, but she didn't glance his way even though he was backlit in the kitchen window.

She let herself in and stopped the moment she saw him. "Well, I'll be damned." She smiled, tossing him a sexy look. "I never thought I'd see you in an apron."

"I often wear an apron, just not ones with pink flowers on it. I didn't want food on my clothes before it gets to my mouth."

She laughed. "Color me surprised." Not. He started toward her, but she held up her hands. "I smell. Aunt Martha threw up on me, and I have to shower."

"Go ahead. Dinner should be ready when you get out."

He'd made everything beforehand but had waited until she came home to heat the rolls.

Jenna spun around half way down the hall. "You want to watch?" She licked her lips in invitation.

Dear God. Would the women never stop coming onto him? She had to know his willpower would give out at some point. "I need to look after our meal."

She winked. "You know what they say about a watched pot."

Jenna twisted back and sashayed down the hall, telegraphing a clear invitation for him to have sex with her, and his stupid cock stood to attention. Maybe he should be assertive toward her and see how she reacted. He had a feeling Jenna was one big act.

The force of the water banging in the pipes took his imagination in a dangerous direction. He ran a wet cloth over the kitchen counter one more time and tried to think of anything other than his new room-mate, who in about one minute would be naked, with slippery, sweet smelling soap all over her delicate body. He pictured his hands sliding over her perky breasts and down her flat stomach. She'd press her body against his and he'd devour her luscious lips.

He tossed the towel down. To hell with the food. He needed air. The rolls could burn for all he cared. Sam raced past the bathroom to the spare bedroom to grab a sweater. On his way back, the urge to catch a glimpse won. Of course, she'd left the bathroom door open. Tease. Steam streaked the glass door, but her shapely outline stood out.

Don't look. She's trouble.

"Damn it," she groaned.

"What's wrong?" Why did he say that?

"That you, Sam?"

"No, it's the boogey man."

"Funny." She laughed, obviously enjoying the fact he hadn't been able to resist the siren's call after all. "I have a plan," she called out over the hiss of the water. "You want to hear it?"

Trouble flooded her words. "Do I?"

* * *

JENNA DRAGGED Sam down the back alley of *Botanica*. "Don't be such a sissy." God how she loved the adventure of danger. Adrenaline excited her.

"Who's a sissy? Breaking and entering is against the law in case you didn't know."

"That so?" She plastered his back against the brick wall and pressed up against him. Man did he feel good, all hard and strong. "We won't be breaking anything, I promise. Just entering."

"Semantics won't free you if you're caught. Let me hear this bullet-proof plan again."

She rolled her eyes and ran a finger down the tip of his nose and over his lips. "When you were speaking with Deidra a while back, I opened the office window. Stay here and keep watch, while I check out the backroom again. Be out in a jiff."

She was just about to grab his crotch but then resisted. Jenna didn't need to piss off Sam. She needed him. Oh, how Jenna wanted to ravish him right then and there. Forbidden sex was the best, as was the thrill of not knowing if anyone would walk by and catch them doing the nasty. So what if it was sixty degrees outside. Inside, she was hot.

The lamplight on 8th Avenue snuck down the alley and turned Sam's face mysterious. Jenna grabbed the front of his sweater with one hand and dragged his face down to her lips with the other. She kissed him hard.

He pressed her shoulders away, but not before he half kissed her back. "What are you doing?" he whispered.

"Kissing you. I need to relax, remember? Are you sure you have a PhD?"

That must have insulted him, for he spun her around, her back now against the wall, and planted one on her. Yes! Progress. She ground her hips into him, excited to feel an erection. Once she knew he wanted her, Jenna let loose. She opened her mouth to taste his sweetness and raked her fingers through his hair.

"God, you taste good," she said after coming up for air.

"Jenna, this is stupid. Let's go."

Thrusting her chest forward, she made total contact with the planes of his rock solid chest.

A wave of laughter and giggles floated toward them. Shit. Sam must have heard them too, for he stepped back. "They won't mind," she said. "People have sex in alleys all the time here."

Her rookie year she'd followed Sergeant Dustin Fallow around for six weeks and had seen plenty of illicit activity in this part of town.

"Tell me again why you really need to get into the backroom?"

She ran a hand down his cheek. "I told you. If I can get a blood sample off the wall, and if it turns out to be human, maybe the police can get a warrant." Which had nothing to do with Sam. Whoops. "Or there might be more cauldrons inside. More dead bodies for you to work on."

* * *

"I don't need any more bodies." This was the stupidest idea Sam had ever heard. He didn't want to be involved with her scheme, but here they were, nonetheless. There was no way he'd let Jenna go it alone though. If the man who'd grabbed Jenna outside his classroom was the same man as who was in the backroom, she didn't need to go in by herself.

The wind howled down the back alley, and he looked over at her. She'd wrapped her arms around her shoulders. "Are you warm enough?" he asked.

"I will be as soon as I get inside." She pushed on the window. "The sash is stuck."

"Here, let me help." Not wanting to leave his prints or tempt fate since his prints were in the system, he pulled on a pair of latex gloves. "You sure you unlocked this?"

"Yes, I'm sure."

Sam looked right then left before stepping around her. Dried paint caked around the sill. Old buildings made window opening a challenge. Using his knees to help shove the window upward, he forced the sash open but not without a lot of tugging. The window squeaked and he stopped.

"Don't worry. No one can hear. Can you open the window any wider? Even I'm not that small."

When he managed to raise the lower sash far enough, he motioned her in. "You go first. I'll follow."

"You're coming with me?" She smiled, and he knew he'd made the right decision, at least until they were caught.

"I don't want to be responsible for you being hurt."

"Oh."

Damn. He kept hurting her feelings. Before he could explain, Jenna slipped in and turned on her Mag light. With quite a lot of wiggling and Jenna's help, he squeezed through. "Hope we don't need a quick exit."

Jenna strode over to Deidra's desk and pulled open the bottom drawer, and then routed around the contents for a minute. "I can't believe this."

"Believe what?"

"Her keys are gone," she whispered.

"Keys for what?"

She blew out a breath. "Keys to get into the back room." She stood and planted her hands on her hips.

"Looks like that sample might have to wait until the cops get a search warrant."

"Hello. You can't get a search warrant without proof, and the blood is the proof. Assuming the stuff is human."

"And you know about search warrants how?" He cocked a brow.

"Ah, TV?"

Smart ass. He loved bantering with her, only now wasn't the time. "Jenna, why do you care so much about this case?"

She blew out a long breath. "If Deidra, or a former owner for that matter, is involved in using someone's bones for nefarious purposes, and I don't do anything about it, what kind of person would that make me?"

He rubbed her back, wondering what had happened in her life to make her so feisty. "If more citizens were like you, maybe there wouldn't be so much crime."

"A lot of good it does us now."

Sam had given up his bad ways a long time ago—right after his younger brother was arrested for B&E and his father killed himself. Someone had to step up and be the responsible one in the family, and he'd chosen himself. But now? He had more than himself to consider.

Her desperation prompted him to cross the line—a line he swore he wouldn't step over again. "Let me see what I can do."

"Are you going to break down the door or something? Don't tell me you have a black belt in karate."

"Nothing as romantic as that."

He stepped over to the locked door and pulled out his lock picks. Picks he shouldn't have brought, but something told he they'd come in handy. He'd kept them all these year to remind himself he wasn't the same man he had been. At least he was breaking the law for a good reason, or so he hoped.

Jenna stilled his hands. "What are you doing with those?" Her whisper was louder than a shout. "You're a science geek for God's sake."

That stung, but he let it pass. "It's a long story."

"Where did you get those?"

"They're mine from when I was a young thug."

Jenna's hands fluttered in his face, almost as though she'd forgotten their mission. "But your house burned down."

"I didn't want to keep them at the house for fear someone doing renovation might come across them." Sam was surprised how quickly his skill returned. In a matter of seconds, he had the hall closet open. "Whoa."

The stench of decomp hit him hard. Just because he was used to the smell didn't mean the rancid odor didn't burn his nasal passages any less. Jenna covered her mouth, and then pulled a gray cord high in the ceiling. The hallway lit up. "Let's get this over with."

"Kind of creepy in here," he said. "You sure Deidra won't come back for something?"

"The shop closed twenty minutes ago," she said, still keeping her voice low.

"But you can't be sure."

"No."

Great. Sam decided on a new plan. His—not hers. They'd rush in, get the sample, and then get the hell out. Simple. Jenna would want to linger.

Sam hurried to the end of the hall, did his magic trick again on the second door and tugged it open. Oh, boy. The odor was close to a body assault. "There's something dead in here all right."

"It's far worse than before. I think Deidra's been in here." She flashed her light on the red streaks.

Sam whistled. "Looks like Indian cave paintings."

"Or a math class gone bad."

He chuckled. "Now what?"

"Why don't you get the sample while I look around for the source of the decomp?" she asked.

"Suit yourself."

Sam scraped the blood off the wall with the cotton swab and shoved the specimen back into the tube. He thanked his lucky stars he wasn't a crime scene investigator. Give him bones any day.

"Let's get out of here, Jenna."

"Oh...my...God. Come here. Look what I just found."

CHAPTER THIRTEEN

JENNA'S HEART RACED. "It's another cauldron. The bitch is guilty of murder."

Sam grabbed her shoulders and moved in front of her. "Let me have your light." Under what looked like blood, a skull bobbed at the bottom of the black pot. "Just because she possesses this skull doesn't mean she is a killer. This could be a fake."

Her mind flashed to the torso of the man at Ballast Point. Christ. Could this be him? She wasn't supposed to know about that murder.

Sam reached down to pick up the cranium when she stopped him. "Don't touch anything."

"Why? I just want to see if the head is real or a hunk of plastic."

"Plastic doesn't smell like this."

"The smell might not be coming from the head." A muffled noise reverberated down the hallway, and Sam grabbed her arm. "What was that?"

Every muscle tensed. "Deidra? Shit. Maybe she forgot something, or else she's coming back to practice her witchcraft. Could be that guy with the gun again though."

"You never told me about a gun."

"Forget it." She bent down to lift the cauldron.

"Leave it. I'll notify the police to come get it. You have your cell phone for a picture?"

"No."

"We have to get out of here now."

Jenna raced toward the door the best she could. The cuts on her face pulsed from the exertion, and her breath was harder to find than a killer.

Sam closed the first door behind them. "I can't lock the door with picks."

Crap. They didn't have a key. "I hadn't thought that far ahead. Forget it. Come on."

They made it down the hallway without making much noise. At the end, Jenna peeked her head into Deidra's darkened office. She turned to Sam. "All clear."

Voices sounded outside the office. Adrenaline was having a hay day in her body as Jenna slipped out the window. When she landed on feet, her knees buckled, and she dropped to the gravel alleyway. "Dammit."

Sam crawled out after her, though he had a more difficult time than she did squeezing through the narrow window, but at least he managed to land upright.

"You okay?" he asked.

She didn't have time to investigate the damage. Her father's voice echoed in her head about showing no emotion. "I'm fine."

He closed the window most of the way. "It's stuck."

"It doesn't matter. Deidra will realize soon enough that something is wrong when she goes into the back and finds all the doors unlocked."

"Go." He pointed to the road.

They'd made it. Actually, made it. They raced down the alley a hundred feet and stopped. Jenna planted her hands on her knees, her back heaving. "That was a such high, wasn't it? My God, my heart's going one hundred miles an hour. Wow." She couldn't help but laugh. "I don't remember when I had such fun."

"Jen-na. We need to get away from here."

Before she could chastise Sam for being such a fuddy duddy, the light in Deidra's office clicked on, flooding the road behind the building. Oh, shit.

Sam plastered himself on top of her, the hard brick walls biting into her back. His breath came out in rapid bursts next to her face, and her traitorous body reacted to his presence.

"Don't say anything," he said.

Talking wasn't on her mind. Escape was.

When Deidra failed to poke her head out the back window, Sam motioned they continue down the alleyway toward the road. The window squeaked open behind them making Jenna pump her feet faster. If Deidra caught them, everything would be ruined. She couldn't get enough air. That damn elephant was sitting on her chest again. Blood gushed down her cheek from the cuts on her face opening up.

"Hey you. Stop!" Deidra shouted.

Crap. Jenna couldn't let her catch them. She could only hope the light didn't bounce off her blond hair and give her away. They reached the end of the alleyway, hopefully out of sight from the back window. "I have to stop. I can't breathe."

"Deidra could come out the front and find us. We have to hide."

She swallowed hard and sucked in the needed oxygen. "Which way?"

Sam tugged on her hand to go right. They were halfway down the block when she pulled to a stop again and bent over to catch her breath. Pain ripped through here, and tears welled in her eyes, but she refused to complain. "The...the...car's in the other direction."

"I know, but we can't go toward the store."

Jenna agreed. "You lead. Take it easy, though." *Don't be a wimp.*

Sam wrapped a possessive arm around her shoulder and led her away from harm.

Maybe breaking into the store to get the sample hadn't been such a good idea after all.

* * *

WEARING HIS WHITE LAB COAT, Sam pulled up a chair next to her. "Jenna." He dragged a hand down his face. "I wasn't able to sleep last night."

There were circles under his eyes and his skin had a yellow cast to it. "Because?" She figured it wasn't due to his overwhelming need to be with her. In fact, after they were nearly caught, he'd been a little cool toward her.

"Call me wimp, a goody-two-shoes, or whatever, but I could never live with myself if I lie to Phil about breaking into the store. While I was waiting for the blood analysis, I called a cop friend of mine and asked him about the legalities of obtaining a search warrant if we attained the evidence illegally."

He had to be kidding. "And?"

"The judge wouldn't grant one, he said."

"We don't have to say we broke in, you know."

"That would be lying."

Now he has to grow a conscience? "So?"

"I don't lie." Sam stabbed a hand through his thick, sandy hair.

"Even for a good cause?"

"No."

"You knew this would happen as soon as I told you why I needed to get in the backroom. Why are you changing your mind now?"

He cocked a brow. "Because my conscience fought the battle against justice, and my conscience won."

"That sounds like a country western song. Nobody will ever know if we don't tell her. It's not as if Deidra will report the break in."

He leaned forward, and she could smell his aftershave lotion and almost forgot what he'd been saying. "Lying is lying, no matter the reason. To me, there's nothing worse than someone not telling the truth."

Jenna forced her face into a neutral position. She pressed a hand on her stomach to quell the acid that was eating away her insides. Their whole relationship was based on a lie. He'd hate her for sure if he ever found out.

"What do you propose?" she asked with a lightheartedness she didn't feel.

"Find another way to catch Deidra Willows at her own game."

Like she hadn't been trying to do that for a month. "What if we just say that while I was working, I happened to notice an offensive smell—which is the truth by the way. When I went to investigate, I found a cauldron full of remains."

"Deidra's attorney would cut holes in your theory."

The man had no imagination. Jenna crossed her arms and leaned back in her seat.

Someone punched the buttons on the lab door and Phil wheeled in. He glanced first at Jenna, and then at Sam. "Howdy folks. How are things going?"

She wasn't in the mood for his cheeriness this morning. She was tempted to tell Phil the truth and see if he had any suggestions.

Sam moved away from Jenna. "Nothing much."

What? Sam the confessor was keeping quiet?

"Well, I learned about an interesting development from Tampa PD. Seems they found a torso over at Ballast Point Pier. John Ahern, the ME in downtown, said the man's head was severed in the same manner as Creighton Jackson—all clean lines and no tool marks."

Oh, shit. She was the one who told her boss about the coincidence of the two bodies. Would Sam wonder how the TPD learned of the similarities?

"Did you tell him them about Creighton?"

"No."

"How did they find out about the clean lines, then?" Sam asked.

"I'll have to get back to you on that."

"Is the body coming here?" Sam asked.

Jenna studied Sam's face. No mental machines seemed to be spinning. Maybe he never would know how the connection was made.

Phil lifted his right leg with his hands and changed positions. "I'll ask."

"Good. I'll compare the style of amputation to Creighton's Jackson. With Eric Markowitz's help, I might be able to connect the two."

She looked over at Sam wondering why he hadn't spilled the beans about finding the new cauldron. There was a lot about the man she had yet to learn.

* * *

JENNA TRIED to block out Sam's mumblings as he tested various weapons against the dent in skull that was, in theory, Carla's sister. The DNA had not come back to see if there was a match, but regardless of whether Carla was related to the victim or not, Sam had to find the murder weapon.

Her butt had fallen asleep and her face itched from the gauze pads pulling on her cheeks every time she talked. She couldn't wait for her injuries to heal. "Potty break. I'll be right back," she said.

Once out the door, she called Marlon Giombetti. Given the number of times he'd asked her out, she figured he'd do this favor for her. She explained she needed to find Richie Raden, a man she suspected of being involved in the recent grave robberies. Okay, not directly involved, but if he gave Deidra money to do a curse, she'd need bones, bones that might have been procured from graves.

"You owe me, Holliday."

"Fine. Just do this, okay? But I don't want Raden apprehended. I need to find out where the guy's holing up in order to follow him. I need some information from him, that's all."

"You say you saw him with Willows, right?"

The man didn't listen. "Yes, which implies your Jackson case might be related to this Raden guy."

"Okay." She couldn't believe he hung up first. Whatever.

She actually used the bathroom before returning to the lab.

Sam dropped something heavy onto the metal gurney, and it sent out a strong ping. He blew out a breath.

Jenna walked over to him. "What's wrong?"

"Nothing." He stabbed a hand through his luscious sandy hair. "I'm not finding the weapon that crushed the skull. I've tried a crowbar, a hatchet, and a hammer. None of them match."

She ran through some of the weapons used during her training. "What about a baseball bat?"

"Too round. This injury has beveled edges."

Jenna studied the instruments he'd placed on the counter. "May I?"

"Sure."

She picked up the hatchet, turned the blade toward her and slid the back of the hatchet into the large grove.

"I'll be damned." Sam's smile reached his eyes and her heart lightened.

"Do you think this could be the murder weapon?" she asked.

"Not the exact one, but I'll tell the police what they should be looking for. Good job."

"Thanks. Tell me the story about how you learned to pick a lock."

Sam's hands stilled, and he glanced to the ceiling and then ripped off his gloves. "It's not interesting."

"It is to me."

Sam stepped around the gurney and took Jenna's hands. He walked her over to the two computer chairs and arranged them to face each other. Stress lines marred his perfect face.

"I was born in a small town in southeastern Ohio. Marietta to be exact, which is on the Ohio River. My father worked across the river, in West Virginia, at a packaging plant. My mom stayed home with my younger brother and me. We lived in a trailer, ate a lot of Spam, and went to school in clothes that never fit."

What a depressing childhood. "My family didn't have much money either, but at least we had a house and a fenced in yard." Jenna moved her chair closer. "Were you a happy family?" She'd pictured Sam as a shy child who liked to smile.

"At first. Dad was a rough-around-the-edges kind of guy. He didn't treat Mom very well, or us, for that matter, but she never complained. We didn't either. Hell, we didn't dare, unless we wanted the belt. When Dad lost his job, I was nine and Eddie, my brother, was seven and a half. We had to move up to Akron, Ohio where Dad found another job."

She'd gone through a change of schools after her mom died. It sucked. "Was it hard to leave your friends?"

"I didn't have many, so, I guess no. I never fit in at either school. I liked science and found dead people fascinating. No one else shared my passion."

She almost laughed as his self-assessment, but her heart hurt too much for him. She wanted to console him, but she also needed to hear more. "What happened next?" She kept her tone as soft as possible.

"We did okay for the next three years until Dad lost his job again.

He started drinking and we had to go on welfare. I... felt... I guess lost, would be the best way to describe it. I needed control in my life."

"Ohmigod. That's why you have to be neat and fold your clothes."

"So I've been told. At least I didn't go in the other direction and save every newspaper and piece of mail."

"Hoarders are the worst." She reached out and clasped his warm hand, hoping he understood she was there for him. "Did your dad find another job?"

He shook his head. "No one wanted to hire a drunk."

"How is he today?"

Sam's face pinched. "He's dead."

"Oh, Sam, I'm so sorry." His father couldn't have been very old. "What happened?" She sat back abruptly. "You don't have to tell me if you don't want to. I don't want to pry."

"It's okay. It might be good to tell someone."

And he chose her? Talk about guilt. "I'm listening."

"I was having trouble sleeping one night when I heard a noise coming my parents' bedroom. Mom was out of town visiting her older sister, so I went to investigate. I thought maybe Dad had fallen. He'd slipped before. I guess he didn't hear me when I knocked, because as soon as I stepped into his bedroom, all I remember was the loud explosion of a gun."

Jenna sucked in a breath. "He killed himself?"

"Yes."

"So did my mom."

His eyes widened. "How?"

"Pills. I never saw her dead, though. Dad found her and called the cops. She was gone before I woke up." Sweat beaded on her forehead as chills put bumps on her arms. A boy so young would be scarred forever. Hell, she was too. "What did you do?"

His soft chuckle held no humor. "At first, nothing. I turned on the light and saw him lying there. I didn't know what to do. I was thirteen, almost fourteen, and I was scared. It must have been two, three minutes before I had the courage to check him out. His face was half gone, but I still thought he might be alive. Dads didn't die in my world. They lived forever."

"Please tell me you called 9-1-1 for some adult help?"

"Eventually. It took years before I got over my hesitation. I thought if I'd acted quicker he might be alive today. The doctors told me my dad had died instantly, but I never could be sure."

Jenna's eyes watered. "What about your mom and your brother?"

"I didn't call her until the next morning. I thought she'd be mad if I woke her up. I'm not sure she's ever accepted my father's death. The guilt from being away at the time of his suicide ripped her in two. You see they'd fought right before she left. She was convinced that's what made him take his life." Pain skittered across his face. "My mom took up drinking too and never stopped."

Jenna sat there absorbing the terrible chain of events. "I can't imagine such horror. How did your brother handle losing a dad?"

"Andy hurt the worst I think. After the gun went off, my brother apparently woke up and came in. I didn't hear him until his sobs registered in my numb brain. I came to my senses and blocked his view with my body, but he'd seen Dad. That's when I realized I needed to call for help."

"That's horrifying." What else could she say? No words could express the trauma this man had been through. "And your brother. What happened to him?"

His eyes turned a dark, steely gray. "Eddie never recovered. For some reason, he decided that with Dad gone, he had to be the man of the family and bring in the money."

"He was what? Eleven or twelve?"

"Twelve. We're not quite two years apart."

"The pain your family went through was incomprehensible." It was similar to what she went through after her mother took her life. "What did your mom do for a living?"

"She worked as a hairdresser. After dad died, her job was to drink."

Jenna swallowed. "How did you pay for school?"

"I served in the Navy for four years, partly to get away from the bad family dynamics and partly for the GI Bill." He shook his head a few times. "I was a Navy Seal in fact. Or should I say, I went through the first seven of twelve months of training until an accident put me behind a desk."

"An accident?"

He said nothing for a long moment. "It was stupid really. I was more than halfway through the course, when I went to a quiet lunch at a friend's restaurant. There were maybe three customers at the place, max. A crazed man rushed in, gun in hand, with a mask over his face. He raced into the back where my friend was cooking." Sam squeezed his eyes shut and gripped his fists tight.

She laid a hand on his. "What did you do? Did you have a gun or don't Seals carry guns?"

"No gun on me. I called 9-1-1, but the cops would need at least ten minutes to respond. Two shots were fired and I reacted, giving no thought to the consequences. I charged in. I should have known better, but Gus was my friend and I'd seen his sixteen year old daughter in the back too."

"What were you thinking dashing into danger?" She regretted the words the minute she said them.

"I wasn't."

"I'm sorry. I didn't mean to judge." She softened her voice. "So then what?"

"I pushed open the door. The other three customers were a lot smarter. They ran to safety. To my horror, Gus was sprawled on the ground, blood pouring out of his gut. His daughter, Marie, was sobbing, begging for her life."

Jenna sucked in a breath. "Ohmigod."

"It gets worse. I shouted at the man to put his gun down. Me, the hero. The shooter didn't hesitate. He turned the gun at me, fired, and then spun around to the daughter and shot her in the head."

A salty tear streaked down her cheek. He was a hero, even if he didn't believe it. "How badly were you hurt?"

He lifted his shirt and showed her a three-inch scar near his waist. She hadn't noticed the injury when they were in bed. "The wound was the least of my concerns. I keep thinking if I hadn't gone in, Marie might be alive today."

"You don't know that." Her father had told her too many stories like this one. "What happened to the shooter?"

"He shot himself."

From the small tick that lifted Sam's jaw, he'd punished himself ever since. Poor Sam. "Maybe the attacker did you a favor."

"How's that?"

"It forced you to end your military career. You could have been sent overseas and died."

"Sometimes I wish I had."

He couldn't mean it. She leaned back and inhaled, needing to learn more about him. "Why forensic anthropology? It seems a million miles away from being a Navy Seal."

"Not really. I grew up wanting to help people. If I couldn't save the world from terrorists, I could bring closure to the families who'd lost loved ones. And remember, I had a fascination with dead people for some reason."

Like her reason for being a cop. "I understand." Except she didn't like the dead.

Sam scrubbed a hand down his face. "I've never told anyone this story before." Tears shimmered in his eyes.

Jenna's heart nearly exploded. "Thank you for sharing." The urge to hear the rest of the story prompted her to push him a little further. "You never told me about the lock picks."

His brows rose. "Ah, yes, the infamous lock picks. That's how this saga started, wasn't it? Well, after dad's death, we went on welfare, but the money barely kept food on the table. When mom became sick, we couldn't pay for her medicine. It was then that Eddie started stealing. He was the one who bought the picks."

"How did you get involved?" Sam was so straight-laced, she couldn't imagine him doing anything illegal—until he'd helped her.

"When I was sixteen and Eddie was almost fifteen, he wanted me to help him break into a convenient store. I said no. Wondering if he had a gun, I searched his room. I found no gun, but I did find lock picks, and I became fascinated with them. I learned to open all kind of doors, just to see if I could, but I never did anything illegal."

Jenna looked deep into his eyes. The ache coming from him tore at her soul. "Then something bad happened, didn't it?"

"Yes. Eddie stole some money from a bunch of older boys at school. They found out about the theft and beat him up real bad. Said if he didn't return the money, they'd kill him. I thought I had no choice. I had to help. I'd already lost my father, and I didn't want to lose my brother too."

"So you broke into the store and took the money."

"Yes."

A sob caught in her throat. He'd grown up without knowing love, kind of like her after Mom died. Something inside her nearly broke. A deep yearning to connect with him nearly drowned her. "Did you get caught?"

"No, but after I gave my brother the amount of money he needed, I returned the rest to the store. They never found out who was responsible. After that, I retired my lock picks."

"Then why did you keep them?"

"I guess to remind me that when things become bad in my life, it's a lot better than it used to be."

She took both his hands in hers, stood up, and pulled him to her. With as much tenderness as she could manage, she cupped his face in her hands. She wanted to give him comfort, give him everything he never had. She stepped back and unbuttoned her blouse and shrugged it off. Sam's eyes widened. For once, he didn't protest or say now wasn't the right time for sex. They'd shared an unbreakable bond, and she could sense Sam felt the strong connection too.

He slipped his thumbs under her bra and raked his thumbs over her hardened nipples. Excitement rippled through her. With her gaze locked onto his, she stood on tiptoes and dragged his head down to hers, hoping he wouldn't push her away. He needed to know someone cared. The moment their lips locked, Sam seemed to transform into a man full of passion, wanting to release all his fears, his guilt, his anxiety.

He backed her up to the counter opposite the door and lifted her onto the flat surface. The cold metal froze her rear, but she wasn't going to complain. He unhooked her bra and slid the strap down with such care, she wondered if he thought she'd break if he went any faster.

"Jenna, we shouldn't." His words said he wanted to stop, but his actions didn't. His hands fondled her breasts and his lips pressed against hers.

For the first time in her life, she wanted them to make love together, not the one-way street she'd been traveling all these years. Sam seemed to need to touch her at his own pace. He needed the control. It would be her gift to him.

"Touch me more."

Sam didn't hesitate. He raked his fingers over her breasts until the nubs peaked from pleasure. A moan escaped deep from inside her throat, and she pulled his buttoned down shirt from his pants and threaded her fingers up his rippled chest, causing lust to pool between her thighs.

Maybe it was the hunt or perhaps his tortured story, but Jenna wanted him like she'd never wanted another man. He dragged his lips down to her neck, his kisses as soft as butterflies. His thumbs flicked over her nipples, igniting her blood on fire. As much as she itched to touch him below the waist, but she wanted him to set the pace.

When Jenna opened her mouth to invite him in, he took the offer with enthusiasm.

He stopped only for a moment to whisper in her ear. "I can't stop thinking about you."

His admission sent her over the edge.

Four little beeps shattered her dreams.

Shit, shit, shit.

She had just enough time to grab her shirt and cover her breasts, when the door swung open. Chance Tavares rushed through the door, anguish flooding his face.

"Oh, shit. I'm sorry, guys."

Sam pulled up his zipper, his face tinting red. "What's wrong?"

"It's Carla. You've got to come."

CHAPTER FOURTEEN

SAM AND JENNA raced behind Chance as they sped up the stairs to Carla's unlit office. The glow from the computer screen provided the only light in the room, and Sam rushed to Carla's side. Her computer dinged, indicating she had mail, but she didn't even glance at the incoming message, her gaze unfocused. The girl's hands and body shook as tears streaked her face.

"What happened?" Sam asked.

Carla mumbled something as she handed him an envelope. The same kind of envelope Sam had received, and Jenna's stomach choked. This time he didn't bother with gloves, probably because the first note had been fingerprint free. He emptied the letter onto the counter and flipped open the page.

"Chance, would you mind turning on the overhead lights?" he said, his voice thick, but still strong. "This looks similar to what came before."

Jenna looked up at Sam. "Read it to us."

"You've crossed the line. May the Dark Ones make your days end soon." He handed the note to Jenna. "That's just as stupid as mine." His words didn't match the worry that pooled in his eyes.

Carla swiped a tear from her face. "Stupid to you maybe. Did you forget someone threw a rock through your windshield and then tried to burn you to death? This person is serious."

Jenna moved next to Sam. "I have to agree with her on this one. It's not about whether you believe in curses. This note is someone's way of sending a threat. I'm thinking Carla must be close to finding this person's identity, and he or she wants her to stop the investigation."

Carla sniffled. "Fat chance."

Chance dragged a chair next to Carla and looked at her with such caring, Jenna's heart skipped a beat. "Tell them how you got the note," he said.

She swallowed hard. "I was coming back from getting something to eat when I noticed Harold wasn't at his station. I thought that was rather strange, so I stepped over to his counter and saw the envelope with my name on it. Curious what was in it, I picked it up and headed upstairs. If Harold had been there I would have asked him who delivered the note."

Chance shot them a pleading glance. "Sam, why don't you and Jenna see if Harold knows who delivered it? I think I should stay with her."

Sam nodded. "We'll be right back."

A strange tightening in Jenna's chest made breathing more difficult than usual as they took the elevator to the first floor. Fresh floor polish filled the air.

Sam placed a comforting hand on her back. "I bet Harold was taking a leak or something when Carla happened by."

"Let's hope."

Sam and she exited the elevator and rounded the corner. Harold wasn't there.

"I'll check the bathroom," Sam said.

Jenna stepped behind the counter, looking for some kind of message indicating where he'd gone. A cell phone and a set of keys lay on the desk, and her stomach soured. This wasn't good.

Sam traipsed back, looking right and left. "Nothing."

"Sam, look." She pointed to Harold's personal belongings.

"Unless he was called to another part of the building in a hurry, he'd never leave his things here. Without his keys, Harold couldn't go far. Let's check outside. He took a lot of pride in his Chevy truck. Maybe he wanted to check on something."

Jenna could tell he didn't believe a word of what he'd said. The Chevy required a key and Sam knew it too. As they headed out to the parking lot, the cooler than usual breeze slapped her in the face. The setting sun only added to the chill.

Sporting a new windshield, Sam's car sat in the middle of the near empty parking lot—untouched, thank goodness. He'd retrieved it from the shop this morning. At least he wasn't the target this time.

Sam pointed to a white truck with souped up wheels and black trim. "That's Harold's."

"I wouldn't have expected someone his age to be driving something so sporty." Jenna hurried to the truck and checked inside. It was empty.

Sam edged up behind her. "I'm worried. Lab protocol dictates that if he needs to leave his post, he has to find a replacement. Once I even saw Gina man the desk." Sam flipped open his phone. "Phil, it's Sam." He told him about Harold.

A moment later, Sam disconnected. "Phil's calling campus police. He received no notice from Harold that he'd be leaving."

Sirens blared outside less than a minute later, the noise coming toward the lab. Both of them watched as campus police drove past close to breakneck speed.

"They never respond that fast," Sam said.

"Maybe someone else called about Harold."

He stared at her for a moment as if she was way off base. "Let's see. Hop in my car. I'll follow them."

Jenna tried to jog toward his vehicle but had to stop to catch her breath. Sam raced back to her. "I'm sorry. I keep forgetting you're not up to par. Why don't you head on into the lab and wait inside? I can see what the cops are up to."

Hollidays didn't let a little thing like smoke inhalation stop them from doing their job. Besides, she'd need his fob to reach his lab. "Hell no. I'm going with you."

"Suit yourself."

The sirens made following easy. Few cars were on campus, allowing them to catch up to the cops. Two campus police cars pulled to a stop next to a grove on the far side of campus, their lights flashing, where a student-aged male stood near a tree-lined copse waving his arms.

Sam got out. Jenna knew they'd be denied access to the scene, so she stayed put. Although she was pretty sure she'd never met any of the campus police during her investigations, she didn't want to chance being identified.

"Don't you want to talk to them?" he asked.

She rubbed her chest for effect. "You find out what you can."

"Be right back."

Sure enough, the cops stopped Sam. He spoke with them and flashed his badge, but they wouldn't let him into the cordoned off area.

He returned to the car. "A kid discovered a body—a fresh one. That's all they would tell me. If I hadn't been with the lab, I doubt they would have told me that much."

"Do you think it's Harold?"

"I sure as hell hope not." Sam slapped the steering wheel. "I have to stop this person." She'd never heard such conviction in his voice before.

"And I want to help."

* * *

CARLA PACED SAM'S LAB. Her curly hair hung over her forehead, and she'd eaten off half her lipstick.

"Come sit down with me, Carla." Jenna felt sorry for her, all tense and anxious.

"I can't. Not until Chance gets back. I'm worried about him."

"Nothing will happen to Chance. He's with scads of cops, checking the body."

"I know, but what's taking him so long?"

Jenna knew the tedious procedure of documenting the scene, taking Trace evidence and trying to determine cause of death. He'd have to bring the body to the lab and do an autopsy. That alone would take hours. "He might be working on the body right now." She saw no reason to give any details.

Her face brightened. "Maybe I should go see him."

"I think he'd want you to stay here." Jenna didn't think seeing an autopsy would do Carla any good. She gently clasped Carla's elbow. She led her new friend over to where she and Sam were seated.

"Take my seat." Sam pushed back from the computer. "I'll go check on Chance."

"Thank you."

Once Sam left, Jenna tried to console Carla. "So what are you going to do about the threat?"

She dropped her head in her hands. "I don't know. I'm afraid to go back to my place. Even before the killing began, the campus wasn't safe —at least not for me. The lab used to be my haven but not any more." Carla pushed her glasses up on her nose and sniffled.

"Did something happen on campus?"

"Yes. I've told Chance, but no one else knows." Carla's words shot out in short bursts.

"Told anyone else what?"

"Two and a half months ago, I was raped on campus."

The horror took her breath away. "Oh, Carla. I'm so sorry."

"It was my fault in a way."

Jenna didn't do Vice, but she'd heard victim's often believed they'd caused the attack. "It wasn't your fault. Did you report the attack?"

"No."

Now wasn't the time to lecture her about proper procedure. "Where on campus did this happen?" She hoped it wasn't nearby. Jenna knew she sounded like a cop, but some things couldn't be helped.

"I was working really late at the lab. Past ten, I think. I should have asked Harold to escort me to my car, but I was on campus. What could happen to me here?"

That's why most campus's had emergency phone centers. No campus was safe from sicko's. "Go on."

"I'd parked at the library when I arrived that morning to do some research. The weather was dry and cool when I finished so I decided to walk back to here instead of driving the half-mile and battling to find a parking space. I didn't give a thought to the fact it would be dark when I left work." She bit her thumbnail. "That night, the moon was hiding and the wind howling. A storm was brewing. I kind of got spooked and wanted to reach my car as soon as possible, so I cut through the buildings instead of staying on the sidewalks. I don't know if he targeted me, or I was in the wrong place at the wrong time, but the next thing I knew I was on the ground."

Jenna could only envision the fear and sense of helplessness that ripped through Carla at the time of the attack. "Did you get a good look at him?" Please say, yes.

She nodded. "He was African American, and very strong. He shoved my face into the ground and held me down with his knee. He told me if I screamed, he'd kill me." Carla lifted her hair to expose a red scar that hadn't faded. "He cut me here."

"Oh, God. You poor woman. I can't imagine what you went through."

"Then he...he...burned me with a lit cigarette." She slipped her sleeve up a notch to reveal a scar the size of a dime.

Perhaps that's why Carla feared fire. "Before he raped you."

Carla nodded again. The pain of talking about the incident must have been traumatic for her. "I stayed on the ground for an hour before I had the courage to drive home."

"Oh, sweetie, why didn't you tell anyone?"

"I couldn't. He took my purse. He knew my name." She choked out a sob. "Every night I fear he'll find me and come back."

Jenna's heart ached as she grabbed Carla's hand. "I hate to ask, but did you at least take a morning after pill?"

Carla squeezed her hand tight. "No. I wish I had. I'm...I'm pregnant." Tears streamed down her cheeks. "I don't know what to do."

How much more could this woman take? "Tell me what I can do to help."

"There's nothing anyone can do. I don't believe in abortion, so that's out of the question. Chance has been very kind to me though. He seems to understand."

Four beeps sounded on the entry door, and Sam and Chance entered the lab. Exhaustion lined Chance's face. "The body was Harold's. Someone must have lured him outside then attacked him from behind. They bludgeoned him to death—in plain sight."

Like Carla's sister? Jenna slumped back in her chair, sickened by the violence. "Do you think the killer drove Harold to the grove and dumped the body?" Dumb question. "Never mind. I don't imagine someone would just heft Harold over his shoulder and walk him down the road in the middle of the day."

"Oh my dear Lord." If possible, Carla dropped lower in her seat. "When will this nightmare end?"

If Jenna had been lead on this case, what would she do? "Did anyone check the security cameras in the lobby to see what happened to Harold?"

Sam nodded. "Phil checked. The perpetrator knocked out the system beforehand."

A shot of fear bubbled through her. "Then the killer has free reign in the building?" Was no place safe?

Carla choked in a sob. Dumb move. Jenna hadn't meant to scare Carla to death.

Chance rushed over to Carla and helped her up. "Come on."

She sniffled. "Where are we going?"

"I want you to stay with me until the killer is caught."

For probably what was the first time all day, Carla's face relaxed.

Jenna's cell phone rang, and all eyes turned to her. "Excuse me." She checked the ID. Giombetti. He couldn't have called at a worse time. "Hi, Dad."

"Still undercover, huh?"

"Yup. Everything okay?"

"Never better. I found your man, Richie Raden." He gave her the address of a restaurant in South Tampa. Great. "If you hurry, you can catch him."

"Thanks." Jenna disconnected and tried to figure out a plausible lie for the three-person listening gallery.

"Something wrong?" Sam asked.

"Aunt Martha again. She had a little set back. Dad asked if I'd check in on her. Do you mind?"

Jenna stood when the big steel door swung open. Phil rolled in with a pretty young woman behind him. Apology covered his face. "I'm sorry for the intrusion. Sam, since you have your hands full. I thought you could use an intern."

Jenna swung around to Sam. His eyes were smiling, but not his mouth. Sam stepped past her and shook the woman's hand. "Lara. I'm delighted."

He knew her? Well, Jenna wasn't delighted. "I need to go." She would have preferred to stay to see what these two had going, but duty called.

* * *

As soon as Jenna reached her car, she called Marlon back and asked if he could keep watch on Raden until she got there. It would really suck if the man she planned to tail finished eating before she arrived.

"You owe me big time, Holliday."

"You don't have to remind me. Look, this guy might be the key to everything. Including finding the man who murdered Jackson." *Please don't let him cop an attitude now.*

"Let's hope."

Twenty-five long minutes later, she pulled into the restaurant lot. Marlon emerged from his white Kia. The car wasn't a give away, but his blue uniform sure was. Idiot. How had he managed to pass the test to become a detective? Life wasn't fair.

She jumped from her car and immediately regretted the quick move. Her ribs had been bruised when the fire blast had tossed her to the ground. Not wanting Giombetti to take note of her injured status and tattle to the captain, who surely would notify her dad, she straightened and sucked in a breath. Damp, cool air slipped down her top and she shivered.

She motioned Marlon away from the restaurant windows. Apparently, the man had no sense.

"How long has Raden been in there?" Her stomach grumbled. She needed food and wondered if she'd have time to order the salad bar.

"Forty minutes."

"Thanks. I'll take it from here."

"You want me to hang around?" He stepped toward her, but all she could think of was sexy Sam.

"I'm cool."

"Call if you need me." From his puppy dog expression, she almost reconsidered having him keep her company.

"Will do."

The moment Giombetti pulled out of the lot, Richie Raden emerged. The nearly full lot shared space with the bookstore next door, so Raden didn't glance her way. Good.

Jenna pulled out her phone and pretended to have a conversation as she watched him stride to his car.

Here we go.

She never prided herself on being invisible when tailing someone, but the heavy traffic helped her stay close behind without being too obvious. Richie turned right toward downtown. At this hour, she couldn't imagine where he was headed. The moment he passed through Channelside, she suspected his destination was Ybor. Following him down the narrow streets would be trickier.

He drove down 7th Avenue and pulled into the parking garage next to the movie theatre. Great. If he went to a show, she'd have to split. Sam would become suspicious if she came home too late since her imaginary aunt could need only so much care.

She wasn't ready to confront Raden yet though. She wanted to get a feel for his lifestyle—or so she tried to convince herself as the trepidation of interacting with him crept down her spine. He parked on the third level, she on the fourth. As not to look too noticeable when she followed him, she peeled off the gauze bandages. She flicked on the overhead car light and examined the damage. Red streaks zigzagged across her cheeks and forehead. She looked like freaking Zorro had left his mark. Oh well. Nothing she could do about her face now. Too bad she wasn't into makeup or she would have plastered her face with concealer.

She turned off the car's overhead light and eased out of the seat. She'd taken two steps when a hand covered her mouth.

She couldn't breathe. On instinct, she elbowed her attacker and stomped on his instep. He groaned and dropped his hand.

"Bitch."

He got that right. She swung around and reached for her gun—only her gun was in the car. Shit.

CHAPTER FIFTEEN

"RICHIE RADEN." She held up her hands and backed away, praying he hadn't come prepared for a fight. A quick scan of his body convinced her he most likely didn't have a weapon.

The confusion that crossed his face almost made her laugh. "You know me, lady?"

"In a way. Can we go someplace to talk?" This dark, empty parking garage made her uneasy.

His face muscles sagged, and his eyes darted right and left. "Sure, but I only got a minute. I'm meeting someone."

She hoped it wasn't Deidra. That could be the death of her.

Keeping her distance, Jenna walked to the side of Raden. Despite the cold, Jenna insisted they sit outside at the restaurant. It made for an easier escape. When the waiter came by for drinks, Raden waved a hand. Jenna asked for water and a menu. She needed food.

"So why were you following me?" he asked.

"I wanted to know what you were discussing with Deidra Willows last week."

"Deidra? You know Deidra?"

She couldn't tell if admitting she worked for her would be a good or bad thing. Decision time. She was convinced Deidra had fingered her for a cop, which would pretty much ruin her chances of ever working undercover again. Her dad would stick his fingers into her affairs to make sure that would happen since Captain Lucas and he were best buds. Deidra would never give her permission to explore the back, so what did she have to lose?

"Yeah. I work for her." No use using the past tense.

"That so? Then *you* talk to her." Richie stood up. She grabbed his arm with one hand as she reached into her pocket with the other. She drew out her badge and flashed it. Richie Raden's eyes widened.

He sat back down. "What do you want to know?"

This guy had no record, held a fairly good job and could be on the level. "I'm not here to hassle you. There has been a rash of deaths lately, and I'm kind of afraid." That sounded good. "I don't want what's been happening to other people recently happen to me, or to you."

"Such as?"

"Theft, arson, rape, and murder." No need to mention dismemberment, head bashing, and other assorted modus operandi.

"For real?"

"Yes." Jenna held her breath, hoping he'd give her some piece of information to help with the case.

"I haven't done anything, so I got nothing to hide." Richie scrubbed a hand down his face. "Just don't tell Deidra I told you, okay?"

She crossed her heart. "I promise."

"I, ah, asked Deidra to put a curse on someone—someone who raped my sister." He flinched.

The image of Carla being held down on the ground jumped into her mind. "Did the curse work?"

She didn't believe in curses, but maybe the rapist did.

"Hell yeah it worked. The man ran into the wrong end of a bullet the next day."

If he knew that much, he must know the man's name. "This bullet catcher got a name?"

His gaze darted right, then left. "Yeah. Rodrico Evans."

Well, I'll be damned. The man they found at Ballast Point. The pieces were coming together.

* * *

JENNA FACED Captain Lucas across his desk. He leaned forward on his elbows. "So you think the same person who killed the HOPEFAL guard, Harold, also killed the people in the cauldron?"

"I have no proof, but my gut tells me, yes."

He scribbled something on a pad. "You learn anything more from your new boyfriend about who's in the cauldron?"

"He's not my boyfriend, but yes. One set belonged to the sister of someone who works at the lab. The victim was Daphne Pendowski. She was a nun who was bludgeoned to death."

"A nun? Dear God. What are these people into?"

"I have no idea. Sam is checking to see if the second set belongs to Franklin Manchester, since both he and the skull were about the same age."

"Did you tell him about your mom's skull being stolen?"

"No." She leaned back in her seat not wanting to address her deceit or the pain. "I think you should send Rodrico Evans's body to the lab so Sam can compare him to Creighton Jackson."

"Why?"

She blew out a breath. "If the two have the same cut marks, we'll know we have a serial killer on the loose."

He took a sip of his coffee and stared off in space, as though he were putting together everything she'd told him. "You thinking a nun bludgeoned to death and two chopped up men are related? How did the HOPEFAL security guard die again?"

"Knife to the kidney." She held up her hand. "I know the M.O.'s are different, but between the curse for Sam and the curse for Carla, I'm thinking the same person is responsible."

"Bring me proof. And bring Marlon up to speed if you think these cases are related."

"I already have."

"Good. Be careful. And don't overtax yourself. I need you healthy. The last thing I need is your dad on my back because I let you work before you were ready."

"I promise to keep an eye over my shoulder at all times." She stood.

"One more thing. You said you saw a head floating in another caul-dron in the back of the store. Did anything come of that?"

"We can't obtain a search warrant if the head's some plastic decoy."

"You sure it was plastic?"

"No."

"Then find a way to take another look."

"I already spilled the beans about being a cop to Richie Raden, the one who paid Deidra to put a spell on someone who raped his sister. I can't waltz back in there." She told him about Rodrico Evans, the corpse at Ballast Point, being the rapist.

"Shit. We'll talk to Raden. You think he had anything to do with the Evans' death?"

She shrugged.

"You sure you can't find some way to get into the backroom? With Deidra's permission, of course."

"As soon as I learn to leap tall buildings." Jenna rolled her eyes and walked out.

She was sick and tired of running into brick walls. She prayed Sam had made some progress today. Being at the lab with him relaxed her probably because he never put any expectations on her to perform.

Jenna flashed her temporary HOPEFAL badge that Phil has provided her with at the new guard and marched to Sam's lab, frus-trated the captain never seemed satisfied with her progress. Sam had provided her the code to the door, as well as a spare fob, so she wouldn't have to disturb him every time she wanted to visit. As the door swung open, she spotted a near perfect woman bent over the metal gurney, her head practically touching Sam's, and a jolt of jealousy jabbed her.

They both looked up at the same time. Sam smiled. "Hey."

He must have suspected all was not right, for he peeled off his gloves, stepped around the gurney and wrapped an arm around her waist. Even though he'd been playing with bones, he smelled fresh, like a morning shower. Every muscle relaxed in his tender embrace. If only she could convince him he wanted her—in the biblical sense—all would be right with the world.

Sam turned her around. "Jenna, you remember Lara Romano? She was a student of mine and has been a big help."

Super. The girl was everything Jenna wasn't. Lara was tall, thin, had flawless olive skin and dark straight hair that snaked down her back in a ponytail near her waist.

"Hi."

Lara ripped off her glove and shook Jenna's hand. "Nice meeting you. Sam told me how much you've helped him with the case." She had a slight nasal twang to her speech as if she was hard of hearing.

What a crock. Jenna had done nothing to help, but she smiled in return. "So, what are you two working on?" Jenna glanced to Sam and kept her tone upbeat.

"Just investigating all the bones in the cauldron."

Before she could ask another question, four beeps rang out and Chance hurried into the lab. After a quick introduction to Lara, Chance's mouth pinched. "I'm looking for Carla. She's not in her office and not answering her phone."

That didn't sound good. Carla practically lived at the lab. "Did you check with the guard to see if she checked out?"

His shoulders relaxed. "Good call. I don't know the last time I've slept. I'm worried about her. We were up half the night talking." He turned to Sam. "Maybe you can convince her to take some time off. She's a nervous wreck what with the baby and the curse. She should be with her family right now."

Sam's brows rose. Apparently, Carla hadn't told him about the baby. "I'll try, but don't get your hopes up."

Chance saluted. "I'll let you know if I find her."

* * *

CARLA SAT in the university's student center, indulging in a large chocolate shake. Chance had made sense last night, but there was no way she could go home and face her parents. Not now, at least.

"Miss?" A young woman shifted from one foot to the other.

Startled, her muscles tensed. "Yes?"

The girl handed Carla a folded note and dashed away. The slip of a girl was gone before Carla could push back her chair and chase after her. She glanced at the white envelope, and her hand trembled. The paper wobbled. Was it another curse? She couldn't take much more. Holding food down had even become a chore.

She took another sip of her drink to delay reading the message, but the cool, chocolaty drink did nothing to calm her nerves. She sat up straight and checked out the remaining tables. Two guys were laughing at a corner table. Had they been there when she arrived? She couldn't remember. Her mind had been on the curse, on the baby...on Chance.

A man who looked like a professor was on the phone, another guy with a hairy face was sipping coffee while reading a newspaper. No one seemed to notice her. Three girls huddled around a table, punching numbers in their calculator.

Convinced the sender of the note wasn't nearby, Carla peeled open the note.

She read the neat handwriting. "I have a surprise for you. Meet me in the Campus Police parking lot." It was signed, Chance.

"Aw." She couldn't help but smile. Her birthday wasn't for another week, but perhaps he wanted to give her an early gift. She grabbed her half empty drink and headed to the parking lot, and then cut across the grass instead of taking the path. Giving up a good parking place might be dumb, but her swollen feet made walking farther than a few hundred yards uncomfortable.

Two minutes later she pulled into the mostly full police lot. Not seeing Chance's car, she walked over to wooden bench and sat. The clear day and slight breeze lifted her spirits. She reread the note to make sure she hadn't misunderstood. Wait a minute. How had Chance known she'd be at the food court? Had she mentioned something to the guard at the front desk? And why did Chance send a note instead of surprising her in person?

Then again, he knew she loved mystery and intrigue. Cars whipped down the street seemingly unaware they were driving past the police station at unlawful speeds. She tried to relax, but the questions zinging through her brain wouldn't let her. Sunlight shot through the leaves and warmed her face. She closed her eyes for a moment, dreaming of what Chance had in mind. Carla shifted in her seat and a hand clasped over her mouth and nose. She moaned and struggled, and her hands flew to her attacker's hands. Oh, shit. She needed air.

Carla tried to pry his fingers off her, but they didn't budge. Her throat constricted and her vision blurred. Another surge of pain ripped through her as the sharp slice of knife dug into her back. He yanked her head to the side, and blackness engulfed her.

CHAPTER SIXTEEN

"CHANCE, stop pacing. I'm sure Carla's fine." Jenna said, even though she didn't believe it herself.

He stood still, his hands clasped behind his head. "Whit, the new guard, said she left over an hour ago. Why hasn't she checked in?"

"Maybe she had a doctor's appointment and didn't think to tell you."

He relaxed a bit. "Maybe."

Gina rushed in, her breathing ragged. "I just received a call from University Community Hospital. Carla's been stabbed." Her hands fisted as her sides.

Chance gasped. Sam stiffened. Lara looked frightened. When no one moved, Jenna jumped up. "I'll drive."

Sam turned to Lara. "Do you mind staying here?"

Lara's cheeks softened. "Not at all. Call if I need to do anything."

The four of them left and loaded into Jenna's car. Given the hospital was less than a mile away, they arrived at the emergency room in less than five minutes.

As the HOPEFAL representative, Gina went to find out about Carla.

Chance pulled out his phone. "I'd like the number of a Robert Pendowski in Wheeling, West Virginia." He slipped outside.

Poor Carla. She'd be upset that Chance had notified her parents, but what choice did he have? If a relative of hers had been injured, she sure as hell would want to know.

Gina came back into the waiting room. "Carla's still in surgery."

Jenna sucked in a breath as a deep ache twisted her stomach. Sam looked worse than when he'd arrived. Carla was a dear friend of his.

Sam's jaw clenched. "Did they give you her chances?"

"No."

"Who found her?" he asked.

"Campus police. Can you believe she was sitting on a bench next to the station when the motherfucker attacked her? Excuse my language." She shook her head. "Someone sure was arrogant to do this in broad daylight."

"I trust they didn't catch the bastard?"

Gina pulled out her notepad. "No. Officer Terrance McNally found her slumped down on the bench. At first he thought she was sleeping until he saw the patch of red on her back."

Chance returned, his eyes vacant as he sat down without saying a word. The difficult conversation with Carla's parents must have put a strain on him. Sam settled next to his friend and relayed the information.

For the next hour, no one said anything. No speculation, no outpouring of sympathy. Nothing. The pain ran too deep to express what anyone thought. First Harold, then Carla. Sam's house had been set afire and his car damaged. Who was next?

At three thirty, a man in green scrubs exited through the electric doors. "Are you relatives of Carla Pendowski?" He scanned the group.

"Her family is in West Virginia. We work with her," Gina said. "How is she?"

The doctor's lips pursed. "The surgery went as well as expected."

Bullcrappy. The doctor took so long to answer he must have been debating whether he should tell the group anything. Jenna wanted details.

Chance leaned forward. "And the baby?"

The doctor shook his head. "Unfortunately, she lost the fetus."

"Thank you for letting us know." Chance's voice came out hard. "When can we see her?"

"She's in ICU." He glanced at his watch. "She should be in her room in about an hour. I'll have the nurse let you know when you can visit." He nodded to them, his face full of sympathy. His pager went off and the doctor disappeared back into the main hospital.

His absence left a void. "So now we wait," Jenna said. "If you three want to go back to work, I can wait here and let you know what happens."

"No way I'm leaving," Chance announced. "Besides, you drove."

Her mind wasn't functioning well at all. "There is that."

After what seemed like hours, a chunky nurse in a flowered uniform came up to them and asked who was here for Carla. All four of them raised their hands.

"Ms. Pendowski is in her room. We can only allow two of you to see her—"

Chance jumped up. "I'll go first."

As it should be. The two seemed to have grown a bond as strong as she and Sam had.

Sam stood. "I'll come with you. Then we'll let the girls visit."

Jenna didn't mind. From the brittle way Chance held himself, he needed Sam's support.

* * *

WITH EACH STRIDE SAM TOOK, his legs grew weaker, but he forced himself to keep up with Chance. What if it had been Jenna on the bench instead of Carla? His friend's face had paled the moment the doctor delivered the news, but now his steps were rushed.

The familiar smell of antiseptic churned his gut as Sam remembered the last time he walked these halls. Jenna had been in the bed, cut and burned—because of him. Now it was Carla. Had her stabbing been a message for him? This insanity had to stop.

Two chairs were positioned by the bedside. Chance sat in one, but Sam stayed back, letting his friend have time with her first.

Chance lifted Carla's hand and held it tight. "Carla?" he whispered.

From the side, Sam noticed a single tear streak down his friend's face. Empathy swamped him. Carla and Sam had developed a solid friendship, and now she barely clung to life.

Carla half opened her eyes. "Hey." She winced and Chance leaned forward.

"What happened?" Chance's Adam apple moved up and down.

"I got your note. It said you wanted to meet with me." One corner of her mouth lifted for a brief moment before falling.

"Aw, honey, I never sent that note." She wet her lips and Chance dropped her hand, reached for her water, and fed her the liquid through a straw. "But I wish I had."

"I know that now."

"Did you see who did this?"

Carla coughed and Chance's back stiffened. "No, I was facing the other direction watching for you." She took another sip of water. "I didn't hear anyone, but suddenly this hand came out of nowhere and covered my mouth and nose."

Sam slid into the chair next to Chance, sensing his friend could use the support. "What did he smell like?" If this person knew that Carla and Chance had something going, he or she had an inside connection to the lab, which was very scary.

Her gaze flicked to Sam. "Hi, Sam. Smell like?"

"Yeah. His hand was over your mouth. Did it smell like tobacco, dirt, sweat or what?"

Her gaze moved down to the right. "He smelled like soap, but not the good kind you can buy at Bath and Body Works." She inhaled slowly as if getting air took effort. "It was closer to an antiseptic smell. I'm sorry. It happened so fast." Her eyelids fluttered.

"Did you notice anything about him? Was his hand large or calloused, Negroid or Caucasian?"

"His palm was calloused. I think he was Caucasian, but it all happened so fast I can't be sure of anything."

"You're doing great," Chance said, rubbing his thumb over her palm.

With her free hand, Carla grabbed her stomach and her eyes widened. She shot a glance at Chance. "Did I—"

Chance scooted the chair closer to the bed and visibly squeezed her hand. "I'm sorry. The baby didn't make it."

A sob erupted. After a long cry, she wiped her tears and sobered. "Maybe it's for the best." She squeezed shut her eyes, and just as fast, opened them. Her mouth rounded into an O. "Drake!"

Chance turned to Sam. "Drake's her dog." Sam shifted his gaze back to her. "What about him?"

"I forgot to take him out yesterday," Carla said. The effort to talk was obvious. "He needs to go out. He needs to eat. Ohmigod. I can't stay here."

Carla tried to sit up, but Chance was too quick. He jumped up and eased down her shoulder. "I'll feed him."

Carla relaxed back on the pillow. "Really? You'd do that?" He nodded. "My key's are in my purse." She made Chance write down the directions to her house.

"Don't worry about a thing. I'll even walk him."

The same nurse who told them Carla was in her room, entered. "Time's up, boys. I need you all to give me some space. I have to give Ms. Carla something for the pain."

Chance and he stood.

"Don't forget about Drake," Carla said, her voice fading fast.

"I won't."

Once they returned to the waiting room, Jenna was pacing in front of a row of visitors, while Gina was flipping through a magazine. They stopped what they were doing and rushed over to them.

"I need to feed Carla's dog," Chance said. "Can I borrow your car keys? I won't be long."

"Sure." She dug in her pocket, unhooked the car key, and handed it to him.

"Thanks." Chance hesitated.

"Go," Sam said. "I'll fill them in on the extent of Carla's injuries." Chance looked grateful and left.

"She looks pretty good, considering the attack. She's pale, but that's to be expected with her injury."

"Can we see her now?" Gina asked.

"The nurse is with her."

"When can we—"

A loud explosion sounded outside the Emergency Room and Sam nearly jumped out of his seat. Before he reached the door to see what had happened, two male nurses raced outside, medical bags in hand.

Sam, Gina and Jenna shot outside and halted at the sight of flames shooting out from Jenna's car.

"Ohmigod," Jenna screamed, sending an arrow straight to Sam's heart.

She leapt forward as if to save Chance, but he grabbed her arm. "Jenna. Don't. You can't do anything. No one can."

The fire had completely engulfed the inside of the car. Chance was dead—as were Sam's insides.

Less than five minutes later, sirens sounded in the background. Someone must have called the fire department. A ton of people poured out of the hospital, gawking at the scene. The stench of rubber mixed with the cloying smoke kept the onlookers far from the accident.

Poor Chance. No fire department in the world could save him now.

Gina looked ready to explode. He figured it was her way of coping with the terrible loss. She stalked off to the right, darted in between the cars, and then circled around the lot opposite Jenna's car, apparently looking for the perpetrator. Someone must have set a charge on Jenna's car. They didn't explode by themselves, despite what television shows portrayed.

Sam pulled Jenna to his chest and held her tight. Her body vibrated against him. As much as he wanted to soothe her, no words would form. Over her bent head, he too checked out the area, trying to identify something out of place—or rather someone he knew.

Jenna leaned back and looked up at him, tears streaking her face. "That should have been me. He meant to harm me."

"Shh. We don't know that." It was a lie, but right now wasn't the time to tell her he agreed with her assessment.

"Sir, you'll have to move inside," a security guard with a strong Boston accent motioned them toward the door.

"Sure."

Jenna grabbed Sam's hand and held it tight. The intimacy was not lost on him. "What are we going to do now?" She looked up at him with tears brimming over her lashes. The strong set of her jaw told him she was mad, which in his mind, was a lot better than sad.

"Find out who did this." He relished the frustration that overtook the grief.

His cell rang. No caller ID. "Bonita."

"Next time it will be your girlfriend." Click. Sam's blood pressure dropped.

Jenna tugged on his arm. "You look liked you saw a ghost."

"Wrong number." Sam tried to smile, but his lips wouldn't cooperate. He'd tell her later about the threat. Maybe. "Come on, I want to talk to Carla's surgeon."

"Why?"

Sam held open the Emergency room door for Jenna. "To see if he could tell the type of instrument that was used to stab her."

"Good thinking. Let's pray the attacker left some evidence near the park bench, like a fingerprint or something. We should check."

She sounded like a cop, but he figured it was Jenna's way of coping with the tragedy. "I'm sure the cops have everything under control."

"They're campus cops."

"Still cops. They're good." He dragged a stray hair behind her ear. "Phil will want to be involved, so there's nothing to worry about. They'll catch the guy." They had to. He cupped Jenna's cheek and a small smile captured her face.

Sam prayed the cops would arrest this maniac before he really did kill Jenna. Dread nearly tripped him. He had to protect her at all cost.

"Are you okay?" She waved a hand in front of his face. "Never mind. That was a stupid question." She grabbed her stomach. "I want to vomit."

"Hold on." Sam led Jenna inside to the waiting room chair hoping once she sat down, she'd be less agitated.

Gina rushed in letting in a gust of fresh air. "I saw nothing. He must have set the device and not stayed around to watch the fireworks."

"We've been here all day," Sam said. "He could have followed us here, set the charge, and left hours ago."

Jenna grabbed his arm. "Do you think they have security cameras on the parking lot?"

"Maybe," Gina said. "I'll check. I need something to do or I'll hurt someone."

Jenna stood and moved away from Sam, wrapping her arms around her waist. "I wish I knew which one of us stepped on this guy's toes. We have to be getting close."

Sam stayed put, understanding Jenna's need to put distance between them. "Maybe he's only after me. You've been driving me around." He scrubbed a hand down his chin. "Damn. I haven't found anything to tie these deaths together, so how am I'm a threat to this guy? Or you?"

Her gaze shot to the ceiling. "This guy could be a woman, you know. Let's not leave Deidra out of the equation." Jenna blew out a long breath. "Tell me about this Manchester man—the one whose bones were stolen from the cemetery. Maybe someone wanted revenge against his relatives and want to stop us."

She had a good memory for names. "I know nothing more than the fact his bones were stolen from his mausoleum. You'd have to ask Phil for details."

Gina strode back into the room. "Bastard disabled the video cameras overlooking the parking lot."

"How could he get past security?" Jenna asked.

Gina stabbed a hand over her short-cropped hair. "The hospital staff is trying to figure that out now."

"Oh God." Jenna grabbed her chest. "How are we going to tell Carla that Chance is dead?"

Gina shook her head. "We aren't. At least not until she's healed."

Another lie. When would this deception stop?

CHAPTER SEVENTEEN

ANGER RIPPLED THROUGH HIM. That bitch had more lives than a fucking cat. When he saw the pathologist from the lab get into Jenna's car, he was tempted to stop him, but if he had, he would have blown his cover. Shit. Now he'd have to figure out some other way to kill her.

He had to smile a little bit though. The look on Bonita's face had been priceless when he witnessed his friend go up in flames. For a moment, he thought Jenna was going to faint. Ha. Maybe now they'd get the hint that no one was going to stop him or his brother until they'd touched the lives of everyone Jenna and her dad cared about.

He was actually getting into this killing stuff. It gave him power, and made him feel like a man.

Once he peeled off his rubber mask, he stuffed the latex face into his pocket. He'd burn it later so they couldn't retrieve any DNA off the inside. No sirree. He'd been careful in everything he'd done.

He wiggled his nose and mouth to get rid of the constricting feeling from the rubber. Ignacio had made several realistic masks for him over the years. Perhaps it was time to pay the man a visit. Loose ends had a way of coming back to haunt you.

* * *

GINA RUSHED into Sam's lab. "We have a break."

Jenna jumped up, and Sam straightened. Both rushed over to her. "What?"

"There were security cameras inside the hospital that our man didn't disable until after he reached the security center itself to disabled those. Does that make sense?"

"So we have a picture of him entering the security center?" Jenna couldn't keep her hands from gesturing.

"Yes. The hospital just sent the footage over to us. Edwardo Lopez is going over the film with Phil right now. Our perp is about five ten, a little overweight, has blond hair, a goatee and a bad complexion. Unfortunately, he was wearing a cap, so his eyes won't show."

"Age?" Jenna asked.

Gina shrugged. "I left before Edwardo finished."

That description fit the bill for half of America. "So now what?" Jenna asked, her gaze shifting from Gina to Sam.

Gina's gaze dropped to the ground for a second. "The man was wearing a security uniform."

Sam slapped the counter. "Shit. No wonder he was able to move around without raising suspicion." He snapped his fingers. "That sounds like the man who asked Jenna and me to move away from the fire. I was so focused on Chance, I didn't look at his face. I do remember he had a heavy Boston accent."

"Phil received news that the real security man was killed," Gina said. "His throat was cut."

Sam slapped the counter. "I hate this. I have to do something."

A sizzle of fear snapped Jenna into gear. "You're not a cop. We don't need any vigilantes running around." Both Gina and Sam froze at her attack. "Sorry." Perhaps her tone had been over the top. Her dad's pet peeve was civilians trying to do a cop's job. "I don't want the same thing happening to Sam that happened to Chance, that's all."

Sam stepped next to her and wrapped an arm around her waist, sending a refreshing jolt up her back. "Don't worry about me. I'll be uber careful. I promise."

"That's probably what Chance thought too." Poor Carla. Oh, shit.

"Chance was on his way to feed Carla's dog. He never made it and we don't have the keys to her place."

Sam exchanged a glance with Gina. "Do you know if Carla donated to the key caddy?"

"A key caddy? What's that?" Jenna asked.

Gina shrugged. "It's where you put one of your house keys in a storage closet. In case you lock yourself out, there's always a spare."

"That doesn't sound very safe."

Gina's brows rose. "You have to go through Phil to get to the closet. He may be in a wheelchair, but the guy can fend off anyone."

Jenna doubted that, but from the dreamy way Gina said it, Jenna wasn't going to burst her bubble.

"I'll see about the key and take care of the dog." Gina pulled open the heavy metal door and disappeared down the hall.

Once she left, Sam returned to his bones. Jenna was halfway to the computer station on the other side of the room when he rapped his knuckles on the gurney. She spun around.

"I wonder if the same person who knifed the security guard cut Carla," he said.

Jenna shrugged. "It was the same M.O. Maybe he followed the ambulance to the hospital and waited to see who would come. When he saw us arrive en masse, he decided to take us out—or as many as he could."

"Sick." Sam held up a finger and pulled out his phone. A moment later he discontinued. "Eric Markowitz is in autopsy right now with the guard. He'll be able to tell the type of knife used to slit the man's throat."

"How long will that take?" As a cop, she knew. As a civilian, she needed to ask.

"Not long. Cause of death was evident."

"Did Eric see Carla's wound? He'll need to in order to compare weapons."

"I imagine he'll contact the surgeon for the information."

Jenna sat down, her mind racing through the events. "You do know that we have to sneak back into Deidra's back room, don't you, to see about the head we found?"

A low growl came out of Sam. "No freaking way. It's too dangerous. What made you think of that?"

"Deidra is somehow involved in all of this. That's why I was targeted. Maybe she was mad because I quit." *Or because she figured out I was a cop.*

"When did you quit?"

"I called her two days ago." Jenna smiled.

Sam stepped over to her and pulled her to his chest. "As far as sneaking back into that room, the answer is no. Weren't you the one who said to let the cops do their job?"

"Yes, but—"

"No buts. You are not going to do anything regarding this case. I don't want to have to worry about keeping you safe." Sam ran a thumb over her lips and her mind switched gears. If only Sam would heed his own advice, she could relax.

"Maybe you're right." To argue would be to admit who she was, and that she'd lied.

"Damn right, I'm right. The police will find this guy. Phil will see to it."

Everyone seemed to think Phil walked on water. Jenna wanted to scream that she was the police and this was her case. Unfortunately, she'd grown attached to this neat freak and didn't want to jeopardize what relationship she did have with him.

He kissed each eye and Jenna could feel her jaw unclench. "Mmm. I think I need more of that." She reached up and pulled his face toward her. His eyes were slightly bloodshot and his hair ruffled, but to her, he belonged in a GQ ad. Her thoughts traveled south as she pushed away the horrors of the day.

When she lifted her lips to his, Jenna pressed her hips forward, relishing the contact—the very hard contact. She liked how Sam found her attractive. Their lips locked just as the lab door swung open. Again. Shit.

As if Sam had been stung, he leapt back. Sam swung around. "Jenna, this is Eric Markowitz. He was Chance's boss, if only for a short time, and who Phil assigned to autopsy the hospital security guard."

Age had not been kind to this man if the number of wrinkles present were any indication. "I'm so sorry for your loss," Jenna said. Dr. Markowitz may not have known Chance long, but he seemed to have touched everyone he'd met.

"Thank you." He inhaled and straightened his shoulders. "I came to tell you I finished. The hospital just contacted Phil. Man's name is... or rather was, Alfred Witterd. I just spoke with Carla's surgeon and asked him to fax over the photos of her injury. From what I could tell, the knife slice on Alfred's throat seems consistent with that of Carla's wound."

"So the same person hurt them both?" Jenna asked.

"I believe so."

* * *

JENNA WOKE up late and out of sorts, which wasn't surprising considering the recent events—Carla's stabbing, Chance's death, and her car being blown to smithereens. To top it off, she'd called her dad —out of Sam's earshot—and told him about her car. Somehow, he managed to twist things to make it appear as if she was at fault somehow.

All in all, today had started off bad. What was worse was the fact that Sam had barely spoken to her when they returned home last night. He'd been moody, agitated, and quite jittery. She'd never seen him like that before. Yes, his good friend from school had died, and one of his coworkers was in the hospital, but when she'd tried to discuss both tragedies, he pretended he had things to do in the bedroom, and that all was well. Now that was a lie if she'd ever heard one.

She carried her bowl of cereal over to the table, hoping he'd be in a better mood this morning. Only a cup of half empty coffee sat in front of him. "Aren't you eating anything?"

His jaw clenched. "Can't."

"You need your strength if you plan to put in a full day." God, she sounded like her dad. Sam speared her a glare. Guess he didn't like to be nagged. "Sorry."

His face softened as he reached over and grabbed her hand. "No, I'm the one who's sorry. It's just that I'm used to being in control, and whoever is attacking the lab workers is pissing me off." He withdrew his hand and dragged his fingers down his unshaven face. "I feel helpless." He turned to her. "I don't want to lose you too."

His heartfelt comment nearly toppled her. Jenna searched his eyes for the depth of his caring. She blinked then cast her gaze downward. Did she want him to care? Was she falling under his spell?

Reason intruded. He'd dump her once he found out she'd been lying to him. *Tell him. Now.*

Sam touched her shoulder. "Jenna, are you okay?"

"Peachy." Her courage disappeared with his dreamy look. Before she did or said something dumb, she shoved her chair back. "I'm going to see Carla."

"Aren't you going to finish your breakfast? Or is eating important for only me and not for you?"

"I'm not hungry."

Sam stood. "Let me clean up, and I'll drive you."

"Crap. I forgot I don't have a car." Until she received her insurance check, she couldn't afford to buy a new one. And she sure as hell wouldn't ask Dad for a loan. She threw the cereal down the disposal and left the dishes in the sink. After picking out a warm jacket, she stepped outside to wait for Sam. The cold, overcast day matched her mood, since she didn't want the good weather to bolster her depression. For some reason, she needed to wallow in her pain for a while. She deserved it. If she'd been able to tie Deidra to the killings, none of this would have happened.

Sam trotted out the door. "I want to install a security system for your place."

"You going to pay for it?" She hadn't meant to sound bitter, but her Holliday spirit was beginning to flag under the pressure. She waved a hand. "It's a good idea. I'll call for quotes on Monday." And figure out later how to pay for it.

"I want to stop at the lab first if that's okay."

"Sure."

When they pulled up to the front, Marlon Giombetti was standing by the main entrance. Crap. What the hell was he doing here? He'd give her away for sure.

"I'm...um...not feeling well. Would you mind taking me home?" Jenna covered the side of her face with her hand to prevent Marlon from identifying her.

First his brows furrowed, and then rose. He must have seen through her deception. "What's wrong?"

She rubbed her belly. "My stomach is suddenly upset."

Stupid Marlon was waltzing toward them. Damn, damn, double damn. He'd blow her cover for sure. Guy never could keep his mouth shut.

Sam's gaze shot from her to Marlon and back again. "You know him?"

Think. Think. "Yes, we went out a few times."

"Good, then you'll feel comfortable having him shadow you."

Anger ripped up her spine. "Shadow me? As in by my bodyguard? Are you sh—kidding me?"

"Nope."

"Is this your doing?"

"I asked Phil to find someone to escort you. I know you have places to go, and I have work to do. I'm not taking any chances that something might happen to you."

Sam's tender tone did soften her frustration. "Did he have to find Marlon of all people? The guy couldn't shoot the side of a barn, and he's afraid of his own shadow."

Sam tilted her face toward him. "How do you know how well he shoots?"

"He, ah, took me to a shooting range once." Good catch.

"Fine. Then Mr. Straight shooter can take you to see Carla. Tell him to keep his gun in his pocket." A quick lift of his lips implied he meant the double entendre. Super.

Arguing would only make things worse. "Fine."

Marlon—of all people. If the cop touched her, she'd have to deck him. She took a peek at Sam. He didn't seem the least bit concerned someone she dated was going to be spending time with her. Maybe she had misread his interest.

Before Marlon blew her cover, she took the offensive. She eased out the car and waved to him. "Hey, Marlon."

The guy smiled. Really smiled. "Hi, Jenna." If he hit on her, so help her God, she might have to deck him, or tell him the truth about why they never could be a couple again—Sam or no Sam.

She turned to the man who held her interest, leaned up against his solid chest and gave him a peck on the cheek. "We'll be back."

The moment Sam ducked inside the lab, she dropped the nice act. "Who picked you to be my bodyguard?"

He held up his hands. "I volunteered. I figured we could work on the case together. After all, you're the one who said the Jackson case might be related to the theft of your mom's skull."

She didn't need this aggravation. "Me and my big mouth." She wanted Sam to guard her, not Marlon. "I need to visit my friend at University Community Hospital. Do you mind driving me?" As if she had a choice.

He pointed to his squad car. "At your service."

When they arrived, Jenna tried to smile, to show she appreciated his willingness to keep her safe. "I'm not sure how long I'll be."

"Take your time." He patted a racecar magazine next to him on the seat. "It's a new issue I've been wanting to read."

Some bodyguard.

At the front desk, Jenna asked for Carla's room number. Even though Sam had told her which room Carla was in, Jenna hadn't been able to remember her own name yesterday, let alone which floor she was on. She sped past her old room where she'd spent time recovering from the fire at Sam's house. That seemed like forever ago his place burned down. A small tremor rattled inside her chest at how close both of them had come to death.

Room 329 loomed in front of her. Jenna knocked and entered. Carla's face was waxy white, and her body limp. At least her chest rose, albeit slowly and evenly.

"Carla?"

Her friend's eyes opened halfway. "Hey." Her gaze looked behind Jenna. "Did Chance come with you?"

"No." Guilt slammed her. How could she tell this weak woman that Chance, the man of her dreams, was dead?

"He said he'd feed Drake and be right back." Carla's eyes widened and her mouth opened. "Did something happen?"

Rapid feet sounded outside the door. A second later an older man and woman burst in. Both of them rushed to Carla's side—well, the man rushed, the woman shuffled. Jenna let out a long breath, happy she didn't have to answer Carla's question.

"Oh my poor baby." The woman, an older version of Carla, collapsed on the edge of the bed and took Carla's hand. "What happened?"

Time to disappear. "Carla, I'll come back later." Jenna waved goodbye.

A flash of fear crossed her friend's face. "No, don't go, please?"

Obviously, the two new visitors were her parents. Jenna didn't know why Carla wanted support from someone she'd only met a few times, but she didn't mind staying if Carla needed her. "Sure."

Carla turned to her parents. "Mom, Dad, what are you doing here?"

The older man sat on one of the chairs. "Your boyfriend, Chance, called us and said you'd been stabbed." He clasped a hand to his heart. "Mom and I jumped in the car and drove all night to get here."

Carla grimaced. "I feel so bad you came all that way, especially this time of year, with all the snow on the roads. You didn't have to come. I'm fine. Really."

Her mom pushed back hair covering Carla's face. "You're our daughter. We love you. You needed us and we came. The weather didn't matter."

"I don't deserve you." Carla sounded unconvincing, but her parents didn't seem to notice.

Mr. Pendowski cleared his throat. The mother turned back to look at him. "The doctor told us how sorry he was that you'd lost the baby."

If possible Carla's face paled even more. "Yeah, about that."

"Why didn't you tell us you were pregnant?" her mom said. "Is Chance the father?"

Jenna's body stiffened. An emotional war was about to ensue, and Jenna was sitting in the middle.

CHAPTER EIGHTEEN

JUST AS THINGS began to turn dicey between Carla and her parents, Jenna slipped out of her newfound friend's hospital room. Hearing confessions were not her thing, and being in the middle of chaos was the last place she wanted to be.

Outside the stuffy hospital, she inhaled the clean air. When had the gray sky disappeared? Marlon sat in his cruiser, windows up, seemingly oblivious to the world around him. She rapped on the passenger side window to get his attention, and he jumped. Wonder cop opened the door.

"You're back so soon."

She curled her lips. "Didn't I give you enough time to finish the magazine?"

"You don't have to get snippy with me. Where to?"

"To HOPEFAL. Just drop me off. I'll stay with Sam for the rest of the day." If she needed to go anywhere, maybe Gina could give her a lift.

"You sure?" His fists tightened on the wheel.

Marlon seemed upset that she wasn't desperate enough to go out with him. Whatever. "Yes." At least he was a careful driver, which counted for something.

When she entered Sam's lab, Eric Markowitz and he were huddled over a pile of photographs spread out on the counter.

"I think they're different," Sam said, tapping one of the photos.

Jenna cleared her throat. He looked up and smiled. "How did the visit go?"

She shrugged. "Carla's parents showed up so I split."

"They came, huh. I'm glad for her sake."

"Me too." Ever curious, Jenna stepped over to where the 8x10 glossies were displayed. Bloody shots of a dismembered man were next to photos of Rodrico Evans. "And these would be?" She kept her voice even, pretending she didn't recognize the lime encrusted man.

Sam pointed to a pile on the left. "Creighton Jackson before he ended up as bones. And these belong to Rodrico Evans who was found mostly dismembered at Ballast Point."

"Any comparison?"

Sam glanced at Eric who shook his head. "Eric and I have agreed to disagree. I think two different people did the deed. He thinks the same person hacked them both."

"That's scary. Do you know how this one died?" Jenna pointed to Rodrico Evans.

Eric nodded. "Most likely shot in the head—which we don't have. There were no other wounds that would indicate cause of death. It's the only logical conclusion."

Somehow the image of Deidra wielding a gun didn't compute. Did that mean the woman was innocent?

* * *

AFTER EATING a malnourished snack from the machine, Sam thought a real lunch for them was needed. To save money, they headed back to Jenna's where he made a ham and Swiss on whole wheat for both of them. The moment they finished their meal, the doorbell rang. Jenna dropped her napkin and froze. Sam held up his hand. "Let me check it out."

He raced to the kitchen window and looked out. "It's a woman and a baby."

"Ohmigod. Maybe it's Shelby!" Jenna jumped up and winced.

Sam was by her side in a flash. "Take it easy. You sit, and I'll answer the door."

The short redhead smiled brightly and introduced herself. "Is Jenna home?"

"Yes, come in."

With the baby huddled between them, Jenna and Shelby hugged. "Ohmigod. He's so cute. What's his name?" Jenna tickled the baby's belly and beamed when the child smiled.

"Dominick."

For a split second Sam wondered what it would be like to have a family. The problem with that dream was that he'd never get out from under his debt to afford one. He slipped into the spare bedroom to catch up on some reading while the women chatted. When he heard the visitor's car door close an hour later, he returned to the living room. Jenna was watching television, looking like a vision in her pink tank top and short shorts. Her hair was the way he liked it, all spiky and sexy. The red marks on her face were fading and, except for her sore ribs, she seemed to be healing well.

She looked up, smiled, and clicked off the television. Lust grabbed him hard as Jenna rose and slinked toward him. He didn't move a muscle. When she ran her hands down his chest, he grabbed her hands and kissed her knuckles. "I need to shower. Then we can talk."

The sparkle in her eyes faded. "What have you been doing for the last hour?"

You're a cad, Bonita. He could have washed up then. "Doing calisthenics?"

"Right."

After turning on the water, he slipped into the shower, dumped a handful of shampoo on his head and lathered his body. In mid scrubbing, Jenna opened the bathroom door. Even though she'd seen him naked, Sam shifted his body away from the glass shower door. "Jenna?"

"I was getting lonely out there." She slipped the tank top over her head.

"Jenna, this isn't a good idea."

The phone rang. "Aaargh. I'm not getting it."

"It could be the lab. Would you mind?" *Please obey for once.*

Jenna shook her boobs, ran a hand over her hips, and smiled. "For you I will."

Once she disappeared, he turned the water colder and willed his erection to shrink. As he was toweling off, Jenna rushed into the bathroom, her gaze not on his crotch, but rather on his face.

Panic and horror collided on her features. Tears streamed down her face. "My dad's been shot."

CHAPTER NINETEEN

SENDING Sam back to the house after he dropped her off at the hospital had been the hardest thing Jenna had even done, but she knew if he learned her dad was a cop, Sam might put two and two together and figure out she was one too. She'd told Sam she needed to be alone and convinced him she'd be safe once she was inside the hospital, promising to ask the guard at the hospital to escort her to her father's room. He seemed mollified, and thankfully didn't insist that Marlon be by her side.

The moment she learned of her father's injury, her pent up anger toward him had evaporated. She still wasn't ready to forgive him for cheating on Mom, but he had raised her, and blood was blood.

Marlon Giombetti was in the waiting room when she arrived. He rushed up to her and grabbed her hands. "I'm so sorry."

"What are you doing here?" He'd met her dad once when Marlon picked her up for a date, but that was it. He ran his hand across his eyes and down his jaw. For a moment, he reminded her of Sam—tall, sandy blond hair, and good Italian coloring. Too bad, he had no social skills.

Marlon stopped his pacing and sat next to her. This time he locked his gaze with hers and visibly inhaled. "I was at the scene when your dad was shot. I'm waiting to see him."

"Why were you at the scene? My dad would only be there if the sheriff's department was called in." Marlon was police.

"Someone got their wires crossed and both the sheriff's department and TPD were called in about a dead body. I responded to the call as I was close by." He leaned forward on his elbows. "It was like a blur. Mrs. Eades, she's the neighbor lady, said she'd heard gunshots. She ran next door and looked in the window and could tell the guy was dead, so she called 9-1-1."

"Did he look dead?"

"Definitely. His face was mostly gone from a gun blast to the face."

Jenna tried not to show any emotion. "Then what?"

"Your dad and I arrived at the same time. Not wanting to get in a pissing match about whose jurisdiction it was, we both went in to clear the scene before we could let the paramedics in."

"Standard operation procedure." So far Marlon had done nothing wrong.

He leaned back, his eyes misty. "Your dad took the kitchen where the victim was, and I checked the two bedrooms. I swear to God I didn't see the scumbag anywhere."

Obviously he didn't check thoroughly enough. "Go on."

"I went back into the kitchen and told your dad the place was clear —only it wasn't. As I went to find the paramedics and to call for the CSU team, I heard gunshots and sprinted back inside." His voice wavered and she thought he'd start balling. "Someone had shot your dad in the back. Blood was pumping out. I heard footsteps and the back door bang shut, but I had to tend to your dad first."

From the amount of blood on Marlon's pants, he was telling the truth. She placed a hand on Marlon. "Thank you."

"I'm sorry it went down that way."

"Me too."

The air mostly cleared, Marlon sniffled, stood and headed toward the snack machine. He brought her back a candy bar and a soda and handed it to her as a peace offering, she guessed. Man, her blood sugar would spike for sure, but she didn't want to turn down his attempt at a reconciliation.

An hour later, an older doctor dragged through the hospital swinging doors. Shoulders slumped, his eyes were slightly blood shot. "Ms. Holliday?"

"Yes?"

"Your dad's out of surgery."

Jenna jumped up. "How is he?"

"It was touch and go, but I believe he'll pull through."

Her legs nearly gave way. Thank God. "How extensive were his wounds?"

"He took two shots. The first ripped through his right kidney, which we had to remove. The other bullet lodged in his intestines, but we were able to remove the bullet and patch him up without any significant damage."

Poor Dad. "When can I see him?" She knitted her fingers together.

"Maybe in an hour, but only for a few minutes. He's still groggy. He needs his rest."

"Thank you." How had her anger for her dad disappeared so quickly? Was it because the thought of losing him was too much? She squeezed her eyes shut and forced her mind to sort through her issues. Marlon cleared his throat. Shit. She didn't need him to see her fall apart. "You don't need to stay."

"You sure?"

"Yes, go change."

He pressed his lips together and nodded. "Call me if there's any change."

"I will."

She waited the required hour before tiptoeing into her father's antiseptic smelling room. His normally ruddy complexion was wan, his cheeks sagged, and his mouth hung loose. Despite the pent up anger she'd built around her heart, her stomach nearly heaved. Seeing him broken made her defensive shield crumble. Just because he'd been wounded shouldn't erase what he'd done to Mom, but having him so close to death unnerved her.

Jenna pulled up a chair and studied the attached tubes and beeping monitors. She wasn't going to wake him because he needed to sleep. Lifting his cold hand, she squeezed his palm, wanting to let him know she was here for him.

He coughed and his eyelids fluttered open. She leaned closer. "Daddy?" She hadn't called him that in twenty years.

"Jenna." His eyes opened. "I messed up real good this time, didn't I?" He winced and her insides turned to mush. Stupid emotions.

No way would she discuss what happened in the shoot out. Getting nailed in the back meant he was losing it. Her dad would become defensive, pushing his blood pressure to the limits. He'd blame Marlon for not having his back. For that, she'd agree.

"Don't worry, you'll be at your desk in no time." What was one more lie?

He shook his head. "I'm dying. I've been shot before. I can tell the energy is seeping out of me fast." He coughed again and grabbed his stomach.

"The doctor said you'd be fine." *Please let it be true.*

"Not this time." He squeezed her hand. "I love you, Jenna. I know I've never told you before, but I do."

She nearly choked. A tear dribbled down her cheek, and her eyes flooded with water. Dammit. Now wasn't the time to break down. Staying angry helped keep the emotions locked up tight.

She glared at him. Just like her old man to croak before she could ask the one question that had been ruling her life. "Why did you cheat on Mom?" Christ. She hadn't meant to speak those words.

He flinched. "She cheated on me first."

She slapped the bed. "That's bullshit." Though why would he lie now?

After licking his lips, he squeezed his eyes shut. "I deserved it. I was never home. She needed someone, so she took a lover and I found out. I'm not proud of how I reacted, but I slept with someone to get back at her."

"Mom really cheated first?" Impossible.

"Yes, but I promised her I'd never say anything."

If what he said was true, retaliation wasn't the answer, but that was just like her dad to pay Mom back for hurting him. "Then why did Mom kill herself after I told on you." *See if you can answer that one.*

"She was dying." He held up a hand, knowing she was about to call his bluff. "She had stage four cancer and knew she didn't have long to live. Dr. Pullman was her oncologist. You can get the records if you don't believe me."

The air deflated from her lungs. Her head swam with denial. "Why didn't she get treatment?" *Why did she have to leave me?*

"She didn't want to put you through the torture of seeing her become sicker and sicker. There was no cure."

"Why didn't you tell me before?" His silence was a bigger betrayal than when he'd cheated on Mom.

He turned his head to the side. "You hated me enough. I was in shock after your mom's death. Keeping quiet seemed best for both of us."

"I always thought you believed it was my fault Mom killed herself."

He grabbed her hand. "No. Never. I loved you more than life."

He never showed it. "You wanted a boy." Now why did she bring up that sore subject? For closure perhaps?

"A boy? You're wrong."

"You never bought me dresses or dolls. Instead we went to the gun range and the police station and the morgue."

Her dad glanced away. "Oh, honey. I didn't know how to raise a girl. I wanted to teach you what I knew and loved." His breath grew ragged, and she tensed. "You turned out a tad strong-willed, but that's a good thing for a cop. Don't ever change. Be proud of who you are." Her father's words turned her life upside down. He reached out and took her hand. "I was hard on you to make you stronger."

Strong? She needed a lot more strength than she possessed right now. "Daddy?" She let the silly name slip out again.

Her dad's snores ended the conversation. She watched his chest rise and fall. When she was convinced he'd be okay, she slipped out of his room. Her emotions clashed with every step. Her whole life had been a lie. Talk about a shock. Dad had completely trashed her belief system. Now, she didn't know what to believe.

Instead of returning home and facing Sam, she punched the hospital elevator button for the second floor, wanting to see how Carla was doing from her stabbing. Jenna needed to stop the falsehoods and misunderstandings in her life, but it wasn't the right time to confront Sam with the truth. Maybe Carla could help her get her thoughts in order.

The television glowed in her friend's darkened room, but the sound was muted. Carla's eyelids were closed, but her hands were weaving a web.

"Carla?"

Her eyelids popped open, and she smiled. "Company! I'm so bored. Come sit down."

She patted the bed, but Jenna opted for the chair. "You sound so much better."

"I am. Drugs help too."

"It's past visiting hours, I know, but I came to see my dad and thought I'd visit while I was here." Jenna told Carla about her father being shot.

"Oh, Jenna." Carla grabbed her hand and squeezed. "I'm so sorry." Carla raised the electric bed so they'd be eye-to-eye. "I didn't know he was a cop."

"No one did." Given how the truth seemed to set her free with her dad, she figured she'd dip her toe into the truth waters once again. "As a matter of fact, so am I." She held her breath awaiting the censure.

"I know."

Jenna couldn't have been more surprised. "You do? Did you tell Sam?"

"No. I figured that was your job."

Jenna squeezed Carla's hand. "You're right. I'm going to tell him. Tonight." She gave Carla the Reader's Digest condensed version of her undercover assignment.

"I know you wanted to protect Sam from the truth, but trust me, lies only end in tragedy. Chance convinced me to tell my folks about Daphne and about the pregnancy. I thought they'd fall apart, but they didn't. In fact, they were relieved to have closure. As for the rape, they didn't blame me or anything. I never would have guessed they'd react so favorably. I'm betting Sam will take the news better than you think."

"I hope so." Jenna didn't want to talk about it anymore. The emotional vibes in the room nearly choked her. "When did the doctors say you could go home?"

"Hopefully, by Monday."

"That's great."

Sam would be thrilled to have Carla back at work as soon as possible. He mentioned his new intern, Lara, was rather handy with the computer, but he considered Carla the queen.

Not wanting to tire Carla, Jenna said her goodbyes. Once in the lobby, she called Sam, hoping he hadn't gone to bed. Her stomach refused to calm, awaiting the impending confession. "Can you pick me up?"

"Of course."

"I'll wait in the lobby until I see you drive up, okay?"

"Be there in about ten minutes."

When he arrived, he acted so caring about her father's shooting that Jenna's courage began to fail. He'd turn on her for sure when he learned the truth.

They pulled into her driveway and Sam turned to her. "I want you to stay here for a moment."

"Why?" The smirk on his face told her he had something fun in mind.

"Trust me."

While Sam dashed inside, she sat in the car, practicing the words for when she told him the truth. Her hands wouldn't stop shaking, which wasn't a good sign.

Five minutes later, he dashed out of the house, a half-grin on his face. His skin looked refreshed, as though he'd put the tragedies of yesterday behind him. The tension in her neck disappeared, and she focused only on how her body would melt in his arms, and her heart would turn to mush the moment he kissed her—if he ever kissed her again.

He opened her passenger door and held out his hand. "What's going on?" she asked.

"You'll see."

He lightly tugged on her hand for her to follow him inside. "Oh my God." The lights were off, but in its place were about ten small battery driven candles scattered throughout the kitchen and the living room. Cinnamon and jasmine wove a scent so sensual, and her knees weakened. She snuggled up against Sam. "This is incredible!" The flickering light gave the drab house a cozy glow.

All the times she'd tried to seduce him, he'd not responded to her sexually like she'd wanted. Now, he'd flipped the tables by creating an amazing environment, and her mind boggled at the thought of him wanting her.

"I'm glad you like it." His smoldering eyes and sexy smirk told her he knew he'd wowed her.

"I'd say so."

This might be the last and only time he'd want to be near her. Once he found out about her lie, he'd split for good. She swallowed her concern and followed him into the bedroom, putting off the admission one more day.

The anticipation of what was in store made her wet between the legs. She couldn't believe she'd finally make love to him. When he pushed open her bedroom door, she halted. The piles of clothes on the floor were gone. "What have you done?"

"It's called cleaning."

She laughed and her ribs protested, but at the moment, no amount of pain would dampen her excitement. Three more candles sat on the floor surrounding the bed.

She leaned over, touched something pink on the spread and held up one leaf. "Rose petals?"

"I figured you'd had a really crappy few days. It's the least I could do for you."

She couldn't figure out if this presentation was a pity gift or if the whole set up was meant as a romantic gesture. Hell. She'd go with the romantic gesture any day.

"I can think of a few things you could do to help make my pain go away."

The wind picked up outside the windows and rapped on the panes. She shivered.

"Come here," he said, sounding like a lion in wait.

She slinked toward him, excited to be his prey.

CHAPTER TWENTY

WORDS FAILED Sam as he peeled off Jenna's top. Her perky breasts begged to be suckled, but he wanted to wait until every inch of her delicious body was under him before he partook in the carnal pleasures.

"Hurry, Sam."

"No way. I want this to last a long time." He grunted as he slipped off her flowing skirt and gently coaxed her to the bed. "You're amazing."

She closed her eyes. Perfect. He gathered her clothing and placed them neatly on the corner chair before he strode over to the bed. "Want to help me?" Her lids sprang open and he hooked his thumbs in his pants.

She sat up. "Undress you?"

He laughed. Here she'd tried to seduce him the moment she met him. Surely, she wasn't chickening out now. "Yes."

In a flash, her deft fingers undid his belt and unzipped his pants. Her assertiveness must not have been an act after all. With a tug, his trousers fell to the floor. He stepped out of them and scooped up the mess.

Jenna's hands flew to her face. "You're going to fold them, aren't you?"

"I'd planned on it."

She laughed. "I give up. Go. Hurry. Do your thing."

She leaned forward and watched his every move. He whipped off his shirt, placed it on top of her clothes and eased back over to her. Standing in front of her, his erection strained against his boxers, and he willed her to take them off.

To his delight, she did just that. It was when she ran a finger down the length of him and squeezed his shaft that lust grabbed him so hard he failed to breathe for a moment. "Jen-na, why don't you lay back on the bed?" His breath quickened.

He didn't want to admit his willpower had disappeared. He wanted her, needed her, desired her—now. She deserved better than some rutting male, but his patience had been tested too many times to count, and at the moment, it had flown the coup.

When Jenna scooted back onto the bed, he plied open her thighs. His chest on the cool, clean sheets, his tongue did a dance over her swollen, enticing clit.

"Oh my God." She sucked in a loud breath.

Her hands flew to his shoulders as her hips vibrated up and down. The light from the flickering candles played across her features. Open mouth, eyes closed, back arched, Jenna moaned and groaned with every thrust and parry of his tongue.

"I can't take it anymore," she panted. "Please, I have to have you."

Sam grinned. Her eagerness turned him on big time. To half satisfy her, he slipped a finger into her.

"That's wonderful." She seemed satisfied, oohing and aahing until her hips quieted. "You have anything...bigger?"

He worried her ribs might not take the pressure of him on top of her, so he pressed up on his arms and hovered over her. His erection brushed her stomach.

"Wait," he said, as he reached over to the nightstand.

"If you pull any kind of stopping shit on me, I'll have to kill you." Her lips pressed together, but the corners wobbled as if she were trying not to smile.

He laughed and held up a condom. "You want to do the honors."

Jenna dropped her head back and howled. "Yes."

Her fingers worked like a race driver—fast and quick—slipping the protection on in seconds. Jenna grabbed his cock and guided him into her sweet sex. As he slid inside, cinnamon and spice filled the air. Their lips met, and then their tongues parried. The rhythm of their frenzied thrusts grew. Blood pounded in his ears as the lovemaking reached a crescendo.

Her moans rang out as she clawed his back. With each thrust his climax threatened.

"Yes! Yes!" she shouted.

Jenna screamed, and Sam came a second later. Their breaths had turned ragged as if they'd run a marathon. Once they caught their breaths, Sam rolled to the side and gathered her in his arms.

"That was amazing," he said.

"See what you've been missing this whole time?"

Sam kissed her again, not satisfied with the few kisses she'd bestowed on him. "I'll guess I'll have to make up for lost time and do this again."

* * *

JENNA AND SAM huddled over the computer screen in the technician's lab. When she ran a hand over Sam's cute butt, he swatted it away, but she didn't mind. Jenna could tell by the turn of his lips he was trying not to laugh at her less than subtle seduction. Thank goodness, Edwardo Lopez, the video technician wasn't able see them play lovebird behind his back.

The tech leaned forward and manipulated an image on the screen. He pointed to an enlarged version of the fake cop's neck as he strode down the hospital corridor toward the AV room. "Your cop killer was wearing a latex mask."

Sam moved in closer. "You're kidding. So we have no idea what he looks like?"

"He wore a blond wig."

"Shit."

"But look here." Edwardo pointed the mouse to a spot near the man's collar. "Underneath, his hair is curly and dark."

"That's good." Sam tapped the screen. "Hey, is that a tattoo on his arm?" The man's long-sleeved shirt was unbuttoned at the wrist, exposing the partial image.

Edwardo zoomed in closer. "Half of one."

"Can you tell what it is?"

After a series of filters, the image cleared. "A spotted tail of some kind wrapped around a spike. The tail might belong to a snake."

"Can you print a couple of copies for me? And how about an overall shot of the guy?"

"Sure." Edwardo's fingers clacked away.

"Run the film one more time for me, will you?" Sam said once the tech hit the print key.

Jenna leaned into Sam. "What are you hoping to find?"

"I want to check out his gait and also compare his height to the objects on the wall for a more precise measurement on the guy."

As they viewed the film, acid burned in her stomach. "He looks familiar."

Sam faced her and placed his hands on the side of her shoulders. "How so?"

"I've seen him before. Only I don't know where. Here maybe, or at the store. I wish I could be more sure."

"I'd vote for here. Think about it. The guy seems to know all of our employees. He burned down my house, stabbed Carla, and blew up Chance. A guy off the street wouldn't pick three employees of HOPEFAL for no reason."

"I wouldn't consider Chance a target."

"I know." His voice lowered to a whisper.

"In some way, *I'm* the common denominator. The cauldron, or at least *a* cauldron, is associated with *Botanica*. I worked there. It was my car that was blown up. The killer might have seen me with you and Carla and is sending me a message."

Sam gathered her into his arms and squeezed tight. "Then why send cryptic notes to me and Carla and not you?"

"I don't have an answer for that one yet."

"Every time I think of what could have happened to you, it makes me sick."

Jenna leaned her head on his shoulder and breathed in his spicy scent. Sam was worming his way under her skin, something she knew was about to end in heartbreak.

Four color images spit out of the printer. Sam rushed over to grab them. "Let's go." He grabbed her hand.

"Where to?"

"First off, I want Phil to ask the head of Human Resources to go through all of our employees here at the lab to see if anyone matches the man's gate, his height, and his coloring."

"Don't forget his tattoo."

He smiled down at her. "I doubt tattoos or body piercings are on the application. The head of each department might be able to identify the man's markings, unless he never rolled up his sleeves."

"Don't all employees here get background checks?"

"Sure, but all that means is that the person hasn't been caught."

"Scary." Once Sam thanked Edwardo, he and Jenna delivered the information about the latex mask to Phil, who promised to find out about the employees and their markings. They left Phil to track down evidence. They headed to the elevator. "What's your next move?" she asked.

"To see if our guy had the tattoo done in Tampa. We find the parlor, we find a name."

"Why not ask Phil to ask the cops to do the legwork?"

"I don't know how much interaction you've had with the TPD, but finding a man with a tattoo might not be their highest priority. We need action."

So the fine men, or women, in blue apparently did not rank high in his opinion. "The cops work fast when a killer's on a loose, especially one who might be a serial killer." She couldn't let his slight go unchallenged.

"I'm not taking any chances. If you want to get something done right, do it yourself."

She moved away from him. "What is it with you? Do you have to control every situation?" If so, she and Sam would never survive together.

Hold it. Is that what she wanted?

Before she could answer the question, he ran a finger down her face, and her anger flew away. "I want to find this guy so bad I can taste it. Time is not on our side. I won't be able to sleep until he's behind bars. If anything happened to you..."

She smiled at his depth of caring. "It won't."

Argument apparently forgotten, Sam pushed the down button. "Listen, I promise that if we find a name of someone with this tattoo, we'll pass the info to the cops, and I'll let them deal with this guy."

Sounded fair. "Okay."

The moment the elevator reached the first floor, she hit the number two button. He cocked a brow. "We'll need to get a couple of addresses for all the tattoo parlors in Tampa—unless you know where they all are. Since I've investigated every inch of your delicious body and didn't find a drop on ink anywhere, I'm guessing you've never even been to one."

He winked. "Are you positive you've seen every square inch?"

"Maybe not."

He leaned over and kissed her. Only when the doors opened did he end the magical contact.

Fifteen minutes later, Jenna and Sam were heading downtown. She waved the stack of paper. "There are more than twenty parlors here."

"Look through them and see where you want to start."

"If the killer is one of Deidra's minions, he might have had the work done in Ybor. There are four of them on 7th Avenue. I say it's as good a place as any to start."

"Sounds like a plan."

At the first shop, they showed the owner the photo of the blurry tattoo. "Haven't done one of those. I've only been in business a little more than a year, but I've seen the design though."

"Who else might do this kind of work?"

"Anyone of the other artists in Ybor. You just have to ask around."

Once outside, Jenna shielded her eyes against the bright sun. She put an X by that shop and headed to the Dog-Bone Tattoo Parlor.

Three artists, crowded around a table near the back of the store, were enjoying a smoke. The exchange of glances told her they thought they were tourists who must be in the wrong spot. Jenna slipped the paper from Sam's fingers and strutted over to the only guy who didn't look high.

"Help you?" The tall, beefy man stood and pulled up black jeans that were full of holes.

She flashed the photo. "This man is a killer. Have you seen this tattoo before?"

"You shittin' me?"

"No."

Holey Pants took the image over to his cohorts. The heavyset girl, with the thick, black eyeliner nodded. "Yeah, I did a tat like that maybe two, three years ago."

"Guy got a name?"

She jutted out her hip. "If I could remember every client's name, I'd be in Mensa."

"Can you try? Please?" Jenna softened her tone, hoping the fact a killer was on the loose might appeal to her sense of duty.

She took a long drag on her cigarette, stamped it out, and stood. "Could take me a while to look through the records."

"Thanks. We can wait." Sam nodded.

Too edgy to stand still, Jenna scoped out the photographs that plastered the walls. Some people had tattoos on their faces and others had colored ink over every exposed surface of their bodies. Who would do that?

"Here it is." The girl handed Jenna the receipt.

Crap. "He paid cash." The receipt was dated three years ago.

"Many do."

"There's only a first name here."

The girl shrugged and retrieved the paper. "Probably not his right name either. Some people like the anonymity. We're cool with that."

Sam stepped around Jenna. "This is only a partial photo." He nodded to the paper Jenna held. "Do you remember the rest of it?"

"Sure. It's common enough. Just a sec." She ducked into the back room again and came out a minute later. "Here's what the design looks like. It's a medical staff."

Now she recognized it. One of her friends wore a medical alert bracelet with the symbol on it. "Can I keep this picture?"

"Sure. Good luck in finding the creep. If only I'd known."

Once outside, Jenna took in a cleansing breath. "I can't take cigarette smoke any more."

"Me too. What was the guy's name again?"

"Joe. No last name."

"That doesn't narrow it down much. We need Carla."

* * *

"Thanks for springing, me," Carla said.

Gina had had the unfortunate job of breaking the news to Carla about Chance's death. She'd held up well, Gina said, but now a deep sadness filled Carla's eyes, nearly breaking Sam's heart. He couldn't bring himself to mention the same man who killed the hospital guard probably set the car explosion.

If they were to crack this case, however, Carla had to be involved. He'd explained how they needed to find the identity of the masked security guard killer. "You want to work from the lab or from home?"

Jenna shot Sam a stern look and leaned over Carla. "You don't have to go back to work right now. The doctor said you're supposed to be in bed for the next few weeks—resting, not working."

Carla looked over Jenna's shoulder to him. "I won't be able to rest until this guy is caught. I'd prefer being at the lab, but I hope you don't mind if I order a pizza? The hospital has nothing but healthy food, and I'm absolutely starving to death."

Sam chuckled. "Order two and we can share."

Jenna planted her hands on her hips as her mouth turned down into a cute little pout. "For the record, I'm not for Carla going back to work so soon."

"Thanks, Mom." Carla huffed out a friendly laugh. "Like you rested after you barely survived a burning house?"

Jenna clamped her mouth shut. "HOPEFAL it is."

Carla used Jenna's phone to place the food order as Sam wheeled her downstairs. Once she stood, she walked like she was eighty years old. He wished Jenna had been able to talk her out of going back to work.

"I promise I'll be fine," Carla said.

Once they arrived at the center, Seth greeted them from the front desk as Carla inched her way to the elevator. In her office, Sam leaned a hip on Carla's desk. "Phil asking HR to find an employee who fits the bill of our killer, but I think you can do the work quicker."

"I know how slow HR can be." Carla huffed out a laugh and turned on her computer.

When her system booted up, she logged on. "Give me a sec to pull up the names of everyone who works here. Unfortunately, there's no database or I could sort by nationality and height."

Jenna leaned into him. "How many people work here?"

"Including maintenance, I'd say close to one hundred," Carla answered. She glanced back at Sam. "You said he was about five foot ten, right?"

"From my best estimates. He could have worn lifts to make himself taller, but he couldn't make himself look shorter."

"I'm going to start with maintenance." She typed away. "Does this Joe have a last name?"

"No," Sam said.

Carla rolled her eyes as Jenna pulled up a chair. "But if he had a medical symbol on his arm, he's either allergic to something or he could be a doctor."

Carla groaned. "I'll widen my search."

The phone on her desk rang. She answered and then listened for a moment. "Great. I'll send someone down."

She turned around and smiled. "That was fast. Pizza's here." Her stomach grumbled. From her purse, she extracted a twenty-dollar bill. "Would one of you mind—"

Jenna grabbed the money. "I'll go." She waved a hand. "You two do your thing."

Once Jenna left, Sam took Jenna's chair. Carla clicked on the first male on the list. "John Abdulla."

The job description listed him as chemist. "Any photo?"

"No."

"Height? Age?"

"Can't put that stuff on an application."

Sam leaned back in his chair. "Maybe we can ask the heads of each of the divisions to tell us who matches the description. Who's the head of maintenance?"

Her fingernails scurried over the keys. "Terrance Muley."

"Does it say if he's working now?"

"He should be. His office is on the first floor. But let's have lunch first. Then you can find Joe with the medical tattoo."

Jenna bounced in a moment later, and the aroma of cheese and pepperoni filled the small office. Carla cleared an area on the side table and Jenna set down the box. "Here's your twenty back. The pizza was just sitting on the guard's station. Maybe Seth paid the guy. After I eat, I'll bring him the money."

Sam lifted the lid and his hands froze.

CHAPTER TWENTY-ONE

SAM'S FACE paled and his fingernails dug into the cover.

"What is it?" Jenna asked.

He pressed his lips together. "Someone sent a message."

Jenna rushed to his side and stared at the underside of the cover. *YOU'RE NEXT HOLLIDAY.* A large grease stain had bled through her name.

"Oh, shit." Now she'd have to explain that she was Jenna Holliday.

He glanced at her. "You know who this Holliday person is?"

"It's me. I'm Jenna Holliday."

"I thought your last name was Richman?"

Tell the truth. No. Her heart was going too fast. "Holliday was my married name. Richman's my maiden name." She blew out a hard breath. "I was married for less than a year." She waved a hand. "It didn't work out."

Sam starred hard at her for a long moment. "That means this guy knew you back then."

"I guess so." Dear God, how many lies could she tell before Sam shut her out completely. And she needed him. Heart pounding, Jenna grabbed onto Sam's arm.

He enveloped her and held her tight, his scent seeping into her pores. "We'll find the bastard, I promise." Sam's jaw clenched. "He'll slip up, and we'll get him." He turned to Carla. "Could you call the pizza place back and ask for the name of the delivery person?"

"Sure. You think he saw this guy?"

"Maybe."

With shaky fingers, she punched redial. "This is Carla Pendowski again. Could you tell me the person's name who delivered my pizza?...I, ah, forgot to give him a tip...okay, got it, thanks."

"Well?" Jenna asked.

"Just a sec." Carla looked down at the number she'd written and dialed again. "Hi, my name is Carla Pendowski. You just delivered a pizza to the HOPEFAL lab... .Can you tell me who paid you?" She tapped the half-chewed pencil on the desk. "Would it be possible for you to come back to the lab? We'd like to ask you some questions. Thanks." She disconnected. "Someone met him outside the lab. Medium build, sunglasses, and wearing a hoody."

His jaw tightened. "That could be our man."

"Oh, shit. If Seth wasn't at his station, I wonder if our killer took him out like he did Harold."

"Carla, stay here and lock your office door," Sam said, as he grabbed Jenna's hand and pulled her into the hallway.

"Be careful," Carla called after them just as she closed the door.

Jenna pushed the elevator button ten times before the damn thing arrived. Sam was the first one out the door on the bottom floor. Thankfully, Seth was sitting in his chair reading a book, and relief weakened her knees.

"Seth," Sam said.

The young guard sat up. "Yes, sir."

"About ten minutes ago, someone came through here carrying a pizza. Did you see him?"

His face turned blank. "No, sir."

Jenna stepped toward the guard. "When I came down a moment ago, the pizza was on the counter and you weren't here."

He glanced away and chewed on his bottom lip before facing her. "I heard a buzzing sound down the hall and went to investigate. That must have been right about when the pizza man came." He reached below his desk and pulled out a device about the size of a desk of cards. "Some prankster left this in the hallway." He pushed the button and a screeching sound emitted. He immediately shut it off.

Sam turned and tugged on her arm. "Thanks, Seth." He wrapped an arm around her waist. "Let's check out the video room. Hopefully, the guy didn't disable the camera this time."

Sam and Jenna rushed Edwardo Lopez's video lab again. They knocked on his door and entered. When she saw Edwardo was seated in front of his computer and not dead with his throat slashed, she blew out a breath.

Sam clapped a hand on Edwardo's shoulder. "Can you do us a favor and look through the video of the guard station?"

"Something wrong?"

Sam told him about the threat on the box and the absent guard.

"Sure, what time frame?"

"The last hour."

"Give me a sec." Edwardo brought up the digital image from his computer. "Here ya go."

Jenna stood behind Edwardo, her gaze glued to the screen. "Here he comes." She squeezed Sam's hand for comfort.

"Damn," Sam said. "He has his hood pulled too low for us to see his face."

"Looks like he has red hair," she said.

"I'm betting it's another wig."

"Maybe he runs a wig store."

The man bounded past the empty guard station and turned left. He disappeared down the hallway where Seth told them he'd found the noisy device.

Sam leaned closer. "He's coming back. See how he's tilting his head away from the camera and toward the floor? He knows where the security system is. Guy must have scoped out the place before."

"Like when he killed Harold."

"Perhaps, but we can't be certain he's the same person."

The movie continued to roll. "Well look there. Seth didn't tell us the whole truth. He wasn't at his station a number of times. It wasn't just when the guy came to put the device in the hall or when he delivered the pizza."

"Rather convenient if you ask me."

"So you're thinking he's in cahoots with our mystery man?" Jenna asked.

"Hard to tell, but something's not right. I'll ask Carla to dig up any dirt on this new guard."

Jenna's shoulders turned heavy. "I think it's sad we have to suspect everyone here."

Edwardo looked up and held up a hand. "Hey, don't look at me. I was here the whole time."

For some reason his expression made both of them laugh.

Sam's phone rang. "It's Carla," he said to her. "Kid who delivered the pizza is waiting outside for us."

This time when they left the lobby Seth was standing at his station, and they hurried out.

Pimply faced and thin for his age, the delivery boy paced in front of his car. Sam flashed his HOPEFAL badge, but the kid barely glanced at it. He straightened his shoulders as if Sam were some kind of FBI agent. Sam asked him about the man who took possession of the pizza.

The delivery boy shoved his hands in his pocket and glanced toward the ground. "Like I told Ms. Pendowski, I drove up and some guy came out of those doors." He nodded to the ones Jenna and Sam had exited. "He handed me a twenty and said to keep the change. I was so excited I forgot to tell him who the pizza was for." The kid shrugged as if it was no biggie. "I figured Ms. Pendowski asked a coworker to pick it up."

"Did you get a look at his face?" Sam asked.

"Nah, not when he was waving a twenty spot under my nose."

"There was nothing remarkable about him? Any scars, tattoos, a limp maybe?" Sam practically attacked the kid, but Jenna was glad he was asking the questions and not her. Her occupation would have been evident to everyone if she had been.

The kid crossed his arms and bit down on his lower lip. "He had a tattoo, that much I do remember. I was thinking of getting one, so I've been watching for one I liked. His had a snake wrapped around a stick."

It's him. Oh, God, the killer was close. Real close. She couldn't catch her breath.

He handed the kid a ten-dollar bill. "Thanks."

The boy smiled, jumped in his truck and zoomed off. Sam lifted her chin. "You okay? You're pale."

"Death threats have that affect on me." As a cop, she shouldn't have weakened. Damn.

* * *

BIANCA HID behind her bedroom door, her hand clutching the loaded gun. Every time her uncle came over, her father suffered from his wrath. She refused to stand by any more and watch the vicious man hurt her dad. It didn't matter her uncle was blood. Nor did it matter he carried a gun or that the world thought he walked on water. To her, he was scum.

She pressed her ear to the door, listening to the heated exchange. For the last month, she'd told her father she was staying late after school to be in a play, when in fact she went to the Hillsborough gun range twice a week for lessons. If he knew, he'd be real pissed, but she was proud she could hit her target with relative accuracy.

Her uncle was an evil man, but her father would never stand up to his younger brother-in-law no matter how many times her uncle hit him. Well, she'd stand up to the bastard. Only maybe not today.

"I want something to cover my hands," her uncle snarled, his voice softened by the closed door. "Make me look like a black man."

"I've never made hands before."

Bianca shook at his father's weakness. He should tell her uncle he wouldn't do any more work for him and to get the hell out of his house. She'd heard the threats her uncle had made against her and her mom if Dad didn't do what he'd asked. The evil man would never get near her. Oh, he tried to act nice when he was around her, but she knew his sweet-talking was an act.

"You can make masks. You can make hands. Do it."

"But—"

The sound of the flesh meeting flesh twisted her gut. Her hands grabbed the door handle, ready to charge out.

"I need to be able to walk around the lab without anyone taking notice. Every time that Jenna chick passes me in the hall, she looks at me, like she's trying to remember where she's seen me."

"She the cop who used to work for Deidra?"

"Yeah."

A surge of hope made Bianca lower her weapon. Jenna might be someone who could help.

The sounds of feet scuffling made her crack open the door. Her bedroom had a direct line of sight to the kitchen where her dad and uncle were talking, or rather arguing.

"Why do you need so many masks?" her father asked. "Are you hurting people again?"

By hurting, her father meant her uncle was killing people. She needed to stop this insanity before he came after her and her mom.

"You don't need to know what I'm doing with the masks, you understand?" He grabbed her father by the throat.

She clutched the gun hard. Her fingers itched to pull the trigger and end his miserable life, but what would Mama do if Bianca landed in jail?

"Okay, okay."

Her uncle's face came within an inch of her dad's. "If you ever breathe a word about who you gave these masks to, I'll kill you. I don't care that you married my sister. Got it?"

Her father dropped back against the kitchen counter and nodded. Her uncle lowered his hand and stalked out.

Bianca wanted to rush to her father, but she understood he'd be embarrassed that she'd witnessed the exchange. She slipped into her desk chair and booted up her computer. This Jenna woman shouldn't be too hard to find. Bianca Googled the Hillsborough County Sheriff's Department. Dang it. No Jenna appeared on the roster. Then she searched Tampa Police Department. Bingo. That was too easy. Well, almost too easy. The problem was that there were two Jenna's. One was Jenna Holliday, the other Jenna Salvadore. One looked young, the other old. She did a Zabasearch for both addresses, and then printed out the directions to both houses before shutting down her computer.

Bianca stuffed her gun into her backpack, pushed her hair from her eyes and stepped out of her room.

"Hi, Pops." She smiled, pretending she hadn't heard her uncle come and go.

"Where are you going? You haven't eaten dinner. Mama will be home shortly."

"Didn't I tell you? I have a big economics project due tomorrow. My group and I are getting together at Tessa's house. I'll pick up something on the way."

"Does your mother know?"

No. "I think I told her."

"Don't be late. And call if you're going to be out past ten, okay?"

He must have sensed the blood on his lip for he ripped off a piece of paper towel and dabbed it. She said nothing about his slightly swollen eye or bruised cheek. She leaned over and kissed his face. "I won't be too late. I have to get up for school tomorrow. Bye."

She rushed out the door before he found an excuse to keep her home and jumped in her beat-to-shit Volvo. She couldn't complain. Half her friends didn't even have a car to call their own.

Bianca tried to decide what she wanted to say to the cop, unsure if she should say that her uncle killed people or just that he hurt them. Too bad she didn't have any proof nor had she ever seen him kill anyone, but she knew he was evil. She'd seen the blood on his pants one time when her uncle had stopped by. She had to tell the lady cop that he'd threatened to kill Jenna. That should make her interested in helping.

Bianca motored down the two-lane country road, avoiding the main thoroughfares since the evening rush hour would slow her down too much. Lights blinked behind her. She looked up, but couldn't see who was behind her. She glanced back at the speedometer. Since she wasn't going over the limit, it wouldn't be a cop.

She eased over to the side of the road to let the impatient jerk get by, and the right side tires edged off the road onto the dirt. The car behind her sped up and came along side.

She glanced over to see the age of the driver, but the person's face was obscured by dark tinted windows. The sound of the gunshot registered first, then the pain in her head. Bianca's hands slipped off the wheel as her legs went limp.

CHAPTER TWENTY-TWO

IN THE MIDDLE of a mind-blowing kiss with Sam, a knock sounded on Jenna's door. If it wasn't one thing, it was another. They were making out in the living room, but she wasn't close enough to see out the window. "I wonder who it is?"

"It's probably for me. It could be someone from the lab." He nuzzled her neck, his musky scent driving her crazy.

She giggled and ground her hips into his hard shaft. "You don't really me need to get that, do you?" She slipped her hands down his pants.

He gently extracted her fingers from his erection. "It could be important." He brushed her lips and untangled himself from her.

"Does the whole lab know you're staying here?"

"The important people do."

"Fine. Go answer it. I know you want to." She stuck out her tongue.

He turned back to her, his face turned serious. "Stay there."

Like she was going to run to the door and expose herself to whoever was out there? Fat chance.

Sam peeked through the security hole in the door. "It's the police."

Her heartbeat raced. Oh, shit. Would this person recognize her? Before she reached the hall to hide, Sam opened the door.

"Is a Jenna here?"

Crap. She spun around. Sam stood to the side and motioned the two sheriff department officers in. Thank God, it wasn't anyone she knew. The man was tall and reed thin, and his partner was a petite Oriental woman. Neither looked older than their early twenties, which could account for why she didn't know the two rookies. She hadn't visited her dad at his department in years.

Uniformed officers came to tell a family member a fellow officer was dead, and her stomach turned over. "I'm Jenna. Did something happen to my father?" She couldn't think of any other reason they'd show up at her house.

"Your father? No. We're here about a Bianca Bello. Do you know her?"

She took a calming breath. "I'm afraid I don't know anyone by that name."

"She was shot and killed this evening. We found two names on the girl—yours and one belonging to Jenna Salvadore—along with maps to both of your houses on her front seat. We've spoken to Jenna Salvadore, but she didn't recognize the name either." The Ichabod Crane cop's pen hovered over the pad.

Jenna racked her brain to see if perhaps she'd covered a case involving Bianca Bello but came up blank. "I wish I could help. How old was she?"

Jenna used to tutor at the local high school. Perhaps she knew Bianca from there.

"Nineteen. She goes to Hillsborough Community College."

She shook her head. "Do you have an address for her? If I could speak to her parents maybe I can remember something."

Ichabod wrote down the address. Someone must have told him she worked for TPD, or he wouldn't have given out the sensitive information. Thankfully, he kept his mouth shut. "Let us know what you find out," he said.

Jenna jotted down the officer's name on the back of Bianca's address. "Sure."

Once they left, Sam placed a large diet Coke in front on her. She took a sip and stared off into space.

He slipped into the chair next to her. "You remember something?"

She glanced up at him and shook her head. "I have no idea why the girl would be visiting me. We didn't even go to the same school."

"Tomorrow, if you want, we can visit the family."

Meeting with grieving parents sucked, but Jenna believed if Bianca had Jenna's name, the young girl's death might be related to the recent events. Jenna took another long sip of her drink, the cold liquid soothing her throat. "If the parents knew something, they would have told the cops."

Sam's cell rang. He moved to the living room to answer it. "Bonita...Where?... Thanks." He disconnected and slid down onto the sofa seat, his face drawn.

Unable to get a sense of the conversation, Jenna waved to him. "Who was that?"

"That was Phil. HOPEFAL did its weekly scan for bugs and found one in Carla's office and one in my lab."

The ramification hit her hard. "So that's how the killer knew so much. When we left for the hospital to see Carla he knew when and where we were going."

"He must have heard her order the pizza too."

"Which was how he knew to meet the delivery man." It all made sense now. What didn't make sense was the fact that the killer had targeted her and possibly Bianca. The connection had to be through Deidra. This case seemed to revolve around the diabolical woman.

"Come on. It's time for bed." Sam stood and held out his hand. "Tomorrow is going to be a long day."

"No kidding."

Jenna followed Sam into the bedroom. She yawned and stretched. "Did Phil ever say if the cops figured out who killed Creighton Jackson or Rodrico Evans?"

"Not yet."

"We better come up with something soon before I'm next."

He wrapped a strong arm around her shoulders. "I'm not going to let anything happen to you."

She bet Chance said the same thing to Carla and look what happened to both of them.

* * *

SAM AND JENNA drove to Bianca Bello's parents' house, but when they arrived only the father was at home.

The Hispanic gentleman answered, his hands caked with some kind of rubbery material. "Mr. Bello?"

"I've already spoken with the cops." His tone came out flat as though someone had ripped out his heart. Sam could hardly blame the man for his depression.

"We aren't with the police. May we come in?" Sam flashed his HOPEFAL badge.

Mr. Bello didn't look at the offering as he waved them over to the kitchen table. "I don't know how I can help you. My daughter is dead."

"I'm Jenna. Did the police tell you they found a slip of paper with my name and address next to your daughter when she was killed?"

"There were two addresses they said."

"One belonged to Jenna here." Sam nodded to the man's hands. "Sir, I see you're some kind of artist. What do you do for a living?"

"I make latex masks for a costume company."

Jenna straightened in her seat. "Mr. Bello, do you know someone by the name of Joe?"

He scratched his chin. "I know a few, but none who would harm my daughter."

The man's eyes held steady, but Sam couldn't quite decide how much to tell the man. "I have something in the car I'd like you take a look at."

Mr. Bello nodded and swallowed hard.

Sam raced outside and grabbed the Manila envelope that contained the pictures taken off the surveillance tape. When he returned, two glasses of water sat on the table, one for him and one for Jenna.

"Thanks." Sam placed the picture of a man hurrying down the hospital corridor in front of Mr. Bello. Even the cops believed he was the one who'd set the explosion that killed Chance. "Do you recognize this man?"

Mr. Bello's face paled as he dropped his hands to his lap. "No."

"Look again, please. The man is wearing a latex mask."

"Many people buy my masks from the costume store. Ask them." His lips pressed together so hard they turned white.

"We will." The fact he admitted the killer wore one of his masks spoke volumes.

"You never said if you knew why your daughter was coming to visit Ms. Richman."

"I have no idea. Bianca was supposed to meet with her friend, Tessa, to work on an economics project for school. She said nothing about a Ms. Richman to me."

"What's this Tessa girl's last name?"

"I don't know. You can call the college. They might know."

Sam made a note to follow up. Perhaps Bianca had confided in her friend. He tossed down his business card. "If anything occurs to you, please give me a call."

THE MOMENT SAM left Jenna alone in the lab in order to check on some DNA results, she called Marlon Giombetti.

"Hey, it's Jenna. I only have a moment to talk, but I wanted to see where you are with the Creighton Jackson's case."

"Funny you should ask. A neighbor, who was out of town for a few days, remembers a woman with dark hair going onto Creighton's boat around the time of the murder."

Her heart sped up. "Deidra has dark hair."

"That doesn't mean she killed him."

"True. Anything else?"

"CSU was able to lift a partial foot print. The killer must have stepped in the blood. There was plenty of it."

"Did they dust for prints on the boat?" she asked.

"Yes, but only those we'd expect to find were onboard."

"So, basically you have squat." She inwardly groaned.

"I wouldn't go that far. This yacht neighbor said he heard shouting, but he didn't think much of it at the time. He also heard Creighton doing some construction work but he couldn't recall if it was before or after the dark headed woman left."

Construction? "Maybe what he heard was the sound of the saw cutting him up."

"Hmm. Even if that were true, that's not what killed him."

Her hand squeezed the phone. "You know the cause of death?"

"Gun shot, most likely to the head. No one saw the bullet at first, but when the cleaning crew came in, they found it lodged in a panel behind a multi-colored curtain."

The shot must have been to the head. "You need to send it over to HOPEFAL right away."

"Already sent it. You thinking the lab can compare it to another bullet?"

Jenna dropped down onto the computer chair. "I can hope can't I?" The same person who killed Bianca Bello could have killed Creighton Jackson, though that was a stretch. "Call me if you find out anything."

The moment she disconnected, the four tones sounded on the door. Knowing the killer wandered their halls, she ran toward the cooler, but she didn't make it before Carla came in.

Jenna's hand shot to her chest. "I thought you were—"

"The killer," Carla finished. She waved a hand. "You're a cop. Bring a gun to work. That's what I plan to do, just as soon as I take some lessons."

"Shh. You haven't mentioned my undercover assignment to anyone, have you?"

Her brows pinched. "No. I take it you still haven't told Sam."

"I'm waiting for the right moment."

"Do it soon."

Carla shoved a few rampant tendrils of hair behind her ear. "I did some searching on Creighton Jackson." Carla's brow shot upward.

"What did you find?"

CHAPTER TWENTY-THREE

/

CARLA PULLED up a rolling chair next to the computers in Sam's lab. "Sorry. I get tired real easy."

Jenna scooted her chair next to her friend. "I hear ya. I'm not even back to normal after the incident with the fire, and it's been a while." She leaned forward. "What did you find?"

Before Carla had the chance to tell her anything, Phil rolled in with Sam right behind him. "I called in a favor and had Bianca Bello's body sent here since the State lab is too backed up to process her quickly. We needed to move on this case."

"Did you find anything useful?" Jenna asked.

"Apparently, TPD found a bullet in the wall of Creighton Jackson's boat. The bullet is a match to the one in Bianca's head."

"That means whoever killed Creighton Jackson killed Bianca." Was this case finally coming to an end?

"That would be my first guess." He turned to Sam.

Jenna had been formulating a plan, but she was hesitant to bring it up. Sam would veto her idea immediately, but Phil might be an ally. "What do you all think of me trying to lure this guy out in the open? After all, he seems to be targeting me." Okay, that was a stretch when one considered she'd never met Creighton Jackson or Bianca

Bello, but her gut told her that these murders were related to her somehow.

Sam slammed his hand down on the counter. No surprise there. "There is no way I'm letting you put yourself in danger."

She held up a hand. "Now wait. How about if I wear a wire, a bullet proof vest, and maybe carry a weapon." She paused for effect. "I'm even willing to have a million cops follow me."

Phil edged toward the group. "I understand you're concern, Sam, but Jenna may be our only hope here. I don't know for sure who he's killed, but someone blew up Jenna's car and someone knifed Carla. Creighton Jackson didn't cut his own head off. Given we suspect he might be an employee here, Jenna's plan might work."

"A bullet proof vest won't stop a bullet to her head," Sam said.

"I agree, but we have to stop him." Phil turned to Carla. "I know you've been working with HR to come up with a match on this guy. Any luck?"

"I've narrowed it down to three men who work here that might fit the bill. Jesus Soler, in pathology, is a lab tech. He could be our man. He knows how to use a saw to cut up someone. There's one guy in maintenance, named Victor Nunez, and another in the footprint lab, by the name of Felix Cardoso. That's assuming we're profiling Hispanics."

"Did you do a thorough background check on them?" Phil asked.

"On those three, yes, and they come up clean."

"Do any of them have a serpent tattoo?"

Carla blew out a breath. "I haven't gotten that far."

Phil turned to Sam. "Let me get with TPD and see what they want to do. The killer could be in our midst, or he could be someone who knows someone here. Jenna, I think we should outfit you with a gun at the very least. Ever handle one?"

"Yes." The less said the better. While she'd never confronted Phil about being a cop, she was quite certain he knew.

Sam stood next to Jenna. "This is a bad idea. There's no way I want her to have a gun. It's too dangerous." Not only did his voice shake, so did the hand on her shoulder.

What could she say? She wasn't about to announce how she'd won last year's annual precision shot award. Going to the range with her dad as a kid had its benefits.

Phil slapped the arms of his wheelchair. "I have another idea."

Sam shoved his hands in his pocket. "What's that?" His tone came out almost hostile.

Jenna glanced up and didn't like the pain that raced across his face.

"Come with me. Both of you. Carla, you know what you have to do." Phil said.

Jenna grabbed her purse and followed right behind Phil. Sam was right behind her.

She, Sam, and Phil took the elevator to the first floor and headed out the back entrance where Phil kept his wheelchair-equipped van.

"Hop in. I'll drive," Phil said.

Sam said nothing as he piled in front. Jenna sat in the back, which was just as well. Jenna needed time to work through her own plan.

"Jenna," Phil said, as he pulled out of the lot. "I figure the safest place for you right now would be the police station. I called a friend of mine, Officer Larry Bernard, of TPD. He said he could fix you up with a loaner car until you get one of your own. He'll brief you on my plan to draw out the killer."

So he knew. God bless Phil. Excitement bubbled up. She'd have a car, and she could work at the station. That was about as win-win as she could get.

"What about Sam? Just because I seem to be the new target doesn't mean he's out of danger. The first curse had been aimed at him."

She looked in the driver's rear view mirror and caught the small lift of Phil's lips. "That's where I come in. I'm going to teach Sam here to shoot a gun."

"I don't need lessons." Sam's sharp retort startled her. "I had enough of that in the Navy."

Phil glanced over. "That wasn't in your employment record."

"I wanted to forget that whole time of my life."

"Hell's bells. Maybe you should be giving me some lessons. I've become rusty since the accident. Mind?"

Sam shrugged. "Guess not, but I hate guns and hate the thought of guns."

The image of the dead friend in the restaurant and the young girl's life cut short flashed in her mind. She understood.

When Phil pulled in front of the station in downtown Tampa, she was never happier to see work. TPD screamed safety—and transportation.

"The Chief promised you security, so we'll meet you back at your house in a few hours," Phil said.

Jenna attempted to keep the joy from her voice. "Okay."

She leaned over the front passenger seat and kissed Sam on the cheek, but his hard jaw didn't soften. Oh, well. In her heart, she believed this was the best way to handle the killer.

"Be safe," she called as she slipped out of the van.

She took the escalator upstairs and almost enjoyed the familiar musty smell and the dingy row of chairs for visitors. Jenna dragged her badge out of her purse and planted it proudly on her chest. The young officer at the desk merely nodded to her as she slipped into the back looking for Larry.

Bernard sat at his desk, two empty cups in front of him along with a half eaten sandwich. He looked up and winced.

"You don't look so sweet yourself, you know," she said.

Larry dragged a hand down his face. "I heard about your dad. I'm sorry. How's he holding up?"

"He was alive the last time I looked." Marlon slid next to her. She didn't need him today. "Hi, Marlon."

"Jenna, can we talk?"

Larry waved them on. "The car's ready when you are, but the Captain wants to speak with you first."

Marlon dragged a hand around her waist, and she let him lead her over to his desk. "Please sit, Jenna."

The light in Lucas' office was on, but the blinds and the door were closed. She had to wait for him to be free anyway. "What's up?"

"I can't sleep. I keep going over the scene with your father in my head. How could I have missed the shooter?"

She didn't want to get into another round with him. "What did Internal Affairs say?"

"They spoke with your dad by phone. He backed up what

happened, so I'm exonerated, but I know I'll be haunted by my mistake the rest of my life."

He'd have to see a shrink before being allowed out in the field. Poor Marlon. She glanced over at the captain's office as the door opened. "Speaking of which I need to go see Dad." She stood, not wanting to listen to Marlon moan and groan anymore. "But first, I need see what the Cap wants." Jenna knocked and stepped in. "Hi."

"Shut the door."

She didn't need this.

"How are you holding up?" he asked, his gaze on a folder in front of him.

Her shoulders relaxed. She thought he'd tell her he planned to keep her locked in the holding cell until the killer was caught. "As best as can be expected given the circumstances."

He leaned forward. "Here's how it's going to go down. Since we have no idea if our killer will attack by gun, knife, bomb, or whatever, we're trying to be thorough. I want you to wear a flak jacket at all times." He lifted up something that looked like a dog collar. "And this too. Assuming he's responsible for all the deaths around her, he likes to cut throats. This will deter him." He bent it. "Good old Italian leather."

"I already have one like that." With spikes.

"Not like this you don't. It's lined with a malleable metal. If he tries to strangle you, he'll have a hard time crushing the band. Wear the collar under a turtleneck. He won't see the protection."

"Are you going to ask me to wear a bullet proof helmet?"

"I wish, but as you can imagine, you'd be a little conspicuous. "He picked up a microphone attached to a wire. "Whenever you go out, put this on. We realize that the best chance of this guy has is getting to you at HOPEFAL, so if we don't see you for a few days, we'll understand. The guy's escalating. Be careful."

Jenna scooped up the two guns, two knives, and the not-so-beautiful handcrafted neck gear. "Wish me luck."

"Larry will show you to the car. You'll like it. It's rigged up special. Not only does it have redundant GPS trackers, it has bulletproof windows too. There are microphones that will pick up every sound, so no singing." A hint of a smile cracked his lips. "We had to disable the radio so as not to interfere with the transmission. If this guy managed to worm his way into the car and holds a gun to your head, do as he says. We'll be nearby at all times."

And here she thought working at *Botanica* was dangerous.

CHAPTER TWENTY-FOUR

PHIL POPPED into Sam's lab just as he was scanning in the skull of a young African American male. A bulldozer had come across the remains of the skeleton two days ago. "What's up?"

"I received a call from the Tampa Police Department."

Sam nearly crushed the skull. "Did something happen to Jenna?" He hadn't been able to keep focused thinking someone wanted to kill her.

"No, thank God. Marlon Giombetti, one of my contacts in the force, told me about a family who's been calling him every week to ask about their missing son—their missing twenty-year old African American son." Phil nodded to the bones on the gurney.

Sam tensed. "You think it's this guy?"

Phil handed Sam a photo. "Marlon faxed this over to me. Does it look familiar?"

The man's broad smile revealed two gold teeth studded with diamonds. "Holy shit. It sure looks like our man. The teeth will be able to confirm it."

"The DNA's already in our Lab."

Sam chuckled. "I knew you were good, but that good?"

"Aw, shucks. Seriously, the victim's name is James Coverson. But here's the spooky part. He worked as a part time gardener for...are you ready for this? Creighton Jackson."

"Shit. Maybe Coverson saw the killer and needed to be shut up."

Phil swiped a hand over his head. "I can't wait for this nightmare to end."

A soft knock sounded, followed by the familiar tones. Carla entered. "I am good," she announced with a smile.

"What did you find?" Phil spun toward her.

"Get this. Deidra's sister's husband was a med student here at Braham University, but he dropped out fifteen years ago after finishing his second year. The registrar is a good friend of mine and told me that according to the records, the guy still owes his last semester's bill."

"I don't suppose she gave a reason for his financial trouble?"

"She didn't, but I hunted down one of his fellow classmates who remembers the husband quite well, claiming he gambled—a lot."

"Carla," Phil said. "You've earned every measly dime I pay you."

A broad smile lit her face. "Such a generous man. I have to go." She saluted and left.

Something tickled Sam's brain. "You know the fact Shelby's husband was a med student fits well with the surgeon angle. Not just anyone could cut off a head and hands and not do any injury to the bones. That takes skill."

"You're right. I'll have TPD put an APB out on the guy and have them bring him in for questioning. I'd like to see him explain away all the coincidences."

After Phil disappeared, Sam's concentration went to shit. He couldn't get his mind off Jenna. They'd spent last night hashing out her plan as the Tampa Police patrolled their street all night long. Having Jenna in his arms gave him a contentment he never knew existed. The woman had definitely burrowed her way under his skin.

His brain sent out a warning. Every person he'd grown close to had either died, gone to jail, or run away. He prayed he wouldn't lose Jenna too.

The bigger question was whether he was willing to give her the last piece of his heart and chance having his dreams crushed.

* * *

AFTER JENNA VISITED her dad in the hospital, she decided she needed to play matador and flash the red cape at Deidra. The woman was connected somehow to this mess and only by confronting her would she find out how she was involved.

The occult shop was actually crowded for a Wednesday afternoon. A new guy was at the counter, and she approached him. "Is Deidra in the back? I need to see about a check she owes me."

He scrunched up his lips. "Yeah. Haven't seen her in a few hours, so knock first."

Whatever. The incense seemed more cloying than the last time she'd been in and a tickle caught in her throat. Jenna stopped at the door, hand ready. She didn't relish confronting Deidra. It was hard to ask someone if she'd hired some kids to rob a bunch of graves so she could do a stupid spell for an outrageous price, but unless Jenna brought up the topic, she'd never learn the truth.

Her rap was louder than she'd planned, but there was no answer. Jenna knocked again, and was one more met with silence. Surprised the knob turned, she pushed open the door and stopped dead in her tracks. A scream lodged in her throat at the bloody sight. Deidra was slumped in her chair, a bullet hole in her head. "Dear Lord in heaven."

Jenna might have been on the force for five years, but she'd never been first on the scene at a homicide. Shit, shit, shit. Now she'd never learn the truth. And here she thought Deidra might have been the one to off Creighton Jackson's head and possibly his gardener's. Deidra still could be guilty, but someone else was definitely at large—someone under six-foot with a tattoo on his arm. The jerk who'd confronted her in the backroom didn't have red hair like the pizza deliveryman, but that didn't mean he hadn't blown up her car, thrown the rock in Sam's window, killed Carla sister, or committed a host of other transgressions. When he'd approached her, he'd always worn a jacket or had on long sleeves—hence no visible tattoo.

A quick call to the precinct about the murder gave her some solace that help was on the way and that she didn't have to deal with the body herself.

A slapping of wood sounded behind the office, and adrenaline rushed through her. Crap. Was the killer in the back? She tugged on the door that led to the backroom, and it creaked open. She debated waiting until backup came, but if the sound was from the perp, and she didn't go after him now, he would get away. She refused to think this was a stupid move. With her vest, collar, and gun, she was prepared—or so she hoped.

She withdrew her Glock from her backpack purse and, as silently as she could, raced down the hallway praying the last door would be unlocked too. Her breaths rapid, she placed an ear to the door. Nothing. Damn. *Go for it.*

When she tugged on the handle, the door swung open. The dim light was on, and the air was a combination of rotten remains and something else she couldn't pinpoint. A quick glance told her no one was here. She turned, and the light glinted off something in the floor. Hand on the trigger, she stepped to the far left side of the room and past the wall with the crazy symbols.

A dull, one-inch ring sat in the dust on the floor. She stepped over to the area and bent to pick up the metal, only to find it was attached to the floor. Wait a minute. Jenna moved behind the ring and tugged. A trapdoor eased open. So that was how he'd been able to escape.

Sirens sounded in the background as understanding flooded her. Rickety steps led to a dark, dirt-lined room. No way was she going down there. Uh, huh. Nope. The killer could be waiting for her.

After releasing the handle, she raced back to where Deidra lay. The stench of death filled the air. Two cops burst through the door—David Hanson and Mike Blansky, both with Homicide. They nodded to her.

David stopped and scanned the room. "Mike, get the CSU team here ASAP." He faced Jenna. "Mind waiting outside. We don't need you messing with the evidence."

Like she would? Instead of flipping him the bird, she scooted out without making eye contact. Neither seemed to think she had anything to do with the murder, thank goodness.

The Hispanic behind the counter had shooed everyone out, so she could shake and worry by herself.

"Is it bad?" The man who had more craters on his face than the moon nodded toward the office.

"Yeah, real bad. You didn't see anyone go in there?"

"Besides you?"

"Funny. Yeah, besides me."

"Nope. Deidra disappeared about three hours ago. I learned my lesson about interrupting her."

Smart man. The front door dinged and the CSU team piled in, including the medical examiner who wore his fatigue both in his face and his bent back. Both techs waved, and Jenna directed them to the back. Given someone murdered Deidra, her ex-boss might not have been the one to do in Creighton Jackson. Whether Jenna's boss had ordered the two teens to break into the mausoleum was anyone's guess.

Mike Blansky strode out wearing his footies like a good detective. "Jenna, I need to get your statement."

"Sure thing."

She led him out of earshot of the cashier and told him what she suspected.

Mike took notes. "Larry and Marlon brought me up-to-speed on Ms. Willows and her connection to Jackson. We'll have to see what the M.E. says about time of death, but I'd say she was killed two to three hours ago."

"Hey, Mike." His partner rushed out with a piece of paper encased in plastic. "I think you'll want to see this." David dangled the plastic enclosed note in front of both of them, his gaze shooting between Mike and her.

"It's a note covered in blood," Jenna said.

Mike lifted the baggie toward the light and read the message out loud. "Jenna's next."

"Oh, shit. Why me?"

Both shrugged. "You worked here. Maybe he thinks you know who's responsible for all the bad shit that's been happening."

"I wish." She and Sam had been over all the suspects and had come up empty-handed.

"Some guy is staying at your place, right?" Mike asked.

"Yeah." Some guy.

On her way from downtown to the lab, Jenna stopped by the deli and picked up Sam's favorite sandwich of rare roast beef on rye with lettuce and tomato. She bought nothing for herself, because Jenna couldn't rid her brain of the vision of poor Deidra. And here Jenna thought she wanted to be a homicide detective. Maybe giving out parking tickets wasn't such a bad profession after all.

A different guard was manning the HOPEFAL's desk. This one appeared alert and friendly. She thought about asking what happened to the last guard but decided to keep quiet. She flashed her temporary HOPEFAL badge Phil had given for her and signed in. Once on Sam's floor, she punched in the code to Sam's door and stepped inside. He and Lara were huddled over a gurney studying a skullcap.

"I'd say between forty and fifty," Lara said.

"I agree." Sam looked up, but Lara seemed oblivious someone had come in or else was too focused on her work to notice.

His heavy perusal and small lift of his lips gave Jenna oohlala goose bumps that implied lots of kissing and touching were in her future. "I brought lunch." Jenna waved the bag.

Sam strutted over to her, planted a tongue tingling kiss on her, and removed the food from her hands. "Thanks. You staying?" He nuzzled her neck. "I miss you," he said soft enough for only her to hear.

For some reason making out with Sam in front of his intern embarrassed her. What was wrong with her today? Was she nervous about confronting the killer? God knows she had enough protection to keep a SWAT team at bay. Or had seeing her former employer shot ruined things for her?

Jenna took a big breath. "Someone killed Deidra. Shot her in the head." Might as well not cherry coat it.

He tossed the sandwich bag on the counter and took hold of her arms. "Tell me everything."

She filled him in on the details, including the threat aimed at her. "All I can say is that it was pretty ugly in there."

Sam leaned in closer. "Are you sure you want to go through with the investigation now that your life has been threatened?" His eyes pleaded with her.

"You mean, again? I have to." She probably should show him the knives and guns, and every other precaution, but he might realize the cops would never give a civilian so many weapons without proper training. If only she was ready to assure him nothing would go wrong, that she was a cop and was trained to handle this pond scum, he might support her decision.

Sam ran a hand down her face. "Let's eat then."

"I ate already." She wouldn't tell him her stomach was doing acrobatics inside, and eating anything would have made her vomit. Sam split his sandwich with Lara who seemed sweet enough and had the courtesy not to look too intrigued by her professor.

Sam pointed to the microphone Phil had found in the lab. "So what exactly is your plan?" Both believed if they filtered their conversation, they could trap the guy.

"I'm going for a jog in Lettuce Lake Park. I need to unwind. Finding Deidra dead has me on edge." No lie there.

"Be careful."

"I promise."

Jenna kissed Sam goodbye and left. Once in the car, she adjusted her earpiece under the headscarf. The leather collar itched like hell and the Kevlar vest weighed her down, but Jenna was determined to get this guy.

She tilted her head downward and spoke into the mike that was pinned to her bra strap. "I'm heading down Fletcher Avenue toward Lettuce Lake Park."

"I read you loud and clear. We'll have our guys there before you even arrive," Larry said. He'd volunteered to run the sting and had four beat cops stationed inside the park. "You have nothing to worry about, but do be vigilant."

"You can count on it." Thankfully, the windows in the car were bulletproof.

Even though the plan was on schedule, Jenna couldn't stop glancing in the rear view mirror every thirty seconds. A white truck followed her for about a mile before turning off. Either the guy was good, or she was going for a nice run in the park—alone. The sun shone bright, the day in the mid-sixties. If nothing else, the fresh air might give her time to think about Sam and how to approach him about what she did for a living.

Jenna pulled through the gate and drove down the tree-lined road to the parking lot. Gnarled live oaks dripping with sphagnum moss extended their long arms and provided some nice shade. Palmetto bushes, intermingled with some scruffy underbrush, dotted the landscape. About six other cars were parked in the lot. Given the cops were in unmarked vehicles, she figured one or two must belong to them.

Her bodyguards were good about keeping out of sight. Deciding to enjoy the clear, cool day, Jenna slipped out of the safety of the car and jogged toward the wooden walkway that wended through the park toward the Hillsborough River. Egrets feasted on snails, seagulls squawked overhead, and lily pads bobbed in the running water. When she reached the peaceful river, she leaned over the handrail and caught sight of an alligator basking in the afternoon sun.

She waited over five minutes, but no one approached her. The person after her must not be as observant as she thought or he would have taken advantage of her supposed isolation.

"No one's here," she said into her microphone. "I'm going to head east before swinging back to the parking lot." Even though no one was close enough to hear her, she felt stupid talking into the hidden microphone.

She trotted around the long pathway until the wooden walkway forked and then stopped to watch a mother with her young child off to the left. The mom pointed to a white bird in the tree and the little boy laughed. Her heart tugged as Sam's face emerged in her mind's eye. Would she ever enjoy such a moment?

Sighing, Jenna edged her hand along the weathered wooden railing and peered into the water, hoping to see some other form of animal life. The sharp prick of a needle and the hand over her mouth sent a surge of adrenaline zinging through her. Her muscles went numb as her fingers attempted to grab the gun at her waist. Her forefinger brushed the cold steel, but before she could grasp the weapon, the strong man pinned her arms behind her back and dragged her in the opposite direction of the woman. Jenna moaned, hoping the cops would pick up her distress or at the very least attract the attention of the woman.

The little boy squealed and pointed to a buzzard flying overhead, over-riding any noise she could make. *Turn around. Please.*

Where the hell were her bodyguards? When she said she was going for a run, did they decide all was clear? Jenna struggled, listening for the pounding footsteps of her fellow officers coming to her rescue, but she heard nothing.

She expected to hear the usual shout of, "Stop, Police." Only she didn't.

"It's no use struggling," her captor said. "The drug will render your muscles useless in a few minutes."

She knew that voice. Oh my God. Her eyes crossed and breath hitched. Her legs gave out and her knees nearly dragged to the ground. In a flash, she was hoisted up and over his shoulder. Her eyelids wouldn't stay open and her body turned to lead.

Oh God, she was going to die, and she'd never see Sam again.

* * *

MARLON GIOMBETTI TAPPED THE MICROPHONE. "JENNA, CAN YOU HEAR ME?"

Derek Wolf, a fellow homicide detective, sat across from him, earphones on. He shook his head, his eyes creased in worry. "Call Prior and Gomez. They're at the park. See what they say is happening."

Marlon tried contacting the two agents. "They're not responding."

"Shit." Derek tore off his earphones and stood. "Let's go."

"To the park?"

"No, dumb fuck to Busch Gardens."

Pisser. Once out the door, Marlon notified Phil how they'd lost contact with Jenna. The string of insults lasted until they were halfway to Lettuce Lake Park. Derek ran two red lights and wove in and out of traffic to reach the park.

"Turn left here."

Wolf tore into the entrance, down the rutted road, and past the guard station. He whipped in next to Jenna's car.

"She's still here," Marlon said blowing out a long breath. "As are Gomez and Prior—or at least their vehicles are here."

"Here's what we're going to do," Wolfe said with way too much authority. "Divide and conquer."

Wolfe shot out of the car and took off down a well worn path as Marlon tried to make contact with Jenna once more. Nothing. He tapped the microphone in case a wire was loose, and then attempted to contact Prior and Gomez again. "Do you read me?"

He waited for a response as he kept his gaze on Wolfe. After ten long seconds of silence, he jumped out the vehicle to search on foot.

He'd gone about fifty feet, when Wolfe shouted, "Giombetti," and waved him over. Marlon traipsed down the path and wiped sweat from his forehead despite the cool temperature.

"What is it?"

"Blood."

"That's not good." Wolfe was a full-blooded Seminole Indian and had the talent to track anything. "I wonder if it's Jenna's." Marlon knelt down and studied the large stain. "It doesn't look good for whoever it belongs to." He glanced around for signs of a struggle. No broken branches, no pieces of torn clothing, and no bullet casings. So far, so good.

Without offering any speculation, Wolfe raced away, stomping through the underbrush. Like a bloodhound, he stepped through the sharp-ended palmettos as if they were blades of grass and stopped about one hundred feet from the path. "Over here." He ran a hand over his head.

From the hoarse shout, whatever Wolfe found wouldn't be good. Marlon raced over. Both Prior and Gomez lay tossed on the ground, their throats cut. "Shit. How could this person have gotten a jump on both of them?" Marlon sank to his knees. "Prior's wife is due to deliver their first child any day now, and Gomez is a single dad raising three young sons. Dear God." His voice cracked. "I'll call it in."

Marlon contacted Captain Lucas, expecting another tirade. Instead, his captain sounded relatively calm, but he could hear the strain in his boss' voice. "Look to see if her phone is in the car," the captain said. "The GPS indicates she's still at the park. Someone needs to check every vehicle leaving the place."

"Yes, sir."

Armed with some direction, Marlon rushed back to the parking lot and peered into her car. Her cell was prominently displayed on the driver's seat. The phone was on, the message light blinking. He tugged on the door handle. It was unlocked. Dumb girl. After donning gloves, he picked up the cell, scrolled through the buttons for the messages and listened.

After two rings, the phone announced the arrival of one message. Three seconds passed. Click. "Jenna's going to die." Click.

"What do you have?" Wolfe said right behind him, and Marlon jumped.

He held out the phone. "He's got Jenna."

"What did he say? Did he ask for a ransom or anything?"

"No. All he said was that Jenna was going to die." Wolfe stood like a stone statue, as if he were in a trance again. "The captain said to stop anyone trying to leave. Why don't you search the park while I talk to the guard on duty?"

Wolfe snapped back into this world, nodded, and took off running again.

* * *

LOUD COUNTRY MUSIC, mixed with the roar of a big engine greeted Jenna the moment she realized she was alive. Her body heavy, she tried to assess the situation. Where was she, and how did she gotten there? She must be in a car because the movement was linear instead of up and down. A rag was stuffed in her mouth and a blindfold covered her eyes. The vehicle stopped, and then jerked forward. From the low-pitched sound of the engine, they must not be going very fast. That meant they probably weren't on I-4 or I-75.

Jenna wiggled her toes and fingers, but little sensation registered until pin pricks of pain raced to her extremities. Too bad her hands were tied behind her back or she could have searched for her weapon. Her face rested against a rough carpet that smelled like dog pee. She inhaled to bring air into her lungs and tried not to gag. Mentally, she ran through her options. Her captor must have found the gun stashed at her waist, but had he located the pearl handled 22 shoved in her boot? She wiggled her thighs together but didn't find the knife she'd strapped to her inner thigh. Damn. The thought of that scum touching her made her skin crawl.

She'd kept her phone in her top pocket but couldn't tell if she still had it. Jenna rolled part way onto her chest to feel for any kind of lump. Damn. Her cell was gone. There went the GPS. A wave of depression assaulted her. Captain Lucas' failsafe plan had failed.

Wait. If she could get the mask off far enough to see, she might stand a chance at finding something to attack him with when he came for her.

Energized with hope, Jenna rubbed her face over the carpet, hoping to move the material an inch. With each swipe, the cloth edged farther upward, but it also scraped her skin. After trying for another few minutes, she finally succeeded. Light filtered in and she blinked. In front of her sat a stained carpet, a pen, gum wrapper and an unused cigarette—but no gun, tire iron, or knife. She was in the backseat of a car, not the trunk as she'd anticipated. That made it easier to escape. Maybe.

At least her feet were free. Assuming she had the opportunity, she could make a run for it—if she ever freed herself and her toes functioned again. She needed to go on the offensive when her kidnapper stopped the car. Without making any noise that would let him know she was awake, she rolled onto her back and tucked her knees to her chest. She stretched her shoulders to the max and managed to swing her hands under her butt and threaded her feet through the loop. Phew. Free at last. Thank goodness for being double jointed.

The vehicle turned off the paved road onto a rough surface. She had no time to spare. The ride jostled her up and down, making maneuvering difficult and rather painful.

Her hands might be bound, but she could reach the gun in her boot —assuming it was still there. Groggy from whatever he gave her, her eyes blurred as she reached along the inside of her shoe. When her tingling fingers found her weapon, she nearly let out a strangled cry of gratitude.

With gun cocked, she propped herself up on her elbows and waited for the bastard to open the door.

CHAPTER TWENTY-FIVE

THE ENGINE DIED, and the music stopped. Jenna counted to ten, expecting the jerk to whip open the door her any second. She concentrated on her surroundings. No sounds of tires whirring on the nearby road, no birds singing, and no feet crunching on fallen leaves. Where the hell was she? Did he realize she was awake yet? Whatever drug he gave her, it made her mouth dry, her vision blur, and her body slow. Most likely, he was relieving himself or readying his weapon to kill her. Jenna tried to squash the horror running rampant through her brain.

A tap on the window behind her locked her muscles. He'd gone around to the side where her back was. Shit. Wedged in between the back and front seat, there was no way she could turn around in less than a second in order to shoot him. Before she could maneuver into position, the door squeaked open. With his hands under her armpits, he dragged her out and flipped her over so that she was on her stomach, the clutched gun trapped between the ground and her ribs.

"Trying to get away my little cop?" His voice dripped with sarcasm. That voice. That unforgettable voice.

Knowing time was critical, Jenna scrunched into a ball, flipped over, and thrust her feet into him, knocking him backwards. In that split second, she leveled her gun and pulled the trigger. Damn. She hit him in the shoulder. Stupid drugs.

His eyes widened, and the knife he'd been holding dropped to the ground with a dull thud. A gust of wind whirred through the trees as life needed oxygen rushed into her lungs.

The man from *Botanica's* backroom stumbled toward her. No way was she going to let him live. With trembling arms, Jenna lowered her gun and pulled the trigger again, sending a pool of blood bubbled out of his crotch, right where she'd aimed.

He dropped to his knees, his eyes vacant. "You bitch."

Relief powered her body to move the hell away from the madman. Holding the gun with wobbly hands, she jumped up and raced ten feet away from him, ready to move back at any second. She didn't need the bastard trying to disarm her. Even with two bullets lodged in his body, he could attack. Unless she'd nicked an artery, his bleeding out would take ten, fifteen minutes—equal to a lifetime of waiting.

She waved the gun at him. "Tell me about the nun you killed." For Carla's sake, she needed to know.

His contorted face made her think her question didn't register. "Don't know."

"Surely you remember You remember Carla, don't you? She was the HOPEFAL person you stabbed. Her sister was a nun."

His eyelids fluttered. "Oh, her. Yeah." He smiled, blood dripping off his teeth. "I killed the nun all right. Gutted her in fact." Red caked his lips. He reached across to his shoulder and grabbed his arm, exposing a tattoo in the shape of staff and a snake. The bastard had blown up her car.

Jenna ground her teeth. "Why'd you kill her?" And Chance.

He winced. "She saw me kill a homeless man who was at the wrong place at the wrong time." His sentences came out in panted bursts. He was dying.

"Then why blow up my car."

"Revenge."

Revenge?

"For what your father did to my mother." The man coughed up blood.

"What did he do?"

"He fucked my mom, so Dad left us. Three kids and he walked about because she couldn't keep her pants on." The man's gaze shot behind Jenna. "What are you doing here?"

Jenna spun around. "Marlon!"

He dragged her behind him. "This killing has to stop."

"You—"

The man never got to finish the sentence. Marlon shot him through the heart and the man's head crashed to the ground.

* * *

SAM PACED PHIL'S OFFICE. "It's my fault. I should have gone with her."

"You didn't know. Don't worry. TPD will find her."

The phone rang and Phil picked up. "It's Detective Wolfe."

Sam stood in front of Phil's desk, his hands clutched in front of him. If anything happened to Jenna, he wouldn't forgive himself. She was a civilian for God's sake. Why the police let her put herself in danger made no sense. Where were the cops who were protecting her?

Phil disconnected and placed the phone on his desk. "Detective Giombetti found Jenna. She's okay."

"Thank God."

Phil leaned back in his seat. "The good news is that the killer is dead."

The relief socked him in the chest. "That's wonderful. Can I talk to her?"

"She's at University Community Hospital."

His euphoria died. "Is she hurt?"

Sam didn't like the way Phil avoided eye contact. "He didn't give me any details. I say we see for ourselves."

Because Sam's assistant, Lara, was down at the DNA lab, he left a note saying he might be gone for the rest of the day. If Jenna needed him, he wanted to be there for her. She'd been through so much.

"Do we know the name of the man who attacked Jenna?" Sam asked as he followed behind the fast moving wheelchair.

"Not yet. He had no identification on him. Marlon Giombetti delivered the fatal bullet before they learned who he was."

Phil punched the electric door button and headed outside. Sam's boss drove and parked in the handicapped spot. The moment Phil cut the engine, Sam dashed out.

"Wait up," Phil called.

Sam realized his insensitivity in rushing off. "Sorry." His mind was barely functioning.

Together they entered the Emergency Room waiting area. This time, the cold, depressing place didn't dampen his spirits. The maniac was dead and Jenna would be safe, and her bright, indomitable spirit would shine forever. After Phil flashed his credentials, they made it to Jenna's room.

To his delight, Jenna was out of bed and dressed. She limped toward them. "Hey, guys! The doctor just released me."

"That was fast." Sam scanned her body for trauma, but she looked good. Too good. He rushed up to her and folded her in his arms. He pressed kisses to her head, drinking in the wonder of her. He leaned back and looked into her eyes. "I was so worried about you."

"I'm fine. Just a little shaken. It's not everyday I get gagged and bound and tossed in the back of a car." She held out her hand, and her fingers trembled.

"Let's get out of here, then." Now wasn't the time to discuss the near death experience. "How about some food, a hot shower, and some bedtime?" He winked.

"Sounds divine." She leaned around him. "Hi, Phil."

Sam wanted to shout for joy, but he didn't want to bring in the nurses. Thankful Jenna didn't seem scarred physically or emotionally, he escorted her out in the required wheelchair.

Once they were seated in the back seat of Phil's van, she tapped him on the shoulder. "Mind dropping us off at Lettuce Lake? My car's still there, I hope."

Phil didn't answer. Instead he made a call. When he was done, he started the engine. "TPD hasn't towed your car yet. Guess they figured you'd be back for it."

After Sam and Jenna picked up her car, they headed home. Home.

Such a nice word. He'd made a large meatloaf the night before, ready for feasting tonight.

Though seemingly upbeat, between Jenna's poor posture and dark circles under her eyes, he figured she must be exhausted. "You sure you're okay?"

He took his gaze off the road for a brief moment and squeezed her thigh. While her shirt looked a bit soiled, he couldn't detect any visible injuries.

"He drugged me," she said to his unasked question.

Sam swerved, nearly running off the road. "Why didn't you tell me?"

"I'm not ready to relive the horror."

Oh God. "Did he... touch you?"

"You mean did he rape me?" She shook her head.

"Thank God." Jenna turned her head and gazed out the window. He understood her need to mull over the event. Hell, when his father died, he'd refused to address the issue for months.

Neither spoke for the rest of the short trip home. If he'd known today would have gone as it had, he would have decorated the house or picked up a bottle of champagne to celebrate her return to a normal life. He pulled into the driveway and helped Jenna inside.

She tossed her jacket onto the back of the kitchen chair and punched the answering machine.

"You have one message. Message one, Wednesday, one PM. This is the Sharp's Dry Cleaners. Your uniforms are ready for pick up."

Until Jenna's shoulders stiffened, the message didn't register. "Uniforms? What are those for?"

She spun around, her eyes looking haunted. "Can we sit? I need to tell you something."

Sam obeyed, his pulse racing. "Shoot."

"There's been something I've been meaning to tell you, but I couldn't think of an easy way to do it."

With the danger over, he could draw only one conclusion. "You're kicking me out?"

Her smile wobbled. "No! You mean the world to me." She wrung her hands together. "I'm not who you think I am."

He didn't like the dreaded tone in her voice, nor did he understand what she meant. "And just who are you?"

"I'm a cop." His eyes widened, and then his brows furrowed. "I was working undercover at *Botanica* on a case when you wandered into the shop."

Only the beginning part stuck in his brain. "You're a cop and you conveniently forgot to mention this?" His voice escalated into a shout.

"I was working undercover. How did I know I could trust you? Undercover cops don't shout they're cops to everyone."

"So now I'm just everyone?" Sam pushed the chair back so hard it fell backwards and clanked against the hard kitchen floor. "We almost live together. I've made love to you. When were you going to tell me about this new profession?"

"I meant to, but somehow the timing wasn't right. I knew you'd be upset."

"Upset? You're damned right I'm upset." He paced the small, galley kitchen, no doubt wearing a hole in the tile. "Do you know what I went through when you put yourself in danger? Why didn't you tell me then you were a cop and save me a smidgen of grief?"

Jenna looked shell shocked. Tough. He hated lies. He'd even told her so when he bared his soul to her.

"I'm sorry."

"You're sorry. Well, I'm more sorry. You know, I'm just a dumb fuck. For a PhD, I've got no common sense. I tell you my life story and what did I get in return? Nothing. Were you laughing at me the whole time when I mentioned how my dad died, how my brother stole goods to get enough money to put food on the table, or how my mom drank herself into oblivion? I thought we had a connection, but obviously I was wrong."

She shook her head. "No, we did."

"Now that I think about it, there were clues. Lots of little clues that I missed." He stabbed a hand through his disheveled hair. "I can't believe I didn't recognize you were a cop. You always had the right words, the right angle on what to look for. You even thought like a criminal. You're good, I'll say that."

"I couldn't turn off my brain." She glanced at everything but him.

"Is there anything else you've lied about?"

"My dad's a cop too."

"Oh, wonderful. So the whole goddamn family is a bunch of liars. I bet you're not even a student at Braham, are you?"

"No, but I do have an undergraduate degree in statistical analysis and a masters in criminology."

Tears streamed down her cheek, but he figured they were as fake as she was.

"And what about us? Did you fake your attraction to me? Was there some underlying reason why you wanted to lure me into your web of seduction?"

Her watery eyes brightened. "Our relationship was real." She swiped a hand across her eyes. "I love you."

"I'm supposed to believe that because?"

When Jenna didn't answer, he stomped into the bedroom, tossed his clothes in a suitcase and returned ten minutes later. He wouldn't be a sucker for those three little words again. Tammy had told him the same thing before she ran off with someone else. She wanted his research. That's all. Look what her little lie had cost him.

Jenna remained at the table, looking off into space. He refused to let guilt overshadow his anger. Of course, he wanted to comfort her, but his heart might stop beating if he did.

"Hope you have a good life." He slammed the front door behind him.

* * *

JENNA STARED AT THE DOOR. Would he come back and say he really loved her, and that he was sorry he'd become so angry?

No, she'd hurt him. Deeply. She deserved this. Lies were always bad.

Her throat clogged with tears. Jenna had tried to tell him that first day about being a cop when his windshield had been broken, but he'd accused her of destroying his property and wouldn't listen. Dummy. She should have taken the hint and left right then, but did she? No. Not her. Being brilliant, how he held himself, and the kindness he showed his coworkers spoke to her. Of course, being hot didn't hurt either.

Jenna dropped her head in her hands, her grief unbearable. Should she run after him and say she hadn't confessed because her life was at stake? It didn't matter. He wouldn't believe anything she ever said to him again. She trusted Sam with her life, so why hadn't she told him a while ago? Because his damn moral compass would have booted her ass weeks ago, and she wanted to stay wrapped in his arms for as long as possible.

Until this case closed, she'd vowed silence about who she was. Her job meant the world to her, but had it been worth losing the one man who made her body sing, the one man who taught her to realize how wonderful life could be, who made life worth living?

No.

Jenna shoved back her chair and poured herself a glass of wine. Wine for God's sake. She didn't even like wine. It was Sam who was crazy about it. He'd bought a few different bottles for her to taste.

She poured a glass, hoping to somehow feel closer to him, have his essence near her. Maybe he left something of his in the bathroom that she could hold and remember him by. When she stepped into the bathroom, the counter top was bare of his shaving cream, his toothbrush, and his razor. The finality of his absence slapped her in the face. The towel he'd used to shower hung over the rod. She brought the terrycloth to her nose and inhaled his scent. Jenna hiccupped. Stupid job.

Shuffling her feet, she meandered into the office hoping to find something he'd left there, something that would give her an excuse to return to him, to see him one more time, but the office too exuded emptiness. She pawed through the drawers, hoping he'd left a shirt, a pair of pants, anything, but she found nothing. He was gone. For good.

A headache pounded against her skull, but she took another sip of wine hoping for oblivion. Her body teetered as her energy took a nose-dive. She needed a nap to give her a new prospective.

She lay down on her soft, unmade bed, still remembering their last lovemaking. The sheets held his scent. She swiped the tears from her checks and forced the image of sexy Sam from her mind as she drifted off to sleep.

When she awoke, darkness had infiltrated her house. Fumbling for the light switch, she took a long, hot shower hoping the pain of Sam's desertion would lesson, but it didn't work.

She slipped into her pajamas and padded into the kitchen for something to eat. A quick glance at the answering machine in the hopes she'd missed a call from him only brought a renewed rush of depression when the light remained unlit.

The book she tried to read didn't interest her either, as the characters appeared flat, the plot dull. Her only option was television, something she rarely had time to watch anymore.

She sat through back-to-back episodes of NCIS, but even the hot operatives didn't boost her mood. After swallowing a sleeping pill the hospital had given her, she snuck back into bed praying oblivion would come soon.

* * *

JENNA AWOKE WITH A KILLER HANGOVER. She never should have that last glass of wine, but then again, she shouldn't have waited so long to tell Sam about her undercover work.

She shrugged into her uniform, only to remember she had to pick up her order from the cleaners. The damned cleaners, the ones who had hastened her loss from Sam. Combing her hair instead of dumping on a half bottle of gel to tame it, she glanced at the mirror. Oh, man. She'd aged ten years since this undercover job had begun. Whatever. What was done was done.

Her life was right back where it was before her mom's skull was stolen. Even with the unknown man dead, she was no closer to finding her mom's remains. Perhaps Larry or Marlon had some news.

Jenna reported to the station on time for a change—early, in fact. Larry wasn't at his desk, but Marlon was there, drinking a cup of hot java. The strong aroma reminded her she hadn't had her caffeine fix for the day.

He tossed a folder on his desk, leaned back in his chair, and closed his eyes.

"You snoozing already?" Jenna tried to keep her tone light, but he jackknifed up.

"Jesus, you scared me."

"You not sleeping much?"

"No. I spent most of last night with your dad."

Guilt swept over her. She should have stopped by, but with Sam leaving, she couldn't bring herself to visit. "How is he?"

"He's getting cranky."

She smiled. He might have been a jerk all those years ago, but he hadn't caused her mom to kill herself. For that she was thankful. Trusting him again and even forgiving him would take time.

"Any news?"

"On the dead guy?"

"No, on the weather," she shot back.

"HOPEFAL's got him. We did run his prints, but nothing came up."

Jenna craned her neck around the corner of the office. "I see Larry's not in yet. I'm guessing no news on where those kids put the skulls."

"None that I heard."

He was no help. "I'm surprised the captain has you working giving the shooting."

"Until I see the shrink, I'm on desk duty." He shrugged.

"Well, thanks again for saving my life."

He smiled. "Does that mean you owe me one?"

She'd been about to say, no, but without Sam, her life held little appeal. "Sure. Maybe dinner next week?"

Something sparked in his eye that she couldn't decipher. Maybe he had a major crush on her, and here she thought all they had was an occasional release session in bed. Nothing like what she and Sam have. Or rather had.

"Sure."

Not wanting more conversation, she trudged off, grabbed some coffee from the break room and settled down at her desk. About an hour later, after many of her coworkers came to congratulate her on escaping the serial killer, the captain stopped by.

"Jenna, can I speak with you in my office?"

Oh boy. Could she be in trouble so soon? Like a puppy dog, she followed him. "Yes, sir?"

"Have a seat." This didn't sound good. "I want you to take some time off."

No way. She'd go crazy with nothing to do but think about Sam. "If you don't mind, I'd rather stay at work."

"You need to see the psychologist and rest. Not only did someone try to kill you, you shot someone. Maybe you should spend time with your father."

"But—"

"That's an order, not a suggestion."

Shit. "Yes, sir." How was she going to find her mother's remains if couldn't access the databases. Do lots and lots of legwork she supposed.

She rushed out, past Derek Wolfe and the rest of the homicide crew, not ready to talk to any shrink. She glanced to where Greg, the partner she'd abandoned resided, but even he wasn't there for support. She didn't mind going over the capture one more time, but her anger over Sam's leaving would surely come up and the subject cut her too deep.

On her way out, Jenna grabbed some folders from her desk, needing to keep herself busy. Given she had the keys to the TPD's loaner car, she took advantage of the situation. Before she chickened out, she shot down Florida Avenue and jumped on the Interstate, toward Braham University.

CHAPTER TWENTY-SIX

JENNA PARKED in front of HOPEFAL and ducked inside.

Some new guard stopped her as she walked past. "I'm afraid this is a secure facility, ma'am."

"I here to see Carla Pendowski." She wouldn't have been surprised if Sam placed a Do-not-let-Jenna-Holliday-pass-this-way notice on each of the entry doors.

"Just one moment."

It took him two phone calls, but eventually he waved her through. Stupid security system. Didn't he realize if she hadn't helped locate the serial killer, his life might now be in jeopardy?

The elevator seemed to take forever to move three floors. The doors opened and before she stepped out, she looked both ways, wanting to make sure Sam wasn't wandering the hallway. She still had the fob Phil had given her, which gave her easy access to the corridors. When Jenna walked into Carla's office, her friend sat hunched over her computer. The techie jumped the moment she spotted her.

"Jenna!"

"Hey."

Jenna sat down, exhaustion grabbing hold of her. The tension from the indecision to come here finally caught up with her.

"Have you seen Sam?" Carla asked with a smug lift to her lips.

"I guess you didn't hear we broke up."

"I did hear. I'm sorry. Don't worry he'll come to his senses." Carla waved a hand and smiled.

Hope rushed through her. "You think?" Damn, she shouldn't have sounded so excited. She didn't want Sam to come back because he felt sorry for her. Or did she even care as long as he came back?

"I'm no expert on men by any means, but he might change his mind once he's had time to think about it. I told him he was a jerk to judge you so harshly, but he's hurt, you know."

Jenna shrugged, despite her insides turning to mush. Talking about what happened burned a hole in her heart. She hadn't come here to discuss her love life, or lack thereof. Jenna cleared her throat. "I found out what happened to your sister."

Carla's apparent joy evaporated. "You learned what happened to Daphne?"

"She was in the wrong place at the wrong time." Jenna told her a sanitized version of what the killer had said.

"Did he admit to killing anyone else?"

"Detective Giombetti shot him before I could question the guy any further."

Carla shook her head. "I guess we'll never learn what really happened to that young African American boy either."

"Probably not."

When Jenna was driving there, she'd dreamed of running into Sam, but now that she was in the lab, she thought better of it. If he cared, he'd have called her. "Look, I better be going." The two hugged. "Don't be a stranger."

"We'll keep in touch for sure."

Instead of taking the elevator and chance Sam spotting her, she darted into the stairwell. Halfway down the stairs, a door below opened and footsteps pounded on the steps coming toward her. A shot of fear forced her to grab the railing. *Stop it. He's dead. He can't hurt you anymore.*

Inhaling, she stepped down. As she rounded the landing to the last flight of the stairs, a dark blond head bobbed up, and her heart raced.

Jenna was tempted to turn around and race back upstairs, but it was too late. Sam had seen her.

"Jenna?"

Like he didn't know who she was. "Hey. I needed to see Carla." Darn it. She shouldn't have answered his unasked question about the purpose of her visit. It made her look like she'd come to see him.

"Are you doing okay?"

Why wouldn't she be? Just because she cried her eyes out last night and her stomach was so upset she had a hard time keeping food down didn't mean she wasn't okay. "Peachy."

He ran a gaze over the length of her, long and slow. She held her breath, waiting for him to tell her he was sorry. He pressed his lips together, ducked his head and slid past her without a touch. And then the faint hint of bleach wafted past her.

Half of her wanted to grab his arm and shake him, but Holliday's didn't beg.

Hurrying as fast as she could, she flew down the rest of the stairs, ran through the foyer, and dashed outside. The cold air slapped her in the face. *Stupid move, Jenna, what did you expect to happen?* The tears nearly spilled over her lashes as she raced to her car.

* * *

FOR THE NEXT four days Jenna's routine didn't vary. She'd sleep until noon, eat a little something and visit her dad in the hospital for an hour or two. Each time she sat with him, their relationship improved. He'd explained, to the best of his ability, why things had gone wrong between him and her mom, and why she couldn't live with dying a slow painful death. Jenna didn't hug him goodbye, but at least she didn't stomp out after the visit like she used to. To her, that was called progress.

Today, however, she didn't have the energy to see him or do much of anything. Christmas was closing in on her and wanted to buy something for her father, even if it was the usual tie she bought every year, but she was too tired to think right now. What she needed was a nap.

By tonight, the crowds should have thinned and she could venture out. Jenna crawled into bed and within minutes dozed off. A knock on the front door entered her dream. It took a series of knocks before full awareness arrived.

Sam!!

She jumped out of the bed with a huge smile on her face and her heart racing faster than an AK15 spitted out rounds. He'd come back! She glanced at the clock, surprised by the darkness outside. She'd slept more than four hours. Who cared? Sam had returned.

She couldn't think of a better Christmas present than making love with him. She flung open the door, and her chest deflated. Not Sam. Damn. In fact, she'd never seen this person before. "Yes?" The older woman's hair was teased into a beehive like the kind Jenna had seen on those old TV shows from the 50's and the lady's form-fitting dress and pearl necklace backed up the ancient look.

The woman held out her hand. "I'm Kathy Bello. Bianca was my daughter. May we talk?"

The mother of the dead girl. Heaven help her. "Of course. Come in." Jenna scooped up the left over meal from the table and tossed the plate in the sink. "Sorry about the mess."

Kathy sat stiffly in the chair. "I probably should go to the police, but I'm too afraid he'll find out."

"I am a cop you know."

"Yes, but if what I believe is true, not only is my life in danger, so is yours."

Jenna's brain hadn't woken up yet. "I don't understand."

"My brother is Marlon Giombetti."

Jenna smiled. "Marlon? He's a good cop. Why not talk to him?"

Kathy leaned forward. "May I have some water?"

"Sure." She recognized the stall tactic for what it was and pulled a clean glass from the cabinet. Jenna set the full glass in front of her guest. "Here you go. Did something happen to Marlon? You did hear he saved my life?"

"That's what your captain said." Kathy wound her fingers together. "Let me begin by saying I'm sorry you had to be the one drugged and kidnapped." She dabbed her nose and eyes. "The police told me how

Bianca had died. I think maybe the same person who killed her, kidnapped you."

"I don't understand." Bianca was shot, whereas Jenna was kidnapped, though had she not had a gun, the kidnapper might have killed her.

"That man who hurt you was our younger brother, Enzio Giombetti. And Marlon directed him—told him who to kill. At least, that's what I suspect."

Every nerve ending exploded. "I don't believe it. Not only did Marlon save my life, he saved my father's too. Marlon is a hero, not a killer." Kathy glanced over her shoulder at the door, looking as if she expected her brother to burst in any minute. Jenna jumped up and locked the door in case the woman was correct. "How can you be sure he's behind the killings?" Jenna sat down again. "He's a cop."

"That's what gives him his power. When your father and my mom had an affair all those years ago, Dad was pissed and left. Mom was saddled with three kids and no job. Then came along this rich guy, Creighton Jackson."

"Oh, shit. Creighton was your step-dad?"

Marlon was in charge of the investigation. What had he said? That he found the bullet that killed the man. "Did Marlon kill him?"

Kathy dragged her fingers down her mouth. "I don't know, but I'm glad he's dead. Creighton was nothing but trouble for our family."

"How?"

"The bastard took out his frustrations on both of my brothers, but we needed his financial support, so Mom stayed. I was twenty-five and married at the time, so I wasn't around to see first hand what he did to my brothers. Both changed after a few years, for the worse."

"And your mom? Why didn't she stop him?"

"The boys never told her. Apparently Creighton said he'd hurt Mom if they did." Kathy opened her purse, dragged out a lace handkerchief and dabbed her nose. "She died a few years after she married Creighton, though I swear there was nothing wrong with her. "I wouldn't put it past Creighton to have poisoned her. He pulled some strings and had her cremated without an autopsy. After that, Marlon and Enzio started to rebel. They killed Creighton's dog, and then set fire to the barn behind his house. Marlon was the one with the brains. Once he turned fifteen, he convinced Enzio to do his dirty work—until recently."

None of this made any sense. "Marlon's always been cheerful around the precinct. He follows the rules. Do you have any evidence he's a killer?" Jenna went into cop mode. She watched Kathy's body language, her eye movement, and her facial expression for some evidence of a lie, but found only openness. If Jenna thought about the ramifications, she wouldn't be able to function.

"He made my husband make him masks so no one would recognize him when he killed." Like the man who wore the mask who blew up her car. "I followed Marlon once to Creighton's boat, but he didn't see me. Deidra, Creighton's newest girlfriend, showed up later. When someone fired a gun, she ran."

"But you stayed."

"Yes. Marlon came out about half an hour later. I wanted to call 9-1-1 but knew if he found out, he'd kill me."

Jenna absorbed the information wondering if maybe Kathy was the killer and not Marlon. There could be some kind of transference going on and that she lived in denial. Perhaps she orchestrated the whole affair, and Marlon figured the only way to get justice in this life was to become a cop. No way would Jenna have slept with a man capable of killing so many.

Kathy finished off the water. "I see you don't believe me."

"Regardless of whether I do or don't doesn't matter, I think you should have protection." From herself. "I'll call the captain to see what he can do." Jenna stood hoping Kathy would take the hint and leave.

"You can't tell him. Marlon will find out." She dragged a finger under eye. Jenna couldn't tell if the tear was real. "I do have proof."

"What kind?"

"I decided to confront Marlon about the killings." Jenna gasped. "I know, I know what I did was stupid, but I had to know if he killed my daughter. Don't worry, I went over to his house, but he wasn't home. I have a key to his place, you see. I figured he had to come home eventually so I let myself in. As I passed the guest room, I smelled something foul coming from the closet."

"Before you continue, tell me why didn't you go to the station and speak with him there? It would have been a hell of lot safer."

"I did, but no one had seen him. Not even Andrea, his partner."

Jenna hadn't gone to work in days, what with the depression and the holidays, so maybe what Kathy said was true. Her mind raced back to the topic of the smell. "What kind of smell?"

"Like a dead body kind of smell."

Jenna stiffened. "Did you find this dead body?"

"I found a head."

She sucked in a breath, the image of Creighton without his head surfaced. "A head?"

"In a box."

"In a box?" Jenna didn't normally repeat everything, but nothing was making any sense.

"Yes, that's what I said."

This time she kept her remark to herself. "And it was a human head? With eyes and lips and a nose and everything?" Or was it all white and plastic, like the one at the backroom of *Botanica*?

"It didn't have a face. It was just the skull. A smelly one. My husband said you were friends with a forensic anthropologist. I was wondering if he could tell me if it's real. I didn't know who else to turn to." Kathy stood and pushed in her chair.

This might be the break they needed to close the graveyard robberies. Her big chance to make the captain proud, and maybe her dad too. "I'd like to take a look."

"Are you sure? For a moment you looked at me like you thought I was a killer."

"For a brief moment only." Jenna smiled. "Let me grab my purse." The purse with the 22 inside. She still didn't think Marlon was capable of murder, but someone could be framing him if they knew Creighton Jackson was his stepfather. Though why would Marlon agree to take the case when there was an obvious conflict of interest? Kathy might have a point.

Whether the skull could be used as evidence, she wasn't sure. However, they wouldn't be breaking and entering since his sister had permission to be in his house. Shit. She could look at least.

Since Kathy's car was blocking the TPD's loaner, Kathy drove. The trip took less than twenty minutes. They stopped in front of an average looking, one-story, cement block home. The lid to the mailbox was gone, and the lawn hadn't been cut in a while.

"This is Marlon's place?" When she and Marlon had gone out, it was to dinner and a movie, and if they hooked up, they always ended up at her house. Now she knew why.

"Not exactly the Ritz, is it?"

The smell of decomp hit Jenna as soon as she stepped inside the front door. "How could Marlon live with this stench?"

Kathy covered her nose. "It wasn't this bad before. Maybe I shouldn't have opened the lid to the box."

Jenna followed her down a low-lit hallway into a back room where a metal box sat on a table. Kathy motioned for Jenna to open it. In case this was a trap, Jenna faced Kathy and held her breath as she took a peek inside the box. Sure enough, a clean, white skull sat inside. Only it wasn't bleached white like the skulls in Deidra's shop. Small bits of tissue clung to the brow and to the hole at the back of the head. The tissue had caused the foul smell.

"Looks like this one might have been shot in the head," Jenna said.

Kathy held a hand over her nose. "How can you tell?"

"By the hole?" Okay, so that came out sarcastic, but anyone could see the cracks radiating from the half-inch opening. Part of Jenna's training involved homicide and cause of death.

"I would have thought if someone shot this person, the whole skull would have been blown away."

That made sense. "Depends on the caliber of the gun and how close the shooter was. Let me call TPD. They can sort out this mess." Then she remembered her fear of Marlon finding out. "If your brother isn't at the station, he won't hear about you breaking in."

"I don't care anymore. Marlon has to be stopped. Go ahead and call."

"What's the address here?"

After Kathy told her, Kathy motioned she wanted to wait outside. Jenna nodded, happy to be able to speak frankly to her fellow officers. She asked for Larry, figuring the head might belong to Creighton Jackson. Sam would be happy to have another part of the body if it did belong to the yacht man. If not, he'd have something else to work on.

Jenna looked around for another metal box, thinking the hands and feet had to be nearby.

"I'll be right over," Larry said. "And thanks for calling me. Stay there. It shouldn't take me more than ten, fifteen minutes tops. Just to be safe, how about getting back in the car and locking the door. You never know if Marlon will come back."

"I plan to do just that."

Once she finished her conversation, she rushed outside, and the fresh air was a welcome relief from inside the house. The temperature had turned chilly and Marlon's front door light had burned out providing little light in the driveway.

Kathy was leaning against the hood of the car, smoking a cigarette. She tossed the butt on the ground and stomped it out, looking like she was taking out her anger on the cigarette. Marlon's sister wrapped her arms around her shoulders. "It's getting downright cold." She stormed over to the driver's side. "I'm going to wait inside the car for the police."

"I'll join you."

Jenna grabbed hold of the passenger side handle, just as a strong arm grabbed her around her throat. Oh, God. Not again. Her instinct kicked in. She stomped on the attacker's instep, and he let out a curse. Palming her fist, she drove her elbow into the man's rib cage. Jenna twisted around to ID the man's face, just as a sharp needle pricked her in the neck and her body froze.

"What the..."

Unable to finish the sentence, her knees teetered and she met the ground with a thud.

CHAPTER TWENTY-SEVEN

SAM FINISHED his bland Christmas Eve meal, left a generous tip on the restaurant table and headed upstairs to his hotel room. While Phil had offered him a place to stay, interacting with his boss and his now live-in Gina would be too painful, especially since they were in love.

He dropped onto the bed, shoes and all. Being alone on Christmas Eve sucked. He'd already called his mom earlier today, but she'd slurred her words so much he doubted she'd remember the call. Fortunately, she didn't chastise him for not coming home for the holidays. Only now he wished he had made the arrangements. At least he'd have been with someone who cared about him.

Though he rarely contacted his brother any more, before dinner he'd called Andy, whose situation in life was a lot worse than his own. At least Sam had a good job and wasn't in jail on armed robbery charges like his baby brother. The conversation had been short, but he knew Andy appreciated the connection. His little brother was growing up and sounded as though he'd learned his lesson. His parole hearing was coming up in six months and Sam promised he'd be there.

With the lab locked down tight for the next two days, he flipped on the TV. After ten minutes, he turned it off, the contents too sentimental for his tastes. Christmas meant family, the one thing he didn't have.

He'd tried to forget Jenna all week but he'd failed. Every petite blond he passed, every bouncy kid he saw and every sweet scent he smelled reminded him of her. The way her lips curled up when she smiled, the feel of her fingers as she ran her hands over his body, and how well she understood what he'd been through, all made his mind focus on her. Without the upbeat woman, his life had turned almost meaningless, but her words *I'm a cop* still rang in his head like the lyrics of a bad song.

The fact she didn't trust him enough to tell him the truth cut the deepest. He held honesty at the pinnacle of his beliefs.

Or did he? *Be honest.*

Hadn't he lied in small ways?

Fine. He hadn't told the truth on his application for the HOPEFAL job when he omitted his service record, but that was because he wasn't proud of how he sat at a desk while his friends fought overseas—or how about how every time he held up his badge, he prayed the viewer would think it was police issued and give him the information he sought.

Aw, shit. At least she lied because of her job.

Face it, Bonita, you're no better than she is. Besides, you're miserable without her. She claimed she loved him. The lonely half wanted to believe her, but his logical side said she didn't. There was only one way to find out. Talk to her.

Sam dug out his phone and dialed her number. He jumped off the bed and paced, his heart racing, waiting for her to answer. What would he say? Five rings, eight rings. Her answering machine clicked on. Damn. "Jenna, it's me. Sam. Can you call me? Ah, bye."

He tossed the phone on the bed, disgusted he sounded so stern, unfeeling, and unconcerned. Hell. Maybe she didn't want to see him again after he raced out of her life.

If he went to her house, knowing Jenna, she'd let him in, and then hopefully forgive him. When he'd seen her in the stairwell at the lab, he'd been so shocked he threw up his shields and walked on by. If he'd held out his arms, he bet she would have come to him. So why hadn't he?

You're an idiot. Go after her.

Sam grabbed his keys. His mind spun with possibilities. He'd bring her flowers, perhaps buy her a card, and maybe even some chocolate. Yeah, that was it. Jenna loved chocolate. She'd appreciate the thought.

Energized for the first time in a week, he ran down the stairs. The elevators took too long.

Thank goodness Wal-Mart was open for the last minute shoppers. Armed with his forgiveness goodies, Sam headed to her house. The drive was the longest fifteen minutes in his life. He couldn't wait to hold her, kiss her, and tell her how much he missed her.

The moment he spotted the police issue car in the driveway, he barked out a laugh and pulled in behind her. After popping a piece of gum in his mouth to freshen his breath, he gathered the dozen roses, sappy card, and box of chocolates.

He knocked, and then rang the bell, but Jenna didn't answer. Shifting his weight, he knocked again, and then stepped in front of the kitchen window to see if she might be asleep on the living room sofa. Lights out, the place looked deserted. He wrapped on the window. "Jenna, it's me. I need to speak with you."

A cold wind sneaked in through his sweater, but he was more worried about the chilly reception he might get than the possibility of catching a cold.

He gave the door one last try. "Jenna, I know you're home." Frustration bit him until concern edged in.

Where could she be? He walked around back of the house and peeked in her bedroom window. The bed was unmade, and she was nowhere to be seen. Maybe she was in the shower. That thought lightened his step.

No wonder she couldn't hear him knocking. Given he'd never returned her house key, he let himself in.

"Jenna?" A sharp perfume bit his nostrils, and his skin pricked at the unfamiliar scent.

He placed the flowers in a vase and propped the card and candy in front. Surprised he didn't hear the water running, he strode to the bathroom. The open was door and the dark interior confused him. She really wasn't home.

Oh, crap. Could she be out on a date? On Christmas Eve? He squashed the jealousy that raced to his gut.

He snapped his fingers. He bet she was at the hospital visiting her dad. Given the University Community Hospital was half hour away, how did she get there? Had a friend driven her, or one of her cop buddies? And why not take the armored car?

He looked up the number for the hospital, dialed, and asked to be connected with her Dad.

"She's not here," Mr. Holliday said. "Hasn't been by in two, three days. Tomorrow's Christmas though. Jenna loves the holidays. There's no way she won't be here to visit. I wouldn't worry about her. She's probably off pouting somewhere. I'll tell her to call you when I see her."

"Thanks."

Sam disconnected. Jenna could be with her dad, refusing to speak with him, but he doubted it. He looked around her house for clues as to where she might have gone. Two glasses sat on the kitchen table, one with red lipstick rimming the edge, which did not belong to Jenna. He wrapped the glass in a cloth to protect the evidence. If nothing else, he could run the fingerprints and learn who she'd last been with, assuming the prints were on record.

Sam stood at the table, his mind working overtime. Something wasn't right. The smell, the lipstick, her car. Before he went back to the hotel, he called Tampa Police and asked to speak with Marlon, the man who'd saved Jenna.

"I'm afraid he didn't report into work today," the desk officer replied.

The hairs at the nape of his neck stood up. "What about," he couldn't remember the guy's name who was working on the cemetery case.

"Would you like to speak with her captain? I can patch you through to him."

Before he could answer, the captain answered. "Dr. Bonita. I was about to call you. I received a call from Jenna a little while ago about finding a skull at one of our detective's houses. When we arrived, Jenna was gone."

"She just left?"

"Probably not willingly." His heart nearly stopped. "We found a woman, Kathy Bello, passed out in the front seat of her car. She'd been drugged."

He grabbed onto the kitchen counter. "Did she know where Jenna went?"

"She doesn't remember exactly, but they'd gone to Giombetti's house to look at a skull she'd found while in his house."

"Why was she in a detective's house?" This was sounding too crazy.

"She's Marlon's sister. The man who took Jenna captive, the one who Marlon shot, was their younger brother, Enzio."

Shit. Marlon wasn't at the precinct. "Kathy Bello believes Marlon has Jenna?"

"That's our first guess, but I find it hard to believe. Marlon's been with the force for quite some time."

"What are you going to do?" Unease took hold of him and his throat tightened, squeezing the air from his lungs. "I put an APB on Marlon's car, just in case."

That didn't sound encouraging. "Call me if you find out anything."

* * *

JENNA CRACKED OPEN an eye and her stomach roiled. Her mouth was dry, and her skull was exploding from a wicked migraine. Bile raced up her throat. *Please don't throw up.* She couldn't sleep in her own vomit. How had this happened? Again? The man who'd taken her the first time was dead.

Oh shit. Kathy's confession about Marlon sprang back to life. It had to be him, but she couldn't reconcile the man who had a crush on her with the man who'd drugged her.

There had to be some way to get out of here. She forced her mind off the pounding and onto her surroundings. Stars shone through the window directly above her and the air smelled damp and tangy.

She tried to sit up, but a series of ropes held her down. Crap. She leaned over the edge of the lumpy mattress and waited for her eyes to adjust to the darkness. The shape of an anchor appeared at the end of the rope. Why an anchor? Was she on a ship? Water slapped against the side of a boat. Damn it. That's why she was so sick. She hated being on the ocean. She needed Dramamine.

She went over the series of events that led to her capture. She remembered someone grabbing her. Kathy had been in the car. Had he taken her too? His own sister?

A giant swell nearly tossed her off the bed. Had she not been tied down, she might have dropped to the floor. She squeezed her eyes shut and thought of Sam. The racket inside her head lessened. He'd been gone a lifetime it seemed. Would he call to wish her a Merry Christmas and leave a message? Would her father call out the dogs when she didn't stop by to see him tomorrow? For all she knew, it was Christmas already. Jenna lifted her wrist an inch, pressed the light button against the rope and read the time. Not yet.

Wait. TPD was on its way to Marlon's house. They'd be suspicious when they arrived and she wasn't there, but would they think to look on a boat? Crap.

She was thirsty, hungry, and royally pissed. Jenna debated whether she should call out to Marlon for food and chance getting stuck with another needle or keep quiet. She'd either starve to death or die from an overdose. And she really needed to pee. Not to mention getting out of this stale room before her lungs rotted from the mildew.

Marlon might agree to her few small demands. It wasn't like she'd jump overboard if she were allowed on deck. The water temperature alone would send her core plummeting. She'd be dead in no time.

Her only consolation was that if Marlon had wanted her dead, she'd be fish food right now. No. The bastard had some diabolical plan up his sleeve.

Jenna swallowed to wet her mouth. "Mar-lon?"

Laughter trickled into her cabin from under the door. A woman's voice—and it seemed as if they were having a good time. His partner, Andrea, perhaps? Or Kathy? Were those two in cahoots? Jenna didn't buy it. Kathy wouldn't work with the man who killed her daughter.

The door opened and light from the main cabin crawled in. A man bent down and stuck his head in. "What do you want?" He didn't sound like anyone she knew.

Jenna had no idea the identity of Mr. Friendly. "Could I have some water? I also have to take a piss real bad." Cop terms. Man terms. Something he might understand.

"Just a sec." He turned around. "Hey, the princess wants you."

* * *

"If you don't stop pacing, I'll never find out where she is." Carla shook her head as she shot her gaze upward.

Sam stood still and balled his fists at his side. "Every minute that goes by could spell Jenna's death."

"Like I don't know that? I didn't come here to spend Christmas Eve with you, you know. I am trying to locate her."

Sam shoved a hand through his hair. "Sorry." He'd already spent too much time driving over to Marlon Giombetti's house in Tampa. The police appeared to be working hard at locating Jenna, but they'd only come up with one dead end after another. Carla was Sam's last hope.

Her fingers sped across the keyboard. "Here's something."

"What?" Sam leaned over her back.

"Marlon has property near Clearwater Beach."

"Do you think he'd be dumb enough to take Jenna to his own house?"

"There's only one way to find out." She hit print. The map spit out a moment later. "Go."

With map in hand, Sam raced to Clearwater in under an hour. Marlon's place wasn't hard to find, but no lights were on and Jenna wasn't anywhere nearby. Defeated, he turned around and headed back to Tampa. Before he reached the Howard Franklin bridge, his cell rang. It was Carla. "You find something?"

"Yes. I decided to look into the lives of all the periphery people. Deidra, Marlon, Kathy Bello, Enzio—"

His fingers turned white from holding the phone so tightly. "Just tell me."

"Did you know that Deidra's sister, Shelby, was a practicing surgeon until about five years ago?"

Sam let the information sink in. "Oh shit."

"What?"

"Remember I told you Eric and I had this little disagreement about Creighton Jackson and Rodrico Evans, the man the cops found at Ballast Point? About whether the same person had killed them?"

"Yes. That's why I'm calling. You said the two men had the same cut marks."

"Not exactly the same, but close. I contended two different people had cut them up. Rodrico's murderer wasn't as precise as Creighton's. Eric claimed maybe the guy was rushed since he left before he cut off the man's second hand." The car behind him honked, before speeding around him. Sam checked his speedometer and then accelerated.

"Whatever. I think Marlon might have killed his stepfather, but he had Shelby hack him up."

"You think she's involved because Marlon's stepfather dated Shelby's sister? Jenna told me Deidra's sister just had a baby. I'm not buying it."

"Okay, how about this?" Carla said. "Enzio Giombetti, the brother, served in Iraq as, get this, a medic. Maybe Shelby killed Creighton, and Enzio killed Rodrico."

Sam rolled down the window to let in the cool air to help him think better. "That's a reach, but if it's true, Phil might give you a metal. How does that help me find Jenna though?"

"Just hold your horses. I hacked into Shelby's records, as well as a few other people's accounts. Shelby withdrew fifty thousand dollars from her account two days ago."

Sam whistled. "Any idea what for?" Carla had a knack for learning all sorts of goodies from neighbors.

"I'm thinking it has to be get-away money."

"Let me get this straight. You think new mother Shelby is involved with Marlon and helped him cut up his stepdad, and that she's willing to leave without the kids? Marlon Giombetti might have been a killer, but children need their mother."

"It all fits. I bet she plans on coming back after the investigation settles down and picking them up."

"In the meantime, they'll spend Christmas alone if she did run off. And what about Shelby's husband? Is he involved too?"

"I'm not sure, but that's not why I'm calling."

He exited the bridge on the Tampa side. "Time is running out. Tell me."

"I checked her tax records or rather my FBI friend did. Shelby had a large sales tax deduction last year. Guess what it was for."

"Carla!" He gnashed his teeth together.

CHAPTER TWENTY-EIGHT

A BOAT?" Phil shouted over the phone. "Where?"

A strong salty wind whipped Sam's hair, and he brushed it out of his way. "Shelby keeps it at a local marina off of Davis Island, no less." Carla had given him all the information on Shelby's new purchase, including its location. "I'm here at the marina now, but the boat's gone. According to one of the workers, the boat's named, *The Gambler*. The guy said he saw two women and two men board a while ago. From his description, the second woman might have been Jenna."

"Did he say if one of the women was being held hostage or anything?"

"He said the woman with Shelby looked drunk." Sam's jaw tightened. Jenna might drink a beer, but not more than one. Drinking gave her a headache.

"Probably drugged is more like it."

Sam steeled his mind against the horrors Jenna might be going through. "He actually chatted with Shelby because she took on a lot of supplies. He was curious where she might be headed, especially with a sick woman on board."

"Did she tell him?"

"Mexico."

"Damn it to hell." From the loud bang that came over the receiver, Phil must have slammed his fist on something. "Let's hope to God Marlon doesn't plan on dumping Jenna's body in the middle of the Gulf."

The moment Phil put the terrifying thought into words, panic gripped Sam. "Don't even think that." Drawing on his special forces training, his rapid pulse slowed.

"You're Mr. Navy Seal. This rescue mission should be right up your alley. What do you suggest?"

"You're asking me? You're the cop." Or ex-cop.

"You have the training for a sea rescue."

"I only half completed the course, so I'm no Navy Seal, but I did train long enough to know how to deal with this kind of situation." His mind raced through the options, discarding most as too dangerous for Jenna. His logical mind latched onto an idea. "Get me near the boat and I'll take it from there."

"How near do you need to be?" Sam appreciated the vote of confidence.

"Drop me off about a half mile away. It's dark. Marlon, or whoever is involved, probably won't think a boat that far off is a threat. Just don't have the name Coast Guard blazoned on the side of whatever you find."

"You want to swim in?" Phil sounded incredulous.

"With a tank, it'll be easy. I don't want anything motorized as sound travels." He listed a few extras he'd like to have.

"I'll see what I can do. It'll be Christmas morning in a few hours. This might be tough to get everything set up in time."

"Jenna needs our help. Besides, you're Phil, the superhero, remember?" At least that's what Gina always called him.

"I'm hardly superhero material, but I'll find something. Don't worry."

The stench of dead fish hit him, and Sam turned his back to the wind. "If you can't get the scuba gear, I'll swim."

"Got it. I'll call Lucas and get back with you."

It was times like these he wished he smoked or drank to take the edge off. The waiting and uncertainty might kill him before he was able to hold Jenna in his arms to tell her how foolish he'd been and how much he missed her laughter. "Hurry."

* * *

CHILLS RACKED JENNA'S BODY. The big man who'd come in to check on her had been nice enough to let her use the head. Most likely, her captor was worried about having to clean up any messes if he hadn't let her go. The man stood outside the door until she was done, claiming he wanted to make sure she wasn't injured with all the rocking. Right. As if she even had the strength to climb out the porthole above the toilet, or head, or whatever the hell it was called.

Her *host* even provided her with something to eat and drink. While Jenna wasn't sure what caused her abdominal pain and fever a half hour after eating, she suspected her captor might have put something in the food. She'd run the gamut of being so hot she could barely breathe, to feeling like someone had doused her veins with ice water. She didn't remember the man giving her any more needles, but hallucinations had a way of changing reality.

Unless she'd caught some horrible disease whose symptoms mimicked the black plague, the jerk had to be responsible for her disturbing condition. Only what would he get out of it? Was his game to make Jenna as miserable as possible? Weren't the ropes enough?

If her captors wanted to do away with her, why wait? Or were they hoping she'd die from this disease and an autopsy would exonerate them? Her mind couldn't focus long enough to come up with a plausible answer.

The door opened to Jenna's small cabin—a cabin where the room was ninety percent bed. "How are you feeling, Jenna?"

That voice. She knew it. "Shelby? What you are doing here?"

"Didn't Marlon tell you?"

Marlon was here? Shit. So Kathy was right. Her brother had lost his mind. "Tell me what?"

"That he and I are seeing each other."

Okay, none of this was making sense. "I thought you just had a baby."

"I did. She's Marlon's."

"But you're married."

She chuckled, but there was no joy in her tone. "You're more naïve than I imagined." Jenna choked on her saliva and Shelby rushed over. "You okay? Are you coming down with a cold?"

"Cold, hell, you drugged me."

"It wasn't my idea to bring you here."

How stupid did Shelby think she was? "So Marlon is behind all of this?"

"For the most part." She waved a hand. "But we need to get you some help. Let's call your boyfriend."

Her mind fogged. "Sam? Why would you call him?" Jenna wasn't going to mention they'd broken up.

"Who else would come out in the middle of the Gulf to save you? The manifold, or something to do with the engine, broke, and we're stuck here indefinitely. I don't want my poor kids to spend Christmas alone, and I'm sure you want to get off this boat for more than one reason."

Shelby was making no sense. "Call the Coast Guard. They'll save us."

"On Christmas?" She waved a hand. "Let's call Sam. What's his number?"

As if Shelby didn't know. Jenna's mind wouldn't allow her to think through her options. More chills wracked her body, and an intense abdominal pain took her breath away. She needed to hear Sam's voice. "You don't have to wake him. Wait until tomorrow morning."

"You need help now."

Was Shelby for real? Jenna would do anything to have Sam by her side. "It's 813-555-9837." Jenna's breaths turned shallower as fear pushed her heart faster. What was happening to her?

Shelby smiled and punched in the number. Her smile turned upside down. "Sam? It's Deidra's sister, Shelby. Did I wake you?...I'm so sorry. We have a problem."

Is that what she was? A mere problem? Jenna strained to hear his reaction. "Sam?" Jenna panted. She stretched out her hand for the phone, but Shelby waved her away.

"You hear that? Jenna can barely talk. We went out for a cruise and Jenna must have eaten something bad. She's quite sick. Can you come and get her? I think she needs to go to the hospital... I wish I could, but my engine died, can you believe it? I have three little ones at home waiting for Santa, and I'm stuck in the middle of the Gulf of Mexico... I know you don't have a boat, but I've figured that out. I've called my mechanic already. He was on his way down to Punta Gorda for some fishing but was willing to take a little detour. He's heading into Clearwater now to pick up some parts." She gave Sam the address of the marina. "When I told him I planned to call you, he said for you to come with him. ...What's that?... He said he doesn't have time to take her to the hospital, but he's willing to drop her off at the docks if you'll babysit her while he heads back."

Shelby actually made sense. They were stranded. Her mechanic, who must have asked for an extraordinary amount of money, was willing to come out here in the middle of the night—on Christmas Eve no less—and save them. She didn't blame the poor man for not wanting to take care of her.

Apparently, Sam agreed and Shelby disconnected. "Well, that's settled."

"I don't understand."

"About what?"

"If you get your engine working, why not take me back to shore yourself?" She knew the answer. Neither Shelby nor Martin had any intention of taking her or Sam back to land. They're goal would be to dump them into the sea. Poor Sam. It wasn't fair he had to be mixed up in this mess.

"I don't have time to go back. I have a date in Mexico."

Jenna's mind latched onto the tropical paradise—sandy beaches, Mayan pyramids, great food, and peace. She'd never been there, but she bet she'd like it. "What about your kids?"

Jenna's eyes rolled into the back of her head and dozed off without hearing the answer.

* * *

"SORRY IT TOOK ME SO LONG." Phil wheeled down the ramp to where Sam and four other officers congregated. "Mr. Pomerantz's personal yacht will be escorting you just as soon as it arrives."

The H and P in HOPEFAL were named after Henry Pomerantz. The man was a true altruist. "Please thank him for me. Did you get any gear?"

"State of the art scuba gear is on the boat."

"Awesome." Sam nodded toward the bank of clouds rolling in. "The fog will help camouflage our arrival."

"Let's hope the weather stays that way."

Now he'd have no problem reaching Jenna and saving her. Hopefully, she'd still be alive.

Sheldon Meyers, Larry Bernard's partner, drove up and raced down the gangplank. "What do you need me to do?"

"Pretend to be Sam," Phil said. "You'll go with the mechanic instead of Sam, assuming the man shows up at all." Phil turned to Sam. "You said Shelby has never met you, right?"

"Right. Sheldon and I are about the same height, build, and coloring. In the dark Shelby won't realize there's been a switch. I've got a cap in my car that has the HOPEFAL logo on it. Sheldon, the visor will help cover your face."

"If Marlon is on the boat, he'll know what's up," Sheldon said.

Phil shook his head. "By then Sam will be on his way to the boat. Just keep them busy until he arrives."

Sheldon held up his hand. "I'm armed to the teeth, so it shouldn't be a problem."

Phil tapped the arms of his chair. "Good."

Sam raced to his car, returned with the hat, and handed it to Sheldon.

"Thanks." Sheldon slapped it on his head.

"I'll be damned. You two could be twins," Phil said with a smile. "T

The sound of an engine rounded the corner and Phil sobered. "Everyone but Sheldon take cover." He pointed to Sam's stunt double. "You know what to do."

"Yes, sir."

Sam pushed Phil in his wheelchair up to the parking lot where they hid behind his car and waited. The other four men with Sam scattered. One would hide on the trawler, while the others would make sure the repairman was on the same page before they hopped on *The Pomerantz* with Sam.

A beat up trawler pulled into Shelby's vacant slip. A man in jeans with a scruffy beard and thick around the waist, jumped off the boat. He ran a line to the dock.

Sheldon jogged up to the man. "Hey. You going out to Mrs. Vivaldi's boat?"

"You Sam Bonita?" the guy asked.

"Sure am."

"Then hop on. I want to get something from my storage shed. I keep spare parts and other tools there."

Once the owner disappeared, Phil motioned his men to get into position. The tall, muscular cop, dressed in a black vest and helmet, jumped on the boat and slipped into the cabin. Sheldon climbed on board and paced the small deck, looking like an expectant father. Sam had to hand it to him. A casual onlooker would believe this man was Sam Bonita, a man worried about his sick girlfriend.

The boat captain/repairman returned with a duffle bag. Phil waved to the remaining men on the dock. In a flash, two officers came up behind the mechanic and grabbed him.

The scuffle was short-lived with the officers the victors.

"What the hell is going on here?" The mechanic continued to struggle despite being outnumbered.

Phil wheeled down the ramp and flashed his badge. "Can I see what's in the bag?"

"No."

"Arrest him."

"For what? I'm just taking this guy to see his woman."

"How do you know Shelby?" Phil asked.

"I worked on her boat a few times. That's all."

Phil nodded to the bag. "I'll ask once more. What's in the bag?"

One of the officers drew the mechanic's hands behind his back and cuffed him, his bag dangling from his fingers. "My tools. Aw, shit. Here." He dropped the bag and stepped to the side.

Phil scavenged through the contents but acted as though nothing appeared out of order. "Tools."

"Told you."

Sam couldn't help but wonder why the man fussed so much at showing the bag. Before he could question the mechanic, the sound of a large yacht motored toward them.

"Sam, your ride is here," Phil said.

Sheldon emerged from the cabin and hopped off the boat. "I'll need the keys." He held out his hand to the mechanic.

The mechanic, if indeed he could fix a boat, handed them over.

"Uncuff him." Phil nodded and the officer obeyed. "Let's go."

"Why do you need me if you got him on board?" The captain nodded to the tall cop.

"I imagine Shelby would become a little suspicious if we pulled up and you weren't on the boat," Phil answered.

He curled his lip. "What's to prevent me for giving away your little cop-on-board operation?"

"If you're not guilty, why would you?"

The man shrugged. "For the record, I didn't do anything wrong. I'm trying to fix a boat."

"How much is she paying you?"

"Two grand. No one else would give up Christmas Eve to fix a boat." He shrugged. "I ain't got any family, so I don't care. The money's good."

"Did she give you coordinates of her location?" Phil pulled out a pad and pen.

The man shoved a hand into his pocket and pulled out a piece of paper. "Here. I already programmed this into the GPS."

The beat up boat didn't look sophisticated enough to have that kind of equipment, but looks often were deceiving. Before he had a chance to check out the man's claim, Sam went aboard *The Pomerantz*.

"Good luck," Phil said, as he waved to the crew.

Sam stood at the stern as they motored away from the marina. He bet it killed Phil to stay behind. Sam imagined once a homicide detective, always a homicide detective. The need to help never left the soul.

Once the two boats passed the last buoys, the powerboat sped up.

They would reach their destination long before the trawler, giving Sam time to swim to Mrs. Vivaldi's boat. The yacht would drop him off and pretend to head out to sea, and Shelby Vivaldi would never suspect a thing.

The scuba gear was stretched out on the back deck. Without saying a word, Sam took the tank and suit below to begin his rescue mission.

* * *

BLACKNESS SHROUDED SAM'S VISION. He swam close to the surface and headed for the small bobbing light in the distance. The quality gear kept him warm, but his nerves made him shiver. Ten years was a long time without training. Sure, he might run every day, but that didn't keep him in Navy Seal shape.

Maintaining even breaths, Sam blocked out the possibility of failure and pictured sweet Jenna.

Swim to Jenna. Swim to Jenna.

Lights from the trawler cast an eerie glow as the boat moved closer to *The Gambler*. Needing to time his arrival for when the two boats made contact, Sam pushed harder, his strokes smooth. Two people, with their backs to him, stood at the stern, obviously awaiting the mechanic's arrival. The short, round person, was probably Shelby. The man next to her was at least six four, but thin, even with his bulky sweatshirt. He'd seen Marlon Giombetti once, and he wasn't even six feet. That made at least three people on the boat. So where was the cop?

Sam dove about two hundred feet from the boat and resurfaced as he arrived at the bow. The trawler's lights reflected off the water as he drew near. The mechanic called out something, but Sam couldn't quite hear over the rumbling engine noise and the slap of the waves.

"Everything okay?" Sweatshirt Man said to the trawler captain.

"Yup."

Sam prayed the ruse would play out as planned. With Shelby and her accomplice distracted, Sam studied his options. He glanced to the cabin area, but no lights glared. Was Jenna asleep inside or up on deck? He refused to ponder she might be dead.

Treading water, he removed a state-of-the-art grappling hook and attached rope velcroed to the side of his leg and opened the prongs. With a toss, the rubber claw latched onto the metal railing on the first try. Yes. He hadn't lost his touch. Sam gave a good tug to test its stability. It held. Good.

A large swell lifted him up, and then down, making maneuvering difficult. He submerged, lifted off his tank and shot back to the surface. After tying the tank to the end of a rope, which dangled five feet below the hull, he repeated the process with his fins. Now for the hard part. Hand over hand, he inched his way up the thin line, his rubber shoes helping with the grip on the side of the boat. Half way up, he swallowed a groan from the exertion.

"You hear something?" Shelby said. Sam froze and dangled on the side, his hands slipping.

"Hear what?"

"Like something scraping against the boat."

"It was probably a fish. Why don't you get Jenna from below?"

Jenna's alive! His heart sang, but Sam didn't move a muscle until the cabin door banged open.

With renewed energy, he hoisted himself up the rest of the way, hooking a leg over the rail to leverage his body onto the walkway. He stilled, and then listened to see if any of them had noticed his arrival. When no one sent out any warning shouts, Sam crawled toward the bow, away from Shelby and Sweatshirt Man, believing at least one other person was on board—Marlon Giombetti.

He didn't worry about the trawler's crew giving him away as TPD's finest would keep a keen eye on the mechanic. Sam slipped a small stun gun from his waist, ready for action. The loud chatter at the stern made moving around easier. He decided to stay at the bow and wait for the right moment to spring Jenna.

Footsteps, followed by a groan, caught his attention. On his belly, Sam slithered along the cabin roof to look through the windshield. Covered in black neoprene from head to toe, Sam had blackened his face with grease paint to avoid detection. Except for the whites of his eyes, he should be virtually invisible to those on deck.

Shelby's accomplice held Jenna up by the armpits, moving her toward the trawler. What was going on? The mechanic jumped aboard Shelby's boat and smiled. Something wasn't right.

Jenna's head lolled to the side. Sweatshirt Man swore, lifted Jenna up in his arms and passed her over to Sheldon who'd come on board. In good undercover form, Sheldon kissed her forehead. Something inside Sam snapped despite knowing his look-a-like was only acting.

Jenna's legs twitched, and Sheldon carefully stood her on her feet to face him. She appeared conscious. When she swayed, Sheldon wrapped both his arms around her waist. Her hands pushed on his chest. Oh God, he hoped she wouldn't blow his cover.

Sheldon twisted her away from the prying eyes and whispered something in her ear. Her legs gave way and Sheldon scooped her up in his arms. "I'll put her down below."

Sheldon deftly leapt from Shelby's boat to the trawler. Thank God, Jenna was safe.

The urge to run to her overwhelmed him, but Sam stayed put. Giving away his position too soon would jeopardize the mission.

Shelby's motive for handing over Jenna made no sense. Shelby wouldn't have given up this easily. Or had he misjudged her?

Sheldon came out of the trawler's cabin area after placing Jenna in the cabin and picked up the mechanic's duffle. "You need this, don't you, to fix Mrs. Vivaldi's engine?"

Smart, Sheldon. He was testing the captain to see if he was for real or a fraud.

The mechanic held up his hand. "In a minute." He moved across to *The Gambler*, lifted the engine hood and banged on the metal with some of the tools he'd carried over with him. He tugged on a few wires and made more noise than Sam thought necessary.

"Hey, Sam?"

Sam jerked at hearing his name. Thank goodness he didn't respond. Sheldon did. "What do you need?"

"I can use the bag now."

Sheldon tossed it over to the mechanic. Just then, someone else came up from the cabin. From his height and size, Sam guessed it was Marlon.

"What are you doing?" Marlon asked the repairman.

"Fixing the goddamn engine." He held up a wrench. "Hold this."

Marlon obeyed. The mechanic wiggled two of the wires. "I think I found your problem. Start the engine."

Marlon moved the controls and turned the key, and the engine jumped to life. "Well, I'll be," he said. "We didn't need a new engine after all."

Shelby turned to Mr. Sweatshirt. "Be a dear and pay the man."

The tall man stuffed an envelope into the mechanic's large duffle that contained his tools. He handed the bag back to Sheldon who'd been watching intently from the trawler.

The mechanic stood. "You'll all set, Mrs. Vivaldi. Merry Christmas."

"Merry Christmas," Shelby chirped back.

The mechanic unhooked the rope connecting the two boats and slid into his Captain's chair. He waved, acting as if all were well. In less than ten seconds, they were off. Thank God Jenna was safe.

Confused what had transpired, Sam slid back toward the bow and waited until Marlon and his colleagues went below. The cabin lights illuminated the interior, giving Sam further protection from being spotted. On his belly again, he took hold of the grappling hook and lowered himself into the cool water. After unhooking his scuba tank from the rope, he headed back towards *The Pomerantz*. Before he'd gone a quarter mile, a loud explosion rocked his world, and a huge light lit the night sky. Wood showered the sky and he swallowed a mouthful of seawater from the huge wake.

Oh, my God. The trawler had exploded.

CHAPTER TWENTY-NINE

SAM DOVE under the water and kicked and pumped his arms until he made it back to *The Gambler* before they were underway. When he surfaced, the three occupants were cheering.

Motherfuckers.

He'd make them pay.

With scuba tank on his back, he hoisted himself up the side of *The Gambler*, not quite sure what how he planned to stop them. Debris floated alongside and banged into the boat. He squeezed his eyes shut, trying to control the fury racing through his body. No way was he going to let these people who killed the woman he loved get away with it.

Love. He knew for sure the hope and joy that had seeped into his heart from knowing Jenna, was called love. Damn Marlon for ripping her away from him.

From the bow of the boat, Sam glanced behind him and located small pinpricks of light a good one to two miles away. *The Pomerantz* crew wouldn't be much help for another few minutes.

His new mission was to stop Marlon from abandoning those left behind. *The Gambler*'s engine kicked into gear and chugged forward at a leisurely pace—away from the graveyard. Bastards. Marlon and

Shelby would believe all the witnesses were dead, so they could take their sweet time.

No doubt, both Marlon and the giant were armed, so a direct attack wouldn't be wise. Sam crouched low and crept down the walkway toward the stern. Sweatshirt Man didn't seem to notice he had another passenger. Sam dropped onto the deck behind him. With soft rubber shoes to dampen any noise, Sam took three steps forward and dove at the man at the helm.

"What the fuck?" the man said, as he fell forward into the steering wheel, hitting his head on the metal gearshift. The boat veered slightly eastward.

With Sam's forearm around Sweatshirt's throat and a hand over his mouth, the man's oxygen starved body crumbled to the deck a few minutes later. Before the man on the deck came to, Sam needed to secure him. He rushed to the storage unit under the seats at the stern and pulled out a line, hoping neither Marlon or Shelby decided now was the time for an outdoor nightcap. Tying up Sweatshirt Man took less than a minute. Sam's training had kicked into high gear. Finding a greasy rag to gag the guy took longer.

The sound of the purring engine must have drowned out his attack because Shelby and Marlon remained below. A pot clanged. Was she making an early breakfast?

"Sorry, buddy," Sam whispered. He stuffed the cloth into the unconscious man's mouth and wrapped the rope around his face to ensure he wouldn't be able to make a sound when he came to.

While Sam had never harmed a woman, this one might prove the exception. Taking down Marlon would be no problem if he could catch him by surprise. Once Sam reduced the speed of the boat to half to keep him near the wreck, Sam hopped up on the boat's walkway and slipped to the bow.

After taking off his tank and placing it securely on a neatly wound pile of rope, he eased open the door to the main cabin.

With no one at the helm, the boat hit a wake and teetered to the side. Marlon swore. Sam took that moment to attack. Stun gun poised, he slammed open the door.

Shelby's eyes widened as a hand rushed to her mouth. Marlon's gaze shot to the Sig Sauer on the table. Before he had a chance to reach the weapon, Sam pounced. He grabbed Marlon's arms behind his back, glad he didn't have to taser him. Mr. Pomerantz had equipped his suit with the stun gun but also with a pair of lightweight cuffs. Proactive bugger.

Shelby screamed. She stepped forward, but Sam raised the stun gun at her. "Don't even think about it."

Her jaw tight and her teeth bared, Shelby looked like she wanted to claw him to death. "How did you get in here?" She glanced at the helm.

"Your friend will not be coming to your rescue. He's tied up."

"But—"

"As soon as I see about the boat you blew up, all three of us will have a chat."

He secured Shelby and made sure Marlon wouldn't be going anywhere either. With the Sig Sauer in hand, Sam rushed to the helm and turned the boat around. Through the dense fog, he thought he caught sight of a flickering light. The water lapped against the sides and the wind whistled across the stern, sending the canvas flaps in spasms. If any survivor did call out, he wouldn't be able to hear even if he cut the engine.

Shelby shouted something from below, but he ignored her. A quick glance at Sweatshirt Man assured Sam he wouldn't be an issue either.

Once he reached the trawler's debris, Sam cut the engine, fearful a body might be floating in the black water.

"Jenna?" Sam's voice cracked as he called out. Why did he bother? No one could have survived the blast.

Marlon cursed from below. Behind him, *The Pomerantz* forged toward them.

Sam cupped his mouth and yelled again. "Sheldon? Jenna?" It was no use. They were all dead.

A faint shout returned, and adrenaline surged through him. He called again to make sure his mind wasn't playing tricks on him. Was the wind calling to him? Sam raced to the covered storage at the rear and lifted the seat. He pulled out a rope ladder and slapped it over the side.

Blood pounding in his head, he dove under the water and swam in the direction of the faint voice.

When he surfaced, he located the light undulating in the sea. "Jenna?"

"Over here," several voices shouted in more or less unison. He refused to contemplate why he hadn't heard her sweet voice in the mix.

Pumped, Sam raced toward them. As he neared, the fog thinned, exposing a life raft. How could this be? He reached a hand onto the edge of the rubber boat. Sheldon clasped his palm. "God, it's so good to see you. We weren't even sure if *The Pomerantz* would find us." The moon reflected off Sheldon's white teeth.

Sam hung onto the side of the raft, his legs dangling in the cold water. Jenna lay curled in a fetal position on the bottom, her head on a blanket. "How is she?"

"Really sick," the tall cop said. "When Sheldon brought her into the cabin, she was conscious, complaining her head and stomach hurt. She lay down on the sofa and never woke up. Mr. Snyder here," nodding to the mechanic, "informed us Shelby planned to blow up his craft in an attempt to murder Jenna and Sheldon, or rather, you."

"That's why Shelby had readily handed her over."

The mechanic sat across from Sheldon, his hands cuffed behind him, his lips pressed together.

Sam checked out the boat's owner. "You didn't mind sacrificing your trawler?"

"She paid me more than it was worth."

"How was it supposed to go down?"

"The timer was set to go off four minutes after I left. Shelby had the remote. Of course, I didn't expect to have the cops aboard to slow me down."

"We checked the bag at the marina and didn't see any explosives."

"When Shelby's friend paid me, the C-4 was wedged in between the money."

"Clever. So the engine never had a problem."

"No."

Figures. Sam pulled a small flare from a side pocket and handed it to Sheldon. "Pull this tab and *The Pomerantz* will find you."

Sam dropped back into the water.

"Where are you going?" Sheldon asked.

"I need to return to Marlon and Shelby. I didn't want to drive in through the debris field and run over you guys. I never thought you'd be in a raft."

Happy for the first time in days, Sam swam back to the boat with strong, even strokes. As he climbed up the ladder, *The Pomerantz* pulled along side.

* * *

JENNA OPENED HER EYES. The room light hurt her eyes, but seeing the wonderful man sitting across from her hospital bed made up for the pain.

"Hi," she said with cottonmouth.

"How are you feeling?" Sam asked.

She took a quick assessment. "My stomach still hurts a little." She looked around. "How did I get here?"

"Sheldon saved you." He told her about Shelby and Marlon's plan to blow up the trawler with both of them on it.

"And here I thought she was nice. Where is the bitch?"

Sam smiled. "In custody, along with Sweatshirt Man and Marlon."

"Why do you think she wanted me killed?"

"They aren't really talking, but from what I could piece together from Kathy Bello and Shelby's husband, Shelby and Marlon have been having an affair for some time. She wanted *Botanica* for herself, as well as Marlon. Together they devised this plan to kill Marlon's dad."

"Fine, but why me?"

"He wanted to hurt your dad because of the affair."

"That's what Enzio told me. Creighton Jackson must have been one mean son of a bitch to cause this much hatred."

Sam leaned over and took her hand. "Enough talking about the bad people." He rubbed his thumb over her palm and a deep, warm feeling flowed through her. "We need to talk about us."

Joy blasted her. "Us?"

A knock sounded on the door and her nurse came in. "Ah, you're up. I'll send the doctor in."

Ten minutes later, the doctor showed up and checked her out. "He turned to Sam. Will you be staying with her? She'll need someone to take care of her for a day or two."

Sam smiled. "You get."

Then you are free to go home," the doctor said.

"Thank you." Before anyone else came in, she eased out of bed with Sam's help and changed in the bathroom with the clothes he'd picked up from her house.

Another knock sounded. This time it was her dad. "Heard about the harrowing event."

That was a good word. "I'm fine."

"You don't look fine." He wheeled closer, and a tear slipped down his cheek. "I can't believe I almost lost you."

Sam stood, but her father stayed him with a hand. "Stay. Both of you need to hear this. Bill stopped by and filled me in what happened."

"Bill?"

He half chuckled. "Bill Lucas."

Ah, her boss. "And?"

"They did a search in Marlon's house and found several skulls. Since Sam was busy saving you, we had his assistant compare the skulls to those in your mom's mausoleum."

"They found a match?"

"Yup. Your mother's body is now complete, as are the other skulls."

"Thank God Marlon hadn't desecrated them."

He dragged his hands down his face. "I wanted to tell you how sorry I am for all of this."

Sorry? She didn't think her father even knew the word. "Because of what you did to Mom?" She held up her hand. "Because of why you retaliated against Mom I should say."

"Yes. I knew you'd gone out with Marlon, but I thought it was ironic. His mother made me promise not to say anything. When the relationship between the two of you died a month later, I thought I was in the clear."

His cheeks sagged so hard she thought his heart would stop. "It's okay."

"No, it's not. It's all my fault that you almost died."

"You almost died too. I wouldn't be surprised if Marlon shot you himself."

"I was thinking the same thing. I realize that if Louise and I hadn't had our fling, her husband wouldn't have left her, and the kids and the boys wouldn't have turned into such bad men."

"The worst part is that Chance had to die, when Marlon meant to kill me."

"That's true. I'm glad the man who carried out the act, Enzio, is dead."

"Tell that to Carla. She lost two people she loved because of him." Her father's shoulders trembled and more tears streaked down his cheeks. She'd never seen him fall apart like this. "Don't beat yourself up. You didn't know."

"That doesn't excuse all the hurt." He reached up and squeezed her hand. "Whatever you think of me, I do love you."

Before she could answer, he spun away and left.

Sam cleared his throat. "That was intense."

"I never thought I'd ever hear those three little words from him. That's twice in one week."

"How could he not love you?"

The glassiness in his eyes told her something she could only hope for.

"Well I do keep secrets sometimes."

Sam gathered her into his arms. "We all have secrets. It was your job to keep one."

She studied him. "You believe that?"

"Yes. However, I'd like to hear about your mother's skull."

"You know about that? How?"

"Sheldon."

That rat. "It's a long story." From now on, she wouldn't withhold anything from him.

"I've got the time."

Her heart fluttered, and it wasn't from the left over drugs in her system. "Let me finish dressing, and I'll start from the beginning." She might have to leave out one of the reasons she wanted to date him in the first place and focus solely on how much she liked him.

Sam picked up the rest of the clothes he'd brought, and using a wheelchair, guided Jenna down the hospital elevator. "By the way, while you were out of commission this morning, Sheldon stopped by the hospital."

"I'm sorry I missed him. I'll thank him once I return to work."

"I'm sure he'll appreciate it."

Half an hour later, Sam pulled into her driveway. He scooted out and opened the passenger door. Her heart fluttered at his chivalry. She didn't want to ask him about his future plans for fear she wasn't part of them, wasn't part of the *us* he'd been about to discuss before her dad showed up.

The quick change of positions from sitting to standing caused Jenna's blood pressure to drop. She faltered. Sam's strong arm wrapped around her. "Are you okay?"

"Just a little dizzy."

"You should have stayed at the hospital longer."

"No way."

Despite the blazing sun, the chill in the air made her shiver. He hugged her closer as he led her inside.

"Flowers?" Jenna made a beeline to the counter. A card and a gold box sat next to the vase. She turned to him, her heart racing at the implication.

"I came over last night to apologize."

"Apologize?" Her hands sweated. *Please, God, let him say he wants to stay.*

"I kind of overreacted to your announcement about you working undercover."

Her heart pounded. Jenna ran a hand down his arm. "I wanted to tell you so many times, but I knew you'd be upset. Then when I did tell you—"

"Shh. It's over." Sam leaned down and kissed her. Soft, gentle, and oh so nice.

She stepped back. "Ah, while I adore kissing you, you kind of smell of sea water and something else I don't want to think about. And I ain't so sweet either. So..."

Sam's laugh came out throaty. "What do you suggest?" The twinkle in his eye urged her on.

"A shower—together." He wouldn't hear of it when she suggested this at his house. Would he now?

"Oh, yeah, that's what I'm talking about."

Yes! Sam clasped both of her hands and backpedaled into the bathroom. Without taking his gaze off her, he flung his shirt over his head and dropped it on the bathroom floor. Before she had a chance to unzip her pants, he slipped out of his jeans and kicked the material to the corner. He didn't have to remove his boxers for her to see where this was headed.

Sam turned on the shower. "Need to warm it up first." He took a step toward her. "You look like you need help."

"I'm not moving because I'm in shock."

His brow creased. "Over what?" He dragged a knuckle down her cheek and her insides melted.

Sam's brows rose, obviously waiting for her to answer. He unbuttoned her shirt and slipped it over her shoulders. The bra came next. "Spit it out," he said.

"Aren't you going to pick up your clothes off the floor?"

He ran a tongue along the edge of his teeth. "Nope. I have better things to do."

She giggled and stepped closer to him. Stink be damned. "Do tell." Jenna melted into his arms. Her hands slide down his muscular back. Hooking her thumbs in his boxers, she slid them over his hard, luscious rump. Sam stepped back and dropped his briefs, his erection at attention. "Now, that's what *I'm* talking about. She couldn't help but laugh with joy.

He then pulled her into the warm, soothing shower. Facing Sam, Jenna let the pulsating water sluice over her head and down her back.

"Feel good?" he asked.

"The best."

"Let's see if I can make the experience even better for you." He winked and grabbed her liquid soap.

After dribbling the soap on her breasts, he dragged his palms up and down, around and around, causing her nipples to harden and her sex to moisten in anticipation.

While he tended to her front, she shampooed her scalp. Salt and blood had caked her skull. Jenna scrubbed, but her focus was on what Sam was doing to her body and not on the pleasure of getting clean.

When Sam's hands traveled down her waist to the juncture of her thighs, she couldn't help but moan. "I may have to have you wash me everyday."

"I plan to."

Her eyes widened. Dare she hope what that might mean?

He pulled her to him and kissed her with more passion than ever before. Their tongues danced in and out, savoring each other, until he came up for a breath and pulled back. Sam ran his gaze up and down her body. "I love you, Jenna Holliday."

She stilled. Was he kidding? "You mean it?"

"Yeah, I mean it." He ran his fingers through her soapy hair. "I haven't been able to sleep at night since I walked out. Your image is burned into my mind and keeps haunting me. You've become part of my soul." He lowered his hands to her cheeks, kissed her nose, and then dabbed foam on the tip. "I love how you make me feel. You're so free, and so excited about life. For the first time, I'm tempted to throw caution to the wind."

She raised a brow. Leaving his clothes on the floor was the first step to freedom. His eyes turned dark from what she wasn't certain. "Let's not get too out of control, here. You aren't thinking of quitting your job at HOPEFAL or anything are you?"

"No. I love helping people find closure. But I think I'll stay in the lab and let the police do the legwork."

She understood the helping people part. Jenna maneuvered him around and let Sam enjoy the warm water. "My turn," she said, shooting him her wickedest grin.

Jenna dumped a handful of soap on her hands, and starting with his gorgeous chest, lathered his neck, and then trailed a finger down his pecs. The soap slid over his abs and settled into his navel. His cock jumped up and down, making her laugh. "I think someone is vying for my attention."

"He needs to be cleaned too."

"I'll be happy to oblige." With deft fingers, she rubbed him up and down, the smooth, slick soap making the movement easy.

Sam grabbed her hand. "If you continue doing what you're doing, we'll end up on the floor or against the wall."

"And that would be bad, why?"

He nipped at her ear. "While I could stay in here with you for a long time, I want to explore you more thoroughly."

"What's with you and the bed?"

"You'll see."

Sam dragged Jenna out of the shower, but she insisted on drying him. She dragged the thirsty towel down his back, and then over his way too luscious rear end, and finally over his legs. She didn't miss the chance to draw the towel between his thighs either.

"Jenna."

"What?"

He took the towel from her and carefully squeezed the water from her hair. The massaging of her breasts drove her so crazy that she was forced to snap the towel from him. "Okay, enough already. I can dry myself on the sheets." She grabbed his hand and pulled him out of the bathroom. At the entrance to the bedroom, he stopped. "Jenna, before we go in, I need to ask you something."

Dear God, why was he torturing her. "Hurry. What?"

Sam stilled her hands. "I know I don't have much, and my family is a mess, but will you marry me?"

Jenna froze. "You want to marry me?" Her voice rose.

He touched her nipples again, his calloused fingers heightening the sensation. "Unless you want to throw me out on the street, I'm here to stay." He tossed her a pathetic excuse for a frown.

"Oh, no. I have lots of plans for you."

"I hope it involves giving me a few kids."

"For real?"

"For real."

She ran a finger down his chest and past his belly button. "If you want kids, we better get started." Then she grabbed his erection.

"I can handle that, but I've changed my mind."

Her heart nearly wedged between her rib cage and stomach. "About what?"

He smiled. "The bed."

She didn't understand until he pressed her against the door. Total body contact sent every nerve ending into high gear.

"Ever since I met you, I've had this fantasy," he said. His lids half lowered as he leaned closer to her. "Wrap your legs around my waist." He grabbed her butt and helped her up.

His tongue darted in her mouth and she met his every thrust and parry. "I like it."

"I have a lot more ideas like this."

"Do tell." She kissed his still wet cheek, his whiskers rough against her lips. "You need a shave."

"I don't have time. I can't wait to have you." He closed his eyes. "I've dreamed of this for days."

He slid into her, his thick, wide cock sending her body into joyous ecstasy. With her hands on his shoulder, she dropped her head and reveled in the wonderful man. Sam nuzzled her neck and plunged deeper into her.

"God, what you do to me," she gasped.

He lifted her off him and set her down, the void shocking her. "What's wrong?"

"Absolutely nothing." Sam swept her off her feet, carried her to the bed and gently placed her down, wet hair and all. The moment he climbed on top of her, she scooted from underneath and rolled him over. "Now it's my turn."

"For what?"

"To take control. You're just lucky I don't have any handcuffs in the house."

"You wouldn't."

"Bet me." Jenna giggled, spread her thighs and sat on him, taking him inside.

Sam grabbed her waist and tried to set the rhythm but that went against her plan. "Let go. Enjoy the pleasure."

Jenna slid up to his tip and stopped.

Sam grunted. "Don't make me wait."

She leaned over and kissed him. "I love you, and I want you. You make me feel safe." Then she lowered her body and engulfed him.

Lifting his hips, Sam pumped hard. Blood pounded in her ears so hard, Jenna forgot the teasing, forgot the control, and let love wash over her.

A second after she climaxed, Sam sent his seed into her. Sated, she rolled off him and curled up next to him. She then dragged a finger down his lips. "Here's to ridding the world of all the bad and embracing what is good."

"I'm all for that, my undercover wonder."

* * *

EXCERPT-BURIED DEEP

I HOPE you enjoyed Sam and Jenna's story. If you want to be sure to find out about my specials and new releases, sign up for my newsletter or follow me on BookBub.

Next up is BURIED DEEP, and here is the first chapter.

Dead bodies left in plain sight are often the hardest to find.

When Dr. Lara Romano, a profoundly deaf forensic anthropologist, first examines the exhumed skeletons of two Native American men buried in Tampa, she has no idea she's caught the eye of a serial killer.

Missing Persons detective Trevor Kinsey needs a high profile case to land him a job in Homicide. Though he suspects the attractive rookie scientist, Dr. Romano, may hinder his success, he believes the cadavers in her investigation are linked to his current case—eight missing men, all Native Americans, all believed to be dead.

Both are determined to find evidence that will lead the police to the killer's doorstep. What they don't expect is to lose their hearts to each other in the process, or end up as the killer's next targets.

Tampa, Florida

Joe Merrick's worn shirt stuck to his back. He wasn't sure if it was from sweat or the damn muggy air. Didn't matter. He was long past caring anyway.

Slurred curses came from behind the dumpster. What the hell was taking Chester so long? A man could only hold so much pee. Even a drunk couldn't go forever. He took a step to see what was holding up his friend and stumbled over a beer can. *Shit. They never should have bought that second bottle of Jack.*

Let Chester find his own damn way home—if he ever stopped peeing.

As Joe staggered toward his black pickup wedged between two big ass vans, his fingers fought with the keys in his pocket. They were stuck on a damn thread that seemed as strong as a fishing line. *Goddammit.*

He was still struggling when the sound of gravel crunching under a pair of heavy boots came up behind him. *Chester doesn't wear no boots.*

With his hands still his pocket, something sharp shot into Joe's lower back. What the fuck? Red hot pain radiated down his legs and up his back, pressing into his heart. It hurt so bad, he couldn't even take a step.

A forearm clamped hard across his throat, the sleeve scratching his neck. "You filthy Indian."

Joe gasped for air, but all he got was the hot stinky breath of the prick who'd stuck him.

Shit.

Can't breathe. A door clicked open, and Joe's knees gave way. Plastic crinkled under him. Blood soaked his pants, and a bright flame flickered in front of his face. Joe tried to swat at the light, but his arm wouldn't move.

His brain fogged.

His bowels loosened.

He was going to die.

* * *

BURNING to death had to be the worst way to go.

With gloved hands, forensic anthropologist Dr. Lara Romano lifted the charred forearm from a pile of bones and remeasured its width. She should have been pleased her two calculations matched. Instead, her belly ached from the image of the victim's last moments—the heat, the terror, the inability to escape inevitable death.

She squeezed her eyes shut and made herself focus on finding the identities of those in the torched Winnebago and not on their life ending torture. Becoming emotionally involved with the victims would only end in heartache. If she wanted to be a topnotch anthropologist, she needed to leave her heart at home.

As she leaned forward to type the results into her laptop, a blast of cold air burst from the lab's ceiling vent and ran down the back of her neck. She shivered and drew her white lab coat tight.

Someone touched her arm, and she whipped around, pressing a hand to her chest. "Phil."

Phil Tedesco backed his wheelchair away from her lighted work-table. "Sorry. I didn't mean to startle you." Her boss' lips moved, but no sound reached her ears.

"No problem." She smiled and flipped the switch on her cochlear implant to bring her into the hearing world. "What's up?"

He tapped the edge of the table. "You draw any conclusions about the bone yard?"

She brushed some of the burnt embers off the stainless steel counter. Of all days for the lab to look a mess, it had to be the day her boss came to visit. Normally, every countertop in the large room gleamed, but today half the surfaces were smeared with ashes, and the floor needed to be swept. She didn't want him to think she didn't take pride in her workplace.

"Not yet. I don't have enough to identify all the charred remains."

"Can you tell the number of victims at least?"

She inhaled to steady her hands. "I know there are at least five different bodies, three male, two female. There might be more."

"Looks like you've done a great job so far, but time's up."

"You're kidding. I need another few days." She wanted to have the conclusion correct, not only for the sake of her job but to bring closure to the families involved.

He held his palms outward. "The insurance company is bugging me for the results. Our boss is getting worried you're taking too much time examining a few bones. You've been at it three weeks."

Try four. "It's in my nature to be thorough." She'd done postgraduate research at the University's lab for three years and no one ever rushed her. "I'll do my best to finish soon."

"Perfect." Phil sat up straighter. "The other reason I'm here is to get your opinion on some bones that just arrived."

As if he was psychic, the big steel lab door eased open, and he spun his wheelchair away from the entrance. Two men, covered head-to-toe in white protective gear, rolled a pine casket with mud-streaked sides past her workstation into the middle of the expansive room.

The stone-faced technicians lifted the cover and placed it on the bottom shelf of the steel gurney. As a blast of death hit her, she reeled and stepped back. Rotting dead rats baked in the hot sun for days would smell sweeter. The school's research lab mostly had exposed her to sanitized skeletons, not the foul stench of real dead bodies. The times she'd examined remains, the bodies had been completely decomposed.

Phil covered his nose and waved the two men to the door.

She glanced over at him. "The bodies just keep showing up, don't they?"

"Yup." His jaw relaxed. "Hell, when I worked homicide, I often had four cases going simultaneously. I remember when I considered three hours sleep a good night."

She'd been there many times. "I guess the dead don't care about our workload."

He chuckled. "You got that right."

"Who is it?" she asked, wishing she had some VapoRub to put under her nose to blunt the smell.

"Two John or Jane Does."

"Two? In the same casket?"

"I'm afraid so."

She leaned over to look inside. No clothing was visible. One skull had most of the hair intact. Only the second victim, who was hairless, had areas of soft connective tissue, which hopefully would help with the identification.

She stepped back. "Who dug them up? And why?"

He wheeled away from the casket. "One of the workers at the cemetery was preparing a grave when he came across a coffin already in the plot. The parents of the dead girl were quite distraught when they learned the site had been taken over by someone else."

She grimaced. "I'd be upset too. I've never seen two in the same casket before."

"Maybe the family wanted to save money on the burial." He pulled out a yellow pad from the side pocket of his wheelchair. "Can you tell me anything about these two?"

Even though he was a seasoned cop, the double burial softened his shoulders, and her respect for him grew.

Two people in the same coffin wasn't right. She couldn't imagine being that poor and not finding a way to provide a proper resting place for her loved ones. And why no cement vault around the casket? Did these relatives not respect the dead? If she had her way, she'd start—

"Lara?"

"Oh, sorry."

She leaned over the casket again. Keeping her hands tucked behind her back to avoid disturbing the evidence, she noted the slight traces of white powder dusting a few of the bones. Definitely lime, which was very caustic. She moved back to the counter, picked up a metal caliper and held it above each skeleton's hips to get an estimate of the width.

The dimensions fit the standard chart perfectly, and she tried not to smile. "The heart-shaped pelvic inlets and the narrow width tell me you have two males."

"Good." Phil made a note on the pad. "Age?"

One of the craniums faced forward, exposing the top of the skull. Her heart turned heavy when she realized this man had died so young. "The cranial sutures," she said, pointing to the skull nearest to her, "indicate he's between thirty and forty years old." Close to her age. "Without digging out the second head, I can't tell how old the other one is."

Phil edged closer. Manipulating the gurney's pedals, she lowered the level to give him a better angle from his chair.

"Thanks." He peered over the rim of the wooden box. "Race?"

"I'll need to take accurate measurements and do a few tests before I can be sure. Even though I have an intact cranium, I want to run the information through my computer."

He gently squeezed her hand. "A guess is all I ask."

Here goes. Despite the coolness in the room, her armpits began to sweat. And here she thought her exam days had ended four years ago.

"The teeth, which are badly decayed on the top male, are rather crowded together due to the narrow dental arch, and the skull appears smaller than the usual Caucasoid." She searched her mind for details of differentiating between races. "The forehead is somewhat low and slightly sloped backwards—"

"Lara, just tell me."

She looked up. He'd gripped the wheelchair's armrest and tensed his jaw. Not hearing the nuances in people's tones, she had to use physical clues. She rushed to explain. "From the size of the nasal opening and the rather square shape of the eye sockets, I'm going to say some kind of Mongoloid. Native American most likely, given the Tampa area has a large Seminole Indian population."

Phil's fingers relaxed. "Excellent. Can you tell me anything else? When they died? Cause of death?" He kept his gaze on her face.

During her studies she was allowed as much time as needed to draw the correct conclusions. This Johnny-on-the-spot diagnosis set her nerves on edge. One slip and he might think less of her. "As a former homicide detective, when you came across a dead body, could you determine the who, what, when, where and why right away?"

His eyes twinkled. "No. CSU needed hours to collect the evidence."

"My point exactly."

"Do your best. I realize haste isn't always our goal, but I want to give our boss something."

The tension released from her shoulders. "I need to photograph the bones before I move them, but if you look here." She held her fingers above the skull on the bottom. "From the slope of the beveled edges, the hole might have been caused by a gunshot."

Phil smiled. "Now that's what I'm talking about. Any idea when they died?"

His praised bolstered her spirits. "There's still some soft tissue..." She stopped. Only another anthropologist would care about the details. Lara took a leap into the deep end. "Six months to a year."

"Good enough for now. I'll let you get back to work. Let me know when you have a cause of death on both men."

"Will do."

He held up a finger. "I hate to do this to you, but the mayor wants this done ASAP, and Mr. Pomerantz promised him we'd have these men identified by the middle of the month."

"So soon?"

"I know, I know, but Pomerantz pays the bills. It's not like we're some state run facility with a huge backlog. He built this state-of-the-art facility so he could get what he wants, when he wants it."

Her childhood dream was to be a forensic anthropologist at the best private lab in the country. She'd worked extra hard her whole life, and her hard work had paid off, but if she messed up now, she might end up teaching high school science, which for a deaf person, would be a big challenge.

If she came in all day Saturday and a half day on Sunday for the next two weeks, she might be able to finish both cases. "No problem."

"Another thing. Someone from the sheriff's department might be stopping by this afternoon to check on your progress."

She didn't have time to stop her work and explain procedure to a local cop. "Do I have a choice?"

"Nope. I know you won't disappoint me."

"I don't plan to." She'd graduated at the top of her class. She could do it.

The moment he disappeared out the door, she blew out a breath. Ready to tackle the two victims, she flipped off her implant and reveled in the freeing silence.

She spent the next several hours scraping the tissue from the bones and placing each piece in a large vat to finish the cleansing process.

Four hours of bending over the table examining the bones caused her back muscles to tighten into tiny knots. The moment she arched to soothe the ache, her stomach grumbled. It was time to go home and feed herself and her eternally hungry fat cat. Since the bones were still cooking, the remaining tasks would have to wait until tomorrow.

She stripped off her disposable gear and dumped the soiled garb in the waste bin under the portable X-ray machine. To ease the tension building in her scalp, she rubbed her head to loosen the braided strand. God that felt good.

Just as she reached to pull open the heavy door, the stainless steel entry eased toward her and a tall stranger appeared.

As he strode in, she took a step back. "How did you get in?" She quickly flipped on her implant.

The door was key-coded, and only a few lab workers knew the combination. Having worked at HOPEFAL close to a year, she knew everyone, and he was no employee. She would have remembered someone this good looking.

"I put my right foot in front of my left?" He cocked a brow and leaned forward.

"That's not what I meant."

He flashed his sheriff's badge, and then waved a piece of paper with numbers scrawled on the front. "My brother used to work with Phil, so he gave me the combination. Said you might not hear if I knocked." He tugged on his right ear.

Great. Though the newcomer probably would deduce from the slight nasal twang in her tone she was deaf, she didn't need her boss announcing to the world she had a handicap. Out of habit, she tucked her hair over the wire leading to her battery pack to make sure the implant didn't show. She braced for the look of pity she always received when people learned of her deafness. When she searched his face and found nothing but openness, her pulse skipped a beat.

She ran a gaze from his scuffed cowboy boots, up along the faded jeans that hugged his muscular thighs, past the tight T-shirt and to his penetrating aquamarine blue eyes.

She stilled. God that was rude. Had he noticed? How could he not? Thank goodness he had the courtesy to keep his focus off her.

He swiveled toward her. "I'm Trevor Kinsey—Missing Persons detective at the sheriff's department."

Ah, yes, the man to check on her progress. He was running rather late. She extended her hand and a rough palm met hers. His touch was firm, yet gentle. Nice.

"Dr. Lara Romano."

Detective Kinsey stepped past her, halted, and surveyed her lab, his head twisting from right to left in slow motion. Given the high-tech equipment and many gadgets, he probably liked what he saw. The lab still impressed her every time she came to work.

He placed a Manila envelope along with a smaller packet on the counter and walked around the entire perimeter of the lab, first checking the scanning machine, the scale and then the portable X-ray and said nothing the whole time nor asked any questions. In fact, he made no comments. What was going on?

While she enjoyed showing off her new digs, now wasn't a good time. Her cat had needs. "Can I help you with something?"

"I've wanted to see what all the hoopla was regarding this place. Now I know why everyone at the department is gung ho about the new lab."

"I can give a tour tomorrow if you'd like." At the least, she could be friendly.

Then he checked *her* out from head to toe and smiled. "If I have time, sure."

His clear eyes lightened, and she refused to address the tingling that shot up her body at the intimate look. "Are you here to see about the bodies we received today?" She lifted her chin a notch.

He squared his broad shoulders and sobered. "Yes. I've been working on a case involving the disappearance of some Seminole Indians, and I'm wondering if the men we sent over might be two of the eight I've been searching for."

Her muscles tightened. "*Eight* Native Americans are missing?"

"I'm afraid so."

"So many disappearances can't be a coincidence. Are you thinking a hate crime is involved?"

"It's too early to tell." Detective Kinsey headed over to the coffin and peered in. "What did you do with them?"

She pointed across the room to the large pots inside the hooded maceration station. He appeared to be a no nonsense guy. If he could be forthright, so could she. "I'm cooking them." She raised her brows daring him to grimace.

Instead of making a comment, he strode over to the station. If he lifted the clear Plexiglas hood, the escaped smell would fell even the most seasoned cop.

He gazed in, and spun back toward her. "Mind if I wait around to see if your men match mine?"

This man would only get in her way. It didn't matter he looked like some sexy Florida rancher with his dark blond hair curled slightly at the nape of his neck—or that his rough cheek stubble and tanned skin made him appear as though he'd been outside riding all day. Given Tampa was nothing but urban sprawl, he couldn't be a real cowboy, but the impression lingered, nonetheless.

"The bones won't be ready until tomorrow at the earliest. Besides, I don't know for sure if the men are Native American. I need time to study the skulls." The last thing she wanted was to make a fool of herself in front her boss' friend.

She hurried toward the door, pulled open the latch, and swept an arm toward the corridor. He might appear to be a gentleman, but when it came to the job, he'd probably be demanding, over-confident, and insensitive to the needs of the victims.

Okay, that wasn't fair. He hadn't done anything to deserve those labels, but the last two detectives she'd been around fit the bill.

He didn't move. "Did you discover any distinguishing marks on the men?"

"I haven't found anything to help me tell them apart, if that's what you mean, other than the difference in the amount of hair and soft tissue present."

"The families have been waiting for closure for as long as ten months."

She slapped a free hand on her hip. "I just received the bodies."

"I have a few more questions." He picked up the large envelope from the counter, not even blinking at her outburst.

So much for a meaningful conversation. She let the door shut and marched up to him, invading his space. "What makes you think this case is any more important than the arson case I've been working on for the last month?" She didn't need to let him know Phil told her this job needed to be her main concern.

His lips thinned. "I have two dental X-rays and one MRI from three of the families. If you'll just take a look, maybe you'll be able to tell me if one of your cadavers is one of my men." He emptied the X-rays into his hand and offered them to her.

Did he say, his men? Okay. That changed her opinion of him a little. She stepped back. She liked a man who cared, a man who put his heart and soul into the job like she did. Maybe he wasn't the typical law enforcement type like she'd first thought.

Logic sped ahead of emotion. If her two skeletons were among these eight missing men, she'd finish her identification process with time to spare. She'd be the first to admit she was excited to delve into the search, just not with Trevor Kinsey peering over her shoulder. His presence took up the whole room—all twelve hundred square feet of it.

She eased the medical data from his fingers and set the transparencies on the counter. "I was on my way out, but I promise I'll give them my attention tomorrow."

It was his turn to step too close. His body relaxed, and he tossed her a slightly crooked smile, complete with earth shattering dimples. "Sure you can't examine them now?"

"It won't do any good." She'd be damned if she let him use his masculine appeal to get her to do his bidding. "Like I said, the skulls are still..." She couldn't come up with another way to say it, so she merely nodded toward the large vats.

He cocked a brow. "Cooking? I know."

"Yes."

His shoulders stiffened. "Tomorrow then." He took two steps toward the door.

Oh, what the hell. "Wait." She didn't want their time to end. She spent enough time cooped up alone in the lab.

He whipped around, his eyes wide. "Yes?" He closed the gap between them in less than a heartbeat.

She eased back. "Look, I know what it means to want something." *Like friends, success, mainstream treatment.* "While I can't compare the X-rays to the skulls yet, can you tell me a little about these men? Do you know their heights? Ages? Maybe that will help eliminate them." During her preliminary study of the bones she'd estimated the two men's biological profile.

Trevor rattled off the numbers for all eight, his eyes shining brighter with each description. Impressed he'd memorized every detail, she let out a breath.

The muscles in his shoulders bunched as he leaned forward. "Does that tell you anything?"

"Yes. When I first received the bones, I guesstimated the one in his thirties to be about five foot nine, and the older one three inches shorter."

His warm eyes sparkled. "That fits."

"It doesn't prove my skeletons are your men." A small laugh escaped at his naivety. "If only it were that easy."

"I realize that, Dr. Romano."

She couldn't tell if he'd mocked her or if his comment had been tinged with sadness. Before she could get a read on his expression, he rotated around to the counter near the door, picked up the smaller envelope he'd placed there and spread out eight photos side by side. "Take a look at these."

As she stepped next to him, his spicy cologne took her by surprise. She hadn't expected a detective to wear such an enticing scent—strong, clean, and masculine.

"Dr. Romano? Is something wrong?"

This spacing out had to stop. *Look at the pictures, Lara.* "No."

She dropped her gaze and angled the 4x6's toward her. All appeared to be male Native Americans. Two stood next to children, three huddled beside women, and the last few were single shots. Make those blurry, single shots where the heads were either profiles, or tilted to the side. All useless for identification purposes.

He leaned in closer to her, and her breath caught. She forced herself to study the images and ignore the pressure building in her chest. Four were taken at a construction site and the rest were inside what appeared to be a large recreational room. "From their cheekbone structure and the slant to their forehead, I'd say they're Seminole."

"You nailed it."

Lara's stomach sickened. She pressed her eyes shut, not wanting to have a connection to these missing men.

Before they could discuss the case further, his cell rang. The ring tone was some piece of classical music she couldn't identify. It wasn't what she'd have guessed for such a macho man. She had stereotyped him too quickly. Shame on her.

He pulled the phone from his hip pocket and held up a finger. Given he mostly listened, she couldn't get the gist of the conversation —not that she was eavesdropping or anything.

Twenty seconds later, he pocketed his cell and avoided meeting her gaze. "I have to leave. Let me know what you find out regarding the men. Okay?" He slid his business card on the counter.

"Sure, but I—"

Then he was gone, the door closing faster than usual.

She blew out a long, steady breath. "Goodbye to you too, Detective Kinsey."

And here she thought he might want to match the men to her profile. Lara tucked her hair behind her ear trying to figure out if she'd said something wrong. Some unidentifiable and unpleasant emotion swirled in her belly. Her childhood therapist explained that labeling her anxieties would help her cope with the insular world. Fine. The sensation was either frustration at not having helped him or a deep yearning to work with someone. She'd grown up so alone, her dreams were made from the idea of being a part of a team. Classmates had laughed at her, teachers often became impatient, and when it came time to pick lab partners, no one wanted to work with her because she wasn't cool enough for them.

Aw, hell. What did it matter? She had a job to do. Nothing got done by standing around.

Lara had planned to leave, but her need to help pushed her other priorities down a notch, so she slid on a fresh lab coat. If the X-rays and MRI he'd brought didn't indicate the men had the right slant to the forehead, she might eliminate them. If the images did match her men, she'd win, he'd win.

She lifted the films and slapped the first X-ray on the light board. The man's dental work showed he was missing the second and third premolar as well as one incisor. She opened the computer files of the digital images she'd shot of both skulls. The first one wasn't a match, the second inconclusive, and a shard of disappointment stabbed her.

The next X-ray didn't match either. Damn it. Lastly, she peered at the MRI. And froze.

The End

ABOUT THE AUTHOR

Love it HOT and STEAMY? Sign up for my newsletter and receive MONTANA DESIRE for FREE. Click here

OR Are you a fan of quirky PARANORMAL COZY MYSTERIES? Sign up for this newsletter. Click Here

Not only do I love to read, write, and dream, I'm an extrovert. I enjoy being around people and am always trying to understand what makes them tick. Not only must my romance books have a happily ever after, I need characters I can relate to. My men are wonderful, dynamic, smart, strong, and the best lovers in the world (of course).

My Paranormal Cozy Mysteries are where I let my imagination run wild with witches and a talking pink iguana who believes he's a real sleuth.

I believe I am the luckiest woman. I do what I love and I have a wonderful, supportive husband, who happens to be hot!

Fun facts about me
   (1) I'm a math nerd who loves spreadsheets. Give me numbers and I'll find a pattern.
   (2) I live on a Costa Rica beach!
   (3) I also like to exercise. Yes, I know I'm odd.

I love hearing from readers either on FB or via email (hint, hint).

Social Media Sites

Website: www.velladay.com
 FB: www.facebook.com/vella.day.90
 Twitter: velladay4
 Gmail: velladayauthor@gmail.com

ALSO BY VELLA DAY

Ghosts Just Want To Have Fun (Book 3)

SILVER LAKE SERIES (3 OF THEM)

(1). HIDDEN REALMS OF SILVER LAKE (Paranormal Romance)

Awakened By Flames (book 1)

Seduced By Flames (book 2)

Kissed By Flames (book 3)

Destiny In Flames (book 4)

Box Set (books 1-4)

Passionate Flames (book 5)

Ignited By Flames (book 6)

Touched By Flames (book 7)

Box Set (books 5-7)

Bound By Flames (book 8)

Fueled By Flames (book 9)

Scorched By Flames (book 10)

(2). FOUR SISTERS OF FATE: HIDDEN REALMS OF SILVER LAKE (Paranormal Romance)

Poppy (book 1)

Primrose (book 2)

Acacia (book 3)

Magnolia (book 4)

Box Set (books 1-4)

Jace (book 5)

Tanner (book 6)

(3). WERES AND WITCHES OF SILVER LAKE (Paranormal Romance)

A Magical Shift (book 1)

Catching Her Bear (book 2)

Surge of Magic (book 3)

The Bear's Forbidden Wolf (book 4)

Her Reluctant Bear (book 5)

Freeing His Tiger (book 6)

Protecting His Wolf (book 7)

Waking His Bear (book 8)

Melting Her Wolf's Heart (book 9)

Her Wolf's Guarded Heart (book 10)

His Rogue Bear (book 11)

Box Set (books 1-4)

Box Set (books 5-8)

Reawakening Their Bears (book 12)

OTHER PARANORMAL SERIES

PACK WARS (Paranormal Romance)

Training Their Mate (book 1)

Claiming Their Mate (book 2)

Rescuing Their Virgin Mate (book 3)

Box Set (books 1-3)

Loving Their Vixen Mate (book 4)

Fighting For Their Mate (book 5)

Enticing Their Mate (book 6)

Box Set (books 1-4)

Complete Box Set (books 1-6)

HIDDEN HILLS SHIFTERS (Paranormal Romance)

An Unexpected Diversion (book 1)

Bare Instincts (book 2)

Shifting Destinies (book 3)

Embracing Fate (book 4)

Promises Unbroken (book 5)

Bare 'N Dirty (book 6)

Hidden Hills Shifters Complete Box Set (books 1-6)

CONTEMPORARY SERIES

MONTANA PROMISES (Full length contemporary Romance)

Promises of Mercy (book 1)

Foundations For Three (book 2)

Montana Fire (book 3)

Montana Promises Box Set (books 1-3)

Hart To Hart (Book 4)

Burning Seduction (Book 5)

Montana Promises Complete Box Set (books 1-5)

ROCK HARD, MONTANA (contemporary romance novellas)

Montana Desire (book 1)

Awakening Passions (book 2)

PLEDGED TO PROTECT (contemporary romantic suspense)

From Panic To Passion (book 1)

From Danger To Desire (book 2)

From Terror To Temptation (book 3)

Pledged To Protect Box Set (books 1-3)

BURIED SERIES (contemporary romantic suspense)

Buried Alive (book 1)

Buried Secrets (book 2)

Buried Deep (book 3)

The Buried Series Complete Box Set (books 1-3)

A NASH MYSTERY (Contemporary Romance)

Sidearms and Silk(book 1)

Black Ops and Lingerie(book 2)

A Nash Mystery Box Set (books 1-2)

STARTER SETS (Romance)

<u>Contemporary</u>

<u>Paranormal</u>